nicki's girl

Nicki's girl

CLINT BOLICK

Nicki's Girl

Cover art by Marlo Crandall

Published by Wheatmark®
610 East Delano Street, Suite 104
Tucson, Arizona 85705 U.S.A.
www.wheatmark.com

ISBN-13: 978-1-58736-703-8
ISBN-10: 1-58736-703-3
LCCN: 2006932933

prologue

I'M NOT SURE of the day when I finally decided I had to send her away. It was spring: I know that. I remember that the trees were beginning to bud, and the tulips were coming up, which I noticed when she and I took walks in the park.

It's strange, in retrospect, that it happened then. Usually my spirits soar in the spring. The end of winter, the predicate for summer. But as that spring season emerged I found myself in a state of abject despair, for there seemed at last no going back to the halcyon days.

Not that I didn't try to deny it, or that my resolve was unequivocal. On the contrary. Even then, there were entire weeks, maybe, or at least days when I was able to tell myself it wasn't necessary, that the situation somehow was resolvable. But deep down, I knew it wasn't true. I especially knew it wasn't true in the nighttime, when sometimes I would wake up practically screaming, a cold sweat drenching my sheets. In those terrible moments, I would be overwhelmed by the crushing weight of loneliness; not so much in the present sense, but in anticipation of how much worse it surely would get. Always there would be a feeling of dread inevitability.

Yet somehow in the daytime, the situation appeared brighter. Just as in my childhood nightmares, my demons were consigned by day to the closet. But they were there, omnipresent, waiting to come out again when darkness fell.

Of course, she seemed to sense it immediately. I learned that one night when I was hunched over the coffee table in the living room, absorbed in some drawings. As was her habit, she too was drawing, stretched out on her stomach lengthwise along the sofa facing away from me, one foot on top of my leg. From this direction I couldn't see her face, only the ponytailed back of her head.

Her soft voice roused me from my sketching. "Where are you sending me?" she asked.

I didn't hear her at first, and looked over at her above the eye-glasses I recently had started wearing. "What was that, sweetheart?"

She didn't break from her drawing as she calmly repeated what she had said. "Where are you sending me?" The question gripped my heart with icy tentacles. "Are you sending me to the same place as Mommy?"

I leaned back and closed my eyes, taking in what I hoped was a silent breath, my heart racing in overdrive. After I collected myself, I leaned over and tapped her back. "Hey, turn over so I can look at you, young lady," I said.

Dutifully, she put away her pencils and closed her drawing tablet. She turned over, propping her head on a pillow on the arm of the sofa and her feet against my leg. She leveled her gaze at me, the whisper of a cryptic smile crossing her face. Her light brown eyes sometimes, and certainly at that moment, seemed so beyond her nine years, and so much like her mother's. For that reason it was difficult to meet her eyes, but I forced myself to do so.

"Why do you think that?" I asked her.

She looked off for a moment, considering her response. "Well," she began, looking at me again, "I know the things I did make you angry, and scared, like Mommy did." I swallowed at that perceptive observation. "And also, we haven't planned a summer vacation this year like we did last year, and the year before that."

She was right. I hadn't even thought of that. The recollection of those outings brought a momentary smile to my face. They were among our best times together; just Alexandra and me.

"Hey," I said, affecting the most soothing voice I could. "I am not sending you to the place where Mommy went. That is a place where only big people go, when they have really bad problems."

Alex hardly seemed placated. "But you are sending me away. Someplace." She said that calmly, with no visible expression. "Some-place for bad girls. Someplace where girls go when they have problems like Mommy did."

I must have sighed then, as I often do when I'm stressed. I could never lie to Alexandra, just as I never had been able to lie to Nicole. From the moment I had met Nicole, I vowed that our relationship would be utterly truthful; and until the very end I had kept that vow, so intently that it became physiological.

Once a second female had entered my life in the form of our daughter, I found I could not easily lie to either of them. And Nicole knew it and Alexandra knew it. Perhaps if I could have lied I might have saved both. It seems ironic that a quality I thought essential to the most important relationships of my life instead had led to disastrous consequences.

Oh, how easily I mire myself in recriminations. It seems my overriding talent these days.

"Alex, sometimes I don't know what to do with you," I said. "I know you're going through really tough times, and I need some help figuring out how to help you through them. But no matter what happens, I promise we'll end up together, you and me, just like always." I looked over at her face, which as so often was frustratingly impassive. "Because," I added, leaning down to kiss one foot, then the other, "I love you."

I looked at Alex, but now she was looking away. "Can I have a hug from my princess?" I asked. She seemed to think about it for a moment, then reconfigured herself and leaned into me, accepting my hug perfunctorily, more it seemed for my comfort than hers. As she drew away she announced she was going to bed, and without looking at me she scurried off.

I watched as she walked away toward her bedroom in her red flowered pajamas. "I'll be by in a minute to tuck you in," I called after her. She disappeared into the hallway.

The living room descended into silence. I took my glasses off and rubbed my eyes, leaning my head into the sofa cushions. My temple throbbed. I wanted to scream, to cry. But of course I could do neither. I had to maintain the façade of normalcy and stability. But Alex could see right through it. Of that I was sure.

And life emphatically was neither normal nor stable. Maybe it was I who should go away, and get some perspective. And leave the problems to someone else for awhile. It was a seductive thought. But there was no one else to handle these problems. They were mine, all mine.

I must have sat there for a long while, nursing my thoughts. Finally, I raised myself from the sofa and walked quietly down the darkened hallway toward Alex's bedroom. I paused by the door and looked in. She was already in bed, her eyes closed, breathing peacefully, surrounded by her teddy bears. The glow from her nightlight softly illuminated her blond hair and little-girl features, making her appear angelic.

I pushed the door open and quietly walked past her bed over to her dresser, on top of which were two framed photographs: one of Alex and me, the other of Alex and her mother. I picked up the one of Alex and Nicole, and held it close so I could discern it in the dim light.

I thought back to the moment I had taken the picture at a picnic the three of us had in the Virginia countryside. It was a gorgeous fall day, the abundant foliage a cascade of crimson and amber. In the photo, Nicki's smile was brilliant and her eyes luminescent. And in her arms her daughter, four years old then, was a mirror image.

As I stood there for awhile, savoring the bittersweet memory, Alex's voice startled me. "Daddy," she called softly, "come here."

I put the photo down and walked over to her bed. At first I thought she had called me in her sleep, for she did not move as I looked down at her. Her eyes were tightly closed, but her long eye-lashes were damp.

But then, without opening her eyes, she held her arms up, and as I leaned forward she clasped her hands tightly around my neck and pulled me close, drawing my ear toward her face. She whispered so quietly, her voice hoarse and hitching, that I could barely hear her. "But you loved Mommy, too."

I brushed aside a teddy bear and crawled into bed with her. I nuzzled her cheek, now wet with tears. She looked at me pleadingly, her eyes glistening in the near-darkness. "Yes, I loved Mommy," I whispered back. "Very, very much."

I leaned over and squeezed Alex tightly. This time she returned my hug with intensity. Now tears streamed down my face as well, and they dampened the pillow with hers.

I could feel her slender body against mine convulsing with silent sobs. After awhile, her crying subsided, but she did not release her hold on me.

We feel asleep that way, my little girl and I.

PART ONE

1

LONG STORIES OFTEN have ambiguous starts. But this beginning I recall with vivid clarity, as if it was yesterday instead of more than a decade removed from the present. Even the autumny tinge in the morning air continues to reach out from my memory to send a chill up my spine as I contemplate different outcomes that could have supplanted the reality I face today.

As I read the newspaper on the train between Washington DC and New York City, someone caught the corner of my eye. I looked up and watched as a woman lifted some luggage atop the overhead rack in the seat diagonally in front of mine. She was dressed in black from head to toe: sweater, leggings, shoes. The dark color was juxtaposed against her pale skin and the long blonde hair that cascaded around her shoulders. I watched as she arranged her belongings, hoping she would turn around so I could see if she was as pretty from the front as she appeared from behind.

Eventually, she did. And the sight literally took my breath away. I decided she was the most beautiful woman I had ever seen. Big green eyes. Soft eyebrows. Silky, unblemished skin. Delicate nose. Full pink lips.

My heart pounded. With her cover-girl looks, she had to be a professional model, or an actress. I was completely mesmerized, and must have stared dumbly. Her eyes flickered over mine but didn't pause. Her hair flipped as she turned around and sat down. She made herself comfortable: kicked off her shoes, reached into her bag, removed a bottle of Evian, reclined in her seat. She opened the water bottle and took a sip. I watched in rapt admiration. She projected exactly the type of wholesome image I lusted for.

Okay, so I was into pretty women. My ex-girlfriend Jennifer—tall and flaxen-haired, with homespun Midwestern-girl looks—had done that to me, spoiling me forever. Before Jen, most of the girls I dated in college and my early twenties were dark and petite. Jen had changed my tastes irrevocably.

But this woman was more than merely beautiful, for that adjective didn't credit her adequately. She was my definition of physical perfection. She reached inside her bag and pulled out a *New York Times*. She rummaged inside again and retrieved a pair of wire-rimmed glasses. Crossing her legs at the knee, she began reading the front page.

Oh my God, I thought: she's not just a beauty, but my favorite type of beauty—an intellectual beauty. The glasses and reading material iced it.

That was another thing Jennifer had turned me on to: smart women. Jen was a lawyer, though she had only been a law student during most of the time we were together. She was sharp, brilliantly logical. My artistic acumen complemented her intellect, and we had taught each other a great deal. We had often talked into the wee hours of the night, venturing into far-flung topics such as philosophy, religion, politics, travel, music, as well as law and architecture. This combination of beauty and smarts made Jen a tough act to follow.

I lay back in my seat and closed my eyes, smiling. Come on, Kevin, how can you let yourself get so carried away like this? I had barely looked at other women since meeting Jennifer, even after we had broken up. My standards seemed impossibly high, yet in a few seconds' time, I had become hypnotized by the mere sight of this woman. Sometimes I couldn't understand myself. I supposed it was just a guy thing.

I recognized at once that if this woman stayed on the train all the way to New York, I would be able to get no work done.

I opened my eyes and looked at her again. She was kicking her leg rhythmically as she read. A nervous habit. Cute.

Oh man, how painful to observe from this close proximity the most perfect woman in the world, and yet to know I would never get to meet her. She must have a boyfriend, or even a husband, who was probably a professional athlete, or a wealthy Wall Street broker. Or maybe her agent, if she was an actress or model. Certainly not an average-looking, humble, struggling architect like me.

She was absorbed in her newspaper, turning the page now. It appeared she was reading an article on developments in foreign policy. My intellectual blonde Beacon. Unbelievable.

She looked to be about twenty-two. Maybe—hopefully—older than that. She could easily be a college student, or a graduate student. Probably studying foreign policy. Georgetown or George Washington if she lived in Washington, NYU or Columbia if New York. Maybe she'd get off at Baltimore to return to Johns Hopkins, or in Philadelphia for Penn. I hoped not—I wanted her to stay aboard all the way to New York.

I half-returned to my newspaper, glancing up whenever she turned and I could see part of her face. She had finished her newspaper and was now reading *The Economist*. Too much already. I couldn't get over it.

Several people entered our car at the first stop in Baltimore. A woman asked to take the empty seat next to me by the window—certainly there was no way I was going to move over and lose my view!—and I gathered my belongings to make way for her. As I stood to let my new seatmate move past me, I stepped forward alongside the Beacon and glanced down at her. She looked up at me. Brushing some errant hair away from her eyes, she flashed me a radiant smile. I smiled back. The moment passed; her attention returned to her magazine, and I sat back down in my seat.

I removed some sketches from my briefcase and pretended to work at them, still looking up whenever discretion permitted. Eventually the Beacon stopped reading, took off her glasses and rested her head against her seat, her face to the aisle. Before long it seemed certain she was asleep. The steady clackety-clack cadence of the train lulled me nearly to sleep as well, but I forced myself to stay awake. I'd never forgive myself if she got off the train while I was sleeping.

After the stop at Wilmington, Delaware, I made my way forward to the café car and brought some coffee back to my seat. On the way back, I walked slowly past the Beacon's seat and looked down at her. She was dozing peacefully, her lips slightly parted. The sight was erotic and filled me with longing. She was absolutely angelic. I was suddenly and utterly overcome with a desire to nestle with her.

As I returned to my seat and sipped my coffee, I began to think of ways to meet her, counter to all my basic inclinations. Although I am gregarious with people I know, I tend toward shyness with people I don't. I had never picked up anyone at a bar, or even tried to. To find a way to talk to the Beacon—and then to actually do it—would require more courage than I had ever been able to muster in such circumstances, and this was no ordinary circumstance.

It seemed impossible. This woman was probably getting hit on all the time, exactly what I would be doing. It seemed so distasteful. What was I thinking, anyway? She wouldn't have any interest in a guy like me. She might even be married—I'd forgotten to check her ring finger as I walked past. That was the size-up, all right: talking to her would be obvious, embarrassing, and futile.

Yet if I didn't speak to her, surely I would never see her again. Except maybe on television, if she was an actress. That would be frustrating, a lost opportunity. But what did I have to lose? The worst that could happen was that I'd embarrass myself—hardly a novelty for me—and we would go our separate ways. On the other hand, how many times in life do people wish they'd made different decisions, taken risks instead of having played it safe? I was a risk-taker in other realms of my life. I'd left a safe job at an architecture firm and started my own company, and by the time I was thirty the company was grossing over a million dollars annually. In my career, certainly, my risks had paid off.

I marveled at the gravity of those thoughts. For heaven's sake, this was a woman I didn't even know. Was I so enamored of beauty and a particular image that I would go completely bonkers like this? Yes. I was determined not to let the moment pass and regret it later. Particularly because it was the first time I had felt such a powerful desire—even if it was silly and superficial—since Jennifer and I had split up. So I promised myself that if the slightest chance presented itself, I would say something to her.

That being resolved, I was able to begin actually concentrating on my sketches. I leaned back in my chair, inspecting the specifications my colleagues and I had come up with on an apartment building called the Parkside, and ruminated on how best to present them to the owners when I got to New York. My company does architectural designs, specializing in renovations of old apartment buildings. We'd built a niche in the Washington area. What we typically do is to take older apartments that are dark and dreary, knock down some walls and put in lots of glass, restore the hardwood floors, and transform them into units that had lots of light and openness.

As the conductor announced our impending arrival into New

York's Penn Station, the passengers started rising to gather their belongings, the Beacon among them. I gathered my papers to return to my briefcase, glancing anxiously at the Beacon as I did so. She was lifting her suitcase down, and I rose to help her with it as the train rolled to a stop. As I leaned close, I momentarily caught her scent, which was fresh and light. I remember wondering if it was perfume, or soap, or—umm, the image—bubble bath.

"Thank you," she said with a smile, glancing in my direction. Her voice was softly feminine. I smiled back. Here, it seemed, was my opening to say something witty.

Instead I said nothing, my throat constricted by a supernatural chokehold. I couldn't believe it.

She turned away from me and directed her attention toward the woman who had been sitting beside her. I heard her ask, "Excuse me, what's the best way to get uptown?"

As we waited for the passengers ahead of us to disembark, the woman who had been sitting next to the Beacon explained the subway routes. When she finished, the Beacon thanked her and started moving toward the door. I followed behind her, wondering if another opportunity would arise to speak to her. And if so, whether *this* time I would summon the nerve to take advantage of it. Once outside on the platform, she stopped to put her bag down and get a better grip. She lifted it and started toward the station entrance.

I had reached her side and was suddenly seized by a surge of courage. "Excuse me, I overheard you asking how to get uptown. I'm taking a cab, and would be happy to share it with you," I offered. Hooray, Kevin, I thought. You managed to get that out without sounding like you had marbles in your mouth. And it even seemed fairly spontaneous, at least to me.

She didn't seem taken aback at all. "That is so nice of you!" she replied enthusiastically, and for a moment I felt my heart palpitate. "But I'm meeting a friend here, and her train from Boston doesn't come in for another hour, so I'm waiting inside the terminal."

Though I was disappointed, my hopes were stoked by the operative word she used: *her.* Meaning "my friend who is female," as opposed to "my husband" or "my boyfriend."

Suddenly I realized we were walking in stride toward the concourse. "May I carry your bag for you?" I asked, feeling chivalrous.

"Oh, no thanks, it's not heavy." Suddenly she asked me a question. "Are you an architect?"

"How did you know that?" I asked, startled.

"Well, you've got the *Architectural Digest* in your hand and what looks like a tube with architectural drawings tucked underneath your arm."

I laughed. "Well, I guess you don't have to be Sherlock Holmes to figure me out."

We reached the door to the terminal, which I opened for her, and we rode the escalator together.

"What type of architecture do you do?"

"Mostly renovations of apartment buildings in Washington."

"That sounds exciting," she said, sounding genuinely interested. I loved her voice. It definitely matched her looks. "Any buildings I know about? Like maybe the Watergate?" She grinned.

We reached the top of the escalator and paused a few feet away, continuing our conversation amid the bustle of Penn Station patrons rushing toward their trains. I was afraid I was delaying her, yet she seemed interested in the conversation.

"No, nothing so ostentatious as that. Mostly smaller buildings. The Barkley in DuPont Circle, the Smithson/Adams in the Cathedral area, the Pennkurt in Bethesda, places like that."

"You're kidding. A friend of mine lives in the Barkley. I love that building! You did that?"

I beamed. "That was my first apartment renovation, before I started my own company. The owner liked it so much he put up the capital for me to hang my own shingle."

"I'm impressed, considering you're obviously young. I love architecture. Washington is filled with beautiful buildings."

I loved her animation. And her eyes, a gorgeous pale green. Somehow I managed to keep talking. "What's your favorite?" Then before she could reply, I added, "What's your name, anyway?"

"Nicole Petri." She smiled a dazzling smile. "But my friends all call me Nicki."

"My name is Kevin Gibbons. And my friends all call me Kevin." Smiling at my goofy comment, I held out my hand, which she shook, smiling as well. Her grasp was firm, the touch of her skin predictably soft. "So what's your favorite building in Washington, Nicki?"

"The Willard," she said without having to give it a second thought.

"No kidding; mine, too. Sleek, dramatic, grand, unbelievable detail. Now, that's the kind of restoration I aspire to one day."

Even though I knew I was risking a late arrival at my meeting, I didn't want to end this encounter, so I kept talking. It turned out Nicole was a news producer for a radio station in Washington. I expressed surprise that she wasn't in front of a camera instead.

She grinned. Her smile was broad and illuminated her already bright features. "People tell me that *all* the time. But I've never wanted to be on television. I'd hate the way I look." The statement surprised me. I didn't know whether to take it seriously, yet she seemed quite sincere.

Somehow the conversation drifted to our hobbies. I mentioned wine, noting that I had learned quite a bit about California wines from studying architecture in San Francisco, in such close proximity to the Napa and Sonoma Valleys. She expressed similar enthusiasm and tastes in wine, but said she wanted to learn more about them.

Glancing nervously at my watch—more time had passed than I'd feared—I stammered, "Well, uh, maybe we could get together back in Washington for a glass of wine sometime."

"That would be fun." I dug into my wallet for a card and handed it to her. "Horizon Designs. I don't have a card—it's a new job—but I'll call you sometime," she promised.

"I'd like that, Nicole—uh, Nicki. Listen, have a great stay in New York." Again we shook hands, and she flashed her breathtaking smile and gave me a wave as I rushed off to find a taxicab.

Wow, I thought. She seemed even better in person than I had imagined. Very genuine; upbeat personality; incredibly sweet. And unmarried, and obviously older and more established than I originally surmised. In other words, better than perfect.

I was pleased with myself. I had overcome my shyness for once, met an incredible woman, and hopefully hadn't made too much a fool of myself. Not bad for a morning's work. I walked through the doors of Penn Station into the blustery fall day and took in a deep, satisfying breath. It was turning out to be a wonderful day.

2

THE DAY AFTER I returned to Washington from what turned out to be a successful meeting in New York, I shared my experience with my favorite coleague, Samantha, over a glass of wine in her office after everyone else had left for the day. I waxed eloquent about the woman I had met.

"You place too much emphasis on a woman's looks. Just like every other guy on earth."

That stung. First, because I didn't like being lumped with the entire male species. Second, because it was true. "That's not true. I wouldn't have liked her if she didn't seem intelligent and sweet." Boy, that did ring hollow.

"You wouldn't have given her a second look if she hadn't been gorgeous."

"Are you saying your head doesn't turn when you see some hunk walking down the street?"

"Well, of course my head turns, but I don't project positive moral qualities upon them just because I happen to lust over their bodies. Most hunks are jerks."

"You're raining on my sunshine. Just because this woman is beautiful, and blonde, and perfect, you assume she can't be intelligent and sweet."

"You've mentioned that she's blonde about ten times already. I have nothing against beautiful women. It's just there's usually a negative correlation. Stereotypes aren't usually created out of thin air, trust me."

THE SEASONS CHANGED, and work got busier. The winter was harsh; even though there was hardly any snow, there were frequent ice storms that made the always-challenging Washington roadways even more treacherous than usual.

I didn't think much about Nicki, or about much else for that matter. What preoccupied my thoughts was that my mother got sick with breast cancer. Most weekends I took on the weather and drove up to Allentown, Pennsylvania, where I had grown up and where my mother, widowed for the past decade, still lived.

It was a difficult time. My mother had always been vigorous— she was my rock growing up—but now she'd lost weight and grew very depressed as it became clear her condition was serious. She resisted getting second opinions, but gave in to my insistence, though to no avail: the diagnosis was confirmed. In December she had a mastectomy, which would be followed by several months of chemotherapy to get at the remaining cancer. The prognosis was uncertain. My sister, who lived with her husband and two sons in Las Vegas, came out for a few weeks during and after the operation, and she called me to report on my mother's condition on a daily basis. By late January it appeared the treatments were taking hold. My sister had left, and my weekly visits resumed. Though my mother was wiped out by the chemotherapy and had lost her hair, her spirits began to improve.

One night as I was sitting at her bedside, she asked, "When are you going to give me a little granddaughter?"

"Well, I have to get married first, and that doesn't seem imminent."

"You don't necessarily have to be married." I gave her a shocked look. After all these years, my mother sometimes still managed to surprise me. Now that she had the momentum, she kept going. "What about Jennifer? You two would have nice children."

"My mother the geneticist," I mumbled. I held her hand, which as usual imparted a special warmth that mothers seem to emit. "Mom, I'd love to have a little girl one day. Or a little boy, for that matter. But I actually would like to fall in love again first."

"Well, hurry up."

Driving back from Allentown that night seemed especially dark, and the townhouse upon my return extremely cold and empty, even with my cat Elvis there to greet me. As I relaxed on the overstuffed sofa in my living room, listening to the wintry wind and stroking Elvis's silky white fur to her purring contentment, I thought about how fleeting the precious things in life are. I didn't want to lose my mother; and though it didn't look like that would happen soon, her mortality was apparent to me for the first time.

And I hadn't wanted to lose Jennifer. Even though we had lived together only a few years, emotionally I had hitched my wagon to hers, and thought it would last forever. She was too young when we had started dating, and even though we had a wonderful romance, I knew all along that a part of her needed to experience other relationships. So she was reluctant to commit to marriage—a gender role-reversal in the 1980s. When it finally became clear to both of us that it wasn't going to end in marriage, we decided to call it quits. But even a year and a half after we'd broken up, I still hewed to my side of the bed every night, the sheets on the other side remaining perpetually undisturbed. Her absence had left a void in my life that was still as painful as a fresh wound.

THE WEEK GOT off to a quick start the next day. First thing that morning we received final approval from the District of Columbia for renovation of the Parkside. Dealing with the local bureaucracy was constantly frustrating; the bureaucrats were petty, imperious, inept, and unreliable. But like anyone in the District who was crazy enough to own or try to develop property, we had to pay fealty even to the lowliest bureaucrats. Usually if we sufficiently supplicated ourselves before them it eventually paid off. Fortunately, we hadn't gotten big enough to worry about having to bribe people yet, but I knew that day would come.

The news about the project approval came in around ten. I didn't realize the bureaucrats were at work that early, but sure enough, another of my architects, Rich Deeks, came by to tell me we'd gotten the word. Early on I had transferred responsibility of dealing with most outsiders—contractors, city officials, vendors—from Samantha to Rich, because Sam routinely pissed people off. Though six years younger, Rich was considerably more polished, and well on his way to being not only a gifted architect but a successful businessman. I expected that one day he'd move out on his own, but until then I was happy to reap the benefits of his talents and in return bestow whatever experience and opportunities I could.

What the approvals meant was that work could begin in earnest. I called the staff into our conference room and began parceling out the assignments. We planned to start by renovating the lobby—a nice art deco theme, true to the style of many of Washington's apartment buildings—then the apartments, which in this case were being turned into condominiums.

As we were leaving the conference room, our office manager Alice Nance tapped my shoulder. "Everything still set for Saturday?"

For a moment I drew a blank, then I slapped my forehead. "I almost forgot—my new-home wine-tasting party. I haven't even sent out any invitations. Maybe I ought to postpone it for awhile."

"We need to have a housewarming for you for your new condo, and it's your birthday the next week, so the timing is perfect," she argued. Ugh, I'd be thirty-three. Alice continued making her case. "There's been plenty word-of-mouth that you were planning to do this; that will fill the place up. And I can fax out some invitations this afternoon, if you give me a list."

"When am I supposed to get the wine and clean my place up?"

"We'll spend Saturday together, cleaning in the morning and making a wine-buying expedition in the afternoon. It'll be fun."

We stopped outside my office. "So I have no excuses, huh?"

"No excuses. Anyway, I finally found a housewarming gift, and I'm dying to give it to you. Ever since you bought your bed, I knew what I had to buy for you. It's perfect."

After Jennifer and I had split up, I had moved to a townhouse in Old Town Alexandria and exhausted most of my savings buying new furniture. The most recent, and most extravagant, was a beautiful custom-made brass and iron bed. Alice had helped me shop for it, and I recalled her remarking that since it was high off the floor it should have some antique steps to go along with it. I suspected that would be the housewarming gift.

"Well, that's a suitable bribe. I guess it will be fun."

Alice nodded. "I'll come over around ten and you can buy me breakfast."

"Deal."

As I walked back to my office, I reflected on how nice it was to have friends who were determined to make sure I didn't get stuck in a rut, then I sat down and lost myself in work details, trying to shuffle paper out as quickly as possible. After what seemed a short time, I was distracted by my stomach growling. I glanced at my watch: already after noon. It was amazing there had been no interruptions. I got up and stretched, then walked back to Samantha's office to see if she wanted to grab some lunch. I knocked and stuck my head inside, but she wasn't in.

I heard Beth searching me out from the reception desk.

I walked back and turned the corner toward the reception desk. "What's up?"

"Some woman on the phone named Nicole Petri wants to talk to you."

I drew a blank. "Did she say who she's with?"

"She said if you didn't remember her to tell you she met you on a train to New York."

Bam! It couldn't be. "Are you joking? Did Samantha put you up to this?"

"I'm not joking. I have no idea who this person is. Whoever she is, she's been on hold quite awhile."

"Okay, send it in," I said, walking into my office and slamming the door behind me. The phone was ringing as I sat down. "This is Kevin Gibbons," I said tentatively.

"Hi. Are you surprised?"

Even though I had heard it only once for a short time several months before, the voice was unmistakable. "Pleasantly."

"I read about you last week in the *Washington Post* real estate section. I guess you got that project."

Wow. Maybe the *Post* wasn't such a bad newspaper after all. It had done a nice profile of our plans for the Parkside. "Yeah. And actually, we just received word from the District this morning that our plans are approved, so we'll start work very soon."

We ended up talking for forty-five minutes, about nothing and everything. She had lost her job during a downsizing at the radio station, but was doing temporary public relations work—she was calling me from an office where she had a six-week assignment— along with moonlighting on various research projects. She'd been busy, she explained, and had forgotten about her promise to call until she'd seen the article. As I listened to her, I realized I'd broken into a sweat. This woman had quite an effect on me.

She was tapping at her word processor as we talked. Her voice sounded slightly huskier than I remembered, and I told her so. It turned out she was getting over a bad cold. We talked about politics—I learned that remarkably she was an unreconstructed reactionary, just like me—along with architecture, the weather, movies. I told her about my mother's illness, and she was soothingly empathetic. I was mesmerized by the sound of her voice, and didn't want the conversation to end. And I was terrified that we'd get off the phone before I could summon the courage to ask her out. But finally I did.

"Hey, would you like to have brunch together or something?"

"Sure," she replied, and I broke into a huge grin and leaned back into my chair.

Then the thought occurred to me to invite Nicole to my party, and I did, but it turned out she was leaving for the weekend to attend a friend's wedding in North Carolina. So we made a date for the Sunday after, brunch at the Savoy in Old Town. This time I took down her phone numbers—she offered both home and work—and promised I'd call before the appointed time.

As I hung up, I pumped my fist in the air. "Yes!"

Samantha walked by and saw me through the window. She came in. "What's going on?"

"Shut the door." She did and then sat down. I sank down into my chair, my eyes closed. "Oh my God, oh my God, oh my God."

"I think that in male parlance, you have what's referred to as a shit-eating grin on your face. This must have to do with something more than the DC bureaucrats coughing up some development permits. So out with it."

"You remember that woman I met a few months ago on the train to New York?"

Samantha took a moment but then flickered recognition. "Oh yeah, Miss Perfect."

"Yeah," I sighed. "She just called, and we talked for"—I looked at my watch—"we talked for forty-five minutes. And we have a date, a week from Sunday."

"Well, congratulations, I guess."

I sat up. "Come on, Samantha, this is the best news I've gotten in months."

"All right, you're right. I shouldn't pre-judge. I'm happy for you."
I frowned at her. "No, I really am. You're absolutely right. You haven't been out on a date in six months, and you've been cooped up with

your sick mom, and you've been working your buns off. So you deserve a hot date."

"Gee, I hope the Savoy has a Sunday brunch, now that I think of it. It's reputedly the nicest place in Old Town, but I've never been there."

"I'm sure they do. And how nice, you're making your debut there on a first date." She left.

I wasn't ready to return to work just yet. I leaned back in my chair and tried to summon images of Nicki, but my recollection was blurry. Was she as beautiful as I imagined? I marveled that the phone call had seemed so natural, so matter-of-fact. Yet I couldn't remember being so excited about anything so much in my life. Not even Christmastime when I was a little kid. Not even Jennifer. I smiled. Whoa, boy, don't get so excited. Nothing had really changed. This was just a first date. The calculation about my ultimate prospects with this woman—slim and none—remained the same. Better take out the "slow" sign.

3

STILL, HEARING FROM her had put me in a grand mood. I knew why: it meant I had finally, for the most part, put Jennifer behind me. Sometimes it seemed that would never happen, that I would mope endlessly about losing her. But having met Nicki, and feeling my heart literally leap when I heard her voice on the telephone, made me realize that finally the healing process had begun. I could now be open to someone new; or at least to enjoying life without Jennifer. Already it seemed I owed Nicki a great deal.

In fact, combined with the approval of the Parkside project, everything in my life seemed to be coming together. I knew that hard work on the apartment project was ahead. Designing a concept was difficult enough; executing it, particularly on a project this size, was quite another. Dimensions that were approximate on a drawing now must be exact, to the sixteenth of an inch; adjustments would have to be made constantly, always putting the basic architectural premises to the test. It challenged the outer bounds of patience, persistence, talent, and ingenuity.

As my party approached, it seemed a good time for celebration. Alice came over around ten and together we cleaned up my townhouse. It wasn't big—three stories, but only four rooms—and I had a housekeeper who came in once a month, so it didn't get too messy; left to my own devices I was pretty neat.

By noon, Alice and I were already having lunch and then buying wine. I enjoyed making the selections. I wanted wines that would satisfy the discriminating palates of my few discerning friends, but accessible to those who weren't. And of course I didn't want to bust my budget.

Alice had started working for the firm about a year and a half earlier. She was twenty-nine, tall, with a medium build, short hair dyed auburn, and funky glasses. Not my type romantically, but fun.

Alice had degrees in art and journalism. In a way she was an odd fit for an office manager, but that was the opening we had and it seemed to me her talents would allow her to make contributions to the firm beyond office management. My hunch was right. She had a great eye for interior furnishings and a deft touch with the media. In fact, she had scored the *Washington Post* feature for us.

"I'm springing my housewarming gift on you tonight," she said for at least the sixth time.

"Did you bring it with you?"

"It's in my car. Believe me, I wouldn't forget to bring it."

I couldn't imagine why stairs for my bed would be such a big deal; they must be exceptionally nice.

Having some extra time, we browsed some antique shops in Old Town, shopped for some hors d'oeuvres, then returned to my townhouse. We each showered and changed, and then put out plates and wine glasses. The guests were due to arrive starting at eight.

I had to consign poor Elvis to the guest room, wherein she quickly scurried beneath the bed. (The cat—who I named before I knew her gender—had lived with me since she was a kitten. She had strolled into my house in San Francisco just after I'd started architectural school. She'd been a dirt-streaked stray, but after she cleaned herself up, proved to be a pure-white beauty. We had been faithful companions ever since.) After doing that, Alice and I sat down on my huge, white, down-filled sofa—my other major furniture investment in addition to my bed—to enjoy some wine as we awaited our arrivals.

Rich Deeks and his porcelain-beauty Asian wife, Kim, were the first to come. Soon after, Beth arrived, her current Marine Corps boyfriend Brad in tow. By nine-thirty, the party was in full swing. About forty people, half of whom I didn't even know, filled my townhouse. Compliments about the wine were abundant, stoking my confidence. I discovered, though, that parties are events where *other* people socialize; the host, especially a solo host, spends all his time replenishing drinks, directing people to the bathroom, and excusing himself to attend to other guests. But as the crowd and conversation swelled, I grew increasingly comfortable and downright convivial.

After a time I broke away from the party to take a small group— Beth, Rich, Kim, a girl named Meg who was a friend of Samantha's, and two or three others—on a guided tour of the townhouse. Alice trailed the group, making editorial comments on the decorations I'd chosen. There were murmurs of approval for the second-floor bathroom, which featured a Jacuzzi tub and a glassed-in shower with two shower heads.

The iron-and-brass bed in my top floor bedroom was, of course, the centerpiece, and the group gathered around as I described my deliberations in purchasing it. "Alice helped pick it out," I added to her obvious pride. As I glanced over at her, I noticed she was smiling. "What?" I asked.

Now that she was the center of attention, she made the most of it. "Well, as Kevin mentioned, I helped him shop for his new furniture. I was trying to figure out what to get him for a housewarming gift, and when he got this bed I knew instantly what I had to get him. And . . ." she paused for dramatic effect, "now I finally get to make the presentation."

"So where is it?" I asked, looking around for a large box containing stairs for the bed.

Instead, she extricated a small flat box from the pocket of her slacks and presented it with a flourish. I stood there looking at it stupidly in my hand, feeling the group's eyes on me.

"Well, aren't you going to open it?" Alice asked. "Everyone's waiting."

I opened the box, and finding the contents stuck inside, shook it until the contents fell into my other hand. What came out were silvery cylinders, connected by a small chain. I shook them apart, unwittingly holding them up for all to see.

Handcuffs.

Everyone burst out laughing. I could feel my jaw drop and my face turn crimson. I glanced at Meg, who was giggling. Then over at Alice, who managed between fits of laughter to say, "I hope you get lots of use out of them."

I pushed through the onlookers and walked over to my dresser, where I hid the handcuffs out of sight in the top drawer, slamming it loudly. I turned back toward the group and addressed Alice. "If I ever *do* get any use out of them," I stammered, "you're not gonna hear about it."

This got the group laughing again. Secretly, I had to admit I loved the gift.

We all returned downstairs, where periodically someone would ask about the housewarming gift, making me blush repeatedly. The party crested at about ten-thirty, so crowded it was hard to move. Beth presented me with a surprise birthday cake, replete with thirty-four candles—one for good measure—adding to my previous embarrassment but also to the good cheer.

Afterward the party grew more manageable; and by midnight, when my next-door neighbor called to nag me to turn the music down, there were only a few people remaining, sitting on chairs or the floor in my living room. We drained the remaining wine bottles as we talked about politics and religion, with yours truly first shocking my liberal friends with my spirited defense of President Reagan, then my conservative friends by questioning God's existence. It was all great fun. I felt very mellow, relaxed not only by the wine but also by how well the party seemed to have turned out. I thanked Alice for insisting I follow through with it; it was a good night.

4

On the following Monday just after our weekly staff meeting, Beth announced that Art Longley was on the phone. As always I took the call.

"Art!"

"Good thing you're in the goddamned office so early. The competition out there is fierce," he announced

The mental image of the burly developer brought a smile to my face. "Just checking up on my working hours, Art?"

"Nope, just wanna tell you about an opportunity, and get your ass moving on it."

I was always interested in hearing about opportunities from Art. He was my mentor. Back when I had my first job with the Washington architectural behemoth Fielder, Steinmetz & Way, I had worked on apartment renovation projects for the gregarious developer, and a friendship had stuck with the hard-driving construction worker-turned-successful businessman. When I was three years out of school, Longley took me out for drinks. He slugged down multiple Jack Daniels' while I tried to keep up with gin and tonics—he'd never abide me sipping wine—and shocked the heck out of me by telling me to go into business on my own. He'd capitalize me, he promised, and guarantee enough work to keep three architects busy full-time if I'd shave a third off the prices Fielder was charging. "The way I figure it," he'd said between puffs on a cigar, "is that I get all the talent without the goddamn overhead." I thought about it for all of about two minutes, accepted on the spot, and hadn't looked back ever since.

And now he had something new to tell me about. "First, though, congratulations on Parkside."

I beamed with pride. My father died when I was a pre-teen; I thought of Art as almost a surrogate. "Thanks."

"Well, anyway, AWA's annual contest is for a small urban condo concept. The winner gets five thousand bucks and tons of notice."

AWA was the Association of Washington Architects. I knew about the annual contest, and Art was right about the benefits. I had noticed the announcement in the monthly magazine, but hadn't paid much attention because the subject matter was outside my expertise. "I'm a renovator, not a builder."

"Ah, come on, what's the difference? You had to learn it in school. And if you're ever gonna break into the big time, you gotta build. Renovation's a niche."

"I don't want to get big," I insisted, resuming an argument we'd had many times. Art's firm was the biggest apartment and condominium developer in Washington, and he couldn't understand why anyone wouldn't want a big company.

Art played his trump card. "Fergy's got an entry."

"What?!"

John Friedman Fergaman had been my bitter rival at Fielder, Steinmetz & Way. A total jerk; probably the only person on earth I truly hated.

"Word has it Fielder's showcasing him for the big-time," Art added, twisting the knife.

"All right, all right, I'm in. I don't want to lose to Fergaman. When's the entry due?"

"Next Monday at noon."

"Holy shit."

"So what else have you got to do?"

I sighed. Art had me. The guy had to manipulate me to do things that were in my own best interest. And he was superb at it.

"I'll courier over the contest specs right away," he promised. And that, as they say, was that.

I called Samantha and Rich into my office, telling them they'd have to carry Parkside for the next week. Predictably, Sam complained, but Rich thought it was a splendid opportunity for the firm. "Let me know if you need any help," he urged. "Why don't you work at home? There's nothing we can't handle, and you can't afford the interruptions."

He was right, and I was grateful for the offer. I gathered some supplies, told Beth not to bother me with anything that wasn't an absolute crisis. "And if that jerk Longley calls, tell him I'm out of the office, relaxing." Beth laughed.

Then I remembered my date with Nicole scheduled for Sunday. Oh, man. Should I cancel it?

That thought didn't last long. Of course not. If it meant an all-nighter on Saturday, then what better payoff? Man, when it rained, it poured.

Fittingly, the first glimpses of spring were revealing themselves in a balmy and sunshiny day, and I stripped my jacket off as I got into my car. I could wear jeans and T-shirts the rest of the week, and maybe even skip a day or two of shaving, I figured. The obsessed artiste, closeted away like a hermit in his studio. The image made me chuckle.

And that's pretty much how it turned out. My stereo pumped out music incessantly, everything from Saint Saens to the Electric Light Orchestra. I ordered pizzas, drank coffee by the gallon, trekked to the deli for an occasional salad, jogged a few miles each day along the bicycle path, and worked late into the nights, draining a good part of my wine stash in the process.

I was in an expansive, creative frame of mind. Art had been right: it was wonderful to be unshackled from the inherent limitations of renovation design. I applied the same principles—maximize light, space, and function, which were particularly important in urban multifamily dwellings—but for the first time since architecture school I wasn't bounded by existing constraints. It gave me an unexpected feeling of exhilaration.

But for the same reason I was daunted by the task. Renovation was a puzzle, a challenge, to create something good out of finite possibilities. I was always knocking out walls, changing room configurations, trying to find ways of making small, dark spaces seem warm and expansive. But here the possibilities were far less limited. True, the parameters of the project called for twenty-five condominium units in a quarter-block area, bounded on three sides by other buildings. Working as I typically did under tight constraints might actually give me an advantage, because I was used to having to call heavily upon my imagination.

On Wednesday morning, I called Nicki at her temporary job. Her voice was cheerful. She had enjoyed the wedding she'd attended the previous weekend in North Carolina, but was working hard because her project was slated to end in a couple of weeks. I told her about the contest, and she asked if I wanted to postpone our brunch. (I noted with a momentary tug of dismay that she didn't refer to it as a date.)

"Heck, no," I responded. "I'm planning to mostly be finished by Sunday. I'll be in a celebratory mood."

We agreed that I would pick her up at the King Street Metro station at noon. Nicki explained that she attended a Catholic church in her Capitol Hill neighborhood every Sunday, and would catch the Metro at Capitol South just after services. Knowing that she had to return to work, I let her go after firming up the plans. It occurred to me that I'd never dated a Catholic girl before.

By early that evening, I had finally finished a sketch of the basic concept, configuring the twenty-five units in a pleasing design. The plan envisioned five levels around a central atrium, which would allow the units to draw light from the inside of the development as well as the outside. Actually, it was a place I could imagine enjoying, even though I was decidedly not an urban dweller.

As I thought of it, perhaps that's why I was successful as a renovator of urban apartments—I was determined to create an image of space and sanctuary, a place apart from the hustle and bustle of urban life. The units I conceptualized for the contest each had features like vaulted ceilings or stairs leading to loft-style bedrooms to create the facade of spaciousness and increase the privacy available in each room. As was typical, I was willing to create fewer rooms in exchange for larger rooms, especially kitchens, bathrooms, and closets.

The next day I spent a lot of time goofing off, reading magazines and gabbing on the phone. I called Samantha, and then Rich called to discuss some financial issues relating to our Kalorama project. Then the phone rang again—a regular Grand Central Station. I'd never get any work done, not that I really was in the mood to.

This time it was Jennifer, who'd tracked me down after not getting any answer several times on my private line at the office. I told her about the contest, and she was excited and encouraging. That was one of the things I missed most about our relationship: we were each other's biggest fans. Fortunately, I could still count on her for words of encouragement.

Jen was going through a rare slow period at her law office, so she was bored and in a mood to talk. She knew she could always induce me to procrastinate, and we ended up talking for more than an hour. She told me she'd heard my party was successful, which made me happy, though at the same time a bit sad because we weren't able to enjoy it together. I wondered when, if ever, I would stop feeling that way. I asked about her boyfriend, Darren, and it seemed everything was still going well. Eventually, I told Jennifer I had to go, and I returned to work.

Progress was steady until late Friday night, when I was finishing some interior dimensions on the fifth-story units. I was exhausted and getting ready to go to bed when I realized I had made a major structural miscalculation. I looked back at my original notes and saw the mathematical error right away. "Shit," I muttered. The way it was built, the entire structure would come collapsing down. It was a simple enough mistake for a rookie like me, but something the experienced architects on the contest committee would notice right away. And it meant I would have to change everything, literally everything. It all had seemed too easy, maybe because it *was* too easy.

I looked at the clock on my VCR. One-thirty. This was going to take a long time to correct, and I was way too tired to count on myself to do it right this late at night. Dispirited, I decided to go to bed and look at it afresh in the morning.

I set my alarm for six, and woke up feeling amazingly refreshed and reinvigorated. In the back of my mind was my brunch date with Nicole the following day, and I felt like I had to race the clock and dig deep inside to get it done.

I was propelled by an adrenaline rush the entire day. I ordered pizza and drank lots of coffee. In the afternoon, I went for a jog—one of my least-favorite forms of exercise, but I needed to get out and clear my head. It was a surprisingly balmy late-winter day, showing a glimpse of the spring soon to come, and the run was good. Afterward, I showered and returned to work. I didn't look at the clock all evening, and worked late into the night. Eventually,. I applied the finishing touches, knowing I could look the sketches over one last time the following evening. So long as I hadn't made any more structural errors, I was very happy with the final product.

I'd need some time to straighten the place up in the morning, on the off-chance that Nicole would want to see my place. So I decided to set the alarm for ten-thirty. That ought to give me enough time. As I climbed into bed, I glanced at the clock and was shocked at the time: four-fifteen. Great, I was going to be sleep-deprived before the big date. Or whatever it was.

Ɔ

AT THE OUTSET I must describe Nicole's eyes, for they were her most dominant physical feature. Nicki's eyes were the purest green I have ever seen. Not a translucent shade of green, but more like mint. Set off against fair, unblemished skin and delicate blonde eyebrows and eyelashes, her eyes stood out like rare, precious gems.

To say Nicki's eyes were beautiful is to not do them justice. Her eyes were positively ethereal. In isolation, the color would impart a wintry coldness, but in the overall context of her face they suggested softness and warmth.

And yet in truth they were neither cold nor warm. They betrayed no expression at all. They were wondrous to look at, but impossible to gaze into. That is not to say Nicole lacked depth or complexity—far from it—but if eyes are windows to the soul, Nicole's eyes were revealing in the utter absence of what one could find in them. In fact, in all the years I knew Nicki, there was but a single occasion on which her eyes revealed her emotion; and that time I prefer not to think about, at least not yet.

It was at her eyes that I found myself gazing, mesmerized, that early afternoon over brunch. Nicki was talking, but I was not hearing what she was saying. I found it impossible to believe I was in her company, and reveling in the fact that it was real.

It turned out Nicole wasn't as pretty as I remembered—she was even *prettier*. It was an unseasonably warm early-March Sunday, and she showed up at the Metro station wearing a pink blazer, white blouse, and tan pants. She looked adorable, fresh, wholesome. The Savoy turned out to be extremely elegant, and Nicole fit in perfectly with the setting. The food was excellent: I had salmon and scrambled eggs, Nicki had a Belgian waffle, and we both sipped Mimosas. Several of them.

Despite the fact that I was more nervous than I could ever remember on a first date, she made me comfortable as if we had known each other for a long time, and our conversation was easy and animated. Time seemed to stand still. After what seemed no time at all, but must have been hours, Nicki glanced around and announced, "Wow! I guess we ought to be going. We seem to be the only people left."

I realized it was true, then looked at my watch. Two forty-five. The waiter was passing by, and I asked what time brunch had ended. "Two," he said, smiling. We had been talking that entire time, oblivious to the fact that everyone else had finished and left.

Nicki and I exchanged smiles that were at once embarrassed and self-satisfied. It made me feel like romantic co-conspirators.

The afternoon had turned cool and we huddled close as we walked to my Saab, which I was pleased she liked. I asked if she'd like to see my townhouse, which was only a few blocks away. Nicki delighted me by saying yes.

I was happy that I'd straightened the place up that morning before picking her up. Sunshine poured through the French doors leading into my living room. I took Nicki on a tour, and she admired several decorating features. "Not bad for a guy," she remarked. "I guess I shouldn't be surprised, given your line of work."

I positively beamed.

Nicki especially loved the bed. "It's gorgeous. You should get some stairs for it, since it's so high off the floor."

Which made me blurt out the story of Alice Nance's housewarming gift, which I regretted divulging even as the words poured from my mouth. What was I doing, telling this wholesome Catholic girl about handcuffs on our first date? I'd never get her back to my townhouse.

But Nicki's reaction shocked me: She laughed! "I can *imagine* how you'd like to put *those* to use."

Actually, I hoped she couldn't imagine how I'd like to put them to use. I blushed. It seemed I was doing that a great deal lately.

We returned downstairs and settled into the sofa, resuming our conversation as if naturally expecting it to go on forever. Our interests seemed so compatible: politics, travel, wine, art. I wondered at how nervous I was around Nicki, yet how relaxed I was as at the same time. Possibly a good combination; certainly, for me, an unprecedented one.

After awhile Elvis made her customary dramatic entrance,

descending the stairs like a silent-screen movie star, stretching languorously when she reached the bottom. She didn't look at Nicki or me, until Nicki exclaimed, "What a beautiful cat!" Elvis then deigned to prance over toward us, generously accepting back scratches and compliments about her silky fur, followed by a thorough cleansing with her tongue of the spots of fur where we had petted her. She curled up for a time near the radiator, discreetly casting appraising glances at the intruder. I appreciated that Nicki seemed to like my feline companion, and Elvis seemed likewise to approve.

I reached over and pulled out a copy of *Architectural Digest* and laid it on the coffee table in front of us. "Show me what kind of architecture you like."

She leaned forward over the magazine, shifting toward me on the sofa. As she did, I could immediately feel her warmth and smell her fresh fragrance.

That particular issue of the magazine featured recent creations by some of the nation's top architects. "That's the High Museum of Art in Atlanta, which was designed by Richard Meier," I said of the first photo in the article.

"Cool," Nicki remarked. "I like his style."

"Meier's one of my favorite architects. Sleek, light designs. He loves to use white metals on the exteriors. Not very warm, but open. Meier's a modernist. As opposed to a postmodernist, which is the fad of the 'eighties, but I think modernism will come back during the 'nineties. Much less trendy, more functional, timeless." I realized I was on a soapbox and laughed in embarrassment. "Sorry about turning it into a lecture."

Nicki smiled and said, "Don't be silly. I love hearing about creative people." Her face was inches from mine, closer than ever before. I felt flushed. Man, she was beautiful. She turned her attention back to the magazine. "Show me some examples of postmodernism."

I turned a few pages and showed her a classic example. "This one's by Michael Graves. Very cubist. He's actually not too bad; does a lot of stuff for Disney."

As I turned the next page, Nicki exclaimed, "Ugh. What's that?"

I laughed. "That's Eric Owen Moss, who mainly builds in Los Angeles. A deconstructionist, which means weird. He's really left-wing, too. I'm glad you don't like it."

Nicki's hand occasionally brushed mine as we flipped through the magazine. Soft, warm. She was making me dizzy.

I was pleased that our tastes seemed similar. "Hey, would you like to see my contest entry?"

"Sure, I'd love to."

I ran up the stairs and returned with the drawings. "I'm just a beginner at this, so I'm not very optimistic about the contest, but it's given me a chance to expand my horizons a bit."

"I guess that's why you call your firm Horizon Concepts."

"Something like that." I laughed. She leaned forward to look at the sketches I was spreading out on the coffee table. "We had to design the condos under tight space constraints for a densely populated urban setting. My top two priorities, particularly in that kind of circumstance, are sunlight and hardwoods. A feeling of warmth and openness even within a crowded environment. Or at least that's what I was shooting for."

"Wow," she murmured approvingly as she looked at the sketch. "I think you succeeded."

"I conceptualized the interiors first, then constructed the exteriors around them. The idea is not to create a building, but a vertical village, with individual units that have a sense of being self-contained, private, and distinctive, yet part of a community. By making the overall shape uneven and somewhat triangular, I was able to integrate cathedral ceilings and fireplaces even into some of the lower units. And the patios are completely closed off from other units." I hadn't realized how proud I was of the concept, even prouder now that Nicki seemed genuinely to like it.

Nicki was absorbed in the drawings. "Kind of an urban oasis."

"Holy shit."

She looked up at me, smiling but puzzled.

"The name. I came up with everything but the name. I couldn't think of anything that fit. And you just did." Now it was my turn to smile. "Urban Oasis." I liked how it rolled off my tongue, and I liked even more that it was Nicki's inspiration. "Nicki's Oasis."

She grinned even more broadly, looking me in the eye. "You're a silly boy."

"Well, if I win the contest, it's because you suggested the name."

I pointed out some of the details, and she made some suggestions, from a "woman's perspective," as she put it. Bathroom size and location, kitchen configurations, and the like. All her suggestions were excellent, and I relished the feeling of collaboration.

After we finished looking at the drawings, we settled back into our respective ends of the sofa, facing each other. Outside the wind blustered as we talked, ultimately for hours, about everything. Food. Music. Family. Past relationships. Where we'd traveled and where we wanted to go. I learned that when I saw Nicki on the train to New York, she had just broken off a serious relationship with a guy named Carlos, who she'd dated for two years. She had thought it would end in marriage, but now she was happy it hadn't. It sounded like a painful breakup. I told her in turn about my relationship with Jennifer.

The afternoon descended into early evening, and the shadows spilled through the patio doors and began to darken the room, bringing with them an unseasonable chill.

"How about I start a fire?" I suggested.

"That would be great."

"How about some wine?"

"No, but some water would be nice. I ought to think about leaving before too long, even though I'm enjoying our conversation."

As was I, to be sure. I piled some logs into the fireplace—fortunately remembering to open the flue, which I sometimes disastrously forgot—and brought two glasses of Evian from the kitchen. Nicki had excused herself to go upstairs to the bathroom, and I settled back into the sofa. It had been a good investment, I mused; very amenable to conversation, as well as to even more vigorous pursuits.

The fire was already beginning to crackle robustly when she returned, and as she sat down the flames illuminated her face. As we talked more, I let her carry most of the conversation, allowing myself the indulgence of gazing at her. I decided that no matter what, when I dropped her off I would kiss her. Not passionately, but lightly on the lips. She was spectacular, and no matter if we never saw each other again, I wanted to know how it felt to touch her lips.

And admit it or not, I was beginning to fathom romantic possibilities, which were almost too exquisite to contemplate. The rich conversation we were sharing was one of the most enjoyable—and intimate—I'd ever experienced. I admired the combination of characteristics Nicki seemed to embody: dynamic, confident, yet oh so feminine. There weren't many women like that in Washington.

Toward evening I found myself growing tired and, amazingly, losing my voice. I couldn't remember ever having talked myself hoarse. Plus, I knew that sleep deprivation was catching up with me. Nicki seemed tired, too, and I offered to take her home.

It turned out she lived in an English basement apartment on Capitol Hill, only a mile or so from our offices. I pulled to the curb and walked her to her door.

"The light's not on, so my roommate's not home. Let me show you around real quick." The apartment was small and modest, yet nicely decorated. Her bedroom, at which I had just a peek, was frilly and cozy. Laura Ashley, I was sure.

We walked back to the vestibule and paused there. Neither of us seemed to want the evening to end. I wanted to kiss her but didn't know how to approach it. I still didn't know whether it was a romantic date, or just a developing friendship. So I decided to just lean forward, try to touch her lips with mine, and see how she responded. Just like I might kiss a good female friend. But of course, I would respond if Nicki's lips lingered.

I couldn't remember ever having agonized so much over a kiss. Somehow, I suspected this would be a critical moment for us. What if she recoiled and said, "Blecch!" Or burst out laughing?

We stood by the door for what seemed an eternity. Delaying. But delaying what? The awkwardness of the inevitable kiss attempt? Or the departure, the goodnight? Maybe I was thinking too much. Spontaneity is better, right? Just like when I'd started talking to her the first time in the train.

For once I followed my own advice. "I had a great time, Nicki."

Her smile was huge. "I had a nice time, too. Let's get together soon, maybe go to a museum or something."

Then I was leaning forward to kiss her. I wasn't used to kissing a woman who was my own height, and the trajectory was awkward. My gesture seemed to take her by surprise at first. But her lips lingered, and mine did, too.

I slipped my fingers behind her neck, very lightly. Her lips were warm and soft, and I inhaled her fresh fragrance. I thought fleetingly about pressing forward, about exploring her lips with my tongue. But

I held back. The sensation of our lips touching was electric. And it answered my questions, and filled me with wonder. Finally we pulled apart, and my fingers slid around to her chin, which I brushed softly. Again she smiled, looking sheepish and oh so beautiful.

"Sweet dreams, Nicki," I said, my voice barely a whisper.

"You, too."

I let myself out into the brisk night air, closing the door behind me. I was completely exhausted on my drive back to Alexandria. When I finally reached the townhouse, I collapsed into my bed in the townhouse, and sleep greeted me instantly.

I AWOKE IN the morning even before my alarm sounded, ready to return to the office after a week's absence. I gathered up my contest sketches and was on the parkway before seven. During the hour before my colleagues arrived, I went through the mail and messages that had accumulated.

At the staff meeting, I nervously unveiled my sketches, going through one by one and pointing out the details. A painful silence followed; then . . . applause. I swelled with pride.

"Absolutely superb," Rich exclaimed.

Samantha was on her feet, looking closely at the sketches. "This is beautiful."

My colleagues inspected the drawings for the next half hour, offering some last-minute suggestions, but generally bestowing praise as they discovered new details. Eventually all except Rich returned to their desks or offices to allow me to make some last changes before sending the entry to AWA by courier.

As he stood to leave, Rich clapped an arm on my shoulder. "Kevin, you know this isn't just a contest entry." I looked curiously into his dark eyes. "Win or lose that contest," he continued, "this is a new beginning for Horizon. We're going to have to expand into new construction."

I looked at the sketches, then back at my talented young colleague, whose opinions I greatly respected. I was proud of the concept, proud of the execution, but I considered myself out of my depth and hadn't expected this kind of reaction. "You really think so?"

"Gotta follow your talent," Rich said, turning again to the sketches. Then he held out his hand, which I shook.

"Thanks, Rich. I appreciate your confidence more than I can say."

Around eleven-thirty I emerged with the final product and shipped it off with a sigh. After all the intensity, now I had to stop thinking about it. It would be weeks before I heard anything from the contest committee. I knew my chances were slim, especially with the quality and experience of the competition. I stretched and wandered over to Samantha's office and asked if she wanted to go out for an early lunch. Twenty minutes later we were sitting down at the food court at Union Station, Sam over vegetarian sushi and me over delicious greasy fish and chips.

We talked about what had happened in the office the previous week, my date with Nicki.

She listened thoughtfully, asking occasional questions. "It sounds to me like you're very excited about her."

"I don't even know if Nicki considered it a date. She didn't refer to it that way, and I didn't get any definite signs."

"If she's as attractive as you say, she probably doesn't find too many guys who are content to have a conversation for hours on end."

"You're probably right. But I surely was content. And even if nothing else develops, I think I would enjoy a friendship with her."

"Just be careful that you don't set yourself up for a fall."

WORK WAS BUSY that week, with both Parkside and Kalorama demanding a great deal of attention. Beth invited my colleagues and me to a comedy benefit at a local high school that Friday, and I decided to invite Nicki. I called and she seemed happy to hear from me. I told her about Friday, certain that she already had plans. To my surprise she accepted, then added words that made my pulse quicken: "It's a date." I was psyched beyond belief. We arranged to meet at a downtown bar, the Brickskellar, for drinks before the show.

I called my mother later that evening, as a purring Elvis rubbed against my legs. I was pleased to hear vigor in my mother's voice. She in turn was thrilled to hear about my romantic prospect. I tried not to get her hopes up too much. "Nicki's too beautiful," I insisted.

"Nobody's too beautiful for my baby boy." She made me smile, as she did so often.

Friday came and went quickly, and several of my colleagues

gathered with me after work at the Brickskellar. An unexpected late-winter blizzard was forecast that night for the Washington area, but it looked like the weather would hold for the show. I settled into the bar over a beer.

I'd brought a sample of Ralph Lauren cologne that I'd picked up from a department store during lunchtime. Nicki had mentioned the previous weekend how much she liked certain men's colognes. I had agonized over the choice, and hoped she liked it. In the men's room, I dumped the entire small vial onto my hands and slapped it liberally over my face and neck. My colleagues noticed it immediately when I returned, even over the smell of beer and smoke in the bar.

"What *are* you wearing?" Alice asked me.

"I think it smells kind of nice," Beth said.

"It smells kind of *strong*," Rich said.

I hoped the scent would subside a bit before Nicki arrived. She was late, and I was afraid she wouldn't show. But a few minutes later, she made her entrance. I spied her from across the bar before she saw me. She looked dazzling in a conservative but stylish green business suit and long coat. She was wearing wire-rimmed glasses, which I had forgotten about, but which enhanced her gorgeous looks.

Nicki finally spotted me and flashed a brilliant smile. She came over and gave me an affectionate hug. I introduced her to Rich and Kim Deeks, Alice, Sam, Beth, and her boyfriend, Brad. I watched admiringly as Nicki launched easily and enthusiastically into conversation with my friends. It didn't surprise me that she was comfortable in social settings.

After a short time we had to leave for the show. As I helped Nicki on with her coat, I glanced over at Rich, who was discreetly giving me a thumbs-up sign.

The school was only a few blocks away so we all walked together. After a peek of springtime, the March weather had turned frigid, the air clear but bracing. I walked with Samantha as Nicki was engrossed in conversation with Alice. I watched appreciatively as they walked ahead of us; Nicki was making a real effort with my friends.

"Are you listening?" Sam asked. I realized she had been talking and I hadn't heard a thing she had said.

"Of course I'm listening," I replied.

"So what do you think about what I just told you?"

"I think it's *fantastic!*"

Sam stopped in her tracks, nearly causing Rich and Kim to collide with us. Sam cast one of her famous grimaces in my direction. "You think waiting three hours to contest a bogus parking ticket is *fantastic?!*"

I laughed. "I was wondering where you were this morning."

We started walking again. "You are so strange sometimes."

We arrived just before the show began. It was a comedy about political follies, silly but clever, and fairly ecumenical in its disdain for both Democrats and Republicans. Nicki and I both laughed.

I felt Nicki reach across and entwine her fingers with mine. I looked over and she was smiling. Her hand felt warm and soft, and I was absolutely in heaven. After awhile she leaned over and whispered, "You smell really nice." She guessed which brand of cologne I was wearing, which I found amazing. I made a mental note to go back to the store and buy a gallon of it.

I could feel my colleagues' occasional glances, checking us out. I couldn't remember ever feeling so pumped to be seen with a woman. Was it just because she was the most beautiful woman on Earth? No, I hoped not: she was turning out to be special in more ways than physical beauty.

When the show ended, everyone wanted to get home before the storm, so we all made for our cars. I offered to walk Nicki to hers, which turned out to be parked a few blocks away near mine.

We snuggled close against the gusty cold wind along the way. As we walked, snow flurries began to fall. Too quickly, we reached her car and paused awkwardly next to it. The snow was already cleansing the streets with a blanket of white. The street lamps illuminated the flakes as they streamed to earth. It reminded me of a surrealistic yet magical scene from the movie *Edward Scissorhands*; and as I contemplated my surroundings I thought that it was one of the most intensely romantic moments I had ever experienced, so much that I was nearly overcome with passion.

All at once we were holding each other and kissing, passionately, sweetly. The world was spinning. It was like a dream come true, pure ecstasy, delectable, divine. I lost myself in it, hoping the sublime experience would never end. Kissing is for me the most intimate act on earth. To really enjoy it, it seems to me, you have to be deeply attracted to the person you're kissing. You can have sex with someone while fantasizing about someone else, but kissing is undeniably personal. So close, tasting not only your lover's taste but inhaling her breath, her scent. Exploring adventurously, playfully, lustily, losing your self in ecstasy. If I had to choose to forever give up either kissing or sex, the choice wouldn't be a tough one.

And then suddenly a voice from behind: "I see you found your cars!" Not releasing my hold on Nicki, I turned my head to see Rich Deeks opening his car door across the street. I hadn't noticed his car parked so close to ours. Rich was beaming, as were Kim and Alice. We waved as they pulled away, then turned to face each other again.

"I wish the evening didn't have to end," I said hopefully.

"They're predicting as much as a foot of snow."

"Well, I'd better let you go." I gently slipped my fingers underneath her chin and lifted her lips to mine, kissing her again. "Drive carefully."

I held her car door and closed it after her. She waved as she drove off, and I stood there watching the taillights recede into the distance, savoring both the moments that had just passed and the possibilities that suddenly seemed to lay ahead.

After returning home I bunkered inside the townhouse, listening to the stereo, reading magazines, and petting Elvis. Around midnight the phone rang, startling both of us.

The voice was soft and familiar. "I can still smell your scent on my hands," Nicki said without greeting.

"I hope that's good." Did I say that I intended to buy a gallon of it? How about stock in the company?

Nicki chuckled. "Even my roommate likes it."

We talked for several minutes, promising to check on each other over the weekend to see how we were weathering the worsening storm. Then we signed off. I felt positively pumped. A call from the Beacon at midnight! That she felt familiar enough to call—and motivated to do so—was exhilarating.

It turned out to be a nesting weekend for the cat and me. The storm lasted until Saturday noon, dumping fourteen inches on the Washington area, less than a week before spring was slated to appear.

The next afternoon Nicki called. "I have cabin fever."

"Me, too."

"Can you get your car out?"

"A mere fourteen inches of snow never stopped a Saab."

"How about going out for Chinese food?"

THE NEXT FEW months were a blur, for so much happened so quickly.

It wasn't just Nicki; it was simply, wonderfully, my Midas Touch time. It seemed that everything—*everything*—went right, from my career, to my mother's health, to romance. Even the days seemed brighter, the spring flowers more vibrant, the Washington landscape crisper.

But in fact, really it was a time of payoffs from past investments. The dividends from my personal life were reinvested into my professional life, and vice-versa. I'm sure my face during that time wore a permanently goofy grin.

I spent a great deal of time with Nicki; and what time I didn't spend with her I spent talking to or thinking about her. And those thoughts in turn fueled me in my other endeavors, inspired me, made me better. I felt like a total stud in every way. On the Monday after the outing where they had met her, I discreetly asked each of my colleagues what they thought of Nicki. Rich was unequivocally favorable. Beth hedged, but said she seemed very nice.

Samantha dissented. "I just don't like her. I get a really bad feeling about her."

"C'mon, Sam, you're not being specific. Give me a reason."

"Can't you just chalk it up to female intuition?"

Actually, I did place quite a bit of stock in female intuition. But I'd also observed lots of female cat fights. And I wasn't sure into which category these comments fit. "I could, but it would be nice to get something a bit more tangible than that."

Samantha's brown eyes were tentative, but she voiced her thoughts anyway. "She seems superficial. Nobody can be that upbeat all the time and really mean it."

There was hardly a day over the next few months that I didn't see Nicki or at least talk to her on the phone. She proved to be a world-class talker, enjoying long conversations in person or on the phone, especially as an antidote to her occasional middle-of-the-night insomnia. My phone rang frequently in the wee hours; followed by a spirited "Hi, I can't sleep," no apology, and a stream of conversation as if it were the middle of the day. I grew to enjoy the nocturnal interruptions. It made me feel intimate with Nicki; and besides, at that time of night she didn't expect me to hold up my end of the conversation.

We mostly spent our time eating out at restaurants, drinking lots of wine, taking walks in the blossoming springtime, and renting movies to watch at my house. Except that we almost never finished watching the movies. The combination of wine and a very comfortable sofa seemed invariably to lead to snuggling and kissing.

Yet therein emerged the bundle of contradictions that was Nicole Petri. She made it clear from the beginning that as a Catholic, premarital sex was a big deal and not something she engaged in without a great deal of certainty. As a result, she announced (and I was all ears) that she never slept with anyone until three months into the relationship, because at that point she would know that she loved him.

Personally, from the perspective of sin, I couldn't see much difference between premarital sex one month or three months into a relationship, but I didn't mention that to Nicki because I didn't want to dash any prospects by alerting her to a contradiction. The fact that she had brought it up at all filled me with exuberant anticipation, and I certainly didn't mind waiting if there was a prospect of making love to her. Which I wanted to do, very badly.

Anyway, during one of our first evenings together, we were kissing and touching, very erotically, and quickly we reached the point of no return. So in an effort to cool things off, I maneuvered behind Nicki and began gently massaging her shoulders.

"What are you doing?" she asked curtly.

"Massaging your shoulders." I thought perhaps she was irritated that I had stopped necking with her, though I was trying to accede to her wishes not to go further than that.

"Well, stop. I don't like massages. I'm German on my mother's side, and we don't like to be touched."

I was flabbergasted. Here was a woman who loved to kiss and

caress for hours at a time, but she couldn't stand to have her shoulders massaged. By contrast, not only Jennifer but her sisters literally had lined up for my massages, but of course I acquiesced to Nicki's demand.

She remarked upon the incident when we had dinner with one of her friends, Karen Simmons, and Karen's husband Doug. "Kevin likes to give massages, but I hate to receive them because I'm German," Nicki announced cheerfully.

"You're kidding," Karen exclaimed. "I wish Doug liked to give massages. You don't know what you're missing." Karen, an attractive blonde of about thirty, was an advertising executive who had worked with Nicki at the radio station. Doug, who was about thirty-five with a short-cropped gray beard and thick glasses, was a divorce lawyer in Fairfax. I hit it off extremely well with both, particularly Doug, who was shy but had a terrific dry wit. It also turned out he played racquetball, which I also enjoyed, and before long we had established a regular game.

One Sunday, the four of us also drove up to the picturesque foothills of the Shenandoah Mountains to taste wine at Hillside Winery, which I considered Virginia's finest. It was a beautiful day, and we indulged in delicious Chardonnay and paté as we sat on the winery's deck. Nicki and Karen went for a walk among the grapevines as Doug and I talked about politics. When Karen returned to the table and Nicki was in the ladies' room, Karen announced, "Nicki's crazy about you."

I beamed. I wanted to believe it, but I wouldn't allow myself to, at least not yet.

That she genuinely liked me was something I could have inferred from many of Nicki's actions, but not from her words. She had a habit of conveying feelings—including feelings about herself—not directly, but in the third-person. In certain respects, Nicki was self-deprecating. She considered herself fat, even though I thought she had a nice figure. Sometimes she would push her nose back in a parody of a pig, which I thought was quite amusing. Overall, she had a favorable self-image, which she rarely expressed directly but usually by attributing the views to others. She frequently told me what people said about her—always beginning the quote with her name, as in, "'So,' he said, 'Nicki, you are such an attractive woman,'" or 'Nicki, you are so intelligent.'" I got a kick out of it; especially the exuberant way she pronounced her name, with a strong emphasis on the first vowel.

She also conveyed feelings about me that way, telling me about compliments other people gave me, but never giving me one herself. By contrast, I had no trouble expressing my affection directly through words or actions, and did so often, to Nicki's apparent embarrassment. In such situations, Nicki would typically say, "You're silly," making me wonder whether her feelings were reciprocal.

One evening we were lying on the sofa and sipping wine, and she told me about a conversation she'd had with her mother about me. "My mother asked about you. I told her, 'I think I'm falling in love with him.'"

I nearly fell off the sofa, but collected myself and didn't say anything, though it made me ecstatic.

She also talked about wanting to have children, a desire I strongly shared. One time I remarked, "I'd like to have a little girl, just like you." The mental image of a cute little blonde-haired version of Nicole filled me with awe.

"You mean crazy, just like me?"

"No, sweet and beautiful, just like you."

She shook her head back and forth, a serious look on her face. "You don't know me very well."

I wondered about how such a wonderful woman could harbor such negative thoughts about herself. To me, it just made her seem even more mysterious and alluring.

That episode wasn't the only time that Nicki revealed contrasting sides of herself; in fact, she did so repeatedly. On one hand she was exceptionally generous. She was constantly buying thoughtful gifts for people, and seemed to derive enormous gratification from it. By no means was I the only beneficiary, but I was frequently the object of her bounty. Over time and for no occasion, she gave me a beautiful shirt and tie, a bottle of cologne, and chocolate-covered strawberries, all of which were totally on target and amazingly generous, considering that she wasn't working.

She was an avid volunteer, spending several hours each week at the Washington Children's Hospital giving care to babies with AIDS— something I admired enormously but couldn't imagine having enough emotional reserves to do myself. She was close to her family, often babysitting her sister's children and staying in daily contact with her mother.

And yet . . . it was odd that at the same time she seemed to revel in her dark side, to which she frequently made references. Apparently she was one to exact vengeance for indignities that were visited upon her. She told me that she'd sent dead roses to her old boyfriend Carlos's new girlfriend, which I didn't know whether to take seriously. Nicki disclosed in passing (indeed, it seemed that every revelation was made in passing—Nicki was someone you had to pay close attention to lest you missed the choicest morsels) that she regularly visited a therapist named Amelia. In one of her third-party endorsements, she announced excitedly, "Amelia thinks you're good for me!" I took that as good news. I never knew what to say about these revelations, and chalked up much of what she said to exaggeration and a need for self-deprecation.

She was an avid churchgoer, and actually got me into it. We found a wonderful Catholic Church in Old Town, St. Matthew's, with short and upbeat Sunday services. I had to admit to Nicki that it made me feel some spiritual tugging on my heathen heartstrings.

We attended an elegant benefit there that was well-attended by Washington's top social strata. The mayor was there, dapper and over-the-top ebullient as usual, along with such tipsy denizens of the Washington political community as Ted Kennedy and Bob Packwood. As always, Nicki was charming and ravishingly attractive, hanging on my arm and making me feel like a million bucks. I could feel the envious eyes of many men in the room, a feeling I came to expect whenever I was with her.

I was pulled away at one point to talk shop with some former colleagues from Fielder, Steinmetz, and glanced back to see Nicki talking earnestly with the parish priest, Dennis Newman, for whom I had designed some renovations as a volunteer a few years earlier. Eventually she moved to a different conversation and, with a glance to make sure Nicki wasn't watching, the priest came toward me, a big grin on his face.

"That beautiful young lady who was hanging on your arm asked whether it was possible for a Catholic to get married to a non-Catholic in the Catholic Church," he said. "It seems she wants to marry you, and she wants to do it in a Catholic Church." I looked at him blankly.

"That's the obvious implication, anyway. She wanted to know if the church would give its blessing to a marriage outside the fold." He smiled broadly.

"So what did you tell her?"

"Well, I told her that although you couldn't be married in the church, a priest could marry you outside the church if he were willing." He slapped me on the back.

"Well, we'll see. We've only been dating for several weeks."

Even though I was thrilled by the direction our relationship was taking, it suddenly seemed awfully fast. Part of what was sounding alarm bells was that it was clear Nicki wasn't fully over Carlos. They'd dated for several years and had even lived with each other, and had moved apart only the previous fall, just before I'd met her.

Nicki talked about Carlos incessantly, and I knew there was always a comparison going on. It didn't bother me too much, particularly given that I talked about Jennifer a great deal as well. But what was strange were the contradictory statements Nicki made about their breakup. Sometimes she insisted she had instigated the end of the relationship; other times she intimated that Carlos had broken up with her.

I'd met her family. Her mother and father were nice, simple people who lived in a working-class neighborhood in Baltimore. Nicki had remarked one time that her father had wanted a son, and was disappointed about having two daughters. Neither of her parents seemed demonstrative, which made me understand where Nicki's hesitancy about physical affection came from.

Nicki's younger sister, Kim, was a tall, attractive blonde married to a police officer in Baltimore County. They had two young kids, a boy and a girl, who Nicki adored. Nicki was especially close to Kim, and they frequently exchanged conspiratorial whispers, which made me smile. The family was apparently used to Nicki bringing boyfriends over—I wondered whether they were unhappy over Nicki's breakup with Carlos—and they treated me politely but without great warmth or curiosity.

Nicki was such a challenge, yet I felt like I was applying important lessons I had learned from my relationship with Jennifer. First, truthfulness: in my early, fleeting relationships, I had thought nothing of infidelities or white lies, thereby confirming a well-earned negative image that many women have about the entire male species. It wasn't until Jennifer that I learned how comfortable and enriching a relationship could be if built upon trust. And with Nicki I made it a habit always to be truthful.

The second lesson, which I had also learned from Jennifer, was that a relationship has to be balanced, in that it was unhealthy for one person to have stronger feelings for the other. Not that Jennifer didn't love me deeply and sincerely, but I had decided quite early that I wanted to spend the rest of my life with her, and Jen never quite reached that point with me, which led to frustration and resentment. So I was priding myself in my gradually developing feelings for Nicki, which seemed reciprocal. I told myself that I wasn't growing too attached to her, that I was keeping my feelings in check.

Meanwhile, the positive synergy from my relationship with Nicki was spilling over into my work. I was on a roll, scoring about every job we competed for. About six weeks after entering the AWA contest, I learned that my entry had won first place. Everyone was ecstatic, especially Art Longley, who had goaded me into entering, and Rich, who saw it as opening huge new opportunities for our firm. Nicki was thrilled, too, though it seemed less for the award itself than for the black-tie event in June at which I would receive it. Spontaneously, I popped an invitation to celebrate with a long weekend in Bermuda after the event; and to my utter delight, Nicki agreed.

It was a wonder that I could accomplish anything at all at work, considering my constant state of sleep deprivation. Nicki wasn't working, and we were spending lots of late nights together, drinking copious amounts of wine and snuggling late into the night. I could kiss Nicki for hours. And it didn't bother me to wait to make love to her, because holding back induced creativity and lush fantasies.

One night we were eating a late dinner on my sofa. As was our habit, we were drinking a superb bottle of wine, in that case a California Meritage. The usually serious Nicki was laughing more than usual, about the silliest things, and making repeated sexual innuendoes.

"You don't know what drinking red wine does to me."

"Oh, yes I do. And I like it, a lot."

"But this is *really good* red wine."

"I think you should have some more," I said, draining the remainder of the bottle into her glass.

I was tempting danger, though, I knew. We would probably end up making out on the sofa into the wee hours, and I had an eight o'clock meeting the next morning. My colleagues were surely noticing my bleary-eyed mornings lately; in fact, I could count on Samantha to comment on them.

But Nicki clearly had contrary ideas. After she had finished the last sip of wine, she announced, "I think we should open another bottle."

That was unprecedented: we almost always finished the bottle of wine we opened, but never had we opened a second. I merely smiled and retrieved another bottle of Meritage from the wine rack.

After I poured two glasses of wine, I snuggled close to Nicki. "What's the occasion?" I asked.

She smiled sweetly, our lips barely an inch apart, and she whispered, "Wine helps me overcome my inhibitions."

The remark sent me into overdrive and I leaned over and kissed her deeply, my mind suddenly filled with possibilities.

We pulled apart and Nicki took two deep swallows of wine, almost gulping. She looked at me again, an uncharacteristically sly expression on her face. Man, is she beautiful, I thought.

She stared at me.

"What?"

"I think we should go upstairs."

It hadn't been three months yet, so I was incredulous. "Are you sure?"

"Definitely."

I rose slightly, but Nicki put her hand on my knee and I sat down again. She licked her lips. "Wait. There's something else." Was she having second thoughts? I looked at her expectantly. Finally, her emerald eyes huge, she continued. "I think we should use the handcuffs."

If ever I were more jolted by a remark in my life, I couldn't remember it. "Seriously?"

"I think it will help me go through with it."

I wasn't about to argue. "Okay," I happily agreed, my mouth suddenly dry.

My head began to spin and suddenly I wished I hadn't indulged so recklessly. I began to rise abruptly from the sofa, but as I did, I lost my balance slightly, knocked my full glass of wine into the air; it cartwheeled and spilled its contents in spectacular fashion all over the floor and the white sofa. The spectacle roused Elvis, who had been napping near the fireplace, and she fled from the room just as the glass was coming to rest on the carpet, intact but completely empty.

After a moment of stunned silence, Nicki and I burst into peals of laughter, breaking the tension. "You are so clumsy!" she said, as if I didn't already know that already. "We'd better clean it up right away before it stains." She ran to the kitchen. I stood waiting for her dumbly, wondering whether I'd blown my sexual prospects as utterly as I had destroyed the romantic mood.

After she returned, we both got down on our hands and knees to scrub the damage. I couldn't believe how much wine had spewed around the room. Finally we couldn't find anymore (though I would discover errant traces in odd places for months after), and as we stood at the sink rinsing the sponges, Nicki took me into her arms and kissed me. The taste of red wine made the kiss especially delicious.

As I pulled back, still holding her, I asked reluctantly, "Do you think that was an omen that we shouldn't do this?"

Nicki smiled. "It's an omen that you're a total klutz, and that I should be very careful that you don't break any bones while we're making love."

We went upstairs, Nicki stopping at the bathroom. I went to the third floor bedroom, where I lit a candle on the table next to my bed and retrieved the handcuffs from the dresser drawer where they had been secreted since my party.

Nicki came upstairs and undressed in the dim light of the flickering candle, then slid between the sheets. I took off my clothes and joined her. It was the first time we were completely naked together, and the contact of our bodies was electric.

We kissed for awhile, but Nicki seemed anxious. "Put on the handcuffs," she whispered.

"Are you absolutely sure?"

"Put on the handcuffs," she repeated; and as if to punctuate the remark, she raised her hands above her head and grabbed two of the iron bars.

That was all the prompting I needed. I kneeled on the bed, unfastened the cuffs and locked one over her slender wrist, then slipped the chain around a bar and reached for her other wrist.

"Just keep the keys handy," she said.

"I know. I once read this book by Stephen King—"

"Just put the handcuffs on. I don't want to hear about Stephen King right now."

I obliged and looked down at her. With her hands and wrists bound to the metal headboard she looked vulnerable. And unbelievably erotic.

I slid down next to her and kissed her lips lightly, then worked my way down to the side of her breast, which was exposed by her arms above her. She squirmed and moaned softly. I explored every inch of her, drunk not only on the wine but with the euphoria of discovery. Her body was splendid. Soft, round breasts, creamy white skin, firm round hips. She trembled as I explored the expanse of her body first with my hands, then my tongue. My fingers errantly brushed between her legs, making her shiver. As I moved to kiss her mouth, I slid my fingers gently inside her, stroking her rhythmically, making her gasp. She squirmed and urged me on more quickly, but I wanted to linger, to savor, to make her need me, crave me.

And finally when I perceived she could stand it no longer, I shifted on top and slipped inside her. She was moist, hot. She moaned, pushing her head back into the pillow, exposing her neck to my probing mouth and teeth. We entered naturally into a steady, enthusiastic rhythm, all the while kissing deeply, hungrily.

I pulled my face away from hers to watch her in rapture, her eyes closed and lips parted, golden hair shrouding the pillow. The sight of her this way made me unbelievably excited, impelling me to thrust harder, deeper, more urgently.

She moaned loudly between quick breaths, tossing her head back and forth. I stared raptly at her face, licking the perspiration beading at her temples. We went at each other with animal energy. Though Nicki was bound to the iron railing, her hips thrust toward me with fervor, drawing me deeply inside her. Her eyes were closed tightly, her mouth now wide open and rasping for breath. Her moans were louder and more frenzied now, choking and almost painful. Her eyelids opened ever so slightly. The sight made me start, for I could see only the whites of her eyes, making it seem that they had rolled back into her head. I could feel her heart pounding into my chest so hard that it seemed it would burst. In tandem with her desperate moans and gasps, all at once I wondered if Nicki was experiencing some kind of seizure.

I slowed my thrusts and examined her face, worried that she was on the verge of passing out. When she realized what I was doing, she opened her eyes with a panicked look and clamped me with her knees, pulling me back inside her. She whispered huskily, struggling to catch her breath, "Don't stop. Sometimes I can't breathe. It's okay; it heightens the intensity." She licked her lips. "Don't stop. Please."

I obliged, reluctantly at first. But the musky scent of our lovemaking aroused me anew. I switched positions on the bed, lying with my head by her feet and scissoring my legs between hers so that I could touch her while I was pumping into her. The combination seemed to drive her into even greater frenzy, and her breath and moans quickened again as she pounded her head into the pillow. "Oh, Christ," she managed to gasp.

After a while she raised her head slightly and commanded, "Come back." I extricated myself and mounted her again, my face close to hers. The sight of her parted lips and rapturous expression took my breath away. I slipped my hands under her shoulder blades, entering her again, slowly at first. She encircled me with her legs, goading me to go at her harder, deeper. All at once I was seized by a powerful surge of physical passion and thrust so hard I thought for sure I'd hurt her. Once again she moaned painfully, but this time it incited me even more. I clamped my mouth over hers, pumping inside her with pulsating intensity. She thrashed forward, then back into the pillow again, yanking painfully against the handcuffs. She moaned loudly and louder still, sounds of anguish and ecstasy, until finally her body shuddered violently. Her orgasm brought me simultaneously to a long, deeply fulfilling climax.

I remained on top of her for a moment, both of us panting heavily, then pulled out from her. She lay with her eyes closed, her chest heaving, covered with our sweat.

I kissed her lightly on the cheek where damp strands of her hair lay matted. Then I leaned over and retrieved the keys to the handcuffs from the nightstand. I fumbled to open the cuffs and release her hands. As she was freed she rolled over and embraced me, her tongue probing and entering my mouth. As we kissed, she slipped her hands down my back to my hips, drawing me back toward her again.

At first I thought I was so spent I could not possibly make love again, maybe ever. But the kiss was so erotic I felt myself stiffen instantly, and before long I was inside her again. Skillfully using her hands to guide me, she set a slower, gentler, more rhythmic pace than before. I was sore, which seemed only to make the experience all the more exquisite.

She raised her face to kiss me again. As she did, unexpectedly she raked her fingernails down the length of my back, so deeply and painfully I thought I could feel welts start to form. I jerked my mouth away from hers, but she clasped her hands behind my head and pulled me even closer. The combination made me shake uncontrollably, both for its pain and its eroticism. I directed my intensified energy between her legs, and we rolled across the bed, first Nicki on top, then me, then Nicki again, in an ardent sexual wrestling match that we fought to a draw. Minutes later her body and mine shivered again, this time in unison.

I extracted myself from her, more sated and exhausted than I had been in my whole life. Nicki snuggled against me, her arms encircling my shoulders. I could feel the hot tingling sensation from the welts on my back, and Nicki's heart racing against my chest. I gently caressed and kissed her face, then stroked her hair, which was drenched at the edges with sweat. Neither of us could speak, or wanted to.

Gradually, Nicki's breathing slowed as she descended toward exhausted sleep. I stayed awake, propped on an elbow looking down on her, still stroking her face and hair. The moon streamed through the window, bathing Nicki in a celestial light.

"Holy shit," I murmured, shaking my head in disbelief as I stared at her. Then added, to my surprise, "I love you," knowing that she was not awake to hear it.

As I gazed at the beautiful woman sleeping contentedly beside me, I pondered over the enigma she presented in so many ways. This first sexual experience with her had been literally incredible. At moments it had terrified me. But it had also awakened something deep inside me, a forbidden, almost primordial lust, that I had never experienced before.

I lay back in exhaustion, still holding her. As I finally surrendered to sleep, I realized that whatever mysteries Nicki presented, however bizarre were some aspects of this woman with whom I was falling in love, what we had just experienced had opened up whole new vistas, an exhilarating combination of pleasure, decadence, and danger.

And I acknowledged then that I would pursue it, whatever the costs.

7

SEX WAS TO become a permanently defining part of our relationship. It was hot, raw, and constant. Sex was the only perfect symmetry between us. The reason we were so well-matched was that we shared a common goal: the primary object of my lovemaking was to pleasure Nicki—and so was hers.

That remark is not a criticism of Nicki, nor an expression of self-lessness on my part. To the contrary. Nicki's needs were ravenous, and I was only too happy to try to satisfy them. To be sure, Nicki in bed was monomaniacally focused on her own sexual fulfillment. But so was I, for the most selfish of motives. Something about physically pleasuring Nicki brought me to heights of ecstasy I had never before experienced. I came to crave the sight of Nicki's lips parted in sexual bliss, the sound of her gasping for breath, the pounding of her heart. The greater the sexual frenzy, the louder the moans, the closer to passing out I could bring her, the more exquisite my satisfaction. We were perfectly matched as sexual partners. And I grew utterly addicted to it.

And though Nicki persisted in the facade of sex as some sort of pristine act, both of us seemed increasingly to want it to be as decadent as possible. The more formal the setting—the more earnest the conversation that preceded it—the more inspired we were to go at it afterward. We interrupted dinner to have sex on the floor, we pulled over on the road and made love in the car; even once at a crowded party we furtively (but perhaps not so discreetly) disappeared into a bathroom and made love on the tile.

I recount all this not to be exhibitionist, but because it was the first relationship for me in which sex was so central. But despite the fact that sex was obviously and constantly on both of our minds, we never discussed it or followed it with the lingering pillow talk Jen and I had so enjoyed. To the contrary, Nicki seemed embarrassed over her voracious sexual appetite. It was almost like Jekyll and Hyde: the modest proprietess juxtaposed against the decadent sex addict.

I was mesmerized by the relationship. I felt myself in a dream state as I went about my business. I wondered how long it could last; and decided I wanted somehow to make it last forever.

One Wednesday morning when work was slow after a particularly blissful night with Nicki, I found myself in Samantha's office, telling her just that.

"I'm in love. I'm not holding back anymore. I'm incredibly happy."

Samantha regarded me with a dubious expression, her chin resting on her hands which were propped on her desk. "Well, I'm still a little bit skeptical, but I'm really happy for you."

For Sam that was akin to an unqualified endorsement, and I beamed. I gave Samantha a big hug. "Thanks."

"Aww," she said, patting my back. When I pulled away, her eyes were moist.

"I need to go see Rich," I said.

My mission with Rich made me apprehensive: the painful fact of the matter was that if I was going to pursue my relationship with Nicki, I needed to make more money. Her last boyfriend, Carlos, was wealthy and had gotten Nicki accustomed to a pampered lifestyle. Together, Nicki and I had extravagant tastes, and my monthly credit card bill had grown from several hundred to more than two thousand dollars a month, mainly for dinners and wine. And Nicki wasn't working, so she couldn't contribute to our outings. If I was going to propose spontaneous romantic adventures like Bermuda, I would have to bring home a bigger paycheck.

ALTHOUGH ALICE NANCE was the office manager, Rich Deeks had superb business sense, and served as the firm's de facto business manager. He was happily unruffled by my request. "No problem," he said. "You're only drawing about two-thirds of what you could." He was right: I'd tried to leave as much capital inside the company as possible. "You could easily pay yourself an extra twenty-K a year and we wouldn't skip a beat."

"That's great, but I don't want to put the firm in a precarious position. So let's go after new business."

I knew I was saying what Rich had long been waiting to hear. He was always after me to expand the firm, and plainly hated it when we turned potential business away. And I knew Rich was both talented and ambitious, and that we'd lose him if we didn't allow him to grow within the firm. "After all, our name is Horizon. That means even the sky isn't a limit."

"That means we'll have to hire some new architects."

"Tell you what, I'll take ten-K a year more now, and nothing more until the new architects pay for themselves with new business."

"And I'll tell *you* what: I'll guarantee you can give yourself an even bigger raise a year from today."

"If I do, Rich, you do, too."

And with that we sealed the deal with a firm handshake.

I was feeling tremendously pumped, but wasn't able to share it with Nicki because she'd driven out to the countryside to visit some friends. That evening I played racquetball with Doug Simmons, who was rapidly becoming a close friend. That was terrific: most of my best friends were women, and it was great to have a guy friend. Doug was a steady, precise, and relentless player; I was dramatic, energetic, and prone either to make a great shot or come up embarrassingly empty. The result was that Doug won most of the games, but I usually pushed him to exhaustion.

We had great conversations in the showers. Politics usually, a subject on which we mostly agreed, but this night Doug said, "Karen says Nicki has never been as smitten with a guy as with you."

"Well, I am totally, head-over-heels in love with Nicki," I replied, hoping that would get back to her. It was fine with me if we communicated these things through friends. As we were getting drinks afterward, I asked, "What's the deal with her old boyfriend, Carlos?"

"Well, I never met him. They were breaking up just as Karen and Nicki were becoming friends. It sounded to me like it was a very obsessive relationship. Unhealthy."

"On whose part?"

"Nicki's. She was gonzo over the guy."

"So you don't know what he was like?"

"No. We met a couple of the guys Nicki dated after she and Carlos broke up, and they were as different as night and day. But it was always clear that Carlos was lurking somewhere in the background. They seemed to use people they were dating to torment each other."

Doug said all that nonchalantly, but it hit me like a ton of bricks. I was surprised that Nicki had dated in the few months between Carlos and me—and not just one guy, but several. More disturbingly, was Carlos still around, even now? Was I just a ploy to get back at Carlos? It was a deflating thought.

I felt unsettled on the drive back to Old Town. After I reached my townhouse and fed Elvis, I tried Nicki on the phone. I didn't think she would be home—she told me she'd be returning late—but I really felt like talking to her. I left a message telling her I missed her, and asked her to call me no matter what time she returned. A tinge of doubt struck me: what if she wasn't with friends, but with Carlos? I brushed the thought away. Nicki seemed scrupulously honest. I had no reason to doubt her.

I wasn't hungry, so I pulled out a bottle of chardonnay from the refrigerator that I always had on hand. Turning on the stereo to some Yanni, which Nicki loved, the wine mellowed my mood and summoned romantic thoughts. With a contented Elvis purring beside me, I decided to do something I hadn't done since I was a little kid: to write a love poem.

It took me to the wee hours of the night. I agonized over the rhymes and cadence. Of course, only certain words rhyme with Nicki—sticky, picky, and of course hickey—so the poem turned out both sweet and silly. But when I finally completed it around two, I was very happy with it. I hadn't even spoken to Nicki, but I went to sleep feeling that I'd spent an intimate evening with her.

Nicki still hadn't called by noon—surprising, because she usually called me two or three times each day—so I thought perhaps she had spent the night with a friend rather than drive home at night. I decided to surprise her by having the poem couriered to her house. I went out at lunchtime and bought some velvet ribbon and a card, and sent it off.

By five I decided to call her again. She answered on the second ring.

"Hey," I asked, "how was the trip?"

"Fine. I decided not to drive back last night, so I stayed over and came back this morning."

"When did you get home?"

"Oh, around eleven."

That stung. Why hadn't she returned my calls? I didn't ask that, and the conversation drifted off into other subjects. But it wasn't the normal easy tone. I asked if she'd like to have dinner, and she begged off. "We're going out for drinks tomorrow with your friends, right?" I said yes. "Well, I don't feel like going out tonight. I have a headache. You know how much I hate to drive."

"No, I didn't know that." She hadn't driven much since we'd been together.

"I've told you that a million times."

Finally, I couldn't stand it any longer and asked, "Did you get anything from me today?"

"Oh yeah, the poem. You're silly." She didn't sound amused.

"Did you like it?"

"It was cute. You know, you really need a girlfriend who has a sense of humor."

Her remark was like a kick in the solar plexus. Did she really mean that? I didn't know how to respond, but I felt like a deflated balloon. "Well, I guess I'll see you tomorrow."

"I'll come by your office around six."

"Okay." I paused. "'Bye."

"'Bye," she said, and hung up.

I was blown away. Had I done something wrong? Nicki was moody, but I'd never encountered anything like this. Had my poem somehow offended her? I couldn't imagine that; it was so gushy, so innocently romantic. Perhaps she'd had a bad experience on her visit. Hopefully she would call later. But she didn't, and I tried to put it out of my mind. When she arrived at my office the next day after work, looking radiant in a sundress, it seemed as if nothing had happened. Her smile was as bright as the day.

We gathered up Rich, Alice, Beth, and Samantha to go out for drinks at Tony's, a nearby bar that had a good wine selection. We ordered and Nicki told everyone about her road trip. I listened for clues to something that had gone wrong, but there was nothing. After three rounds of drinks, the conversation turned to politics, and eventually to the curfew recently adopted for teens in the District of Columbia.

That was an issue that united my colleagues, liberal or conservative, in opposition. But not Nicki, it turned out. Emphatically not Nicki.

My colleagues were accustomed to frank debates. "What happens to kids who have to work or go someplace legitimately?" Alice asked. "I mean, like church, for gosh sakes?"

"I think it's the parents' responsibility," Samantha agreed. "Not the government's."

Nicki disagreed angrily. "You people have obviously never worked in a hospital." Everyone looked at her curiously. "I volunteer in a hospital, and I see the people who get brought in at night. The police should keep those people off the streets at night."

"You work with AIDS babies, not in the emergency room," I said.

"They're the same people who are having babies and they shouldn't be having babies, either."

"Are you suggesting, like, involuntary Norplant for welfare recipients?" Beth asked.

"Why not?" Nicki answered defensively, her voice choking with emotion. "Some people aren't fit to be parents." Everyone but me laughed.

Though I strongly disagreed with Nicki, I felt like my colleagues were ganging up on her and that the atmosphere was getting a bit too tense. "Listen, Nicki sees this from a perspective that none of the rest of us has. There are serious social costs to freedom."

"And there are serious social costs to authoritarianism," Alice lectured me. "If you have a curfew, the only people who are affected are the law-abiding ones."

Nicki's tone turned icy as she said, "You people are either incredibly naive, or incredibly stupid. My cousin is a cop in Baltimore, and he'll tell you what it's like to try to keep order without a curfew."

Alice snorted derisively. Only Samantha had the presence to respond. "Yeah, I'm sure a curfew would make every cop's job easier."

Nicki turned to me and announced, "I want to go home. I have a really bad headache." She punctuated her demand by standing up and walking away from the table.

I shook my head but couldn't bear to look the others in the face.

As I gathered our jackets, I heard Samantha mutter, "She's giving us a headache, too."

Nicki practically screamed at me in the car. "I can't believe you didn't stand up for me!"

"My friends can be harsh, but I agree with them. You can hold your own, and I did try to stick up for your viewpoint."

"You let them humiliate me."

"Would you like to go somewhere so we can calm down?"

"No, I just want to go home."

We reached her house after a few minutes of driving in silence. She got out of the car immediately, and I followed her to the door of her apartment.

"I just want to go to bed." With a flip of her blonde hair she disappeared inside, bidding me goodnight only with the sound of the deadbolt.

I was stunned. What was going on? I drove home miserably, and tossed and turned in bed for hours that night. Elvis sensed I was troubled and crawled up to my face several times, purring loudly to let me know everything was all right. But I pushed her away, not wanting any solace. I couldn't shake the feeling that I had somehow jinxed everything by letting down my guard and allowing myself to fall in love with Nicki.

But there it was: I was stuck now. There was no way I could walk away. I wanted Nicki, desperately. More than that, I needed her. Yet I damned myself for having allowed myself to think it was possible to have her. I was bleary-eyed and drained when I had to get up for work that morning and concerned about the reaction from my friends would be. Uncharacteristically, Alice was the first to arrive that morning, and I waved her into my office.

"I hate to tell you this, Kevin," Alice said as she settled into a chair opposite my desk, "but your girlfriend is a total bitch."

So the fallout was as bad as I feared. "She didn't attract many new members for the Nicki fan club, huh?"

"She may have lost a few members, actually. I was speaking to Rich afterward, and he was totally offended. And none of us were thrilled over how she treated you, either. You can't let anyone treat you like that. I don't care how pretty you think she is, you can't have a good relationship with someone who doesn't respect you."

I sighed. It was comforting to have friends like Alice, but I wasn't enjoying what I was hearing.

OVER THE NEXT few days I saw Nicki several times, and at the surface our relationship seemed back to normal. We snuggled and made love, but it seemed perfunctory, and Nicki maintained emotional distance. She wouldn't open up, and denied that anything had changed. But in her typical manner, she dropped hints that she attributed to others. "Amelia doesn't think you give me enough space," she commented after one therapy session.

I wasn't sure I liked Nicki's therapist after all. "Nicki, I'll give you as much space as you want. Just tell me what you need."

"That's the problem. You should *know* what I need. Carlos always sensed when I needed space and gave it to me."

I was tiring of her constant references to Carlos. "If Carlos was so perfect, I don't understand why you're not still together."

"It's just very complicated," she answered, terminating the discussion. But it wasn't a denial that she still harbored feelings for him—a denial I wanted badly to hear.

I was tempted to throw in the towel and just give up on our relationship, or at least to give her the breathing room she seemed to want. The trouble was that our trip to Bermuda was coming up the next weekend, following the Association of Washington Architects dinner. Whenever I brought up the subject of the dinner, Nicki seemed genuinely excited. But apart from that, there seemed no pleasing her. She fretted constantly about her inability to find a new job—a common problem among Washingtonians during the economic downturn—and about her weight. I tried to help her with the former and dismissed the latter, but she wanted neither my assistance nor my empathy.

She was also increasingly critical of me, from my driving, to my ideas for spending time together, and even to my work. I had enjoyed sharing my drawings with her, and appreciated her ideas, and now she merely complained that I didn't understand what people wanted. When I said that she rarely had anything positive anymore to say about my work, she snapped at me. "Don't you understand? You're going through such a successful period right now, you're on top of your profession, right when I can't even find a job." She glowered at me, her eyes moist. "I'm jealous, okay?"

Her remark made me feel like a total idiot. It had absolutely never occurred to me that she wasn't reveling in my success. I reproached myself for my insensitivity. "I'm sorry. We're both talented people, and we're both going to have our career ups and downs. You're an important part of my success, I want to be there for you when things aren't going well, and also when they are going well."

I leaned over to hug her, but she pushed me away. "I don't want your sympathy. I just don't want you to rub my nose in how good your career is going. And we barely know each other; I don't know how I can be a part of your success."

Again, Nicki left me speechless–and feeling like I was in total free-fall.

One evening when she was visiting her folks in Baltimore—she didn't invite me, and I thought it a good opportunity to give her the space she seemed to want—I called Jennifer; and we talked for hours.

"How's the surveyor?"

"Darren is doing fine."

"Darn."

"Hey, I thought you were in the midst of a blossoming romance."

I emitted a long sigh.

"Okay, tell me about the troubles in paradise," Jennifer said, and I unburdened myself. Somehow, though the conversation lifted my spirits, it made me feel lonely as well.

I picked Nicki up for dinner after work the next evening and brought her back to my townhouse. I had pumped myself into a good mood and gave Nicki several suggestions for dinner. She rejected all of them.

As I puttered around the kitchen, she noticed a sponge in the sink. "Oh, I hate it when you do that!"

"Do what?" I asked, genuinely stumped.

"Leave a sponge in the sink." She picked it up by the edges, making a face. "It stays all wet and smells."

I couldn't believe my ears. If Nicki had a sense of humor, I'd be sure she was joking, or even making fun of herself. But, as Nicki repeatedly reminded me, she didn't have a sense of humor.

"Nicki," I said steadily, "I didn't know that bothered you. Now that you've told me, I won't do it again. Okay?"

Nicki flung the sponge back into the sink. Pushing past me to retreat to the living room, she exclaimed, "You just don't understand. Carlos understood things like that."

Carlos. Goddamned Carlos. I stood there silently, resting against the counter, my temple throbbing rapidly. This was not going well. I removed the sponge and placed it on the edge of the sink to dry, and calmly walked into the living room, where Nicki was sitting on the sofa reading a *Wine Spectator*, her legs crossed and her foot kicking. "Do you just want to get something and eat in?" I asked.

"No, I want to go out."

"Well, I don't really care where we go. I'll be happy anywhere, as long as it's with you."

Nicki looked up at me, her face expressionless. "Why can't you just make a decision?"

"Because I want to go somewhere that makes you happy."

"It would make me happy for you to make a decision."

For some reason her remark made me lose it. It wasn't that particular remark, of course, but the accumulation of Nicki's negativity. I raised my voice sharply to her for the first time ever. "Goddamn it! I just want to make you happy. I don't give a *shit* where we go so long as you get out of this awful mood you've been in for the past week." Nicki was wide-eyed and silent, her expression undecipherable. Was it anger, defiance, fear—or curiosity?

I trembled with anger, but slowly brought myself under control as I glowered at her. "I'm going upstairs to change clothes. If you want to go out for dinner, let me know where you want to go when I come downstairs. Otherwise I'll just drive you home." I wheeled away from her and went upstairs.

In the bathroom, I stared at myself in the mirror and tried to calm myself. What was going on? Why was I allowing this woman to treat me so badly? I understood that she was going through a rough period. But no matter how hard I tried, she wouldn't allow me to help. I was embarrassed that I had lost my temper—something that had never once happened during my several years with Jennifer. I was relieved I had finally drawn a line, and I was quite prepared to take her home, but was I genuinely prepared to call it quits? That *was* the suggestion implicit in my threat.

At that moment I was so fatigued by all the nonsense that I felt the answer was yes: if this was the end, so be it. Thus fortified with resolve, I returned downstairs, expecting Nicki to ask that I take her home. Instead, she announced brightly, "Let's go to Costner's."

Costner's was our favorite Old Town restaurant. I was still feeling irritated, but I said, "Okay, let's go," and I led the way out the door.

The evening was mild and still light. Nicki unexpectedly took my hand as we walked the several blocks to the restaurant, slowing my pace. Over my brooding silence, she chattered cheerfully about all sorts of subjects, from friends who were getting married to the dress she planned to wear to the AWA dinner. I wondered about her sudden and complete transformation. It was as if all at once a demon had been exorcised. I was slow to warm to her again, but felt my irritation melting as we reached the restaurant.

We sat in Costner's lovely outdoor patio, enjoying the balmy evening. We ordered a calamari appetizer and a superb sauvignon blanc, which mellowed me considerably. Nicki hadn't been so loquacious in quite some time, and before I realized it we were engaged in easy, animated conversation. Our banter the whole evening was light, punctuated by laughter.

My anger dissipated more than I believed possible, and I found myself gazing at Nicki with renewed fondness.

Nicki spent the night and our lovemaking was luxuriant. As we finally fell asleep in the middle of the night, I felt calm and contented. Whatever the problem was between us seemed resolved. Still, unsettling thoughts tugged at me. What was this Jekyll and Hyde personality Nicki was displaying? I didn't like how she had seemed intent on provoking my outburst, nor that she rewarded it with a positive reaction, almost as if she enjoyed watching it happen. Did she goad me into losing my temper in order to exert control over me, or merely to see if I was capable of it—or because she drew some sort of perverse pleasure in it? Or was I perhaps making a mountain out of a molehill?

Whatever the explanation, I didn't like what Nicki had brought out in me; I didn't aspire to a relationship that depended on arguments to clear the air. And after all, I surely didn't understand Nicki any better than before we had argued, so what was the point? Or was that Nicki's intended point: for Nicki to remain a mystery to me?

I found those thoughts too overwhelming to dwell upon just then, dog-tired as I was from the combination of an emotional outburst, half a bottle of wine, and energetic lovemaking. Instead I moved over and slid my arm around the slumbering beauty next to me, and allowed sleep to take me.

ð

THE NEXT WEEK was a blur. The AWA ceremony was scheduled for Tuesday night, and the days leading up to it were filled with well-wishes, apologies from friends who couldn't make it to the event, and futile efforts to get work done before leaving on Saturday for Bermuda.

I barely spoke to Nicki until it was time to pick her up for the event. Whenever I did think about her, I had to sweep aside the butterflies in my stomach. It still felt like the whole thing was falling apart. I hired a limousine to take us to the AWA event—a real luxury for me in those days—because I didn't want to worry about parking. Samantha and her date, Stan Kohler, came along. It was a gorgeous spring day, the tulips in full glory. We pulled up at Nicki's house as scheduled at six-fifteen, and I stepped out to knock on her door.

After a moment Nicki opened the door and stepped out. She looked stunning, so much so I must have gasped: she was clad in a long black sequined dress that flattered her figure. Her hair was arranged in an intricate style atop her head, and glittering dangles cascaded from her ears. She pecked me on the lips, having to bend down slightly because her high heels made her taller than me. I couldn't believe this was my girlfriend.

Samantha and I took pictures of each other with our dates. Nicki snaked her arm through mine, and her smile was bright. Whatever had darkened her mood the previous week had plainly dissipated. Her good mood fueled my ebullience. We arrived amid tremendous bustle. Most of the people in attendance didn't know me, but there was still plenty of glad-handing. I felt like a peacock in full plumage, particularly with Nicki on my arm. She was easily the most beautiful woman among hundreds in the room.

"Gibbons!" The nasal bellow made me turn. I wished I hadn't. It was John Friedman Fergaman, my old nemesis from my previous firm, Fielder, Steinmetz & Way.

"Oh, hello, Fergie," I muttered.

Fergaman was chomping a cigar. I couldn't believe it: smoking was forbidden in all public buildings in Washington, but Fergaman flouted laws and social conventions as easily as he did the bounds of good taste.

Nicki could clearly perceive the sudden change in atmosphere, and she looked at me inquisitively. "Nicki Petri, this is my former co-worker, John Fergaman."

"Nice to meetcha," Fergaman said.

"Oh, *that* Fergaman," Nicki said. Fergaman preened over her recognition. "You're one of the architects who competed unsuccessfully against Kevin for the prize."

Fergaman turned crimson, and it was all I could do to keep from choking on the sip of wine I'd just taken.

"Yeah, well, you know, it's all subjective, you know, bias against the big firm," Fergaman stammered.

"Of course, it could just be talent," Nicki said, twisting the knife. "I find Kevin's designs brilliant. But since you're friends, I'm sure Kevin would give you some pointers sometime."

Fergaman's jaw was clenched. "One competition does not a career make," he muttered, sounding like some sort of oracle, and then disappeared into the crowd.

Nicki and I looked at each other and burst out laughing. I drew her toward me, hugging her and inhaling the light scent of her cologne. Nicki beamed and took my hand, pulling me back into the crowd as more voices called my name.

I was on top of the world. I felt my very being crackling with intensity. All my colleagues were there, friends from other firms, and some of the top Washington-area architects I'd never previously met. Several made their way to meet me, and more than a few were familiar and impressed with Horizon's work. The pocket of my tuxedo pants bulged with business cards. But it was Nicki's presence, her arm in mine, her charm, her laugh, that magnified the evening for me, making it one of the best of my life.

Just before dinner, a beefy arm grabbed mine and whirled me around. "Art!" I exclaimed.

"Howya doing, big guy?" he asked, though he towered over me by nearly a foot. Art's wife Joanne trailed behind him, smiling broadly.

"Nicki, I'd like you meet my mentor and friend, Art Longley, and his lovely wife Joanne," I said.

"I've heard so many wonderful things about you, Mr. Longley," Nicki gushed, extending her hand to greet Art and Joanne.

"Well I've been wondering where Kevin's been hiding lately. Now I know," Art replied, taking Nicki in from head to toe.

"Congratulations, Kevin. It's a gorgeous design," Joanne said.

"Thanks, Joanne. I wouldn't have entered the contest without Art's, uh, gentle prodding." Everyone laughed at that comment, given that Art was never gentle about anything.

"So whaddaya gonna do to celebrate?" Art asked.

"Nicki and I are leaving on Saturday for a long weekend in Bermuda," I answered.

Art laughed. "Well, I know what you two are gonna be doing." He winked at Nicki lasciviously, then turned back to me. "This is a gorgeous one, Kev," he said. "I know what I'd be doing with her behind closed doors."

Suddenly I felt very uncomfortable. Art was obviously drunk, and embarrassing both Nicki and me. In my peripheral vision I could see Nicki smiling, but from experience I knew it wasn't a happy smile. She turned away when I glanced in her direction.

"Nicki is a radio producer," I said in an attempt to demonstrate that there was more to Nicki than her looks.

"That's one radio producer you're lucky to be taking to Bermuda," he replied.

"It will be our first time over there," I stammered. "I hear it's a beautiful island."

"Heck, you're not gonna see the island at all. You'll be in the hotel room, going at it like rabbits. And I don't blame you."

"Art," Joanne began, obviously embarrassed as well.

"Art, I really don't think—"

Nicki squeezed my hand, hard. "I think they're calling us over to the head table," she said, and pulled me away without anyone saying goodbye. She released my hand as we pushed through the crowd toward our table at the front of the ballroom.

Moments later we were at the table, exchanging greetings. Nicki's cheeks were flushed as she introduced herself to our table companions, not waiting for me to do the honors. I went through the motion of shaking hands in a haze. What had happened? Why had Art acted like that? I had never seen him behave like that. Sure, sometimes we discussed women, and his descriptions were a bit crude for my tastes, but I'd never imagined that he would talk like that in front of a woman. My date, for Christ's sake. Nicki was clearly steamed, and it seemed directed at me as much as at Art.

As we sat down to dinner, Nicki talked to the woman sitting next to her, who was the wife of the AWA president. She steadfastly ignored me, except to tell me I was using the wrong bread plate. The incident preoccupied me through dinner and it was difficult to make the requisite small talk.

After the program started and the master of ceremonies was speaking, Nicki leaned over to me and through a forced smile said icily, "I can't believe you didn't tell him to shut up."

"I'm sorry. It was an incredibly awkward situation; I didn't know what to say."

She looked squarely at me, still smiling but her green eyes blazing. "I will never forgive you for that."

After awhile it was time for the award, and the AWA president got up and said nice things about my design. I had prepared some witty remarks, but when it was my turn I stood up and merely mumbled some thanks to my colleagues and to the association. I was given a standing ovation, but all I wanted was for the evening to end.

And it did, mercifully, about a half hour later. We extricated ourselves quickly, making our way to a side exit and finding our limousine parked conveniently outside. Samantha and her date were taking a cab home, so it was just Nicki and me.

I was pummelled by disparate thoughts during the mostly silent ride, all of them bleak. Why hadn't I stood up to Art Longley? But wasn't Nicki overreacting? Was our relationship over? How could I atone for my mistake? Or could I at all? What about our Bermuda trip? I couldn't bear to lose this woman. No matter how difficult, how perplexing our relationship, I wanted her. Was she already gone? As we pulled up at her apartment, the eternal optimist inside made me think I might be able to convince her to pack some overnight things and drive back to my house, or perhaps she might invite me to stay the night.

As we approached her door, she turned around and kissed me.

She pulled back and said, "You'd better go," then pecked my lips again and let herself inside her apartment.

THE NEXT SEVERAL days in the office were becalmed by anticlimax. Rich interviewed potential new architects, and as he passed them along to me I found myself having to fake an enthusiasm for the firm's future of which I found myself—momentarily, at least—bereft. All I could think about was Nicki. Perhaps the sunshine of Bermuda—if the trip was still on—would repair our wounded relationship.

But I found it impossibly difficult to talk about my feelings with Nicki. That put me at a loss. With Jennifer it had been so easy to communicate, even about feelings that were embarrassing. But with Nicki the communication was mostly physical, and so it was ambivalent: what could be taken for affection or love could just as easily be animal lust. Nicki's comments about such topics were oblique: she had insisted that she would never have sex unless it signified love. So through her actions I supposed she loved me. But why did she convey it so indirectly? And if she no longer loved me, would the lust dissipate as well? The onset of that particular question gripped me in paralysis, for I realized that perhaps more than anything I could not bear to lose the raw physical aspect of our relationship, which made me both ashamed and terrified.

I finally called her. She wasn't home, but returned my call later that night, and did not fill me in on where she had been. She was aloof and grouchy, having had no success on the job interview front.

"Don't worry, Nicki," I murmured in an attempt to be soothing. "The job market is tight right now, but you're talented, so it's just a matter of time. And you're temping again, so you've got some money coming in."

"I don't *want* to temp anymore. I want something permanent."

"I feel really badly for you. When we get back from Bermuda, I'll make some calls and see if I can pull some connections."

"I have to get jobs by myself. It's bad enough that everyone assumes that if you're blonde, and attractive, anything you have you must have gotten because you slept with someone. It's important to me to know that anything I have I earned myself."

It was a lecture I had heard from Nicki many times before, but I tried to defend myself. "When I graduated from architecture school, it seemed like nobody wanted to hire me. So I know how rough it can be. And as for connections, that's how this town operates."

"I'm thinking of moving to Seattle." My jaw dropped on the other end of the phone. "A friend of mine works for a public relations firm there. He told me, 'Nicki, you're so talented and qualified, you could get a great job here in about five minutes.' Not the kind of entry-level positions I'm interviewing for here, either. An assistant account executive position, starting at thirty-five thousand."

I didn't point out to Nicki the inconsistency of accepting help from her friend in Seattle, but not from me. I was too aghast for that kind of response. The thought of Nicki moving three thousand miles away was devastating. And the salary she was talking about was a lot more than she was looking at in Washington, so there would be a substantial financial incentive. And who the hell was this friend, and what were his motivations?

"Do you want to move to Seattle?"

"I think it would be nice to have a change of scenery. This city is too political, too superficial."

"Well, on a more short-term note, are we still on for Bermuda this weekend?"

"Of course. I bought two beautiful new sundresses."

I felt like every sentence out of Nicki's mouth was battering me. Not "Of course, I can't wait," or "I'm looking forward to spending time with you," but "I bought two new sundresses." So of course that meant she had to go. How else could she show off her new purchases in appropriate style?

Before I could say anything, she delivered another zinger. "But I'm not sure we should spend so much time together for awhile after that. Amelia thinks you're suffocating me."

"Amelia."

"Yes, my therapist."

"I know who Amelia is." I was so irritated that I blurted out the first thing that came to my mind. "I think Amelia is in love with you."

Nicki chuckled. "So do I."

I was incredulous. "How can you take professional advice from someone who's in love with you?" Nicki merely laughed again. "And how can she say I'm suffocating you? We haven't even slept together for a week. I hardly see you."

"I just need a lot of space."

"Then let's not go to Bermuda."

"No. I want to go to Bermuda."

"So you can wear your sundresses?"

"So I can have a relaxing weekend." Pause. "With you."

I decided to give it up. "Well, I'll come over and pick you up on Saturday at six-thirty."

"Why so early? The flight isn't until eight. "Pick me up at seven."

"I'll pick you up at seven."

I sank into the sofa, utterly depressed. Good grief, what the hell was I doing with this woman? I followed my goddamn dick into this relationship, and the results were all too predictable. I should've listened to Samantha. Nicki was turning out to be a consummate prima donna, and a total pain in the ass.

Some time later the phone rang and startled me awake from my restless sleep. It was Nicki; she had insomnia again. I looked over at the clock and saw it was midnight. I tried to shake the cobwebs, as Nicki had already launched into an animated conversation. She never apologized for her late-night calls, and rarely asked if I had been sleeping. Nor did she explain or apologize for her recent mood.

I quickly fell into the rhythm of the conversation. Nicki was as upbeat as she had been downcast the previous evening. She asked my advice about job interviews, and actually complimented me on what I had to say. We exchanged the latest Ronald Reagan jokes and had each other laughing.

Suddenly, she almost shyly proposed, "You should come pick me up."

"What?!"

"I think we should sleep together tonight."

It couldn't have been more than five minutes before I was behind the wheel of my Saab, a huge grin on my face, en route to pick up my impatient lover, with nary the slightest thought about Nicki's latest 180-degree turnaround.

Q

Nicki was shrouded in morning sunlight that streamed through the window as we jetted across a narrow stretch of the Atlantic toward Bermuda. Watching her, one leg crossed over the other and tapping as she read a magazine, conjured images of the first time I had set eyes on her. She seemed as oblivious to my attention now as she had then, so I indulged in a rapt stare.

I could feel the accumulated stress of the past several weeks dissipate as Washington receded. Though Nicki was engrossed in her article, occasionally stirring to share some interesting fact, I sat quietly, a residual smile on my face that had occupied it for the past three days or so. The middle seat between us was unoccupied, and Nicki had raised the armrests and taken hold of my hand, letting go only to turn a page and then returning it.

As she finished the article, she laid down the magazine and turned to face me. She was wearing her glasses. "One place we should eat in Bermuda is Howard's," she said. "I loved that place when I ate there before."

"What?"

"We ate there when Carlos and I went to Bermuda."

I pulled my hand away. "You've been to Bermuda already?"

"Yes, almost exactly two years ago, with Carlos. I told you that."

"No, I had the impression that this would be your first trip to Bermuda."

"I'm certain I told you."

"I remember every word we've spoken about this trip since we made plans, and you never told me you came here before. I'm absolutely certain of it."

Nicki sighed, plainly irritated. "No, I told you before that. When we were discussing our previous relationships. I told you that Bermuda was where Carlos and I decided we could never get married."

Oh shit, I thought, maybe she had said that. Who knows, maybe that's when the idea of taking Nicki to Bermuda had planted itself in my mind. After all, I was always competing with the ghost of Carlos, wasn't I? If not, for all I know, with Carlos in the flesh as well. And isn't this terrific, I thought: Now I get to re-live Nicki's greatest moments with the love of her life. This place was supposed to be pristine, untainted, restorative. Ours. But it couldn't be ours, not when it already reposed memories and emotions for Nicki. Damn it!

"Would you mind terribly much if we didn't repeat any of the experiences you've already had?" I asked.

"No, I don't mind," she answered, "but that will be difficult. We spent an entire week there, during a convention he attended, and I think we did almost everything. We certainly explored every beach, that's for sure."

Suddenly the three days loomed not as an escape but a confinement. I felt myself withdraw from Nicki, even as I silently admonished myself to make the best of it. After all, the experience had ended badly for Nicki and Carlos—even though their relationship persisted for another year and a half after that. Is that what would happen to us, a lurching off-and-on relationship?

"Okay," I said. "How about a compromise. If we repeat an experience you had with Carlos, don't tell me about it, okay?"

"Sure." She returned her attention to the magazine, but this time she didn't reach out to take my hand.

The weekend turned out to be as painful as I feared. Nicki developed a migraine headache, which caused her to sleep away much of our two days, leaving me to explore beaches on my own. We had sex but it was perfunctory; for once, it seemed Nicki derived no fulfillment from it. For the entire weekend she was detached and introspective.

Finally, as we were eating dessert after dinner on Sunday, the last of our nights there, irritation overtook me. The night was balmy, and a sultry breeze flowed through the open-air deck. Nicki looked virginal in an off-white Laura Ashley sundress, but her mood was bored and distracted. She complained about the service, and about how much she had eaten over the weekend even as she nibbled at her creme Brulée. Though the setting was romantic, Nicki's mood was anything but, so I felt I had nothing to lose by venting.

"Well, Nicki, this weekend certainly hasn't turned out like I planned," I said, knowing that the accumulated bitterness had seeped deeply into my voice. "Do you ever think you are going to get beyond Carlos?"

Her look turned angry, as did her voice. "How dare you say that! Carlos and I dated for four years. You don't get over a relationship like that in a matter of months. You're certainly not over Jennifer."

"What?"

"Come on, you talk about her all the time. I don't think I could ever live up to your conception of her." Nicki had raised her voice so loudly that the restaurant's other patrons were glancing in our direction, but she seemed oblivious. Her words astonished me—it never had occurred to me that Nicki might be jealous about Jennifer.

When I spoke, it was in a hushed tone in hopes that it would bring down Nicki's decibel level as well. "I am in love with you, Nicole Petri. You know that. Jennifer is a memory for me now. You are my present and, I hope, my future." I took her hands across the table and held them. "I love you, Nicki."

She pulled away, and tears abruptly appeared in her eyes. Her voice was no quieter than before, but now was choked with anguish. "I don't *want* anyone to be in love with me. I'm not ready for it. I *told* you that. You didn't listen."

"You've told me so many inconsistent things. I never know where I stand with you. I've let you set the pace of this relationship from the beginning. You even talked about marriage."

"Yes, but in the distant future. I thought I was falling in love with you, but then I realized I couldn't fall in love with anyone. Not yet. But you had to push so fast."

My head was spinning. "Why don't you just get back together with Carlos? I don't understand why you guys didn't get married."

"Because he's already *getting* married," she blurted, her words dissolving into a heart-wracking sob. Now she was bawling. "In two months. To that bitch!" Her fists pounded the table. "All right?!" She looked at me through reddened eyes. "Are you *satisfied* now?" She dabbed at her eyes as she sobbed again, then looked at me again. "Excuse me, I'm going back to the room." She got up abruptly and left, nearly toppling her chair in the frenzy to leave.

I could feel my skin turn crimson and the stares of other patrons boring into me. The waiter brought the check, and I pulled out a credit card without even looking at it.

The restaurant was propped onto a cliff, and as I stepped out into the balmy spring air I could hear the surf pounding below. I knew that Nicki needed to be alone. I maneuvered through the darkness and made my way to a slippery boulder, where I sat with my feet dangling down. The waves pummeled the rock, spraying me with occasional light mist.

After a long time I returned to the room. It was dark, though Nicki had left the sliding doors open to the balcony. The sheer curtains were billowing in the breeze, and I realized that Nicki too had been listening to the sound of the crashing waves. The moonlight bathed her in its celestial light; she was in bed, turned away from me, the strap of her light nightgown hanging low on her arm. I found the image, even amid all that had transpired—perhaps especially because of it—erotic.

But though at first Nicki appeared to be sleeping, I heard an occasional sniffle that made me think she had been, or still was, crying.

I made my way to the bathroom, where I washed my face and shed all my clothes except my boxers. Making sure the light didn't disturb her, I returned to the darkened bedroom and slid between the sheets. I leaned over and kissed her arm lightly, where the strap of her nightgown lay, and whispered softly, "Nicki, I love you."

She rolled over toward me and faced me. In the dim light her skin was glistening, and abruptly she pulled me toward her and kissed me deeply. I could taste the salt from her tears. The thought flickered through my mind that this was the first time in our relationship that Nicki had allowed herself to appear vulnerable.

But that reflection lasted only a moment, for as if by silent signal we began frantically groping each other. I reached between her legs and found her moist; I entered her as if summoned by an unspoken command. Our lovemaking was even more intense and physical than usual. Nicki seemed to need to connect with me in as many ways as she could, kissing frantically, thrusting me inside her, as deeply as possible, arching her back and urging me on. When I ejaculated only minutes into our intercourse, she kept me inside her. I could tell that she was reaching climax repeatedly, but she wanted it to go on, endlessly. And it seemed like it did, and that every second was fulfilling to both of us. When finally we were sated, she burrowed her face into my chest and fell asleep. Utterly exhausted, and feeling that we had reached some sort of understanding, I fell asleep, too.

Both of us were subdued on the trip home. As I dropped Nicki off, I asked her if the plans we had made some time ago for the next Saturday—dancing with some of our friends—were still on. She said yes, and then, tentatively, "Call me before then."

My responses to my colleagues' inquiries about Bermuda were terse. Samantha confronted me on the afternoon of my return to the office. We had been going over some drawings for the Parkside, and after we were finished, she lowered the boom. "So what the hell is going on with you?"

"What do you mean?"

"You're like an emotional yo-yo lately, one day sad, one day happy, the next day withdrawn. What's going on?"

"Nothing's going on, Sam. Everything's fine."

She harrumphed. "Come on, Kevin. I can read you like a book. Of course you get into down moods, sometimes, just like everybody. But lately your moods change on a daily basis, from one extreme to the next. And the explanation can only be one thing: little Miss Prim."

"Come on, Sam. You saw us together at the AWA ball last week. Everything was fine."

"Yes, she couldn't take her eyes off you, because you were the center of attention, and she was basking in your reflected glory. And you, of course, were on cloud nine, as usual. I don't like what she's doing to you. You're depressed half the time. Something's eating at you, so, out with it, or I'll have to resort to the gossip network."

I sighed, leaned back into my chair, and told her about Carlos and how the weekend ended. "Anyway, she's grown fairly distant, and I think I'm going to have to give her space."

"You should just break up with her. She shouldn't be treating you this badly, even if her old boyfriend is getting married."

"Thanks, I appreciate that," I said curtly. "Well, time to get back to work. Are we still on for Saturday?"

"We're still going dancing?"

"Yeah. I'm not seeing Nicki before then, and maybe it won't put such pressure on her in a group setting. And make nice, okay? There's enough pressure without sarcastic commentary from the chorus."

"Me? Sarcastic? Never!" We both laughed, which broke the serious mood.

I was able to concentrate on my work. The two-year condominium conversion was set to commence at the Parkside in the fall, so everyone was putting in late hours. Each morning I awoke disappointed that I hadn't received one of Nicki's nocturnal phone calls. On Thursday, I called her during the day and reconfirmed our plans for Saturday night. She seemed cheerful but aloof.

I called Jennifer on a whim on Friday and asked if she'd like to come over for dinner. I hadn't seen her in months. Maybe the tonic for a new girlfriend with an old boyfriend hang-up was to see an ex of my own.

Happily, Jennifer wasn't too busy at work and apparently didn't have plans with Darren, so she agreed.

I ordered Chinese food delivery and the food arrived just as Jennifer did. As she entered, we surveyed each other almost warily. We hadn't seen each other since before we had started dating other people. Jennifer looked good: she'd lost weight since we'd stopped dating, and was more slender than Nicki. Even though they were roughly the same age, Jen looked older; probably the burden of being a lawyer.

"Wondering how you ever could have dated me now that you have such a beautiful girlfriend?" she asked with a grin.

I started stammering a denial, then just laughed.

Within minutes, the plates were filled and the wine uncorked, and we settled into the living room. For the next hour or so we talked about my complicated relationship with Nicki. Jennifer gently extracted pertinent information, acting as she had so many times before as my empathetic therapist. She offered little advice, but she did comment, "She sounds pretty messed up, Kev."

The conversation turned to Jennifer's boyfriend. Jennifer seemed torn about him. "He challenges me on a lot of levels. He's well-read, and athletic, and has me eating good foods"—at that, Jen gave me a knowing glance, because our diet during our time together had been atrocious—"but he's not very cultured, or thoughtful, or as intellectual as you."

"I think you can do better." I knew she could do better, given that she had dated me. But although Jennifer was good at dispensing advice, sometimes she was sensitive about receiving it, so I trod carefully on the subject.

After dinner, Jen proposed taking a walk through Old Town for some ice cream, to which I agreed. The ice cream at Ben & Jerry's was delicious and the toppings decadent. We continued walking as we ate, stopping by the waterfront to look out at the lights across the river. The moon was full and illuminated Jennifer softly. We stood there silently for a long time, so close I could smell her familiar scent, our thoughts surely intersecting.

"I miss you, Kev," she said as the evening drew to a close after we got home and she prepared to leave.

"I miss you, too."

I watched as she drove off into the night. I stayed outside on the door stoop for awhile, enjoying the cool breeze and the clear, star-filled night, my mind totally emptied.

The serenity lasted only until the following night. Nicki and I had planned to meet our friends at Lola's, a top-40 dance club near DuPont Circle, but Nicki decided to go out for dinner first with Doug and Karen and meet everyone else for dancing later. So I joined Beth and her boyfriend Brad, Alice, and Samantha at Lola's. The demographics were in my favor, so I got drunk and danced with the women. Lola's had opened the garage-style windows letting in the slightly humid night air, so by the time Nicki, Doug, and Karen arrived, I was sweaty.

"You're disgusting," was Nicki's opening line when she saw me.

That was the best the evening got. Nicki spent most of the time talking privately to Karen, ignoring my friends and me. Doug cast empathetic glances in my direction, signaling me that he was alert to something going on, but we weren't able to talk privately. When Nicki and I danced, she was distant; and she disagreed with everything anyone said to her.

I was flabbergasted when I overheard Nicki ask Karen if she and Doug could drop her off, but before Karen could agree, Doug said, "I think Kevin would probably like to spend some time with Nicki."

Nicki acted as if that were a surprise, and said sweetly, "Oh, I didn't want to put Kevin out."

"I would love to drive you home."

"Sure," she said, left with no alternative.

We drove in complete silence. As I parked near her apartment, she pulled the door handle, but I said, "Don't get out yet. We have to talk."

She settled back into her seat and stared forward, her lips pursed.

"What's going on?"

"You should know what's going on."

"I'm really trying to figure out what you want. But you're not helping."

"I don't *want* to help. I just want to get away. From everything." Her voice was growing steadily more emotional. "Sometimes I feel like my head is going to explode. And you just don't understand."

I opened my eyes to face her. She was still staring straight ahead. Her eyes were moist but there were no tears. As I looked at her, I realized that she was absolutely right: she was unfathomable to me.

"Nicki," I said quietly, feeling my patience receding, "I'm really trying my best to understand you." I paused, wondering whether I would add what I was thinking. I did, tremulously. "But if things don't get better between us pretty quickly, I don't know whether we should continue seeing each other."

Her response was terse. "I don't think things are going to get better."

10

BAD TIMES SEEM to congregate, and the following Monday plunged the firm into turmoil.

Before the weekly staff meeting had ended, Rich ran to take a call from a developer giving us bad news on a condo conversion project we were trying to get. Not only didn't our bid win, but we lost to Fergaman.

We had been riding so high with the Parkside contract and the AWA award that I think we were all lulled into overconfidence. It was the first time I had allowed Rich to handle a proposal entirely on his own, and the news hit him hard. Even though I had warned him against inflated expectations—firms like Fielder, Steinmetz & Way were tough competitors who could offer economies of scale—I knew that Rich had been counting on it to meet his projections for the firm's growth. Plus, he was taking it personally because it had been principally his design and entirely his presentation.

Rich and I closeted ourselves away immediately after receiving the news. His jaw was clenched and I could see his facial muscles working, a sure sign that he was severely stressed.

"Rich, don't take this personally," I urged. "It was a good proposal. Fielder has advantages that allow them to undercut us if they want to. And people's tastes are subjective. The good guys don't always win in this business, even if they have the most talent."

Rich was having none of it. "I let the firm down. It was my first proposal, and it got rejected."

"Yes, and it won't be your last proposal to be turned down, either. You have a long way before you catch up with me in the rejection department. Besides, even though you were our front man, I signed off on this proposal every step of the way. We succeed as a team, and we fail as a team."

Rich was silent, then said, "I think we need to have you out front on everything. Our clients want to know they're getting a piece of the star. A good proposal alone can't win the day."

I saw some truth in it. "You may have a point. I probably do need to be more visible, even if it's for show. But," I added, "this is transitional. I intentionally didn't name the company after myself because I want it to develop its own independent persona. And you're an important part of that."

Rich took that in, then put on a brave half-smile and extended his hand. I took it. "Thanks. That means a lot."

"Your being here means a lot. This firm is lucky, and I'm lucky."

Before we could continue, Beth rapped anxiously on the door, and I opened it. "Art Longley's on the phone for you, Kev, and he sounds angry." Rich and I exchanged anxious glances.

"Okay, I'm on my way."

As I walked to my office, Samantha intercepted me, grabbing my arm. I didn't break stride as she started babbling. "Kevin, Art is a jerk. He says he told me to change specifications on the Kalorama floor plan, but he never finalized them."

"Art's on the phone right now," I replied.

"I really think we should talk before you talk to him."

She followed me to my office, holding my arm as if to drag me backward. As I arrived at my office, I extricated my arm. "Trust me." Her face didn't register much confidence as I shut the door on her.

The phone rang insistently. As I approached it I realized this was the first time I wasn't looking forward to taking a call from Art Longley. Not because he was angry—Art was a fearsome taskmaster, and I didn't mind that at all—but because of the scene he had made with Nicki. I had lost some respect for him. I picked up the phone. "What's up?"

"That goddamned Samantha Benjamin! I asked her two weeks ago to reconfigure the plans so we could squeeze in an extra two-bedroom unit on each floor. And I look at them today and nothing's changed. We've lost a goddamn two weeks in prime construction time!"

"Did you confirm the change?"

"I don't know whether I did or not. If she wasn't sure, she should've checked with me. And we could've had two sets of plans instead of one. But she didn't do anything!"

Art was right. At least she should have checked. "It isn't that tough a maneuver. It will affect two, three units at most on each floor. We'll do it today, have it for you first thing tomorrow morning. You'll lose one day, not two weeks."

"I don't want to deal with this woman anymore. Got it?"

That remark cut a bit close to home. Samantha was mercurial, but a good architect. By contrast, Art's attitudes toward women were Neanderthal. I almost made a retort but stifled it, and instead said icily, "You don't have to work with anyone you don't want to."

"I can't afford to move you to this project, Kevin. I need you on Columbia Plaza."

"I'll take care of it."

"I'm not gonna work with that woman anymore."

"I'll take care of it." I hung up.

I promptly called another staff meeting. Both Rich and Samantha looked pensive. "Four things," I announced. "First, Art Longley wants a Kalorama configuration with an extra two bedrooms. Sam, you need to work that up today, have it by morning."

"Come on, Kevin . . ." she protested.

I put my hand up to stop her. "Give the man what he wants. I'll hang out here tonight to give you a hand. As long as it takes." She pouted but acquiesced. "Second, starting tomorrow, Rich is project manager for Kalorama." He beamed: Rich had never managed a project before. "At this point, it's mostly execution, and Art needs to work with someone who has a bit more testosterone." Samantha glowered. "Third, I'm reassigning Samantha to Parkside." She looked at me hopefully. "You and me, kid."

"Okay," she said. Now both Rich and Sam seemed happy. *Pareto* optimality, or so my old economics professor would say.

"And fourth, I've decided who our new architect will be." Or re-decided. We had two finalists, Charles Powers and Julie Crafton. Top prospects, available to us only because of the tight job market. Charles had strong drafting skills; Julie was the better designer. Rich favored Charles while Samantha wanted Julie. I had inclined toward Charles because of new projects we were thinking of taking on.

"I'm going to make an offer to Julie Crafton," I announced. The decision was my little dig at Art Longley. If he wanted to work with a bunch of guys, he could choose another firm.

I returned to my office and knew I had to get back to work, but even more I needed a few moments' procrastination. I wheeled my chair around to watch the trains through the thick plate glass. If we expanded the firm any more, we'd have to give up our office adjacent to Union Station. Change. Always change.

I LEFT TWO messages for Nicki during the week and sent her a Far Side card, but didn't hear back from her. Though I didn't think about her consciously, I went about the entire week with a hollow feeling in my stomach. I didn't want to dwell on the nearly certain demise of our relationship, nor did I care to reproach myself for my stupidity in persisting in the futility. I was vaguely aware of an inner desire for closure, and I think my half-hearted efforts to reach her were a way of fomenting that. But to no avail.

On Thursday, I played a spirited racquetball game with Doug. I had lots of energy to burn off, and for once I actually beat him, two games to one. As we were changing and showering, I asked if he had any news from Nicki.

"I don't think Karen's heard from her since last Saturday," he said. "You must be pretty sad that she's leaving."

"What?"

"You know, Seattle."

I was dumbfounded. "She's taking a trip to Seattle?"

Doug looked at me with pity. "I can't believe she didn't tell you." And it was clear he didn't want to be the one to break the news. "She's moving."

I returned home that evening with a huge pit in my stomach. I tried Nicki's number several times, but didn't leave a message. At midnight I stopped trying. I was preoccupied with it the next day. Even though I didn't know what I was going to say, I tried calling her several more times without success. Finally, at around seven, after everyone else had left for the weekend, I tried one last time.

"Hello?" Her soft voice sounded impatient.

"Nicki."

A pause. "Oh, hi. Listen, Kevin, I'm just home for a moment to change clothes. I'm going out."

"We need to talk."

"I don't have time right now. I'm going out."

Her petulance was annoying. "Yes, you just told me that. If

you'd returned my phone calls earlier this week, maybe we wouldn't have to be talking now. Why didn't you tell me you were moving to Seattle?"

"I didn't have time," she said, as if she'd merely neglected to tell me about a shopping excursion. "I've been really busy."

"You weren't too busy to tell Doug and Karen last Saturday night."

"I've been really angry at you, ever since the night of the awards dinner. I can't believe you didn't tell that thug to drop dead."

She was still stewing over that? I couldn't believe it. "I've never been in that situation before. I've never seen Art act like that, and I didn't know how to react. He's my most important client. But if I had it to do over again, I'd do it differently."

"Well, I find myself in situations like that all the time. Guys are always making crude comments. Carlos would have told the guy off."

I let the reference to Mr. Perfection pass without comment. "Nicki, the point is that we've dated for four months, and you're about to move clear across the country and weren't even going to tell me."

Nicki sighed. "Look, we had a really nice several months. But it just wasn't going to work out. We're not right for each other."

"Well, not with your attitude. You use relationships to serve whatever needs you have. You don't open yourself up to the possibility of real intimacy."

"How can you say that?" she entreated, her voice turning whiny. "I really care about people."

"You're like Jekyll and Hyde. One side of you is one of the most generous people I've ever met. Taking care of babies with AIDS. Babysitting your sister's kids. Buying thoughtful presents. But the other side of you won't let anyone in. It's like you're not capable of anything but the most superficial relationship." My words were flowing with a life of their own.

"I opened myself up to you," Nicki protested.

"Never, Nicki. You never let me inside. You're a bundle of contradictions. I never know how you really feel about me or anyone else. You speak in riddles. To this day, I don't even know if Carlos broke up with you, or you with Carlos. I've heard it both ways."

"I broke up with Carlos," she whined. "And I told you not to fall in love with me. I didn't want to hurt you."

"That's revisionism. You say wildly contradictory things, so you've got your bases covered no matter what you decide to do. In the meantime, you suck the spirit out of the people who care about you. You revel in their adoration and act like you care about them. But when you've taken all you can, you just walk away."

"I can't believe you're painting our relationship like that! We had a romantic relationship. It was really special. I can't believe you're taking that away! I really cared about you."

I laughed. "You don't really care about anybody but yourself, Nicki." I was shocked at the words that were coming out so easily, and at the accumulated bitterness they imparted.

"What do you know about being good to people? You don't even believe in God," Nicki blubbered, trying feebly to fight back.

"Ha! I can't believe what a hypocrite you are. You go to church, go to confession, manufacture these ridiculous rules about sex to justify your behavior, and then you pronounce yourself moral. Doesn't God say something about the Golden Rule? That's the one rule you break with impunity."

Now Nicki was crying out loud. "My God is forgiving," she stammered.

"That's your only hope." I could not remember ever having been this verbally brutal with anyone in my entire life. I almost felt like a schoolyard bully, an unfamiliar position, opposite the normal equation for me. Amazing the unknown qualities Nicki could bring out in a person.

Nicki now was crying uncontrollably. I was surprised that she hadn't hung up on me. Now she was saying something again, but her sobs made her words difficult to understand. "What? I didn't hear what you said."

"I . . . can't . . . believe . . . you're . . . saying . . . these things."

Surprisingly, I found myself utterly without sympathy over Nicki's discomfort. I said nothing.

"Why . . . can't . . . you . . . let . . . it . . . end . . . nice?"

"Right, so you can add this to the litany of your storybook romances, all sweetness and happy endings? No. I want you to acknowledge the consequences of your actions. I want you to know how much damage you inflict on people. I'm not going to let you just scurry off into the night. You led me on until you didn't want me any more, then you discarded me, without even the courtesy of letting me know I was no longer needed. I'll never forgive how you treated me. And apparently you treat everyone that way; not just lovers, but even the people you call friends." I paused, letting the words sink in. Then I continued. "So much for your pseudo-Catholic moralizing. The reality is you're not a very good person."

She gasped and totally lost it, her voice raising several octaves, raw with emotion. "*DON'T . . . JUDGE . . . ME!*" Her scream was blood-curdling, even as it was choked by sobs. Even louder now: "*DON'T . . . JUDGE . . . ME!*"

Her hysteria was unnerving, yet apart from a sheen of cold sweat, somehow I remained completely calm in the face of this emotional outburst. I wondered what it would be like if we weren't separated by distance. Would she pound me with her fists? Slash me with a knife? Or just fold up into herself and cry?

Regardless, I found myself almost taking pleasure in the reaction I had provoked. I was finally reaching her. Really reaching her. Now that it was too late.

She was blubbering more words, but they were indecipherable.

"What?" I asked.

"You've . . . ruined . . . our . . . relationship."

"*You've* ruined our relationship."

That got her crying even harder, and her voice was quaking. "I . . . never . . . want . . . to . . . talk . . . to . . . you . . . again," she managed to get out. More sobs. Then with a sniffle, she briefly collected herself. "Ever. Do you understand that?" Then it sounded like she pulled the phone away, her cries racking again.

"Okay," I replied, but by then the phone had clicked loudly in my ear.

I hung up, and lay back on the bed. Though my voice had been steely calm, I realized now that my whole body was shaking. Wow, I put a clean end to that one. Ordinarily I could never seem to manage putting such an emphatic end to a relationship. Precipitated by Nicki, yet punctuated by me. With an exclamation point. Still, it all seemed fitting, and inevitable.

Yet Nicki's reaction—not to our breakup, which seemed not to faze her, but to my accusations—turned out to be unpredictable, and scary. Plainly I had touched a raw nerve. But how? And why? If Nicki didn't care about me, why had she reacted that way?

As I tried to keep my mind focused on that, tears welled in my eyes. I wiped them away, but new tears quickly replaced them. Stop it, Kevin, I told myself: She's not worth it. You're much better without her. It's a good thing that it's over.

Over.

Something deep inside me disagreed profoundly with that assessment. The relationship might be over, but that surely wouldn't be the end of the matter for me, even if I never encountered her again.

11

THE DEPTH OF pain from my breakup with Nicki was far more profound than I could have expected. Perhaps it was the accumulation of two failed relationships. But even though the outcomes were the same, the situations had been starkly different. With Jennifer, the decision to break up had been mutual. It was an excruciating decision, but one that I knew was inevitable. With Nicki, by contrast, to the finish I had allowed myself to hope that it would work out; that the difficulties between us were aberrational and temporary, owing to turbulent times that Nicki was going through; and that somehow, in the end, Nicki would wind up being my soul mate, my lifetime partner, the mother of my children. That illusion had been so horribly and completely shattered that it had shaken me to my core. All I wanted to do was run away . . . to anywhere, as long as I wasn't here.

Unfortunately, the timing made escape impossible. The Parkside renovation was underway, and it needed lots of my personal attention. So I buried myself in the work, avoiding my friends' attempts to draw me out of my solemnity.

Nicki dealt with things differently, apparently. A couple days after our tumultuous final telephone conversation, I came out in the morning to discover that the windshield on my Saab had been smashed. Not smashed in, as if to gain access to the car, but smashed as in a wanton act of vandalism. There had been a single blow delivered powerfully—or perhaps just angrily—to the center of the windshield, causing spiderweb cracks in each direction over the entire surface. As an emotional commentary, if that's what it was, it was a work of art.

And it had its intended effect. It made me terrified of Nicki, even as I stupidly mourned her loss. My first instinct was to call her, but I knew she would deny it. And who knows, maybe it was a neighborhood thug overdosing on drugs. My Old Town neighborhood bordered some seamy areas, and an act of wanton vandalism certainly wasn't beyond the pale of possibility. Maybe I was just turning paranoid.

The incident intensified my desire to get away.

The respite I needed came unexpectedly from a chance call from an old friend, Andrew Tournus. Drew and I had roomed together in San Francisco when he was a law student at Berkeley and I was in architecture school in the city. Drew was now a prosecutor in New Jersey, and he and his wife Leslie had a cabin up in the Adirondacks to which they frequently invited me, but I'd never been able to make it. When Drew discovered I was reeling from a disastrous relationship, he encouraged me to spend Labor Day weekend, about eight weeks hence, at the cabin with Leslie and him, and then to stay up by myself for awhile after that. I accepted.

The prospect of the Adirondacks trip also had the effect of focusing me on my work so that I could afford to take ten days off. The firm was nose-to-the-grindstone all summer. Nights were the most difficult time for me, though. My months with Nicki had made me a restless sleeper: when we were together, her insomnia often interrupted my sleep; when we were apart, her nocturnal phone calls did the same. Each night since our breakup, it seemed, I would wake up, and realize the bed was empty of human companionship. It usually took awhile to purge myself of the bleak thoughts that inevitably assaulted me in the middle of the night.

By the time Labor Day came, I needed a vacation desperately. I flew up to Westchester County and rented a car to avoid the predictably horrendous traffic between Washington and New York. I arrived at the cabin before Drew and Leslie, which gave me a chance to explore the place; it was a two-bedroom cabin backing into the woods, with a stream flowing through the property. The kitchen and living room had soaring cathedral ceilings, and large windows afforded a superb view of the trees and the hills beyond. Very relaxing. Though the cabin was rustic, the decor was elegant, reflecting Leslie's professional skill as an interior decorator.

Before long they arrived and as always in the past, the three of us grew relaxed, particularly when we uncorked a Navarro zinfandel and Leslie served up a scrumptious steak dinner.

On Sunday, I borrowed Leslie's bicycle, and Drew and I went for a thirty-mile bicycle ride in the mountains that nearly killed me. The weekend was the perfect escape. Drew, Leslie, and I spent most of the time telling stories and laughing. I tried not to think about how much I wanted a woman like Leslie. Drew was a lucky guy.

They departed on Monday and I was left in the solitude that I had craved for months. Drew left his bicycle behind, and I went for several short rides, and wandered on foot into the woods around the cabin, managing somehow to avoid getting lost. Mostly I read vacuous novels, channel-surfed, and emptied my mind of everything. On Wednesday and Thursday it rained and thundered relentlessly. I thought the cabin would float away, and during the night I wished I hadn't read so many horror novels.

The week in the Adirondacks began to replenish me emotionally and help me put things back into some sort of perspective. Even if it turned out that I wasn't cut out for serious romance, I had a thriving business, and wonderful friends, and a mom who had survived a horrible ordeal, and even a sweet cat.

When I returned to Washington, my smile was easier than it had been for a very long time.

The first thing I did was to plow myself back into my work with renewed enthusiasm. But with a difference: I vowed to leave the office each day around six, and to work out with weights at a gym in Old Town, or—imagine the thought!—to socialize. I started going out with friends again and asked out several women, none of whom ignited any sparks; but I gained new appreciation for the concept of casual dating.

When I remarked about this to Samantha, she attributed it to a necessary healing period, introducing "antitoxins" into my system. I thought it was an apt diagnosis.

My relationship with Sam, in particular, was back to its former self. But not without its penance: Samantha wanted me to know that she resented having been shunted aside, and that my relationship with Nicki had been stupid, but she was nevertheless happy to be buddies again. Life was nonetheless a bit lonely, yet a sense of balance and normalcy had returned. After-work happy hours rediscovered their prominent place in my social lexicon, Elvis's dinnertime came on a more regular schedule, and I saw and talked more often with my mother and sister.

Still, I wasn't able to get away from Nicki completely. Even though I rarely asked, Doug imparted the latest news from the west coast when we got together for our semi-monthly racquetball games. Apparently, she had a new boyfriend and was doing well in her job. Seattle was truly enriched, I thought sarcastically.

George Bush somehow won the 1988 presidential election, and Sam, who had volunteered for his campaign, dragged Beth, Alice, Rich, and me to an election-night party. It was loud, the people were boorish, and I was reminded why I hated politics so much.

As I leaned on a bar nursing a drink and biding my time until I could respectfully leave, a guy spied my nametag and came over and introduced himself. He was young, dark in complexion, and far-too stylishly dressed for the nerdy white-bread crowd.

"Tony Alvaro," he said, offering his hand. "Are you Kevin Gibbons, the architect?"

"Yes," I said, shaking his hand and feeling the twinge of pride anytime someone recognized me.

"I'm a friend of Carlos Echeverria's," he said, but I drew a blank. It must have something to do with architecture, I thought, but I couldn't place the name at all. Sensing my confusion, Tony explained. "He used to date Nicole Petri. We both moved here from Argentina, and work in the same company."

My heart thudded painfully. I hadn't known Carlos's last name, and this was such a bizarre place to make the connection.

As if reading my thoughts, Tony said, "I'm surprised to meet you at this type of function. I thought that architects were apolitical." His English was flawless.

"One of my colleagues brought me here." Scanning the room, I added, "But predictably, she's disappeared." Remembering my manners, I asked, "Can I buy you a drink?"

As we chatted over the cacophony of second-rate bands and third-rate political speeches, I learned that Tony and Carlos worked for a high-tech firm in Reston, and had wired the Bush campaign, accounting for his presence at the victory party. I asked where Carlos was.

"On his honeymoon," Tony said. "He waited until our work was completed and was married last weekend, and should be in Tahiti with his bride by now."

Stupidly, a surge of relief passed through me. "Not Nicki, huh?"

Tony smiled mischievously. "No, not Nicki." He drank deeply from his glass. "Thanks in part to me."

"What do you mean?"

"Carlos is a very attractive man, and he has never had difficulty meeting beautiful women. But there are very few women like Nicole in Argentina. Tall. Blonde. Ivory skin. For us, those looks are exotic. Movie-star. Carlos fell very hard for her."

That made two of us, I thought ruefully. "Why didn't it work out?"

Tony laughed, as if the answer should be obvious. "She's crazy. And the more crazy she was, the more absurd their relationship grew. They would argue, she would hit him, they would break up, then get back together again. He has a bad temper, but hers is worse. They couldn't be together and they couldn't be apart. It was like a drug addiction." He drank some more. "I couldn't bear to see him like that. He started drinking, and it affected our work. Finally, it came down either to Nicole or everything else Carlos valued. I begged him to end the relationship, for his sake. Eventually he came to his senses and told Nicole it was over. He moved, he changed his phone number, we instructed the receptionist not to allow her phone calls or visits." Tony smiled. "But of course she managed to get through."

"How?"

"She stole his car. She couldn't find Carlos, but she saw his car on the street. She had kept her set of keys, so she just drove it away."

I laughed at the image. "I'm sorry, but that's really over the top."

He smiled also. "Actually, it was kind of funny. Living in Washington, of course, we assumed the car was stolen, and reported it to the insurance company. Until a ransom note from Nicole arrived at our office. Nicole said in the note that she had something that belonged to Carlos, and they had to meet to negotiate the transfer. I told him not to go, and simply to collect the insurance money, but of course he went."

"And?"

"Nicole begged him to come back. She was all over the place, talking about having children with him one minute, threatening to kill herself the next. Finally, Carlos told her he was dating someone else, and that his relationship with her was over forever." Tony stopped talking for a moment as the crowd let out a loud whoop over some politician's comment. "She took the news very calmly, handed him his car keys, and disappeared into the night. And despite Carlos's suspicions, it turned out there was no bomb in the car."

We both laughed nervously. That must have been around the time I met Nicole on the train. "But it wasn't over," I said.

"No, unfortunately, not completely," Carlos confirmed. "As you can imagine, they had a lot of mutual friends. So Nicole was able to identify Carlos's new girlfriend, Sandra. Nicole didn't know her, but she found out where she worked. One day a box was delivered to Sandra's office. And inside the box were—"

"Dead roses."

He looked at me quizzically. "Yes," he affirmed. "That's right." He rubbed his chin thoughtfully. "I guess Nicole wanted to poison their relationship. But she ended up just driving them closer together." Then Tony smiled again. "Nicole made sure that Carlos knew about her relationship with you. I know it made him jealous, which was Nicole's intent. You are a formidable rival, very accomplished, which Carlos admires. But fortunately, Sandra is beautiful enough, devoted enough, and . . . stable enough so that in the end Carlos was able to resist Nicole's devices."

Later, finding my way to the garage of the cavernous Washington Hilton was a labyrinthine task, but before long the car and I were out in the brisk night air. My conversation with Tony Alvaro had been unsettling. Contradictory thoughts assaulted me. How could I have been so attracted to someone who was as obviously unbalanced as Nicki? Had I somehow overlooked it, or had I ignored it? Or did she show me, for a time, a different face? How could someone who was so insecure and obsessive as Nicki appear so normal? I felt like an idiot.

As if that weren't enough to send me into a mental tailspin, when I arrived home that evening and retrieved my messages from the answering machine, there was one from Jennifer: "Uh, hi Kevin. I was hoping you were there." Her voice sounded anxious. "I wanted to tell you in person, but I don't want you to hear it through the gossip network." She laughed nervously, then continued. "Um, Darren asked me to marry him. And, um, I said yes. So we're getting married next spring. So, anyway, call me if you want." She paused, then continued with an empathic tone. "I hope you're okay. Give me a call, 'kay?" Pause. "'Bye."

Well, what a night. George Bush was a big winner, along with Carlos Echeverria, his bride Sandra, and some dumb surveyor named Darren who was running off with the first love of my life.

I had drunk too much, it was late, and my head was spinning. I sank into the pillow. Oh, Christ, my relationship with Jennifer really was over. I hadn't realized that I had held out hope against the odds—even against logic. But that hope was snuffed out now.

OVER THE FOLLOWING weeks, the combined effects of my discussion with Tony Alvaro and Jennifer's announcement made me pull inside myself again. I concentrated on my work. I decided to take on a small design project entirely to myself: the Parkside penthouse units. I was involved, of course, in the entire project, but for this facet of it I would be solely responsible. The top floor of the building would be divided into two cavernous twenty-four-hundred-foot condominiums, as compared to six units on each of the other floors. It required converting four units into two, and I wanted to make them showpieces—absolutely elegant, taking full advantage of the spectacular views of the National Cathedral, the park, and the Potomac. It was absolutely therapeutic. I absorbed myself in the task, rediscovering the joy of taking a project from concept to refinement to reality. I was constantly tinkering, visiting the site, discussing ideas with my engineers, then tinkering some more. All to the delight of the building's owners, who were surprised by the amount of personal attention.

In the end, I decided to put the living rooms and master bedrooms in the two corners of the top floor to take full advantage of the panorama. Second and third bedrooms would also have views, and the dining rooms would be slightly elevated and open to the living rooms to give them greater visibility as well. The kitchens were spacious and open; the master bathrooms equipped with marble Jacuzzis; hardwood floors adorned the dining rooms. To make the entire building—but especially the penthouse units—amenable to entertaining, I decided to finish the rooftop as well, gratis. The penthouse and rooftop would be the signature of the mature Kevin Gibbons. It became my conceit, my obsession, my outlet. Once again, I couldn't wait to reach the office everyday, and spent as much time as possible wearing a construction hat at the Parkside.

The economy was slowing—so much for the benefits of voting Republican—but our work was steady. I think the reason was that the hard-work syndrome had afflicted all of us at the same time. Without even thinking about it, all of us were hustling. We'd had to pick up the pace when Alice grew ill from complications of diabetes, which was a constant risk for her. Rich Deeks filled in admirably—not only was he an excellent architect, but his management skills were instinctively solid. He had secured a couple of small commissions and was gaining confidence; and instead of assuming that I would lose him one day to a larger firm, I began thinking of him as a future partner. Samantha was doing well on the Parkside, and we were working productively together. The new architect was doing fine, and even Beth was happy. Both Sam and Beth had steady boyfriends, which contributed mightily to office morale even as it diminished somewhat my social life.

Over time the routine of my life again became comfortable, and I thought less and less about Nicki. As spring approached, I went through a period of melancholy, because it was approaching the anniversary of my first date with Nicki, as well as Jennifer's wedding day. But to my surprise, the period of sadness was brief.

Spring came late to Washington, and on the occasion of the first temperate night I slept with my bedroom window open. The sounds from the street and the billowing breeze lulled me into a deep sleep. When the telephone rang it barely reached me in my slumber. I opened bleary eyes and saw that the clock read two.

I fumbled the phone, then mumbled, "Hello?"

"Hi."

"Hello?" I still wasn't comprehending.

"Are you asleep? Of course, you're asleep. It's only eleven here, and I'm still at my office going out of my mind. This advertising campaign is driving everybody crazy. It's for Acura, but nobody is supposed to know that. So how are you?"

"Nicki?" This was a dream. And in it, Nicki was even more manic than usual.

"So what are you doing?"

"Um, uh, sleeping." A weird dream, but I might as well play along with it.

"You're silly. I don't know how much longer I can take these hours. Last night I was here until one-thirty. They're paying me a good salary, but when you break it down to an hourly rate, it's less than I made temping in Washington. And the cost of living is even worse than D.C. But they don't care. If anyone tells you they're mellow in Seattle, tell them they're out of their mind." Nicki laughed at her own joke.

It really was Nicki. I tried to clear the cobwebs from my brain. Strangely, I felt embarrassed at having been asleep.

"So you like Seattle?" If she was working such late hours, maybe she had broken up with her boyfriend, I thought, and then reproached myself for worrying about it.

"It's okay. The job is challenging, the city is beautiful, I have a gorgeous view of the water from my apartment, even though it rains too much. My boss loves me. He says, 'Nicki, you are the most creative person.'"

Despite myself I felt a surge of nostalgia. I had forgotten about how Nicki conveyed her self-esteem through third-party endorsements. It made me smile.

"But the people here are really superficial. No one knows anything about politics, or art, or current events. Everyone wants to go hiking all the time. I like hiking, but I miss having serious conversations like we used to have, too."

"I miss that, too." I couldn't believe I was saying this, much less talking to her.

"No, I really mean it, Kevin. From the moment I met you, I felt like we were on the same wavelength." I assumed she meant that as a compliment. "We could talk for hours."

"Yeah, that, and other stuff."

"You're so bad!"

"I'm sorry." I wasn't.

"There's just nobody to talk to around here. Even the newspaper doesn't provide any mental stimulation. I've subscribed to *The New Republic*, *The Economist*, everything, just to keep me sane. Of course, I don't have time to read any of them, but I have to have them around."

"Well, you can't have everything. You wanted to leave D.C., and you can't take it with you."

She let that pass. "I worked for the Bush campaign out here."

"That should have put you in touch with some kindred spirits."

"It's not the same out here. It's a social thing. The Republicans in Seattle are old money. It's not like D.C., where people really care about politics, and ideas, and stuff like that."

"I know what you mean."

"See! That's what I mean. You understand me." That, of course, utterly contradicted the sentiment she had expressed in our last conversation many months earlier, but I let it pass. "Were you excited that Bush won the election?"

"Well, he was better than the alternative. But he's still a politician, so I figure it's only a matter of time before he comes to steal my money. It'll just be slower than the Democrats."

Nicki chuckled. "You're such a cynic." I could hear her typing at a computer keyboard in the background. "I would really like to be able to talk to you sometimes. There's no one else—well, maybe some my female friends, and my friend Jason—but almost no one who I can talk to about things I care about." She paused. "Do you think we could be friends again?"

Friends? Again? We were never friends. That was part of the problem.

"Yeah," I said, my voice belonging to some crazy person who obviously was not Kevin Gibbons. "I'd like that." I smiled in the darkness, and sighed. "Ah, Nicki."

"What?" I didn't say anything. "So are you dating anyone?"

"No. I couldn't handle a relationship right now." Summoning courage, I plunged forward. "What about you?"

"I was dating a guy from Portland for awhile. Long-distance relationships never work out very well. It wasn't exactly long-distance—he worked for the same company—but he was pushing too fast, so we broke up." She didn't sound exactly devastated.

"That's too bad."

"I've dated a few guys here in Seattle. They were really nice, but I was really mean to them." She laughed, which actually sent a shiver up my spine. "As soon as they decide they really like me, I can't handle it anymore. This one guy, Greg, was really attractive, in that rugged J.

Crew kind of way—a lot of guys around here have looks like that—
and he started getting serious, so I just stopped returning his phone
calls. He kept calling, and I'm sure he didn't know what was going on,
but I just couldn't call him back. He was nice."

Nicki wasn't finished. "Then this other guy, Louis, from Canada,
really tall and gorgeous. A real gentleman. All the women were crazy
about him, and I decided I had to show everyone that I could wrap
him around my finger. So I seduced him. Well, not literally, of course,
I didn't make love to him. You know my rule about that, I won't make
love to anyone for at least three months, and we were only dating for
a month. But he fell in love with me, sent flowers to the office every
day, stuff like that. My friend Cynthia said, 'Nicki, I can't believe
how crazy this guy is about you! Everyone is so jealous!' He asked me
out for dinner to this romantic restaurant in Seattle, and I was afraid
he was going to ask me to marry him, so I stood him up. I know
that's really awful, but I couldn't handle that kind of pressure. I never
returned his calls, either."

I took a deep breath. "Wow, Nicki, that's a lot of intensity in,
what, seven months?"

"Nearly eight. I feel really bad. They're such nice guys, and I was
really brutal. I'm sure I really hurt them. They didn't deserve it."

I was sure that was an accurate assessment. Her description of her
Seattle relationships seemed almost a replay of ours. Was it possible
that Nicki was, at last, opening herself up to me? In her own clumsy
way, acknowledging guilt and regret?

I decided to press the point. "Nicki, sometimes I've done some
really bad things, hurt people I cared about. And I've always tried,
if I couldn't make up for it, to learn something from the experience,
to make myself a better person from it. If I discover something bad
about myself, I try to change it."

I propped myself up in bed, considering whether to proceed. I
decided to plunge ahead. "You've said some really harsh things about
your conduct, Nicki. You recognize that you led these guys on, and
they were really nice, and you deliberately hurt them. Instead of just
agonizing over it, why don't you change your behavior?"

Nicki snickered quietly. When she replied, her words made my
blood run cold.

"It's not necessary."

12

As Nicki's calls recurred with growing frequency over the next few weeks, I found myself reacting to her with almost clinical detachment. Each time, she mentioned that she missed talking to me, referred to me as a friend, complained about Seattle and the demands of her job, and painted a rosy picture of life back in Washington, D.C. She seemed surprised that I never led a conversation, but merely responded to whatever she was saying. If she asked me questions about my work, or politics, or mutual friends, I answered in detail. But I initiated nothing. Nicki was leading our new relationship; and I was following at what I considered a safe distance, like an abused puppy warily trailing its master home.

So it came as little surprise when Nicki announced during one conversation that her time in the wilderness was ending, and that she was flying back east in two weeks to look for work and prepare for a move home. I found that the news did not even quicken my pulse. Her phone calls were a challenge I had surmounted with surprising ease; I could survive her return as well. I even offered to put her in touch with some contacts in various facets of the public relations business, and she graciously accepted. Stupidly, I offered to let her stay with me while she looked for a place; happily, she politely declined.

I said nothing to my colleagues about the developments with Nicki, both because I didn't want to endure any lectures and because frankly we couldn't afford the distraction. The firm was entering a period of transition. Rich and I had negotiated some significant contracts, and we needed to bring on two new architects a.s.a.p. With the job market slowing, we knew we could hire good people away from other firms, or graduates from top architecture schools.

More urgent was a need to find new office space: our lease was expiring, and to remain in the building near Union Station simply wouldn't suffice for another five years. We would outgrow the space soon, and its peripheral location was proving a disadvantage in the competitive market. Plus, rental rates were good, so we could upgrade and enlarge our space without paying much more. I hated to leave the place where Horizon had been born, and I would miss the tranquil bustle of the trains going past, but a move was inevitable. As Alice was sick and out of the office, I put Rich in charge of finding suitable new space.

He found the perfect venue almost immediately in a beautiful building on the Georgetown waterfront. We would trade our view of the trains for a magnificent vista of the Potomac. As with our current location, the space was on the outskirts of the downtown business district, but the neighborhood was upscale and trendy. Union Station was perfect for upstarts; but the new offices fit our emerging persona as a rising star in the city's architecture business. Equally important, the lease offered periodic expansion options that Rich was convinced we would need.

I had never been as excited about the prospects for our firm. We were gambling by investing our present income on expansion, but it seemed a safe bet. We were in the right place at the right time: the economic slowdown meant less new construction and more renovations and conversions, and that was our niche. But we were no longer just a renovation boutique; an increasing portion of our business was focused on lucrative structural redesigns, such as constructing new facades on older buildings. The new contracts were for new office buildings designed over existing structures, one on Pennsylvania Avenue and the other in Philadelphia. The Philly project was our first away from Washington, indicating that our specialty was outgrowing our previous geographic confines.

Meanwhile, assigning Rich to handle Art Longley's projects cemented our business foundation. Rich and Art hit it off famously, often going out drinking or having dinner together. That made me happy because my relationship with Art seemed inalterably changed since the incident with Nicki. So once again, Art was cultivating the talented young architect, just as he had done with me a decade before. I was wiser than Fielder, Steinmetz & Way had been, though: I gave Rich a twenty-thousand-dollar raise and made it clear that if business continued to expand I would make him the firm's first equity partner. In turn, Rich negotiated a long-term multi-project deal with Art, tying him to Horizon and demonstrating Rich's loyalty to the firm. The firm was solid.

And yet . . . our success was bittersweet. I had broken away from the corporate behemoth because I wanted to vent my creative talent. And my talent was as an architect, not as a businessman. Our firm's growth necessitated for me less designing and more supervising— and, even worse, more schmoozing. We were also losing the camaraderie we enjoyed when it was just Rich and Beth and Alice and Samantha and me. Sometimes we rarely even saw each other. We all spent more time with subcontractors and vendors than with each other. The intimacy lost, I knew, would never be regained.

In the midst of all that, Nicki announced her impending arrival, with a plethora of interviews lined up for her week in Washington. She managed to fit me into a busy social schedule for drinks after work on Wednesday. She offered to come by the office, but I ruled that out. Instead, I asked her to meet me at our new office building, where I would show her the work-in-progress that would soon be the new home of Horizon Concepts, followed by a bottle of wine at nearby Nathan's.

Nicki was late, and I paced around the lobby. She entered without my realizing it, and I whirled around at her approach. The sunlight shrouded her momentarily, but as she emerged it was unmistakably Nicole Petri, radiant in a long blue sundress, and a blue bow in her hair. Her face bore flushed cheeks, a slight sheen of perspiration, and a glowing smile.

"It's hot out there. I'm not used to the humidity anymore," she declared as we embraced in an affectionate hug. As she pulled away, she announced, "I'm really fat. I don't get any exercise with my work schedule. I just eat all the time."

Actually, she was right: she looked to have gained fifteen pounds, but instead of complaining about it, she seemed to have accepted it for the time being. That struck me as refreshing in a strange way. Maybe she had changed a bit after all.

I took her up and showed her around the seventh floor office space, describing how it would look when it was redesigned to our specifications.

Nicki chattered as we walked the three blocks to Nathan's. It brought back memories of our frequent one-sided conversations and made me smile.

A bottle of Jordan cabernet and a spare-rib appetizer made Nicki even more loquacious. "I really need to go on a diet." She munched a rib. The interviews so far had gone quite well, and she told me that she had decided to give two weeks' notice when she returned to Seattle, and to move back to Washington even if she didn't have a definite position lined up. "My job seems to have increased my marketability, so I'm not worried, and I can't stand Seattle anymore. I just have to get back to civilization."

The combined impact of the rich wine and Nicki's announcement made my head spin. This was moving too fast. Six weeks ago, Nicki was a continent away, our relationship seemingly irrevocably consigned to the past. Now she sat before me, familiarly touching my hand, on the verge of moving back to town and re-entering my life in some fashion. For her it seemed as if we had never skipped a beat, but merely reunited after a brief absence in a friendship that had deep and cherished roots. The entire experience was surrealistic.

The time passed quickly and I offered to drive Nicki to her parents' house in suburban Maryland. She accepted. Watching her sitting in the passenger seat, adorning my car with her beauty, made me soften toward her. I pondered briefly whether I would kiss her goodnight if I had the chance. She did not invite me in when we arrived, and she settled the question of a kiss by leaning over and pecking me on the cheek before she got out of the car. Just friends, the gesture declared.

It suddenly occurred to me that for better or worse, if Nicki was coming back into my life in some fashion, my friends and colleagues would have to get used to the idea. "Why don't you stop by the office for coffee sometime during your travels on Friday?" I asked. "I'll be around all day."

Nicki flashed me her trademark smile. "That would be nice. I don't know what my schedule will be, but I'll try. I'd like to say hi to everybody." She snickered. "They probably all hate me."

What was worse: that she didn't really believe that, or that it didn't bother her?

ON FRIDAY, I called an impromptu staff meeting to talk about our office move and other odds and ends. As the meeting was ending, I made an announcement. "We may have a little blast-from-the-past today."

"John Friedman Fergaman's coming by to ask for a job?" Beth deadpanned. Everyone burst out laughing.

"No, but something almost as good." Four faces looked at me expectantly. "Nicki may be stopping by. She's moving back to Washington."

Loud groans all around.

"Who's Nicki?" Julie asked. All eyes turned in her direction.

"Trust me," Rich stated, "you don't want to know."

When Nicki showed up around three, I was a nervous wreck. I tried to usher her out of the office to get some coffee at Union Station, but she insisted on saying hello to everyone. And, to their credit, my colleagues were on their best behavior. When we walked past Alice's empty office, Nicki asked where she was. I told her Alice was hospitalized with severe complications from diabetes. Nicki seemed worried. I had forgotten her experience working with AIDS-infected babies. It seemed I had suppressed memories of Nicki's better qualities.

We had a nice time going for coffee, and I felt myself relaxing. Her interviews had gone quite well for the most part, and she had two promising leads, one as an events coordinator with the Sheraton Carlton, another as advertising executive with the news radio station that was the rival to the one for which Nicki had worked when I met her. Once again she remarked on her weight—"I have to go on a diet and start jogging again when I get back, even if it's hot"—but all in all, she seemed more confident than I had ever seen her, more at ease with herself.

Over the next few weeks, I began a (hopefully) subtle campaign to rehabilitate Nicki with my friends. Meanwhile, Nicki was acting not as if I were an ordinary friend, but more like her best friend, calling me two or three times a day to touch base and plot logistics for her move.

She was offered two positions, and decided to go with the hotel— a challenging job, but that was exactly the attraction. She wanted to prove herself, to demonstrate that whatever she accomplished was by means of talent and hard work, rather than looks or connections. She gave her two weeks notice in Seattle, planned to take a week to bring her belongings cross-country, and would begin work at the hotel a few weeks later just after Labor Day. She had already arranged to move into an apartment on Capitol Hill with a former colleague who was losing a roommate.

I looked forward to her arrival. It would be nice to hang around her, to attract the stares that always greeted anyone lucky enough to be with her—even if she weren't my girlfriend. Everyone seemed to be acquiescing in her return, except for Doug and Samantha, who almost seemed to have coordinated their worries about Nicki's possible "agenda." The fact that Doug and Sam hardly knew each other made their parallel concerns all the more worth pondering. My own feelings about the matter were downright serene.

With all that was going on at work, the weeks passed quickly. Nicki went into radio silence on the road, and I wondered whether she was pulling another relationship change. But she called late on the night of her arrival, exhausted but ecstatic. The next morning I went to her new apartment to help her unload the truck.

We eased into our new roles. She stopped by the office one afternoon in her jogging clothes and seemed in soaring spirits. She had some time before her new job started.

"How's Alice?" she asked.

"Not too well," I replied. "Her situation seems stable, but she's going to be in the hospital for awhile. I stopped by last night; her spirits are low."

"Do you think she'd like some personalized attention?"

"Sure. Her family is in Illinois, so aside from friends, she doesn't have anyone looking out for her."

"Well, I have a lot of extra time," Nicki said, "so I thought I'd volunteer at the hospital, as long as they let me spend some of my time helping Alice."

"That's very generous."

Nicki smiled mischievously. "After all, it's the least I can do for the woman who bought the handcuffs."

On the spur of the moment, I asked her if she'd like to take a ride to the see Parkside, where renovations were almost complete. She agreed and we took a cab over. First, I showed her some of the lower-level units that were not yet occupied. She complimented the openness and the light woods I'd used to enhance the light. "It doesn't feel like you're in a condo at all," she remarked.

Then I took her up to the penthouse units. I made her wear a construction hat, which looked terribly out of place yet made her even more adorable than usual.

She loved the penthouses. "Kevin, this is your best work ever."

"Thanks. It's a special project, and that was exactly my intention: to create a signature. I've sweated out every detail."

"And to think, you did all this even without a woman's touch," she said. She walked from room to room, telling me the type of interior decorating each needed to enhance the design. "This whole place is definitely Ralph Lauren, except for the master bedroom, which is Laura Ashley. All white and cream colors." I smiled, picturing the Nicki-inspired decor. "The views are fantastic." The grand spires of the National Cathedral could be seen from one direction, the lush green forest of Rock Creek Park from the other.

Though we didn't see much of each other once she started volunteering and catching up with other friends, the nocturnal phone calls resumed. She was excited about her new job, despite the fact that it would involve long and sometimes erratic hours. We got together for lunch and drinks a couple of times. On her second Friday back in Washington, I happily accepted Nicki's invitation to indulge her favorite pastime: shopping.

"I'm not going to buy any clothes until I lose weight," she said as we walked into the suburban Virginia mall. "But I need shoes and accessories. Women in Seattle don't care about that." She made a disapproving face. "Everything's *au natural.*" Once inside the mall, blazing past stores as she glanced into the windows toward our destination, Nordstrom's, she said, "I miss shopping with you. You have really good taste, and a lot of patience." She looked down at our hands, which had somehow become intertwined, and held them up. "I love your long fingers. You have very talented hands." She grinned. "In more ways than one."

"Um, yeah. Thanks."

Our dinner was divine. We shared a salad and a pizza, and both were delicious. We drained a bottle of Chateau St. Jean chardonnay and were both pleasantly buzzed.

On our way to her home, when we were just about to drive over the 14th Street Bridge in the District, Nicki gently grasped my arm.

"I think we should take this turn," she said, gesturing to the George Washington Parkway exit toward Alexandria.

Her meaning hit me at once. "Gladly," I said.

We were soon at my townhouse. "I missed this place," Nicki announced as Elvis pranced out to greet us. I quickly gave Elvis her overdue dinner, whereupon the cat seemed content to leave Nicki and me to our endeavors.

I opened a bottle of dessert wine that Nicki and I had bought at a Virginia winery. "Remember this?"

"Umm, yes, I'm glad you still have it."

Nicki put on a Yanni CD. When I came into the living room, her shoes were off and she was comfortably ensconced on the sofa. I said, "I didn't realize how much I missed you."

"I missed you, too."

I put my wine down and leaned over to kiss her. Her lips were warm and moist. She put her arms around my neck and pulled me closer, inviting my tongue into her mouth. The kiss was exquisite, and I thought that I really *hadn't* realized how much I missed her.

We pulled apart and gazed into each other's eyes from only a few inches' distance. "Make love to me," she said. I nodded. We pulled the pillows from the sofa to make room, and began taking off each other's clothes and were quickly naked. We kissed and touched each other, rediscovering one another's bodies. With few preliminaries, I slid easily inside her and we made slow, gentle, affectionate love.

When we finished, we lay beside one another in warm embrace, reaching over to finish our wine. I didn't want to get up to refill our glasses, so we lay there quietly. I didn't want to say anything; I didn't want to think about, much less talk about, the ramifications of this. I wanted to savor the moment, and Nicki seemed to want that, too.

"Would you like to stay?" I whispered.

"This was wonderful, but I think you ought to take me home."

Our drive to Nicki's apartment was mostly silent. What did tonight signify? What did this mean for her?

As if sensing my quandary, Nicki started talking. "I missed you, Kevin. Especially our conversations. I can talk to you so easily, but I realized when we spent time together tonight that I missed you in other ways, too."

I was glad to know she couldn't see my face in the darkness. My facial muscles were taut. I was terrified.

"You were able to touch me in ways that no one else ever has. I don't mean just physically." She paused. "Do you think we can still be friends?"

"Just friends?" I asked hoarsely.

"I don't know. That's a lot. There aren't that many really good friends that a person has. And of course that's the best basis for any kind of relationship."

"I agree with that."

"So?" She poked me playfully in the ribs, and I was so tense that it made me nearly jerk the car off the road. "Uh oh," she said, "I'd better let you drive."

It took me awhile to say anything. "Yes," I said finally, "I think we can be friends."

"I'm glad." She took my hand from the gear shift and entwined it with hers and sighed.

When I dropped her off, we kissed lightly on the lips and said goodnight. I wished I didn't have to face the drive home. Why was I allowing myself to do this? The risks were enormous. Was it possible that Nicki was capable of change? If not, the fall could be devastating. Go slow, I counseled myself. But of course Nicki was setting both the speed and the direction. I was just along for the ride.

SHE CALLED ON Sunday night. "What are you doing next weekend?"

"Labor Day weekend?"

"Yes, silly. That's next weekend."

"I dunno. I usually don't like to face the traffic on holiday weekends. I imagine I'll go cycling a couple times, relax, go into the office."

"Well, I think you should break your habit and we should go to New York. We can fly or take the train."

"Any special occasion?"

"Well, it may be the last weekend time I have for awhile with the new job. As the person with the least seniority, I'll be working conferences on the weekends a lot. So if we're going to spend any time together, it will have to be then."

"Sure," I said. "I'll make plans." And the tingle that had accompanied me ever since our last date gained new intensity.

MAKING THE ARRANGEMENTS was tougher than I expected—New York City is apparently a very popular destination on Labor Day weekend, and most of the flights and hotels were booked solid—but the logistical challenges absorbed my thoughts. I finally found a room at the Helmsley Park at four hundred and fifty dollars a night. Clearly it was back to my high-spending days.

The week in the interim seemed endless. It rained incessantly, which wiped out a crucial week of work at the Pennsylvania Avenue site. The Kalorama project was supposed to be finished, but we spent an entire week trying unsuccessfully to obtain certificates of occupancy from the District of Columbia bureaucrats. Failure to secure the permits would mean that the dozen or so occupants who planned to move in over Labor Day weekend wouldn't be allowed to do so. Finally, I authorized Rich to spread some money around—the first time we'd ever resorted to bribery of public officials to do the jobs they were supposed to do, but it wouldn't turn out to be the last. It came down to the wire, but at four o'clock on Friday, we finally had the permits. Rich and I spent most of the evening contacting anxious and angry occupants. By the time the weekend came, I was stressed, exhausted, and disgusted.

But Nicki's sunny mood on the weekend—and matching weather—lifted my spirits. We left for New York on Saturday afternoon and went straight to the hotel, located across from Central Park, and just as gaudy as I would expect from Leona Helmsley. We changed clothes and cabbed to the theatre to see *A Streetcar Named Desire*.

Afterward, we shared a huge corned beef sandwich and potato knishes at the Stage Delicatessen, giggling over the stereotypically rude service. We walked around the city for awhile, but the night air was too humid, so we returned to our room, showered together, and made love until the wee hours of the morning.

On Sunday, Nicki decided to skip Mass, joking that she had too much to confess. The morning was languorous, breakfast in bed with champagne, chocolate-covered strawberries, and the *New York Times*. We strolled around Rockefeller Plaza in the afternoon, explored the grandeur of St. Patrick's Cathedral, and took in a Degas exhibit at the Metropolitan Museum of Art. The weather had turned markedly cooler, making it pleasant outside. In the evening, we took a cab to Greenwich Village in the evening to eat dinner at One if by Land, Two if by Sea, housed in a rustic old building once owned by Aaron Burr.

When the cab dropped us off at the hotel and Nicki began to go inside, I grabbed her hand and pulled her in the opposite direction. We crossed the street and approached the line of horse-driven carriages waiting for passengers. I had always wanted to ride one through Central Park on a romantic evening, and this was it. We nestled beneath the blanket, cheek to cheek, taking in the sounds of the night. It was as romantic as I had always imagined. Suddenly Nicki sat up, and I did likewise. She was grinning.

"Wouldn't Thanksgiving be a nice weekend to get married? Late fall, the leaves off the trees, a chill in the air. Very romantic."

Speechless, I just looked at her, and she kept smiling, embarrassed. "Well, say something, silly."

My throat was so constricted I wasn't sure that any words would come out. And if they did, I had no idea what they would be. I was on automatic pilot. Finally, I murmured, "Any weekend would be a nice weekend to marry you."

She looked away, suddenly turning serious, speaking without looking at me. "I went through a really bad period when we were dating before, but I've got my mind back together. And as I thought about what I wanted my future to be, I realized that of all the people I'd ever met, you had the most integrity. That means a lot to me."

I thought about the bribes we had just paid to the District of Columbia building inspectors.

She turned to me. "I know I can count on you, no matter what. And that made me decide: 'He's the kind of person I want to marry. And to father my children.'"

My lips were completely dry. "I would love that. More than anything." We gazed into each other's eyes. "I've wanted to marry you from the moment I met you. Maybe even before that."

"You're silly." She smiled. I leaned forward to kiss her, but she drew back. "So are you sure you want to marry me? I could make your life miserable, you know."

"You're not going to make my life miserable. Hey, isn't this where you're supposed to give me a diamond ring?"

She laughed and punched me playfully. "Don't think you're evading your responsibilities that easily, mister. I want a big one, too."

I laughed. "Of course. We can go to Tiffany's tomorrow."

"Why do you think I made you take me to New York?"

We both laughed. "I'm impressed. You had this all worked out." She was sweeping me off my feet. The feeling was intoxicating and terrifying, all at the same time.

"Another thing: I want to live in one of the Parkside penthouses."

"Are you serious?"

"Yes, it's perfect. You couldn't realize it at the time, but you were designing it for us. Subconsciously. It's where I want us to live."

I did some quick arithmetic. I couldn't possibly afford it. Then I realized it didn't matter; we would have it no matter the cost. "Okay."

She beamed. "Really?"

"Nicki, I want more than anything to make you happy."

"Don't worry about the money. I'm going to be very good for your career."

"Hey, can we make a detour to Pennsylvania before we go home tomorrow? I'd like to introduce you to my mom."

"Sure. That would be nice."

"You're gonna make her a very happy lady."

"I'm not stealing away her baby?"

"Yeah, but she wants to trade the old one in for a real one, the cuddly kind that smells like talcum powder. And I can't accomplish that by myself." We both giggled. Then I drew Nicki toward me, and we kissed deeply.

Then Nicki pulled abruptly away. "One more thing." She frowned. "This one is implicit, but I want to make it very clear." I raised my eyebrows. "You understand that when we get married, it's for good. No cheating, ever. No matter what. You know I feel very strongly about that."

I nodded dumbly.

"Once we're married, you're stuck with me forever." She smiled, but her eyes, a deep green in the darkness of the evening, were deadly serious.

The sound of the horses' swift hooves on the concrete seemed to mark a cadence for my pounding heart.

I felt my lips moving, and heard words coming out, but there was no conscious thought behind them. Still, the words were binding. I knew that to the core of my soul.

"Forever, Nicki," I heard myself whisper. "Forever."

MY MOTHER HAD been thrilled by our surprise visit and news, and charmed by Nicki. My sister was happy too, but the office crew and friends were a different story. Though Beth and Rich were supportive, both expressed doubts. Even Andrew Tournus, who had never met Nicki, remembered the things I told him about her at his cabin the previous Labor Day. I told Doug after our racquetball game, in which he had slaughtered me mercilessly. "Are you joking?" he asked in his gravelly voice.

"No."

"You've got to be kidding, I mean, come on, she's crazy!"

Even worse than Doug was Samantha. I took her out for dinner on the Thursday following my engagement to Nicki. We sat outdoors at Bullfeathers, my favorite burger place on the Hill. I had a horrendously fattening but delicious Bullburger while Sam nibbled at the artichoke dip.

"How's Lee?" I asked.

"He's fine. How's little Miss Lucifer?"

"Sam, I have something to tell you."

"Don't tell me you're dating her again."

"Well, we're getting married in November."

"Oh my God, you've gone crazy."

"I'm in love with her. That's all there is to it. I have to follow my instincts."

"Yeah, just like you followed your instincts with Jennifer, and then with Nicki. And they both broke your heart. You can go ahead and do it if you're determined, but I'm not going to be a witness."

This was worse, far worse, than I expected. "You really have two choices. I can marry Nicki and you can find it within yourself to be supportive, or I can marry Nicki and you can throw a fit and ruin our friendship."

"I choose option C," Sam declared, and she got up and left the outside seating area, and walked to the Capitol South Metro station a block away.

Though the incident pervaded my mood, I couldn't dwell on it. There was too much to do with a wedding in twelve weeks, juxtaposed against an amazingly busy period at work, and a brand new job for Nicki.

The wedding plans consumed our limited free time. Nicki and I decided on a small but elegant ceremony and reception in Old Town. Her family plunged into the planning with Nicki, and I was clearly along for the ride. But that was fine with me, because the ceremony mattered far more to them than to me. All I really cared about was the woman I was marrying.

Meanwhile, I put my townhouse on the market and negotiated a surprisingly good price on one of the penthouse units in the Parkside. The building's owners were thrilled that I wanted to buy it, expressing the view that I must think highly of our handiwork if I was set on living there. They knocked one hundred thousand dollars off the selling price, which still left me with a mortgage more than twice as large as my previous one. Between Nicki's income and mine, I thought we could manage it, but it would be a stretch. I had to pledge some of the firm's assets as collateral for the loan, but our growth forecast was sufficient to provide me with solid income potential.

Nicki's job was consuming. The training period was two months, and during that time she worked seven days a week, ten to twelve hours most days. She seemed to be thriving, though, and her supervisor generously agreed to give Nicki the entire week after Thanksgiving off for our honeymoon. We made plans to go to the British Virgin Islands, even though the trip would be fairly short.

Our frenetic schedules, especially Nicki's, prevented us from spending much time together. Nicki was enduring frequent headaches, which we both attributed to the heavy stress and dieting for the wedding, and she often found making love uncomfortable.

One night she confided the fears that were fueling her urgency. We were curled together on my sofa, half-watching a television movie. In a remarkably matter-of-fact tone, she announced, "My doctors think it will be hard for me to have a baby after I'm thirty." She would turn thirty in January—two months after our marriage.

"What do you mean?"

"You know I take medication for problems with my endocrine system." I nodded. "Well, it's more complicated than that. My whole reproductive system is a mess. Even under the best of circumstances, it's going to be difficult to have a baby, they say. And it will get worse the older I get." She imparted that information without expression, as if sharing the diagnosis of someone she didn't know. But then she added gravely, "I want a baby. I want a daughter."

"Me, too." I reached out and gently touched her face, smoothing back her long blonde hair. "And no matter what it takes, even if it means making love to you ten times a day, I'm up to the job."

She smiled. "I'll bet you will be."

As I pondered it later, her revelation made a great deal come into focus for me. Her desperation not to lose Carlos. Her sudden decision to move back east. And her even more sudden decision to ask me to marry her. Nicki wanted me not primarily as a husband, but as breeding stock. Yet as I reflected upon it, I realized there were far worse reasons for marrying someone. If she held me in high enough esteem to want me to father her children, that actually gave me solace about the stability of our marriage.

But I had little time to contemplate the implications. In addition to the wedding plans, my work was especially demanding. Among other things, we had to put the finishing touches on the Parkside penthouse units so they'd be ready for occupancy when Nicki and I were married. And the Pennsylvania Avenue project was proceeding quickly, with the construction company wanting to get the facade finished before winter.

Complicating matters was Samantha's anger. At the office, she refused to engage in any personal conversation, and spoke to me in clipped tones. It made life difficult because we were working together on the Parkside project. Beth also confided to me that Sam was sending out her résumé. As it was, we were bringing in two new architects, and it would cripple us if Samantha left.

I spoke to Rich about it and asked him to intercede. He was sympathetic but didn't hold out much hope. "If you go through with the wedding, I think we're going to lose her, no question."

As I walked back to my office after that conversation, I heard Beth speaking to someone on the phone. "Oh wait," she said, "he's finished. I'll put you through."

"So I hear you're marrying the Nickster," Jennifer said as an opening salutation. "I heard through the grapevine that Nicki had decided to make an honest man out of you, so I thought I'd call and congratulate you."

"Thanks. How goes married life for you?"

"It's okay. Darren is a good person. I think if I had dated him before you rather than after, though, I would have married you."

Jennifer could be so blunt sometimes it took my breath away. "Thanks, I needed that."

"Oh, come on, Kevin, lighten up. You're marrying a beautiful woman, right?"

"I don't know. I'm taking a risk."

"Marriage is inherently a risk. Sometimes I don't think it's natural for two people to mate for life. People change, sometimes as soon as they're married. But you can't know whether the change will be good, or bad, or whether it will parallel the ways you'll change. So it's a risk."

We talked for a long time about politics, and work, and what movies we'd seen, and books we'd read. I hated to say goodbye.

"I can't call too often, because Darren worries about you."

"Seriously?"

"Yes. He knows we shared some pretty special experiences."

For some reason, that made me smile. "Actually, I think the same thing with Nicki. Well, not actually. She just made it clear that she values marital fidelity. And if ever she'd perceive a threat, it would be from you."

Jennifer chuckled. "So we'll talk occasionally—and very surreptitiously."

I ASKED DOUG and Drew to stand with me. The night before the wedding, while Nicki was out God-knows-where with some of her friends, the two of them took me out with several other male carousers to a strip club and an endless series of bars.

Through it all there were jokes about giving up my single life, and each one made me wince.

Around two, when I was so drunk I thought I would spent the next day puking, Doug drove me home. When we arrived, he turned off the car and looked at me earnestly.

"You know, you don't have to go through with this. It's not too late to back out."

I managed a thin smile. This was not what I wanted to hear on the eve of the most important day of my life. "I really appreciate your concern," I replied, trying to dismiss an uncomfortable subject.

"Kevin, Karen and I started out as Nicki's friends, but we've come to really care about you, and wonder about Nicki. I've never seen a prospective marriage where one of the person's friends were so united in the belief that it's a bad idea. Not for Nicki; for you. She's unstable. She's vicious. And it's not likely to get better." He smiled sweetly. "I predict a short honeymoon."

I sighed. "Doug, I know you have my best interests at heart, but you don't see the side of Nicki that I do. I think she's finally ready to settle down."

"Kind of like a spider settling in to her web," Doug remarked. I said nothing as Doug stared at me. "Kevin, I implore you. On behalf of everyone who cares about you. Don't go through with this."

But I did.

PART TWO

nicki and alex

14

THE WEDDING WAS tasteful and fun. My friends made the best of it, all except for Samantha, who refused to attend and quietly left the firm. But even that didn't ruin the affair. Nicki looked so radiant it made me feel lightheaded and positively giddy. Nicki seemed very happy, and I felt lucky.

Our honeymoon in the British Virgin Islands was too short, but sun-drenched, relaxing, and romantic. Nicki wasted no time informing me she had cast away her birth-control pills; and though she continued to suffer headaches, we set about our marital lovemaking with ardent enthusiasm. Nicki nearly succumbed to sun poisoning one day when she exposed her fair skin to the Caribbean sun for too long, but even that led only to greater conjugal creativity. We returned home to our busy lives sated and physically exhausted.

As I DROVE the Saab into the garage after work one evening, my thoughts turned to our penthouse condominium and how well it had turned out. We had moved in four months earlier, and it was a delight. We spent nearly every spare moment decorating it—or more accurately, yours truly trailing Nicki around as she made decorating choices—and by now I felt like I shared my house with another couple, namely Ralph Lauren and Laura Ashley. It looked great, and felt very comfortable. And expensive as hell.

Nicki looked up briefly from her magazine as I walked into the living room. "Hi," she said tiredly. She was lying on the sofa, clad in pajamas and wearing her glasses with her hair pulled back into a ponytail. She looked fresh and adorable. She made room and I settled on the end of the sofa. "How was your day?" she asked, setting the magazine on the console.

I released a deep breath. "Intense. We decided to bid on the art museum renovation."

"Oh," she said, dismissing my news. "I had two big events today. The European Auto Dealers, and the American Political Science Association. That one is going on all weekend. It was insane. I'm absolutely exhausted." Closing her eyes, she laid her head back on the arm of the sofa.

I lifted one of her feet and began kneading it through her thick pink sock. She lifted her head and opened her eyes. "What are you doing?"

"Massaging your foot."

"You know I don't like that."

"Sorry. I forgot," I lied. I still could not believe she did not like massages. I stopped rubbing her foot and she removed it from my lap. Rising, I said, "I think I'll change clothes."

"The food should be here any minute," she said, returning to her magazine as I walked toward our bedroom.

The master bedroom suite contained its own large bathroom, and I quickly washed my face and changed into sweatpants and a T-shirt. When I returned to the kitchen, Nicki was arranging the food on the table in the kitchen nook. I glanced around and noticed she had not opened wine. "Vino?"

"Sure."

I went to the refrigerator and examined its viticultural contents. Nicki and I had purged red wine from our repertoire, hopefully temporarily, on the suspicion that it contributed to her frequent headaches. "Some Sattui Riesling?"

"Too sweet. How about some sauvignon blanc?"

I uncorked the wine and poured two glasses. I brought them into the breakfast nook and wrapped my arms around Nicki. "Tough day, huh?" I murmured.

"Yeah," she said, gently pushing me away, "And I want to get to bed." As I pondered the different possible meanings of that statement, she padded off into the kitchen to retrieve serving spoons. When dinner ended, Nicki announced she was going to bed. I glanced at the clock on the stove, which said nine o'clock. Early.

"Do you want me to join you?" I called after her.

As she was about to leave the kitchen, she turned back and gave me the full benefit of her eyes. They weren't seductive—they never were—but they were beautiful, as always, and Nicki knew it. "Of course," she said.

Since we had returned from our honeymoon, lovemaking had evolved into a combination of anxiety and disappointment. Though she didn't speak it, I knew Nicki was obsessed with becoming pregnant. I needed to look no further than the cabinet beneath Nicki's sink, which was stacked with home-pregnancy kits.

Her constant anxiety robbed the experience of much of its spontaneity and ardor. That along with her recent difficulty in attaining orgasm often made it a frustrating ordeal, but Nicki kept on pushing.

As I entered the master suite, Nicki was propped in bed watching *Beverly Hills 90210*. Nicki clicked the television off, turned off the light as well, and I knew she was ready for business. Perfunctory kissing substituted for foreplay. I wanted to slow down the proceedings, but Nicki read my mind. "C'mon. I need to go to sleep." She reached between my legs, not to stimulate but to check the carnal temperature. Finding it limp, she asked, "What's wrong?" and began to stroke it without skill.

I pushed her aside and started attacking her with kisses on her lips, her face, her neck. Breathing her scent, watching her eyes close and lips part, provided an immediate aphrodisiac, and I felt myself begin to harden. Nicki felt it too, and it fueled her own anticipation.

Now Nicki pushed me aside, pulled her nightgown over her head, and straddled me. She leaned forward and kissed me roughly. Pushing herself up on her knees, she lowered herself onto my erection. We began thrusting in familiar unison. Her moans began at once and she buried her face in mine. I could feel her soft hair shrouding my face, and its clean scent enveloped me.

Though physically stimulated, I hadn't achieved the mental focus that would have occurred with more deliberate foreplay. My thoughts wandered. We had so much work to do at the firm. Would we have to hire someone to service our ongoing clients while Rich and I developed the museum project? What would happen then if, as was likely, we didn't get the contract? Would we have to lay people off due to the slowing economy? Who would it be? What if we lost the competition to Fergaman? What if Nicki got pregnant just when the firm was having trouble? What was Jennifer doing at that moment?

Wait, what was that last thought? Why had I thought of Jennifer? I hadn't thought of her, except maybe fleetingly, in months.

Suddenly I realized that Nicki had ceased thrusting, and was kneeling astride me looking down at me. Her expression was inscrutable in the darkness. Had she somehow detected my errant thoughts? No, I must have grown soft, and I supposed that Nicki was pissed off.

Then suddenly she burst into tears. She flung herself onto her side of the bed, gathered into herself and faced away from me.

I slid over toward her and propped myself up, groping for her hand. I found it and slid my fingers into hers. This was only the second—no, third—time I had ever heard her cry. "What's wrong, honey?" I asked, still irrationally worried that she had intercepted my thoughts.

"I don't know what's wrong."

"Hey, turn over."

She did. As I looked through the darkness at her glistening tears, I thought that this could have been a much more erotic encounter if Nicki hadn't rushed things. But I reproached myself for that thought. Nicki was in turmoil, and we needed to find a solution together. We lay next to each other, looking into each other's eyes, Nicki sniffling.

"What's wrong, honey?" I asked again.

"I don't know what's wrong with me. With us." She looked at me pleadingly, as if I had an answer. But I wasn't even sure of the question. "I can't bring myself to orgasm. I've never had that problem with you before. And these headaches. And I'm nauseous half the time. I'm never going to get pregnant."

"If you're nauseous, maybe you're already pregnant."

"I test myself every time we make love. I'm not pregnant."

Had I thought to myself in the shower that Nicki was obsessed with being pregnant? I hadn't known the half of it.

"Maybe we're trying too hard. Rushing it."

She propped her head on her hand. "I'm thirty. Men can have babies until you're eighty. For me it's now or never. Every time I see the doctor he asks me when I'm getting pregnant."

"I'm sure a few months won't make a difference."

"You just don't understand. Every month makes it harder for me to carry a baby to term. It's risky enough already."

"I do understand. I want to have a baby, too. But maybe we're going about it the wrong way. Trying to make a baby rather than making love."

"Maybe we should go to a fertility specialist. My OB-GYN recommended some good ones."

"It's only been a few months."

"We don't have time to waste. If one of us is sterile, we ought to find out as soon as possible."

Defensively, I said, "Nicki, I know I'm not sterile." And regretted the words as soon as they came out of my mouth.

Her gaze turned sharp. "What do you mean by that?" Then she shook her head and lay back into her pillow, looking up at the ceiling. "I don't want to know what you meant by that."

"It was a long time ago, Nicki."

"Believe me, I don't want to know about it. I'm Catholic, remember?"

Oh, what an idiot I am, I thought. But as I wallowed in my stupidity, Nicki spoke again. "I know I'm not sterile, either." Now it was my turn to be surprised. Very surprised. "Although what you threw away, I lost."

I reached across the sheets and touched her shoulder. "I'm sorry." And all at once I understood, far better than before, why she was consumed with anxiety. And maybe I finally understood a great deal more than that. I wanted to know the details, but I also knew better than to press her for them. What Nicki had just imparted was a revelation, which was a big step for her. But as to the present matter, Nicki's worry was unquestionably complicating the desired outcome. I lay there thinking, my fingers gently caressing Nicki's skin. Then leaned over and kissed her naked shoulder tenderly. "I love you."

"I love you, too." Her words were perfunctory, and I hoped she meant them.

"Are you working Memorial Day weekend?"

"No, Jill Kenard is working."

"Wanna go away for the weekend? Out to the countryside? It will be our first time away since our honeymoon."

"Okay."

"I'll make some special plans."

"Mmm," she replied, and I knew she was falling asleep. Nicki possessed a remarkable capacity to say something shocking that would keep me up the entire night, then easily fall asleep herself. It seemed almost a transfer of anxiety from one person to another, and now I was "it."

For good measure, she rolled onto her side, away from me.

"Hey," I said, leaning over her. "I want a kiss goodnight, Nicole Gibbons. My mom only gave me one piece of marital advice, and it was that no matter what, you should kiss every night before going to sleep."

Sleepily, Nicki rolled back toward me and raised her face. I kissed her softly on the lips. She lay back down and quickly went to sleep.

I marveled at how Nicki was able to do that. I think the emotional drain exhausted her. But her penance was that she would inevitably awaken in the middle of the night.

Was this what marriage was supposed to be like—a complicated cauldron of mystery, revelation, and anxiety, flavored with occasional bliss? Our wedding had happened so fast, in the midst of such busy times, that we barely had time to catch our breath and explore our new relationship. Whenever I did have time to think about it, I got scared.

13

I AWAKENED TO the soft pulsing sound of our alarm clock and quickly reached over to extinguish the sound. Before long I was standing beneath a near-scalding torrent, my shoulders turned toward the pelting shower, my eyes closed.

I opened my eyes and was startled by a looming shadow. An arm reached for the glass door to the shower. She circled her arms around my neck and drew my mouth toward hers in a luscious, deep, lingering kiss. Immediately I felt an erection growing, and to my incredulity, Nicki reached down and stroked it; clumsily, but to noteworthy effect.

I pulled away from her kiss and asked, "What's the occasion?"

"I think this is a preferable way of making a baby," she replied huskily.

I was dreadfully late for work that day; and I'm sure my smile belied whatever feeble explanation I managed to muster. But I'd noticed that lately that my presence or absence no longer determined the flow of work at the firm: it was an independent entity now, with a life of its own, separate from mine. That night I played racquetball with Doug, and he beat me so badly that I wanted to hang my head in shame. We went a third game and he destroyed me in that one, too. My game was wildly inconsistent compared with Doug's steady play, and that night it was especially off.

"Sorry I couldn't give you a better challenge," I remarked as we barged into the locker room.

"Yeah, I barely broke a sweat." A quick glance at his dry T-shirt confirmed his claim. He asked how married life was going.

"It's an emotional roller-coaster," I exclaimed, not realizing my frustration until the words left my mouth. "It has its truly wonderful moments. Nicki seems to be settling down, and doing well in her job. But she's obsessed with getting pregnant."

"Well, maybe you should stretch this period out, because once she gets what she wants, you might never have sex again."

Doug's comment was terrifying—the thought of having Nicki and all of her anxieties and mood swings but without the sex was a sobering one. "Oh, she'll probably be fine once she has a baby."

"Right," Doug said, pulling on his clothes. "A howling baby crying for food at two in the morning. I'm sure Nicki will handle all that very calmly."

I sighed and found it advisable to change the subject. When I returned home and found that Nicki was out with girlfriends, I made some calls to bed-and-breakfast inns in the Virginia countryside and made reservations for Memorial Day weekend.

When Nicki returned home late that evening, bearing a serious wine buzz, she beckoned me at once toward the bedroom. She remained in her amorous mood for the entire week and a half before Memorial Day weekend, kissing me constantly and sensually, waking us up early, coming home from work if she knew I was home.

On Saturday as I was packing for our weekend away, Nicki came out of the bathroom with the results of her pregnancy test. "Okay, buster, you have to work overtime this weekend. I'm still not pregnant."

The weekend was idyllic. The Virginia countryside had become our special place. Only an hour or two away from Washington, any tension seemed magically to melt away. I think both of us cherished it for that.

As always, our lovemaking benefited from relaxation. I hated for the weekend to end. It was still spring, and as we drove back to Washington on late Monday afternoon, the sunshine streamed down upon us through the sunroof. "We're going to have to get a convertible after this car," I commented, "to take advantage of the magnificent spring and summer days out here."

Nicki smiled back. "Yes, but a convertible isn't very practical for a family."

"Whaddya mean? Any daughter of ours has to tool around in a convertible. Or a son, for that matter."

"Daughter. I was thinking more of a Land Rover. But you can have a convertible, too, I guess, if you want it."

"Are you planning on maintaining a high income after you're a mom?"

"No, I'm planning on you becoming a millionaire very soon," she answered, deadpan. I glanced over to see whether she was kidding or not, and fortunately she was grinning. She pulled her sunglasses down to bat her eyelashes at me.

My penance for all of our frolicking playtime came quickly. I rose at sunrise the next morning to get into the office an hour or two before my colleagues. The forthcoming summer was doing nothing to reduce my workload, and all of us at the firm would be shouldering a heavier load as vacations arose.

Like most beginnings of the week, the day was busy and discombobulated. It went by rapidly, and when I checked my watch in the afternoon I was shocked to see that it was already four. Too much to do; I'd have to work late, or at least bring work home with me. Fortunately, my home studio, combined with Nicki's propensity either to work late or make phone calls, were conducive to getting work done at the apartment. On the other hand, Nicki's amorous designs had made that pretty much impossible of late. Better that I order some pizza and stay late at the office. If I was going to earn millionaire status in the near future, I'd have to exercise some self-discipline. Even if I didn't want to.

Nicki called and got immediately to the point. "I need you to come home."

"Is something wrong?"

"No. I just want you to come home."

I let out a long breath. "Okay. Do you want me to pick up some dinner?"

"No," Nicki said, annoyance infecting her tone. "How many times do I have to tell you what I want?"

"I'll be home in twenty minutes."

"Don't waste time," Nicki instructed, then hung up.

I wondered what was going on. Unlike recent evenings, Nicki sounded impatient, not amorous. I figured it must be some problem with her job. That would be a shame, because Nicki seemed to be doing well.

Whatever her particular whim, as usual I would indulge it. I glanced around my office to see what work I could bring home, then decided against taking anything with me. I could get up early the next morning to make up for not working that night.

Unfortunately, my departure occurred at the height of rush hour. By the time I arrived at the Parkside, twenty-five minutes had passed.

When I exited the elevator, the floor's only other resident, Mona Beeman, was waiting for it. She was a nice elderly woman distinguished by her Lebanese accent and a disconcerting black patch over one eye. She occupied the other penthouse suite alone except for when her son Arnold, a jeweler who lived in New York City, stayed with her.

"Hi, Mrs. Beeman," I said as I held the elevator door for her.

"You and Nicole are home early this evening," she observed as she walked past me. It was clear Mrs. Beeman didn't miss much.

"Just a rare chance to spend some quality time together."

She smiled. "Maybe I'll hear the pitter-patter of little feet before long."

I turned to my own door and opened it with a key. Inside, Nicki was not in the living room. "Nick?" I called.

"Coming!" I heard her call from the hallway. I shed my jacket as Nicki entered the living room, wearing a beautiful green silk bathrobe that I had bought for her, along with incongruous pink bedroom slippers.

As she closed the distance between us, I noticed how the jade-green color of the bathrobe set off her creamy white complexion and deepened the color of her eyes. Nicki was smiling and planted a wet kiss on my lips. "Hi!" she said cheerfully, her tone completely changed from our earlier brief telephone conversation. I could tell she was freshly showered, her hair fluffy from washing, and perhaps that had relaxed her.

"How was your day?" I asked.

"Fine," she replied, standing before me grinning broadly. When Nicki smiled, she exhibited both rows of teeth, making for a huge smile.

"So, what's going on?"

"I saw Dr. Sykes today," she announced, her grin not breaking a bit. Nicki had so many doctors that her statement at first didn't mean anything to me, and I shrugged slightly. Then recognition dawned: Dr. Sykes was Nicki's gynecologist.

"Are we having a baby?"

"Yes, I'm pregnant," Nicki replied, and before I knew it I had my arms around her, lifting her off the floor, and we were both laughing hysterically. "Be careful!" she demanded.

I dropped her onto the sofa and descended upon her, smothering her with kisses. "I love you! What're we going to name him? Or her?"

"Her," Nicki said back. "I'm sure of it."

We talked about names, and which of our friends and relatives to call first, and of course how we would decorate the baby's room.

We talked and snuggled on the sofa for what seemed eternity. I breathed in her fresh scent and wondered over the magnificent miracle that was taking place inside her body. It was stupendous, wonderful.

As I nuzzled my wife, alternately kissing, tickling, and caressing her, the thought dimly began to take hold that our lives were about to change unalterably, forever.

10

FOUR DAYS LATER, sunlight streamed in on me as I lay alone in our bed on Saturday morning. The news of our impending arrival was still only four days old, and I hadn't at all grown accustomed to the thought of being a father. Wow. I'm sure I bore a goofy grin as I lay there staring up at the ceiling, my hands clasped beneath my head. A son or a daughter? Which did I want? I guess that as a male, my instinctive desire was for a son. To have a little guy with whom to throw a baseball, to discuss the facts of life, to scope out chicks. The image brought an even bigger smile to my face.

For Nicki, of course, the matter was preordained. "We're only having one child, and it will be a girl," she said with certainty during our scrumptious celebration dinner at Jean Louis. Sans wine, of course—Nicki already was becoming fastidious with her diet.

I chuckled. "How can you be so sure?"

"I just know. That's how it's meant to be for us."

A shiver ran up my spine, and not for the first time. If it turned out to be a girl, Nicki's mystery would grow even greater in light of the certainty she conveyed.

"And what shall we name her, assuming you're right?"

It seemed that Nicki had everything worked out, which frankly was a touch annoying. "Alexandra," she declared. "I've always wanted to name my daughter Alexandra. You know, after the last Russian monarchs, Nicholas and Alexandra. Nicki and Alex."

I laughed. "So the two of you are the reigning royalty in our household, huh?"

Nicki laughed. "That's right." Nicki turned serious again. "Seriously, that's what I want to name my daughter. If I have a boy, you can decide what to name him, okay?"

Nicki left on Friday evening to spend the weekend with her family. Their suburban Maryland home was close enough to make a day trip, but Nicki wanted to make the announcement of her pregnancy over the course of a weekend. I was not disappointed that she failed to invite me. I had work to do, and frankly I still felt very much the outsider in Nicki's family. Nicki's brother-in-law seemed to fit in naturally, but I didn't, and I couldn't understand it. Nicki didn't make much effort to integrate me, and her parents were cordial but aloof. I would have to ask her brother-in-law out for drinks sometime to ask him what I was doing wrong.

Not surprisingly, even amidst her euphoria, Nicki already was growing neurotic about the pregnancy. She was consumed with worry that she would miscarry. Nothing I could say would reassure her.

It was going to be a very long nine months.

As I stood at my sink, I spied Nicki's stash of prescription drugs. There were a lot of those, too. I took a look at them. All were indecipherable to me. There were pills from Dr. Sykes, her gynecologist, and Dr. Fabian, her endocrinologist at Johns Hopkins. Man, all those pills must have cost a fortune. I was glad we had invested in a good health insurance plan at Horizon. What were these? Lithium. That sounded familiar. But the prescription had expired six months previously. Who was Dr. Liechtenstein? I didn't recognize that name. Whoever it was had a phone number in the District of Columbia. Here was another one I didn't recognize: Zoloft. Sounded like something out of Star Trek. The prescription was current and had been issued by a Dr. Strachian, another name I didn't recognize. This one was in Bethesda. I didn't realize Nicki had any doctors in Bethesda. How odd.

Nicki treasured her privacy, such as her marathon phone calls taken in her "office" in our apartment, and frequent outings with unspecified friends. I never begrudged Nicki that space, because I knew her personality needed lots of outlets. But she was also oblique about her medical situation. She made a monthly visit to Baltimore to deal with her endocrinological problems, and visited her gynecologist every six weeks or so even before the pregnancy. I gathered that there was a tenuous balance between the two sets of medical treatments. And, of course, prior to leaving for Seattle, Nicki had been under the care of a psychiatrist. Certainly I didn't fully fathom the nature of Nicki's medical situation, and she resisted illuminating me. I had offered to relieve the tedium of her trips to Baltimore with my company, but she turned me down. As usual, she rejected anything smacking of empathy.

That would have to change now that Nicki was pregnant. This was one medical situation we were in together, whether Nicki liked it or not.

As I held the mystery pills in my hand, I considered whether to confront her about them. With our baby growing, I felt I needed to know what kinds of medication she was ingesting. Plainly, Nicki's medical situation gave her enormous anxiety about the pregnancy, and I wanted to know why.

As I left the bathroom, I jotted down the names of the drugs and the doctors I had seen, intending to check them with my own physician. I needed to get a better handle on Nicki, and this information might provide the key.

I didn't think about the situation much over the weekend, instead immersing myself in work at the office. Rich was there both days as well, and we enjoyed a rare chance to catch up with the firm's business. Despite a burgeoning recession, the renovation side of architecture firm was doing very well. I was pleased with the amount of progress I was able to make in Nicki's absence.

Nicki returned on Sunday evening, ebullient from her visit with her family. She reported enthusiastically about her family's reactions to her pregnancy and about her shopping excursions. I told her in turn about my mother's and sister's enthusiastic reactions to the news of our expanding family. My mother, in particular, was thrilled over the prospect of finally having a granddaughter to accompany her two grandsons, and so she had weighed in on Nicki's side on that question.

Then, as she did so often, Nicki took me completely by surprise. "I almost forgot to tell you," she announced brightly. "I have an appointment with Dr. Sykes on Wednesday morning, and he's going to examine me with his obstetrician partner, Dr. Medici, who specializes in difficult pregnancies. Can you take the morning off and come with me?"

"Of course! I would love to." I walked over to where Nicki was sitting and kissed her neck, making her squeal. She chuckled and reached up to lightly touch my face. I nudged her aside and sat down beside her. "I'm really glad to be meeting your doctors. I want to support you any way I can. We're a team in this."

"Well, of course, silly. I couldn't have done this by myself."

"No, I mean, you've never wanted me to come with you to a doctor before."

"That's because those are *my* problems, as opposed to this, which is our problem."

I thought that was an odd choice of words, but brushed them aside. "Nicki, we're married now. Your problems *are* my problems. Not just some of them."

As usual, she dismissed the subject with terse and easy rationalization. "My physical problems are boring. This is exciting." She pushed me aside and rose from the table. "I'm hungry. I still have to watch my diet, but it's nice that I can eat more without worrying too much about gaining weight."

Nicki's invitation to accompany her on Wednesday soothed my anxiety, and I nearly forgot to call my doctor about the mystery pills. But toward the end of a very demanding Monday, I needed a mental break and suddenly the thought returned to me.

My doctor, Allen Parker, had been my physician since I had moved to Washington. We were about the same age and shared similar views on politics, and had become friends. So I didn't feel apprehensive about calling him. Besides, he was not Nicki's physician, so I didn't feel like I was asking him to betray any confidences.

Allen took the call immediately. I asked him whether he was familiar with the doctors on Nicki's prescriptions. I explained that Nicki was pregnant, and I was worried about her secretiveness.

Allen didn't recognize the names, so he pulled out his area physicians' guide. "Liechtenstein," he said. "There're several in the District. The first is Amelia, who's a psychiatrist."

"Amelia! That's her old therapist. I didn't realize . . . okay, that makes sense."

"What was the other one?" he asked.

"Strachian, in Bethesda." I spelled the name.

"Well, there's only one," Allen replied. "Robert. He's a psychiatrist, too. Sounds like your wife wants to keep more than her physical condition from you." His tone was nonjudgmental.

"Well, let me ask you, Allen. I know this isn't your specialty, but why would a psychiatrist prescribe Lithium, or . . ."—I looked down at my notes—"Zoloft?"

Allen emitted a low whistle. "Well, Lithium could be prescribed for a variety of problems. But Zoloft—that's serious stuff. Let me check my drug guide."

I felt my stomach muscles constrict as Allen took several minutes to consult the reference. I had no idea that Nicki had been back to that crazy therapist since her return from the West Coast. And now yet another shrink? One who was prescribing "serious stuff," as Allen had put it. For a serious problem.

"Well," he said, "don't hold me to this, but trying to find the common strand between the two drugs, it looks like they might be treating mixed bipolar disorder, which is manic depression. It could be a lot of other things, but that's my guess as a common denominator."

That struck me like a ton of bricks, but made abundant sense.

"Lithium doesn't concern me too much," Allen continued, "but this Zoloft could be scary stuff. It's one of a new generation of so-called 'wonder drugs,' like Prozac and Elavil. I've been reading about these drugs in the medical journals. They're based on research that suggests that some mental and emotional problems are caused by chemical malfunctions. The drugs all induce the brain to produce more of a natural chemical called serotonin, which is believed to regulate moods and emotions. The drugs are all antidepressants, but at this point they're experimental, and could produce serious side effects."

"Such as?"

"Well, for Zoloft, the DSM-III lists sexual dysfunction, nausea, and headaches, among others," he said. "But messing with the brain's chemistry is risky even without side-effects."

Now my head was spinning. This was much worse than I had imagined, and mentally I was checking off the side effects as Allen listed them. Nicki had exhibited all of them. I tried to keep my composure. "Well, Allen, that's very helpful."

"I don't know how this medication might affect pregnancy. I hope her doctors are coordinating; the health of the baby is paramount. Whatever your wife's psychological problems, I'm sure you can handle them for nine months while you focus on delivering a healthy baby."

I agreed and thanked him and then I slumped in my chair. This was way too intense. But it all seemed so obvious now. Nicki's moods swung like a pendulum gone out of control. Yet sometimes she seemed stable and normal . . . because sometimes she was on serious medication, and sometimes she wasn't.

But apparently whenever she was on successful medication for her mental problems, her physical condition suffered. Sexual dysfunction—I knew about that all too well. Her headaches, too, had been constant. As for nausea, on several occasions in recent months I thought I'd heard her retching over the sound of running water in the bathroom. Usually she denied it, but on one occasion she had joked hopefully, "Maybe it's morning sickness." Instead, it turned out to be Zoloft. And the prescription was current, meaning she might still be taking it.

Oh, man. What had I gotten myself into? All my life, I had never been close to someone with serious mental problems. I had no frame of reference from which to draw. But Allen was right: the stakes were exponentially higher now. I not only had to protect my marriage, and my own sanity, but the baby's well-being.

Why would Nicki hide all this from me? When we were dating, she had mentioned her therapist frequently and matter-of-factly. After she moved to Seattle, she had disdainfully dismissed Amelia as part of the past, even commenting that she thought the therapist had a lesbian crush on her. But Nicki had resumed the relationship after she moved back. Then she switched to a different psychiatrist, who was prescribing stronger, experimental drugs. Which had contributed to physical problems that had created enormous stress in our relationship. Nicki had to know, or at least suspect, that there was a cause-and-effect relationship.

I didn't know whether to pity Nicki or to be angry at her.

But one thing was for sure. Whether she thought so or not, Nicki's problems were indeed my problems. And they were a lot more serious than I imagined.

17

THE NEXT TWO months were difficult, and the troubles escalated steadily.

We had a long and upbeat first visit with her doctors. Dr. Alan Sykes, her gynecologist, was young, handsome, and confident. The obstetrician, Ray Medici, was an older man who projected an air of tremendous competence. Between the two of them, Nicki seemed in good hands.

Dr. Medici had scoured Nicki's medical records (which, frankly, I would have liked to examine, too), and said that so long as Nicki took it easy, maintained a healthy diet, reduced her hours at work and worked no later than her seventh month, we could expect a smooth pregnancy. He mentioned that he was purging her of most of her other medications. He listed them, including the Zoloft, which reassured me that Nicki had provided full disclosure.

Not surprisingly, the physicians scheduled Nicki for regular sonographs and other tests. "Given your medical history," the avuncular Dr. Medici told Nicki, "we want to exercise caution even to excess. The upside is that you'll monitor your baby's progress much more closely than most couples. You'll know how it's doing every step of the way."

"We'll know how *she's* doing," Nicki corrected him.

Dr. Medici and I both laughed. "In this case, the mother seems to have determined the baby's sex," I explained.

"Well, technically that would be a medical first, but your wife seems to be a very determined young woman."

The problems started that very night, a few hours after we had gone to bed. Nicki was stricken with severe nausea and a splitting headache, the combination of which consigned her to the bathroom for several hours. Concerned, I tried to keep her company, but she locked me out. I couldn't sleep and checked on her several times, but as usual she rejected my efforts to help. After I finally went to sleep just before dawn, she woke me up and announced that she would call in sick. I asked her if she wanted me to call Dr. Medici, but Nicki said she would do it. She refused my offer to make toast for her, saying she wouldn't be able to keep it down.

I hypothesized that it might be a combination of severe morning sickness and withdrawal from Nicki's array of medications. Surprisingly, she agreed. "I have such a precarious chemical balance," she admitted. "I take strong drugs for my endocrinological problems, and drugs to counteract the side-effects, both physical and mental."

Ah, I thought, an explanation about the Zoloft. I wasn't sure whether I accepted it, but at least Nicki was giving me more information than before. It was her usual mode of revelation: sudden and unexpected, yet imparted matter-of-factly.

When I returned home that evening, Nicki was lying on the sofa in her bathrobe, paler than usual. She ate some soup and seemed to feel better. But that night was a replay of the last.

Nicki's early euphoria over her pregnancy subsided rapidly as the nausea and headaches intensified. My mother arrived for a long-scheduled visit, and ended up attending to Nicki much of the following week. Nicki was able to go to work twice, but not the other days. By the end of the week, I detected that the relationship between Nicki and my mother was fraying. When Nicki was ill she was insufferable: she complained incessantly yet rejected empathy and most efforts to help. In turn, Nicki made it clear that she would prefer not to have my mother around.

I took Friday off to spend with my mother, and I think it was the only enjoyable part of her visit for her. "Nicki isn't making the grand-parenting role very easy," she remarked.

"Nicki puts everyone through their paces."

Nicki's mother stayed with us the following week, and even though Nicki couldn't go to work at all, the situation eased a bit. Her mother intuited that Nicki didn't want to be fussed over, and she spent her time reading magazines or watching television in the living room unless Nicki wanted something.

Nicki seemed to regain her strength and her mother left. Nicki was able to resume working, albeit with a reduced schedule. Her appointments with her doctors were now twice-weekly, and she no longer encouraged me to join her. On one occasion I did go, and was able to see a sonograph of our baby and hear its heartbeat, which filled me with awe, making the whole situation seem much more tangible. This little being was our flesh-and-blood, mine and Nicki's, our creation. Yet Nicki looked at the picture with seeming disinterest.

If Nicki seemed incurious about the growing being in her womb, she remained obsessed with her health and her ability to deliver, even though her condition had improved. She lost all perspective. She moped around in a dour mood, closing the door to her office to engage in private and endless telephone conversations with friends. She never came to bed when I did, and generally I was unable to stay awake for her. Of course, sex was completely out, but so was any other type of physical affection.

"You don't understand!" she exclaimed one night when I raised the subject in bed. "I can't stand to be touched right now! My body is disgusting!"

"Nicki, that's not true at all." I was lying—Nicki looked positively haggard, with dark circles under her eyes. "Why don't we go away somewhere? Try to get your—our—minds off this for a bit."

Clearly that was the wrong thing to say. "Kevin, *I* can't exactly get away from this problem."

"Yeah, but a change in scenery . . ."

"I just want to get rid of this burden."

"You're worried to death about this baby, Nick. The last thing you want is to be 'rid of it.'"

She turned over and faced away from me, emitting a long sigh. "Just turn out the light. I'm tired," she instructed. And dutifully, I complied.

I reached over and touched her shoulder, stroking it gently. But even in her sleep, Nicki pulled away from me.

THE WEEKS PROCEEDED in like fashion. After two months, we still had not told anyone except immediate family about Nicki's pregnancy. I wanted to; I needed to. On the last day of July, Rich came by my office at the end of the day and asked "Wanna go out for a drink?"

I thought about it for all of two seconds. "You bet," I said. "Just let me call Nicki." As Rich went to get his things together, I called home. It was six, and lately Nicki had usually been home from work by then. Not this time. I too had generally come home fairly early, taking work with me if necessary. Nicki certainly gave me plenty of solitude to attend to it. But I deserved a night out. "Hey, sweetheart," I said to the answering machine. "Rich and I are going out for a drink. Don't worry about dinner. Hope you're feeling okay. Love you."

We went to Sequoia, a massive restaurant a few doors from our office at the Washington Harbor.

"Hey, partner, things have been going pretty well at Horizon, haven't they?" I asked.

Rich grinned. "Yeah, we've gotten the firm pretty solidly on track."

"When this recession is over, maybe I'll indulge your yearning to do some new construction."

He grinned again. "You're singing the right song." We chatted for awhile about growth prospects for the firm, and personnel, and the competition.

Then Rich changed the subject. "Hey, Kev, is everything all right?"

"Whaddaya mean?" The potent Belevedere vodka had kicked in and I was in a very good mood.

"You seem really distracted lately. Unhappy. I just wanted to make sure everything is okay. I don't mean to pry, but you're not your usual self." Just then our waiter came over to inspect our empty glasses. "Do you want to order something to eat?"

"Yeah. How about a bottle of wine, too? It's been two months since I've been able to drink any wine." And then realized how stupid I was for saying that. "Oh shit," I said. I drained the remnants of the Belvedere from my glass and decided to tell him. "Nicki's two month's pregnant. And it hasn't been easy for her. That's why we haven't told anyone. And that's why I've been so distracted. We're not sure Nicki can carry the baby to term, although right now her condition seems okay." And then the words started flowing from my mouth, telling Rich everything. He listened and didn't interrupt me until I had finally exhausted myself.

"Rich, I don't know what to do," I said. By then I was drunk, which probably would piss Nicki off when I returned home, if she noticed. "My nerves are frazzled. Yet I have to be there for Nicki. But she doesn't seem to want my help." Rich grimaced. I could tell he had something to say. "What?"

"Kev, I hate to say this, and I hope you won't take it the wrong way, but I don't know how you put up with Nicole."

"Rich, what she's going through is excruciating."

"That's true, no doubt about it. But she seems to handle her misery by putting you through it. She's amazingly narcissistic, Kevin. She seems worried less about the baby than her own discomfort. Which is understandable to some extent, but not to the exclusion of everything—everyone—else. And this certainly isn't the first time she's acted like that."

"So you don't think I should feel guilty about being selfish?"

He laughed. "Selfish? You? You're consumed with worry about your baby, and your wife, and she pushes you away, closes herself in her office and talks on the phone to other people but not to you. On top of it she manages to make you feel guilty. Not bad for a day's work."

I took the last sip of wine from my glass, thinking about Rich's words as he regarded me silently. Then a bustle caught my attention from the corner of my eye. I turned and saw it was Julie Crafton, making a beeline for our table, a panicked expression on her face.

"Kevin," she said, out of breath as she reached our table, "I've been looking all over for you. Nicki called trying to find you. She was hysterical. Something's wrong; she was rushing to the hospital."

"Oh my God! What hospital?"

"Georgetown."

I was already on my way. "Thanks Rich, thanks Julie," I called back to them as I raced toward the door.

"Good luck!" I heard Julie say.

Good God, I thought to myself. Was Nicki losing the baby? I couldn't believe I wasn't there with her.

Fortunately a cab was waiting by the curb. I climbed in and said, "Georgetown Hospital. Please hurry, it's an emergency." The cabbie raced off into the dusk. As we drove what seemed an interminable distance, I tried to clear my head from the effects of the alcohol, fighting off panic.

When I reached the hospital, I ran into the emergency room lobby and asked the first nurse I saw if she could help me find Nicki. Fortunately she knew who I was talking about. She gave me the basics: Nicki had just been released from the emergency room and was in the intensive care unit in the obstetrics ward. The nurse gave me a pass and I ran for the elevator.

Minutes later I found the unit. A curtain was partially obscuring the only occupied bed. The first person I saw was Nicki's mother. "Mrs. Petri!" I exclaimed. "Mom." I still wasn't comfortable calling her that.

She turned toward me but said nothing. I walked over to the bed and saw that Nicki was surrounded by her sister, the obstetrician Dr. Medici, and a nurse. From the foot of the bed I looked down at Nicki, who was ashen. She opened her eyes, which were milky and momentarily unfocused. Then they turned angry. "You bastard!" she shrieked. "Get away from here!"

I was aghast and looked around dumbly to see if someone else was the object of Nicki's ire. Then I stammered, "Nicki, what happened?"

"I lost the baby!" she bellowed, tears filling her eyes. "I could've died! Where were you, you bastard? Get out of here!"

"Nicki, shh, shh," said a startled Dr. Medici, pushing gently down on her shoulders to restrain her from sitting up.

"He's been drinking," Mrs. Petri observed helpfully. "I can smell it on his breath."

Nicki's sister stared at me dolefully.

"Nicki—" I began.

"Get him OUT OF HERE!" Nicki screamed.

Dr. Medici strode over and grabbed me gently by the elbow, directing me toward the door. "Nurse, I think we should speed up that sedative," he instructed, then said to me, "C'mon, let's talk outside."

I let him lead me to the door, glancing back but no longer able to see Nicki behind the curtain. The nurse was working with an intravenous bottle. I could hear Mrs. Petri assuring Nicki, "Calm down, he's gone."

"What happened?" My head was reeling.

Medici measured me with experienced gray eyes. "Your wife is in shock."

"She lost the baby?"

"Yes, I'm afraid so. Apparently she began to experience cramps at work and came home around six-thirty. As soon as she arrived she started hemorrhaging. She called an ambulance, and fortunately I was already here at the hospital with other patients. We rushed her in to the emergency room, but she had lost the baby by that time."

"Oh, man," I gasped. "Nicki must have been so terrified. Is she going to be all right?"

"Yes, she'll be fine," he assured me. "We'll keep her in for a day or two. She lost a fair amount of blood, so it will take awhile to regain her strength. But I wouldn't worry about your wife regaining her health. Unfortunately, this is not an uncommon situation, particularly for women with your wife's medical circumstances."

"Is it still possible for Nicki to have a baby?"

"Well," Dr. Medici replied cautiously, "the risks increase with each attempt. But I don't see why not. You just need to give her some time to repair. I wouldn't try again for at least six months or so. You probably should completely refrain from sexual relations for awhile, and definitely use birth control. Let her heal."

"Well, I'm glad she'll be all right physically," I said. "But I don't know about emotionally."

"Don't worry too much. Her reaction wasn't all that unusual. She was carrying enormous anxiety along with the pregnancy, and she transferred it to you. But what she doesn't understand yet is that there was nothing you could have done to help the situation, nothing at all. This was a preordained course. She'll look at things differently tomorrow. I promise."

I closed my eyes hard. The combined effects of the alcohol and the shock made my head reel. This was nightmarish.

"In the meantime, why don't you give her some space and go home and get a good night's sleep? Nicki will be heavily sedated the rest of the night, and her family is here with her. She'll need your support tomorrow."

Even though I knew the doctor was wrong about that—Nicki was likely to reject my support no matter when I offered it—I nodded slowly. He was right in the sense that there was nothing useful I could do at the hospital.

As I gathered myself to leave, the doctor touched my arm gently. "One more thing."

"Yes?"

"At this early stage of development, the fetus doesn't really have a well-developed nervous system. So rest assured that he passed with no pain."

I thought about what he'd just said. Finally, I asked, "He?"

"Yes," Dr. Medici replied quietly. "The fetus was a boy." He squeezed my arm, then walked back toward Nicki's room.

18

DR. MEDICI MAY have been a first-rate obstetrician, but he was a lousy psychiatrist: it turned out that Nicki did not want to see me the next day, or the day after that. Each time I left the hospital without being allowed to see her. Then when I returned to try to visit her two days after her miscarriage, I was shocked to learn she had checked out. The hospital receptionist, to whom I had identified myself as Nicki's husband, seemed incredulous that I did not know my wife had been discharged.

I went home and found no sign of Nicki there. I called her parents' house and her mother answered.

"Yes, Nicki is here," her mother replied matter-of-factly to my anxious query.

"Well, may I speak to her?"

"She's resting."

I was losing my patience, if not my mind. "Look, Mrs. Petri," I said, trying to keep my voice modulated, "I really need to talk to Nicki."

"Nicole is very upset. She's upset that she couldn't find you when she began to have problems." The woman's tone was almost spiteful. I wondered if she was feeding Nicki's anger.

"I know Nicki has been through a great deal, but so have I. I lost a baby, too. And I'm worried about Nicki. I love her." Why did I feel the need to establish that obvious fact? "And I'm worried about her. So I would appreciate the opportunity at least to talk to her."

"I'm sorry," Mrs. Petri said firmly, not sounding sorry at all, "Nicki plans to stay here for awhile. And I don't know when she'll call you. I imagine she will at some point, but I don't know when."

It took me a few days even to call my mother and tell her what had happened, and I could hear the pain in her voice as she told me to take care of Nicki.

The weekend came and went with no word from Nicki. It was excruciating. Was this the end of our marriage? I desperately didn't want it to be, but I began trying to reconcile myself to the idea. Nicki's religious scruples made her adamantly opposed to the concept of divorce, but our relationship wasn't particularly stable, and I knew Nicki had a chameleon-like ability to reconcile her religious beliefs with her needs as she perceived them at any given moment. She could probably find some way to annul the marriage, as if it had never happened. After all, she had married a heathen, which meant that in the eyes of the Church, it wasn't really a marriage at all. Who knew what Nicki was thinking, or what she was capable of? All I knew was that I was completely shell-shocked.

When I came home after work on Monday, I discovered that Nicki had come in during the day and taken two suitcases and many of her clothes. Not all of them, though. Furious, I phoned her parents' home again. I was surprised when Nicki answered, her voice full of sunshine until she learned who it was.

"Nicki," I said.

"Oh. Hello."

I kept my anger in check, at least momentarily. "How are you?"

"Fine. My white-blood cell count is low, so I'm tired. But I'm feeling better." This conversation seemed almost normal, except that my wife was fifty miles away a week following a miscarriage. Funny how the bizarre with Nicki almost passed for normal.

But then she jarred me back to reality. "What do you want?"

I was so taken aback I didn't know what to say at first. "Well, I wanted to know how you were."

"Oh, well, I told you."

"And to ask if you're moving out, or what."

Nicki made a tsk'ing sound. "I'm going to Charleston for a week with Amy."

Nicki apparently had this all worked out. It felt like *déjà vu*, the escape to Seattle all over again. Amy was a recent addition to Nicki's constantly replenishing supply of intimate new friends. A single friend, in this case. Did that mean Nicki perceived herself as single again, too?

"What about work?" It was all I could think of to say.

"I quit."

"What?!"

"I just didn't feel like going back there." I was incredulous. "And Ted was always hitting on me. I got tired of it. I wasn't going to have an affair with him."

Did I say I was incredulous? More like thunderstruck. I had no idea her supervisor was hitting on her. Nicki had reported a wonderful working relationship, constantly complementing Ted Simpson's business acumen. Good God, this was getting more insane by the moment.

My throat felt constricted. I could hardly get words out. "Nicki, are you coming back?" I cursed myself silently for sounding pathetic.

"I think we need a month apart. After I come back from Charleston, I'm going to stay here for awhile, and maybe visit some other friends. I need to decide what I want to do. Maybe we can get together on Labor Day weekend. But until then, I don't think we should see each other, or communicate."

I held my tongue. Give her space, I told myself. Then another inner voice exclaimed: Fuck that! But I succumbed to the first advice. "I love you, Nicki," I heard myself telling her. "I'm sorry I wasn't there last week. I hope you can find it within yourself to forgive me. And I hope we can try again to build a family. I really want that."

"I can never forgive you for this," Nicki said sharply. "I was wrong about you. You betrayed me before, and you promised you wouldn't ever do that again, but you did. I can't ever trust you again after this. I gave you two chances."

I swallowed. "So you want a divorce."

Her voice rose an octave. "I told you, I don't want to talk about this right now. I need a month to think about it."

Silence filled the phone line. Was Nicki delivering a reprieve? Or a sentence? At any rate, an ultimatum. And I accepted it, of course. "I'll call you early Labor Day weekend, and we'll arrange something."

"All right. I want to go now. Goodbye."

"'Bye," I answered, but I don't know if she heard me.

And so it appeared that Nicole and I had gone from lust to bliss to estrangement to the brink of collapse in about three months. It must be some sort of record. Or was that merely the normal tempo of our sick relationship, playing itself over and over again?

And yet I knew I would save it if I could.

Finally, after agonizing and internalizing until I could bear it no longer, I called Jennifer. In a sense, she was the last person I wanted to talk to, because her happiness juxtaposed against my misery would make me feel wistful and even more depressed. Yet she was the one person who best understood me, who was eternally nonjudgmental, who truly seemed to have my best interests at heart.

Fortunately, when I called, Jennifer was at home, alone. Her husband was out working somewhere. Jen seemed delighted to hear from me.

Jennifer, it turned out, was fine. Not just fine. Her law career was going phenomenally well—she had won each of the first several cases she litigated—and she seemed to be enjoying everything except the stress. But she also had big news, which seemed to give her distant voice even greater radiance than usual. "I'm going to be a mommy, Kevvy," she announced.

"Wow," I said, trying to stave off the bitter feeling in my stomach. In fact, it was just about the worst thing I could have possibly heard at that moment. But somehow I managed to fake my reaction. "That's great, Jen. How far along are you?"

"Five months," she said. "He should be a November baby."

"You know you're having a boy?" Had Nicki known we were having a boy?

"Yeah. Because I'm over thirty, they've been doing all sorts of prenatal tests, and they determined his sex early-on. Apparently he's pretty well-endowed. Fortunately, it's been a pretty easy pregnancy. I feel disgusting, though. It's unbearably hot out here." All of a sudden I had a mental image of a pregnant Jennifer. Notwithstanding her typical self-effacement, I knew she would be even more beautiful than ever.

Jennifer picked up on my silence. "Is something wrong?"

"Well, we just had a bad experience along the same lines."

"Oh, no. I'm so sorry. What happened?"

Then the words just started spilling out. At first, Jennifer expressed sympathy for Nicki, knowing how it must feel to lose a baby that was growing inside her. But then as I went on to describe the aftermath, and then some of the events leading up to the pregnancy, Jen listened in rapt silence.

When I finished, the phone line was filled with silence. Then

Jennifer spoke. "I want you to promise that you'll do what I say, okay?"

I chuckled. "I don't know about that, Jen."

"You know I have your best interests at heart, don't you?" she asked.

That was funny; that was exactly my thought when I had decided to call her. "Yeah."

"You have to leave Nicki. She's psycho. It's not healthy. You have to get out now, when you still have your own sanity. It's going to have an unhappy ending, one way or the other, so you should cut your losses now." She paused. "I care about you. You don't deserve this. Whatever Nicki decides, you've got to preempt it. You can't let her run your relationship. Believe me, she doesn't have your best interests at heart. She's using you, and sucking the life out of you. I don't want that to happen to you. You have too much going for you to destroy yourself for some crazy bitch."

I sighed. "Thanks. It's good to have somebody who cares this much. I don't know if I can do it, but I know you're right that I should."

When we severed the connection, I felt bereft. As if on command, Elvis jumped up on the bed, purring loudly. She, at least, seemed happy that Nicki was away. The beautiful white cat could return, at least temporarily, to the prominent place she had occupied before Nicole entered our lives.

The sobering practical realities of a possible divorce began to hit me. I could not afford the mortgage payments on this penthouse on my income alone. Plus, whatever small equity we had in the place was basically our only asset. We'd need to sell it just to pay the lawyer fees. I wondered ruefully who would get to use Doug as a divorce lawyer. Maybe he could represent both of us.

My chance for a needed respite came unexpectedly. That week, George Fabish, an old colleague from Fielder, Steinmetz & Way called. He asked if I would be willing to cover for him on a panel at the American Association of Architects meeting in Los Angeles the following week.

"I know it's short notice, but my wife is pregnant and she's had some recent complications, so I decided I couldn't go. The panel is on renovations," he added, "and they want someone to speak on condominium conversions. They should've asked you in the first place, but they don't know your work very well."

Ironically, if Nicki were still pregnant, I would have turned down the invitation for the same reason as George. But I accepted. Workload or not, I needed to get away, and at least this was work-related. My elderly next-door neighbor, Mona Beeman, adored Elvis and agreed to feed her in my absence. So there was no excuse not to go.

Rich was delighted. He was a far better schmoozer than I, and ordinarily would have attended the convention if he weren't so busy. He was pleased that the firm's "star player," as he put it, would attend the event and make a presentation. I decided to stay out for a couple extra days and try to hook up with some old architecture school class-mates who had settled in southern California.

In the week before leaving for Los Angeles, I worked late into the evenings at the office. The apartment was impossibly lonely. There was no word whatsoever from Nicki.

I spent most of the flight to Los Angeles the next day preparing my remarks for the panel. Somehow my speech at the convention, focusing on the Parkside renovation, was a rousing success. I guess I must have channeled my nervous energy into a strong presentation. The sponsors told me they'd ask me back the next year. Even better was the fact that I didn't have to dread the reception that night—confer-ence attendees came up to me to introduce themselves, so I didn't have to mill around trying to seek out the handful of architects I knew.

Toward the end of the evening, a distinguished-looking, silver-haired gentleman approached me. I had noticed him in attendance at my panel. I didn't know him, and was surprised when he introduced himself as Dr. Jule Maguire.

"Doctor?" I asked.

Dr. Maguire laughed, which in his case was a pleasantly earnest sound. "Yes, I know I'm out of place here. I like to expand beyond my ordinary horizons, and I really enjoyed your presentation on renovations. I actually came to hear the other panelists who were talking about house renovations, but I was happily surprised that the principles you use seem to enhance the original structures. I was very impressed."

"Thank you. Are you a physician, or are you a Ph.D type of doctor?"

"I'm a child psychiatrist," he answered. "Here in Los Angeles. Semi-retired. I see by your expression that I really am out of place," he said.

Actually, he misread my expression; I was marveling over the coincidence of meeting a psychiatrist, given that nearly all I had been thinking about lately was the mysteries of Nicki's mind.

He was talking again while my head was fogging. "Beg your pardon?" I asked.

"I was saying that I'm looking to build a dream-house, and trying to get some ideas. I've got a beautiful piece of property on a secluded bluff in Pacific Palisades, and I want to build something special there. Not ostentatious, which is what all the architects I've talked to want to put there. This is *my* house, and I want something that meets my needs."

I chuckled. "Imagine that. Well, that's the architect's job. Sometimes they forget that, unfortunately."

"Yes, that's right. Say, are you by chance free for lunch or dinner tomorrow? I'm a decent cook, and although my present place isn't exactly a dream-house, it's comfortable. I'd like to talk to you about taking on this project."

"That's flattering, but we do renovations, not new construction. And we're based in D.C."

"I don't care where you're based," he said. "Like psychiatry, architecture is a transportable art. I want the right architect, and I think you're it."

The following evening he drove me to see the property. It was a spectacular, isolated bluff overlooking the wild sea, half a mile away from the nearest neighbors.

Then we returned to his house in the hills, where Jule demonstrated he hadn't understated his culinary skills. As we dined on exquisite grilled tuna, we talked about possibilities for his house. He asked me to quote a fee, which was higher than normal because of extensive travel and local consulting costs.

Jule said that the fee was reasonable—even with the extra costs it was less than some that had been quoted by local beachfront architectural specialists—and he counter-offered ten percent higher. "I want you to put your heart and soul into it, Kevin. I don't want you to think me a fantastically wealthy person, but this is my priority."

"I understand. And, of course, I accept."

As we consumed fabulous California wine, we delved a bit into each other's personal lives. I realized that I had been hoping for an opportunity to spill my guts. Maybe I ought to design his house for free, if he could help me rebuild my life. An even exchange?

As I began speaking, he listened intently, then drew me out with questions. Before long, it was clear to both of us that this was turning into a consultation. The conversation lasted a very long time. He scoured Nicki's psychological landscape: her parents, her habits, her past relationships, her moods, her reactions. I finished by telling him about the pills, and the explanation of manic depression offered by my physician.

Jule thoughtfully shook his head. "No competent professional can render a diagnosis without actually examining the subject, but do you want my armchair diagnosis"

"I would be grateful."

"You're playing with fire. Your wife's actions are consistent with a condition known in psychology as 'borderline personality disorder,' or BPD. It's as common as it is amorphous. But like a lot of psychological maladies, it tends to affect not only the person afflicted with it but also everone around, especially those who are closest."

"Go on," I entreated him.

"It's only been relatively recently, going back to the middle of the century, that borderline personality disorder was recognized as a distinct psychological illness, as distinguished from, say, schizophrenia or manic depression. As our society grows more complex, it appears that more people are afficted with it due to inability to cope. I've certainly seen my share; not only in adults, but in children. Very little is known about it; and unfortunately, even less how to treat it."

"But Nicki is really smart, and has had a successful career." As soon as I said that, I realized it wasn't true. Nicki had had a series of jobs, but never really a career.

"Remarkably, borderlines are often high-achieving people. Very talented, high-striving, charming. But they are enormously fragile. They always have one foot in the real world, where they operate at a high level, and one foot in a netherworld fathomable only to them. Hence the term 'borderline,' connoting the boundary between normality and insanity." He drew deeply from his wine glass. "They need to have a lot of friends and lovers, but dispose of them quickly and move onto new ones. On the one hand, they need the validation that friends and lovers give; but once the gambit is up and people grow to know them, they are tossed away like yesterday's garbage." That certainly struck a chord.

"The quintessential borderline," Jule continued, "was Marilyn Monroe. Incredibly successful. But an actress not only by profession, but in her personal life, fooling herself and everyone around her. Ultimately her failure to cope led to her taking her own life."

"How does someone become borderline?" I asked.

"That's a subject of huge dispute. Some experts say it's hereditary and essentially uncurable. Others think that it's a chemical imbalance that can be treated with drugs. Borderlines often go from therapist to therapist, experimenting with all manner of treatment, including the kinds of drugs your wife was prescribed. The problem is that the treatments usually end with everyone, the therapist included, thinking they are successful. But there is rarely, if ever a cure. Borderlines are magnificent actors."

"What about someone who marries a borderline?"

He smiled sadly. "Good luck." I could feel myself turn pale, and he reached out and gently touched my arm. "I don't mean to be so trite. Lots of people fall in love with borderlines. Awhile ago there was a book written about BPD aptly titled *I Hate You, Don't Leave Me.* Lots of borderline marriages end in divorce; lots are marked by affairs. But often the borderline finds the one person he or she wants to hold onto for dear life. In your case, you seem to be the lucky guy."

"So what can I do?"

"Well, if in the short term, the first thing would be to consult privately with your wife's psychiatrist. Bob Strachian is quite well-respected. I've known him professionally for twenty years. It's good at least that your wife switched to him. Amelia Liechtenstein, by stark contrast, is a quack."

I smiled ruefully. "And in the long term?"

"Strap on a seatbelt. You're an awfully talented architect, and I'm looking forward to working with you while you're still on the accessible rungs of an upward-bound career, but you really need to think about whether you can survive someone like Nicki. If I'm correct in my armchair diagnosis, and if you remain married to her, you face a life sentence. I have no doubt that she loves you as much as she's capable of loving anyone. But she also despises you, as a proxy for despising herself." He looked at me gravely as he completed his verdict. "Just be aware that if you stay with her, Nicki will do everything she can to destroy you."

10

THE FLIGHT HOME from Los Angeles was the starkest five hours I can ever recall. Jule Maguire's words were so chillingly accurate; he was right about Nicki, dead right. Not only in his diagnosis, but in his prognosis, as well. He had finally reached me, with clinical precision, in a way that my friends could not.

I sat in the first-class section of the plane and drank one bloody Mary after another. I didn't even like bloody Marys, but the tomato juice tasted good and the vodka felt good. Perfect combination.

What to do in light of the bigger picture regarding Nicki? Was I prepared to subject my entire life to the wrenching tumult a breakup would entail? Hah, too late; I was already there. Regardless, I had a great deal to do to prepare for our Labor Day weekend encounter.

First I had to catch up with my work, which had piled up relentlessly in my absence. Fortunately, most of it was paperwork and administrative stuff. In the midst of that, I sneaked in a call to Nicki's psychiatrist, Dr. Strachian. I left a message with his receptionist. When he failed to return my call after two hours, I tried again. I realized that psychiatrists were busy, but I was impatient. This time I mentioned that Dr. Jule Maguire had suggested that I call. After a few minutes he took the call.

"How can I help you?" he asked in a gravelly voice, his obvious impatience matching mine.

"Dr. Strachian, I'm Kevin Gibbons. My wife is Nicole. Nicki. I believe she's a patient of yours." Silence. I continued awkwardly. "A client of mine in California, Jule Maguire—I'm an architect, by the way—suggested that it was appropriate for me to call you. I'm very worried about my wife. I'm wondering whether I could talk to you about her."

"Mr. Gibbons, I'm sure you understand that as a professional, it's imperative that I maintain my patients' confidentiality, even with their spouses."

"Well, perhaps my wife and I could have a counseling session together."

"That might be possible, if your wife were willing, and if she were still a patient of mine. But she's not; she terminated our relationship"—I could hear him rustling some papers—"about three weeks ago. She asked that I forward her file to her new therapist. Dr. Amelia Liechtenstein."

I closed my eyes tightly. Not Amelia again. The nightmare worsened.

"Perhaps you can contact Dr. Liechtenstein with the same question."

"I don't think so," I mumbled.

Oh, man. First she goes berserk over me, then she quits her job, then she fires her doctor. And returns to a therapist who seems as sick as Nicki.

On the way home, I stopped at Barnes & Noble and picked out two books that dealt with borderline personality disorder, including the one that Jule had mentioned. That night I curled up and read the books in bed, Elvis purring sedately beside me. I devoured the material. Dr. Maguire hadn't exaggerated either the disorder's potential severity or Nicki's symptoms. The prognosis was bleak: If Nicki were a borderline, there was no proven cure.

Remarkably, I did not dwell much on the information. I just let it sink in over the next several days. Nicki still did not communicate with me in any way, and my work occupied my time and thoughts so that I did not have much time to think about her. It also became more natural not to have her home. I ordered pizza, grilled hamburgers on our patio, guzzled orange juice straight from the container, and otherwise returned to a bachelor lifestyle.

But one night just before Labor Day weekend, I found I could no longer escape thoughts of Nicki. I tossed and turned in bed, trying anything to get to sleep: reading a trashy novel, counting sheep, even constructing architectural designs in my head. Nothing worked. It was in those half-awake, half-dream moments that I finally came to a resolution. When it finally occurred to me it had the effect of a crucifix to a vampire: it chased the scary thoughts away.

I was done with Nicki.

I was simply not going to sentence myself to a lifetime of anxiety and despair. As badly as I felt about her illness, I was not equipped to deal with it. I would cut my losses, purge Nicki from my life, banish Nicki's demons along with her.

I would divorce Nicki.

As soon as my mind formed that resolution, whether rational or not, I fell blissfully asleep.

And I awoke to the same thoughts. Were they a dream or had I really conjured them? No, they were real. I really was going to divorce her. This time, the thought brought a smile to my face. I was done with her. It was over. For once I would be the unpredictable one, if I could beat her to the punch.

The day before Labor Day weekend, I called Doug's law office to get the process going. A divorce without kids and less than a year after marriage shouldn't be a problem. It turned out Doug was on vacation but would return on Tuesday. I asked to make an appointment.

My anxiousness remained with me after I returned home. I called Nicki's parents' house on Friday night, got the answering machine, and left a message asking Nicki to call me. Then I drank myself into a wine stupor and fell asleep.

I was sprawled diagonally across the bed dead asleep when the ringing phone woke me early on Saturday morning.

"Hi." *Déjà vu.* Hadn't I been in this identical situation a million times before?

Suddenly the mental cobwebs cleared. "Nicki?" I asked.

"Of course, silly," she replied. Her tone was as if we had been talking every day. "How are you?"

"Fine. What's up?" I asked, inwardly pleased at my matter-of-fact tone of voice. It was authentic.

Nicki seemed taken aback. "Aren't we getting together this weekend? I was thinking of bringing dinner over tonight. Are you busy?"

This was ludicrous. I felt like I was being asked out on a date. "Is it Labor Day weekend already? Yeah, I guess we could get together."

"Oh, fun," Nicki replied. "It's supposed to be nice. Maybe we could eat out on the patio."

"Okay," I said, and hung up.

My resolve was set. I rehearsed over and again the words I would say to Nicki. I was surprised over my composure. Oddly, I felt little anger. Nicki was a sick person, I couldn't really hold that against her. But I wasn't going to allow her any further claim to my life. I took a long, luxurious bath in the jacuzzi tub. I thought about opening some wine but decided that I needed to be clear-headed, and I certainly didn't want to suggest that this was a romantic occasion.

Nicki arrived unexpectedly fifteen minutes early, as I was feeding Elvis. She rang the doorbell rather than using her key—implicitly confessing that she had forfeited the right to let herself in, I guessed—but then bustled in after I opened the door as if she were merely returning from a shopping trip rather than a month's absence. Indeed, her arms were filled with packages, but she lingered long enough to plant a warm, wet kiss on my lips.

Glancing down at the groceries, she said, "I picked this stuff up from the gourmet takeout down the block. We should eat it right away, before it gets cold." As she hurried out to the kitchen, she announced, "I bought a chilled bottle of Chardonnay, Rodney Strong." Before long I could hear her rummaging around, taking out serving dishes and the like. I wished I'd rearranged all of the plates and serving spoons in her absence, just to drive her nuts.

I walked into the kitchen and picked up some plates and silverware to set on the patio. I set the table on our balcony.

Nicki came outside with two generous glasses of Chardonnay. "Here, I thought we could taste the wine before eating dinner." She smiled at me again. She was wearing blue shorts and I could tell she had shed some pounds. She sipped the wine. "Mmm, this is good," she remarked after taking a sip of wine. Then, surveying the surroundings, she added, "I've missed this view."

As I watched Nicki and took a sip of the wine as well, I thought: I've missed this view, too. She looked fantastic, wholesome yet ravishing.

Nicki put the wine glass down, then disappeared to get the food. I followed her to assist. In a few moments we were enjoying a delicious dinner. Nicki kept talking, incessantly, telling me about her trip to Charleston, which had been followed by another trip to Montreal. Revelation after revelation. She hadn't gotten a new job yet, but had sent some resumes to radio and television stations. She wanted to return to media advertising, she said, rather than to the hotel business. "Too many slimeballs, and I know you know what I mean."

I allowed myself to relax and enjoy the meal and the evening. The wine was great and gave me a mellow buzz. By contrast, Nicki was practically manic, moving from one subject to another as if it were an hour newscast squeezed into half that time.

"Well, let's have dessert inside, so we can talk without the neighbors hearing," she said. Man, she has this down to a schedule, I thought. We settled into the plush cushions of the sofa to eat vanilla ice cream with Bailey's Irish Cream.

Nicki took a deep breath. I wasn't sure whether she was nervous, or just full from the plentiful meal. She placed her dessert dish on the coffee table. Though I wasn't quite finished, I did the same. It was showtime.

Surprisingly, Nicki's first act was to slip off her sandals, tuck her legs beneath her, and recline into the sofa. She picked up her wine glass and sipped. "If this sofa could talk, what stories it would tell," she said with a smile.

"Yeah, it's seen some serious action," I agreed. "But not much lately."

"We'll have to remedy that."

I wasn't expecting her to say that. But I refused to let her knock me off stride. I cleared my throat. I was nervous, but miraculously I was going ahead with this. Or at least I hoped so. "I don't think so," I said. I couldn't believe those words came out of my mouth.

"What do you mean?" she asked, swinging her legs out from under her, leaning forward and looking at me seriously. Her soft green eyes were huge and curious. Apparently I had diverted from the script. Ad-libbing was dangerous in Nicki's lexicon.

I looked at her squarely in the eye and said, "We're through, Nicki."

"You've got to be joking," she said with a smile, and she playfully punched my arm.

I drew back from her. "I mean exactly what I said. How much clearer can I make it? We're through."

"Why are you being so hostile?"

"I'm not hostile. I'm just done, Nicki. I've had it."

"What do you mean?"

"I mean it's over between us."

"You can't mean that."

"I do mean it." I leveled my gaze at her, and thought I saw a momentary look of shock in her eyes, or perhaps it was panic. But just as quickly it was gone, she averted her eyes, and stood to pace the room.

"You can't leave. I need you."

I laughed. "Apparently you haven't needed me very much over the past month. And besides, I don't care what you need anymore, Nicki."

"How can you say that? Don't you know I just lost my baby?"

For some reason that comment infuriated me. I rose too and faced her. "Our baby, Nicki. *Our* baby. That's what you can't ever seem to get through your head. There are two of us in this relationship. I know you just suffered the most painful loss of your life. But I did, too. You don't get it, do you?" I looked at her with disgust. My voice rose an octave. "All I can think of is my son who will never get to experience life. The walks in the park. Throwing a football around. Telling him the facts of life. Yeah, I hurt for you, Nicki. A lot. And I'll never forgive myself for not being there. Not because I could have done anything to prevent it, but so that I could be there for you."

I was pacing now. "But it would have been pointless. You wouldn't have let me in, anyway. I'm tired of battering my head against a wall. There's just no reward. And I'm done worrying about it. I grieve for losing my son. Because I lost him, and I can never get him back. But I don't grieve for losing you because I haven't lost anything. Because we never had anything."

"How can you say that? We're married. I need you."

"For what? You need me to have a baby. That seems to be the main point of it. And according to you, I fucked that up, too."

"It just wasn't meant to be this time."

That remark angered me, too, and I turned to face her. "Oh, so now you're forgiving me? After a month of hell?" I was livid. "Is that what your stupid psycho doctor told you to say? Is that what Amelia told you?" She seemed surprised that I knew that she had returned to the therapist. Score one for Kevin.

"She's the only one who understands me."

"Now, *that* I believe," I responded.

"She says that I need you."

I laughed. "What do you need me for, Nicki? Believe me, whatever it is, I can't give it to you."

She looked at me through fresh tears. "I need you. I can't live without you."

I felt a stab, but tried to brush it away. This was the crucial moment. There could be no turning back now. I looked at my wife, despising her. "Too late. I'm done letting you suck the life out of me."

She flew into a rage. "Goddamn you! You can't leave me!"

And suddenly she was all over me, her nails clawing at my face. I cried out in shock, trying simultaneously to shield my face, push her away, grab her arms. She was screaming, incoherently, crying hysterically, all the while trying to get at my eyes.

"Stop it!" I yelled.

She attacked like a demon.

I pushed her toward the coffee table and she stumbled backward onto the sofa. Sensing I could gain leverage over her, I fell on top of her, trying to pin her arms. A thought flickered through my mind that I couldn't dare let her up—there were knives in the kitchen only a few dozen feet away. We were locked in stalemate. Neither her struggles nor her howling dissipated.

Nicki tried to pound at my shoulders with her fists. "No, I won't let you, goddamnit."

I didn't know whether she was referring to my divorcing her or trying to pin her arms. "Quit it!" I demanded, feeling like I was finally gaining control.

"No, you bastard!" she screamed. And somehow she squirmed out from under me, but her legs were still stuck. She tried to knee me in the groin, but I slid off the sofa after her and fell onto the floor on top of her.

She extricated one of her hands and moved it to my face. I thought for sure she would draw blood, but instead she slid her hand around my head and smashed my face into hers. "I hate you!" she screeched into my ear. Then I felt her other hand groping my groin. I twisted away from her grasp momentarily, but was quickly, and dangerously, losing control of the situation.

I tried to get up on my knees, but suddenly I was dizzy from the alcohol and I slid back down. Then I felt Nicki's lips pressed against mine. At first I thought she was trying to kiss me. Then her teeth grasped my upper lip and clamped down, spurting warm blood inside my mouth. I tried to yell and pull back, but Nicki kept her lips pressed against mine. Crazily, her tongue snaked inside my mouth. I tried to extricate, but her hand was holding my head with what seemed super-human strength. So I pressed back as hard as I could, ignoring the pain from my gouged lip. And before I knew it, our violence transformed into an equally violent kiss.

Despite myself, I could feel I was getting hard, and apparently Nicki did, too, for she began rubbing her groin against mine. This was insane, I thought, and again tried to pull away from her, but our mouths and bodies remained locked together.

My attempted retreat lasted only a second. I was growing intensely aroused. And then our hands started stripping away each other's clothes. I couldn't unfasten the buttons of her blouse quickly enough, so I ripped it off her. Almost at once we were almost completely naked. I looked at my wife, her blonde hair cascading around her shoulders. Her face was still furious, and she sat there panting like a wild animal; but one in heat, because it was obvious what was on both our minds.

For a fleeting moment I tried to collect myself. "We're not supposed to do this. The doctor said to wait."

Her pale green eyes were huge, imploring. "Fuck me."

From somewhere deep inside its primordial recesses, my mind summoned crazy images of black widow spiders. But I brushed those thoughts away and focused on my carnal desire.

It was intensely exciting, passionate, violent, self-loathing sexual depravity, driven by the most extreme and conflicting emotions I had ever experienced.

In the act of making love to a woman I had come to fear, I spilled my seed inside her. And in that instant, I sealed my fate forever.

20

I WAS WIPED out as I fumbled with the keys at the door to the apartment. Work that day had been utterly exhausting. Recession or not, it was more challenging than ever. Bringing in new architects had produced diminishing returns: I spent as much time supervising them as I did on my own projects. And as the demands with respect to the latter had not diminished, it seemed, on net, that I was spending ever-escalating amounts of time at the office. That would have to change, and soon. I just didn't know how that would be possible.

It was ironic, I thought as I finally extracted the correct key and managed to insert it into the lock, that the reward for excelling at something was getting to do less of it. I was an architect, not a manager. Yet I was so good at designing that I was spending half my time helping other people do what I wished I could spend all my time doing. Life was unfair sometimes.

The soothing sounds of Yanni greeted me from the stereo speakers as I entered the living room. I dropped my jacket and homework on the sofa and trotted into the kitchen. There was my wife, on her hands and knees, kneeling alongside a bucket, scrubbing the kitchen floor. Her long blonde hair was pulled back into a Scrunchie, she was barefoot, wearing sweatpants and a T-shirt. She was humming off-key and hadn't heard me enter.

I was conflicted between the desire to sneak up behind her, inhale the delicious scent of her hair, and kiss her; or to yell at her for this outburst of domesticity. "You know, you really shouldn't be doing that."

She revolved on her knees toward me, brushing an errant strand of hair from her eye. I found the gesture sexy. "Oh, hi!" she said with a smile. "I'm just scrubbing."

"So I can see."

"Don't get the floor dirty," she protested, but she raised her lips to greet mine. Our kiss was warm and lingering. "Don't worry, I'm just using soap and water," she said as she pulled away.

"That's why we hired a cleaning lady."

"Yeah, but it's never clean enough for me."

I gave up. "How's about I take you out for dinner?" I asked, suddenly replenished with energy.

"How's about you go and pick up some Ben and Jerry's Heavenly Hash?" she asked, a mischievous grin appearing on her face.

I groaned. "Again? You've had ice cream for dinner twice already this week."

"Yeah, but once it was raspberry sorbet." She stuck her arm out at me. "Here, help me up." I did, and she rose to her feet a bit awkwardly. Nicki's pregnancy seemed to have improved her sense of humor. She patted her burgeoning tummy. "She likes ice cream."

The walk in the late fall air was invigorating. If Nicki had been self-indulgent before, now it was boundless. And eating what she wanted, when she wanted, was a big part of it. She had gained ten pounds or so, which mostly reflected in her face, but because the weight gain was modest, it didn't seem to bother her; she positively glowed.

Later, we sat in bed contentedly munching our dinner and watching *Friends* and *Seinfeld*.

"How's work?" Nicki asked unexpectedly during a commercial break.

"Hectic, as always. But Rich is worried about it slowing down with the recession," I added, laying the groundwork for future conversations.

"You have to make lots of money. Alexandra is going to want to live in luxury." Nicki possessed a remarkable penchant for discerning my vulnerabilities and exploiting them. And if it added a little more pressure to my life, Nicki would remain blithely oblivious.

Ironically, though, an opportunity to make more money—a *lot* more money—arose unexpectedly the next day. Rich Deeks summoned me into his office just as I arrived.

"I have an idea," he announced. "The renovation of the National Pension Building."

I was incredulous. "That's twice as big as any project we've ever taken on."

The National Pension Building was a grand, six-story late-19th century structure in the impoverished southeast section of the District of Columbia. Like most everything in that part of town, it had grown seedy over time, and had been empty for a long time. A few years earlier, the U.S. Department of the Interior had turned it over to the city, which planned to restore it and use it to house the Department of Parks and Recreation and to hold official city events, while at the same time revitalizing a once-elegant neighborhood.

"It's a wreck. I've only driven by one time, but it's in a sad state. Have you ever seen it?"

"Just went by yesterday. It looks right up our alley. If we can restore entire apartment buildings, we certainly can restore an office building."

I scrunched my face. "Maybe, but we'd be working for the *government*," I said with venomous distaste.

Rich smirked. "We'd be working for the *people*."

"The *people* we'd be reporting to are *bureaucrats*." We both laughed. "Listen, Rich, this is a huge undertaking, and I'm not joking about the bureaucracy. You know how tough it is to get their sign-off on a private project. Imagine what it would be like to have to answer to them on a daily basis. We'd lose any profit. And *imagine* trying to collect overdue bills from the District of Columbia."

"Well, fortunately, they appointed a design committee with complete authority, but more than that, it's a necessity for Horizon. There's no new work out there. If we don't find a big project, and soon, we're going to have to lay people off."

"We can't do that."

"Or take huge cuts in our draws."

I didn't say anything, but clearly I couldn't do that, either. "Well, let's go over there with Allan Sears and check out the structural soundness." Allan was our engineer.

I knew I was being railroaded, but I also knew Rich was absolutely right. We had a natural advantage on what restoration business there was to be had in Washington; but lately, bigger firms were bidding for every job, no matter how small. That meant we had to reduce profit margins to stay competitive. That was if we could get the contract in the first place—a very big if. Every firm in town would enter the competition.

The three of us inspected the building the next day. Allan loved it. Notwithstanding its advanced age and decades of neglect, the proud old building was structurally sound, except for the horribly outdated heating and ventilation system. But we encountered and dealt with those old dinosaurs all the time.

But oh man, the place was messed up. So many design changes had been made over the years—walls in odd places, everything painted over in institutional colors, makeshift ceilings completely blocking the interior view of the magnificent dome—that it was difficult to envision what the building must have looked like initially. What was worse, the original plans were long gone. Still, it tugged at my heartstrings: the building had been erected in a grander era and still possessed its raw glory. I could envision restoring every inch of it, lovingly.

Rich knew the building would work its magic on me, and he barely said a word. We stood outside for awhile, looking at the place, Allan waxing poetic about its grandeur. "They just don't make 'em this way anymore."

Finally, I sighed and said, "Okay Rich, let's go for it."

He smiled. "I'll get the work-ups going right away."

I wondered if Rich had strong-armed Allan in advance. Whatever, I pumped his hand, then Rich's. We had a deal. "One more thing." I looked Rich. "We need to hire a private detective."

"What for?"

"To find those original drawings. It's a long shot, but that would really give us a competitive advantage."

THE NEXT FEW months were unbelievable. Rich and I, along with the few architects we could spare, worked night and day on the design. Each aspect of the renovation brought a whole new range of dilemmas. I wished I could have the original plans and go back to the essential design, but it was almost impossible to figure out what it was.

The detective couldn't find the plans, but he found something almost as good—a ninety-three-year-old man who had worked as a janitor for thirty years in the building's early days. Roscoe Smith was his name, and he was amazingly nimble both physically and mentally. He spent hours going over the drawings with us, painstakingly recounting the building's original details. Smith refused to take a penny for his efforts, saying that he only wanted to live to see the building restored to its original majesty.

With his help, it might be. It turned out, for example, that much of what appeared to be painted woodwork was actually brass. And the dome contained a fresco by an Italian artist—frustratingly painted over, but restorable. Roscoe Smith's memory filled in what my imagination left blank. His appearance provided the entire team with a palpable boost in morale and inspiration.

Meanwhile, the home front grew stressful. Nicki began to encounter all manner of physical maladies apparently related to her pregnancy, and she was growing fretful and plaintive. She had trouble with her balance, experienced severe nausea, and worst of all, encountered a numbness in her left leg that the doctors were at a loss to explain. Nicki reacted with mild tantrums and by withdrawing into her private world, spending hours on the telephone with friends and disappearing to her parents' house for days at a time. Eventually she quit her outside activities and took to a bed in the guestroom, finding my nocturnal presence intolerable to her already fitful sleep. On top of that, once she was bedridden, she started gaining weight rapidly, and she complained constantly that she would never lose it.

I hired private nurses to stay with her sixteen hours a day, for it was rare with the Pension Building proposal for me to be home more than eight hours a day. The nurses made it plain before long that it was difficult to work for Nicki, but at least they provided an outlet other than me for her frustration and anger, and unlike me they were getting paid for it. We settled on a compromise of sorts when Nicki's mother started coming over on a regular basis, spelling the nurses. When Mrs. Petri was around, I tended to avoid both of them because of my lingering irritation over her role in Nicki's hiatus the previous year.

The stress of our growing financial liabilities was enormous. Nicki managed to exacerbate the situation by hiring a professional decorator for the baby's room, an extravagance I felt obliged to indulge because it gave Nicki something constructive to do. But Nicki was oblivious to our financial straits, and expressed only the barest interest in what was going on in my professional life.

More than ever before my work was my sanctuary. I absolutely reveled in the work. I had long since gone past the feeling of needing this project to wanting it, very badly. I threw myself into it with reckless abandon, and my thoughts were constantly absorbed by it. It had a salving effect because whenever I went home, I was so tired I couldn't worry about anything.

Nicki grew more distant and irritable. She couldn't stand it that I was working long hours, even though she had a nurse or her mother in attendance at most times and really didn't seem to want me around when I was actually home.

One night about five weeks before the due date, I checked on Nicki in the middle of the night to find her tossing and turning. She detected my presence immediately. "I can't stand this anymore!" she complained, kicking the bedcovers off.

I clicked on a lamp on her desk. She glowered in the dim light. "Can I do anything for you, honey?" I asked.

"You can get this baby out of me. She's making me so uncomfortable. I had to give up working and I'm going crazy during the day. I'm fat and bloated. I'm never going to lose all this weight." She balled her fists and struck the bed, her voice rising. "I just want to have this baby already!"

"Nicki, why did you marry me?" I asked, suddenly giving voice to a question that had befuddled me from the moment we had wed.

Her expression turned from anger to curiosity. "What are you talking about?" Her voice suddenly returned to its normally soft tone, and she shifted her legs over the side of the bed so she could get a better look at me.

"I mean, you had dozens, if not hundreds of guys who gladly would have married you. Yet you chose me. Even though I don't seem to be able to make you very happy."

Her mood had transformed so abruptly that it seemed there was a different woman in the bed. "I married you because I love you," she said matter-of-factly. "I married you because you take care of me."

"I do?"

But Nicki certainly wasn't going to give me the satisfaction of elaborating. Instead, she patted the bed beside her. "Come sleep with me." Happily, I clicked off the light, slid into the narrow space on the bed beside her, and kissed her on the lips. When I awoke the next morning, she was slumbering peacefully next to me. She was still asleep when I left the penthouse at seven-thirty, a half hour before the nurse would arrive.

I drove to work absorbed as usual by thoughts of the Pension Building project. The brilliant early spring day further boosted my spirits, which had begun with my sweet and unexpected nocturnal interlude with Nicki.

But that abruptly changed when I arrived to an office in pandemonium. The door to the entryway was ajar, and as I stepped across the threshold I could see that papers were strewn about and chairs overturned. Rich was inside along with several police officers.

"What's going on?"

Beth's head poked up from behind her desk, where she was picking papers up off the floor. "We've been burglarized. Rich and I just came in twenty minutes ago and found the place like this."

"Shit. What did they take?"

Rich frowned. "That's the thing. I took a quick inventory around the office, and it doesn't look like they took anything. They did a pretty thorough job of ransacking the place, but nothing seems to be missing. The computers are all here, all our equipment."

I had never been very security conscious. All our equipment was insured, so I didn't worry about theft. Plus, despite living in the crime capital of the free world, somehow I had maintained a trusting nature. This incident surely would change that, and that probably was a good thing.

"Well, I'm glad it looks like we got off pretty lightly if they didn't steal anything. Maybe someone surprised them and they left before taking anything."

"Or maybe they didn't come to steal something tangible," Rich suggested. I looked at him. "Maybe they came to steal our ideas."

I gasped. "The plans for the Pension Building?" Rich nodded darkly. "Come on, you can't believe that someone would literally engage in espionage."

From behind her desk, Beth laughed. "Listen, you're playing in the big leagues now, with big stakes. Everyone knows we're the up-and-coming firm. Surely you don't expect our rivals to come up with their own ideas when they can appropriate ours."

I glanced at Rich, who frowned. Shit, I would not believe this. The whole idea was too much to comprehend. One of the reasons I had decided on a career in architecture was that it was that it was the closest I could come to making a living as an artist. And artists don't steal from one another.

I sat down in one of the reception chairs and buried my face in my hands. This was too much. The phone started ringing, which jarred me from my daze. As Beth answered it, I looked up at Rich. "Why don't you work with the officers, and Beth and I will clean up, okay?" I suggested.

"Okay," Rich replied.

"Kevin!" Beth said sharply, holding her hand over the phone. At the same moment, my beeper suddenly emitted its sharp-toned whine. Good grief, I thought, what else could go wrong?

Beth illuminated me. "It's Nicki's nurse. They're rushing to the hospital. Nicki's bleeding."

And I thought to myself: dear God, please don't let it be happening again.

21

THE TERROR THAT seized me in that moment was profound and pro-
longed.

Within seconds of hearing the news about Nicki, I was on my
way to Sibley Hospital. For once I was thankful for D.C.'s finest: one
of the police officers who was investigating the break-in offered to
take me there. Siren blaring in his patrol car, I arrived at the hospital
in less than ten minutes. As we weaved through the heavy weekday
traffic, I thought that this time Nicki couldn't begrudge me for any
delay in coming to her side.

But the drive was nerve-racking just the same. There were still
five weeks until the baby's due date. And Nicki was bleeding, just like
last time.

My worries were heightened as I entered the hospital and was
informed that Nicki had just been admitted not to delivery but to the
emergency room.

A nurse walked me to the emergency room but could offer no
information. As we arrived, Nicki's new obstetrician, Dr. Jay Solderholm was bustling inside the door in full surgical garb.

"What's going on?" I asked frantically, rushing over to him.

He paused. "Breach. Nicki is hemorrhaging. We have to try to
deliver the baby."

"Can I—?"

"No," he barked, pushing me away from the door, "I promise I'll
come out as soon as possible." And he disappeared inside the room.
For a second I heard Nicki's frantic protests. I wished I could be inside
there with her. She must be terrified.

The nurse looked at me and took my elbow. "Come on, I'll take
you to the waiting area."

"No," I replied, sinking to the floor. "I'm waiting right here."

Something in my look must have made her decide to override hospital policy. "All right, but don't get in the way."

I sat down inches from the door to the emergency room. The unit was a beehive of activity, with doctors and nurses scurrying from one emergency to another. At the time I was utterly absorbed in what Dr. Solderholm had told me. Breach. Hemorrhage. And worst of all, that they were going to "try" to deliver the baby.

Hot tears stung my eyes, stemming both from worry and frustration. Nurses bustled in and out, their faces anxious, but no one paused to give me information. Each time the door opened, I could hear the low rumble of Dr. Solderholm's voice in the near distance, but I could not hear Nicki's; and craning my neck each time the door opened I could see nothing but frantic activity. The nurse returned with some coffee, which I gratefully accepted, the acrid taste paralleling my mood. Nicki's door opened and closed so often that I thought I was no longer paying attention, but when Dr. Solderholm came out, I immediately detected him and jumped to my feet. He touched my shoulder and lowered me back to my chair and sat down beside me.

His gray eyes bore into mine. "Congratulations," he said soberly. "You have a baby daughter."

My daughter, Alexandra Lynn Gibbons, was born at 2:45 PM on Tuesday, April 16, 1991.

That I can say those words today is the greatest gift God, if He exists, has ever bestowed upon me.

A feeling of relief rushed over me and made me feel lightheaded. "Alexandra," I muttered. "How is Nicki?"

Dr. Solderholm pursed his lips. "Nicki is okay for now. She lost a great deal of blood. A number of things happened simultaneously. Nicki developed a blood clot in her thigh. That must have been what was causing pain in her leg. Meanwhile, the baby moved into breach position. The combination of those conditions, or maybe something else, caused Nicki to hemorrhage. We had to deliver the baby by Caesarian section, which caused Nicki to lose even more blood pressure. We were forced to operate on several fronts at the same time, and I was worried we would lose Nicki or the baby, or both. But ironically, the combination of all those things may have saved both their lives, because we might not have detected the problems if they hadn't occurred simultaneously. They're not out of the woods yet. I'm going to bring in a surgeon to try to determine whether Nicki has suffered any internal damage, either from the blood clot or the hemorrhage. It's too early to say what her situation will be. Dr. McCormack is on his way, and he's an extremely skilled surgeon."

"What about the baby?"

"We sent her over to pediatric intensive care. Of course she was premature, and weighed in at five pounds, eight ounces. That doesn't sound like much, but we've saved babies a third that size. She's actually large for her state of development. But she's very, very weak. She's literally fighting for her life. Fortunately, until the delivery, she seemed to be developing very well, so all things considered, I think the odds of survival look pretty good." Which brightened my spirits a bit. But he wasn't finished yet. "That's not all of it. When the baby was in breach and we were attempting to deliver her, she was deprived of oxygen, so there is a slight possibility of neurological damage. We've called in a different specialist, a pediatric neurosurgeon, to check and monitor her condition."

The gravity of what he was saying struck me hard, but I wasn't sure I comprehended the full scope of it. I had been worried for Nicki, but now suddenly there was someone else to think about. Alexandra. My daughter. No longer an abstraction, but a little human being, introduced prematurely to the world and fighting for her life. Now I was being told that even if she survived, she might be damaged permanently.

All at once I was seized with guilt. "Did this happen because we got pregnant again too soon?" I asked.

"Nicki probably wasn't fully healed from her miscarriage. That may have contributed to her internal problems, but it certainly would have had no effect on the baby. Just bear in mind that both of you knew that it would be difficult for Nicki to bear a child under the best of circumstances. It was a calculated risk." He paused, then added, "And with any luck, one that will work out just fine." I nodded. "Come on," he said, "let me get you to the obstetrics waiting room where you can be more comfortable, and maybe make some phone calls if you want. It will be a few hours at best before you can see Nicki or your daughter, so you may as well relax."

"Okay," I said, and he led me to the waiting room. Fortunately it was bright and cheery, and there was no one else inside. As I sat down in a comfortable chair, Dr. Solderholm looked at me gravely. I knew he had something else to say.

"I should tell you this now, so you can factor it in. Nicki will not be able to get pregnant again."

That seemed to me a foregone conclusion. "I understand," I said. "Thank you, Doctor, for saving my wife's life. And my daughter's."

He smiled, and suddenly looked very, very tired. "I did the best I could. I'll come by later as soon as I know anything more about either Nicki or your daughter. Don't worry, even though we're not out of the woods yet, I think it will work out." He smiled again, and we shook hands and he left.

I was seized by the need to take some action. Called my mother, who fortunately was home, and when I told her the news I could tell she was struggling between obvious concern and the need to reassure me. She had been planning to come and help when Nicki had the baby, but that was to have been five weeks from now. She offered to come right away, and I gratefully accepted. "It will be fine," she said. "And I'm glad to have a brand new baby granddaughter, just like you promised."

I knew I should call Mrs. Petri, but I could bring myself to do it. Instead, I called my sister, whose reaction, not surprisingly, mirrored my mother's. She too offered to come out, but I thought it better not to have too many people out at once, so I told her I'd call again as soon as things got settled.

Then at last I called Nicki's mother, both at her house and mine, but couldn't find her. Fearing I would be accused of dereliction, I called Nicki's sister, Kim. She was home with her kids and took the news with an odd calmness. Good grief, I thought to myself, do these people ever exhibit emotions other than anger?

As I was distracted by that thought, Kim said something I didn't catch. "What was that?" I asked.

"I said that Nicki was born exactly the same way. She was premature and breach, and had to be delivered by C-section. She almost died."

"I had no idea."

As I was trying to find a graceful way to end my conversation with Kim, out of the corner of my eye I saw Mrs. Petri bustle into the waiting room. "Hey, Kim, your mom just came in. I gotta go."

It was three by the time Dr. Soderholm came back. "Well, the news so far is fairly good. Nicki is recovering nicely. And preliminary tests on your daughter seem okay. She's getting food intravenously, and we'll have to keep both girls in the hospital for tests and observation, but they seem to have come out of the ordeal intact and healthy."

"No lasting harm?"

"Well, it will take awhile for Nicki to mend and get her strength back. And I'm concerned about her leg. As for the baby, she's got to build up her strength, too, and we have to run some more tests to make sure there's no subtle neurological damage. But there's one thing I can tell you for certain: they'd both like to see you."

I literally jumped at the chance. As Nicki was still sleeping off her sedation, I started with Alexandra. To visit her, I had to scrub my hands and wear a hospital gown and mask. Dr. Soderholm warned me that she was in an incubator to ward off possible infection, and that I would be able to look at her but couldn't hold her for a few days until she was beyond the danger phase.

Alexandra was sharing an intensive care unit with two other preemies. I was afraid of what I might see. I steeled myself, or at least tried to, for the worst. Instead, inside the incubator was the most beautiful baby girl I had ever laid eyes on. She was perfect—but oh so *small*. Her tiny hands were no bigger than my thumbnail. She lay inside the incubator struggling mightily against all sorts of tubes and wires that were attached to her, her eyes scrunched and her fingers balled into fists, shaking angrily. Her skin was pink and she was naked except for a diaper and white stocking cap.

But she was perfect.

I wanted to hold her in the worst way. As I looked down at her, she looked up at me. Abruptly she stopped fussing, as if I had startled her and she was embarrassed over her behavior. What struck me at once about Alexandra more than anything else was what had struck me most about Nicole: her eyes. Like Nicki's, they were light in color, but instead of Nicki's green they were light brown, a translucent shade of mocha. Like I had been told my father's were. And, very unlike Nicki's, they were remarkably expressive. She smiled toothlessly at me, the look utterly transforming her face.

And as it would forever hence, her smile literally took my breath away.

What a miracle. An absolute miracle.

I stood there, mesmerized, for a very long time. Eventually, Alexandra's struggles against her confinement tired her out, and I watched her fall asleep. Around that same time the nurse came in to lead me away. "Your wife should be waking up pretty soon."

"Nurse," I asked, "are premature babies usually that pink and well-formed?"

"No, but technically she's not premature, being born so close to full-term."

I nodded.

The nurse led me down a corridor to a set of rooms. One of them bore Nicki's name. "I'll let you in, but please don't disturb her if she's still sleeping. She sedated and very weak, and she hasn't even been awake yet."

Again I nodded, then entered Nicki's room. I found her alone, asleep. Her skin was more pale than I'd ever seen, as if she had imparted whatever color she had to her daughter. Her eyes were sunken, and her hair was matted against her face. She looked like she had been through a battle, which was not far from the mark. Still, through her pallor somehow she seemed ethereally beautiful. I felt a surge of affection flood through me. This was my wife, who had just delivered our daughter.

As I looked down upon her, Nicki's eyes flitted open. Usually so vibrant, even her eyes seemed washed out. It took her a moment to focus.

"Hi, beautiful," I said.

"Hi. I hurt. Can you get me some water?"

"Sure." I found a container in the bathroom and filled it with tap water, then found a straw and Nicki sipped several big swallows.

"That's better," she said.

It was comforting for me to be allowed to help her for once. She looked up at me, tired but now more clear-eyed. "How is Alexandra?"

"She's fine . . . and incredibly beautiful."

Nicki nodded. "She's an Aries," she said with a pained smile that appeared almost a grimace. That comment struck me as odd, for I had no idea that Nicki knew or even cared anything about astrology.

I chuckled and replied, "If you say so."

"I'm really tired," Nicki announced. She closed her eyes and fell instantly to sleep.

The door opened, and Dr. Solderholm entering the room. He whispered, "How's she doing?"

"She was awake for a minute, and seemed okay but pretty weak."

"She is pretty weak, but her vital signs are good and she's taking in a lot of nourishment. In a few weeks, hopefully she'll be almost as good as new. In the meantime, you should go home and let her get some rest. She won't really be conscious until tomorrow morning, so why don't you come back first thing?"

We said our goodbyes and walked separate ways down the corridor. As I neared the nurse station, suddenly I was struck by a thought and I wheeled around and called after him. "Doctor! One more thing."

He stopped and turned around. "Yes?"

"I was just wondering, did anyone tell Nicki she had a girl?"

"No, she was unconscious throughout the delivery, until she woke up just now. She couldn't possibly have known."

And yet somehow she did.

22

My mother arrived on the train from Pennsylvania almost instantly, and took control of the home situation, setting up a headquarters of sorts in the penthouse. Happily her presence temporarily displaced Nicki's mom, who stood vigil at the hospital. Meanwhile, my mother prepared the guest room, which Nicki and I had turned into a nursery but hadn't quite finished, and set up Nicki's study so she could convalesce comfortably there. Mother added a bassinet so Nicki could have the baby in her room if she wanted, and for good measure bought another bassinet for our bedroom so I could have the baby sleeping there sometimes, too. She went to the hospital, visiting Nicki and proclaiming Alexandra—who was still in pediatric intensive care—the most beautiful baby she had ever seen, even including her two nephews (though I was sworn to secrecy).

My mother was a huge comfort to me. I hadn't realized that I really didn't have any intimate friends nearby anymore—Jennifer was off in marital bliss with a child of her own, Alice had recovered from her illness but moved back with her family in Ohio, Drew was hundreds of miles away, and Samantha, of course, was gone from my life.

I visited Nicki and Alexandra twice each day during their stay at Sibley. Once both were past the danger point, they were able to room together, although the nurses removed the baby whenever Nicki was sleeping. Fortunately, Nicki was able to breast-feed the baby, and the first time I saw it, the image made my heart leap.

"Alex is a hungry girl," Nicki cooed. It was the first time since the birth Nicki had uttered the shortened version that would become Alexandra's permanent nickname.

"I'm jealous," I said, then realized I was only half-joking. Our affection henceforth would have to be divided three ways. But I sensed that there would be more of it now to go around.

"You're a silly boy." She patted the side of the bed. "Come join us."

I complied. "How's your leg?"

She grimaced. "It still hurts." The blood clot had apparently caused some nerve damage, and it appeared that Nicki was in for a long rehabilitation. In all probability, she would walk permanently with a slight limp. Remarkably, Nicki was enduring that news bravely. On the more positive side, Alexandra was doing well. She had already gained two ounces, and more importantly, there were no signs of neurological damage. Both girls could come home in a few days.

Nicki looked up at me. "Before we come home, you have to get rid of Elvis."

"What?" I asked incredulously.

"I don't want a cat around with a newborn. She sheds, and Alex might be allergic to her, and it's not safe to have a cat around with an infant. The cat will be jealous and try to kill the baby."

I was thunderstruck. "You've got to be kidding. Elvis has been with me for a long time. She's my friend. I can't just get rid of her like yesterday's garbage. And she would never do anything to hurt Alex. She's a good cat."

Nicki rolled her eyes as if I was saying something truly stupid. "She's a *cat*, darling. And that's what cats do to babies." She looked down at Alex, who was finished nursing, and patted her tiny mouth with the cotton towel that was protecting Nicki's nightgown. "You need to get rid of her before we come home." She edged down more deeply inside the bed linens and held the baby up toward me. "Here, please put Alex back in her bassinet. I'm really sleepy."

I took Alex from her. Like her mother, Alex was drowsy and could barely keep her eyes open. I rocked her and patted her back until she emitted a burp that reverberated through her whole body. It made me laugh. I held her up and kissed her and lay her underneath the blanket in her bassinet. She was already passed out, utterly sated and content. I glanced over at Nicki who was snoring softly, and tiptoed out of the room.

As I drove to the office through heavy mid-morning Georgetown traffic, I remembered Nicki's demand that I get rid of Elvis. Nicki was being ridiculous. The cat wasn't going to do anything to the baby. Lots of families had cats and small babies. If there was the slightest indication of danger, of course I would find a new home for Elvis. But she was a member of the household, and frankly a more loyal friend than Nicki. I couldn't just get rid of her.

But that concern was displaced by others when I reached the office. The Pension Building competition entry was due the following week, and the entire staff was busy with final details. Rich Deeks was still certain we'd been the victims of espionage, which would undermine any competitive advantage we had gained from our historical research. Reportedly, six other firms were bidding for the contract, so the competition was fierce. The committee would choose two finalists, but it turned out that the City Council had reclaimed final decision-making authority. It didn't surprise me that the politicians were changing the rules, introducing an overtly political element that made me doubt we could win.

Raising the stakes even further, Art Longley had put two renovation projects on hold due to the recession. They were our main sources of work, with little else on the horizon. If we didn't get the Pension Building contract, we would definitely have to lay off most of the staff. And they knew it, which made a normally upbeat work environment very stressful. If we had to let people go, their employment prospects weren't very good. Top young architects were having to take draftsmen jobs at half their previous salaries. Fielder, Steinmetz & Way had already laid off ten architects, and other big firms were glutting the market. In my own case, I cut back my draw even more, and our savings were completely depleted. Nicki and I would have to take out a home equity loan just to meet our mortgage payments. Fortunately, our efforts in the New York area had opened a new market to us, and there were prospects in Philadelphia as well that Rich was pursuing. But competition was so strong that we were barely able to build any profit margin into our bids.

After work that day, and despite all my other concerns, what mostly occupied my thoughts during dinner was Elvis. Nicki hadn't raised the subject again. "Mom, would you take Elvis if I need to get rid of her?"

She sighed. "I don't know how Lucifer would take to her." Lucifer was my mom's cat. "She still hasn't forgiven me for the time I was in the hospital." Remarkably, my mother rarely mentioned her bout with cancer. She seemed to be in excellent health now, but the experience had made us all realize how vulnerable she was. Yet here she was, being my rock again.

"Ah, Mom, I can't give up Elvis, anyway. Nicki will just have to put up with her."

It was clear that my mother agreed with me, but she said, "If it really bothers Nicki, you'll have to give her up."

"Nicki will have to deal with it," I replied, projecting confidence that I didn't feel.

Still, my mother had the good sense to make sure Elvis wasn't around when Nicki and Alex came home a few days later. Nicki took the trip badly, experiencing severe pain in her leg, and she was exhausted by the time we arrived. We got her comfortably situated in the bed that was set up in her study, but then she announced she needed to take a shower. She wouldn't let me help her in the bathroom, which worried me, but a few minutes later she came out, her hair in a towel and looking refreshed. She propped her head on top of some pillows in bed and started catching up with soap operas while my mother and I played with Alex on the living room floor.

Eventually Elvis came out to the living room to inspect the new arrival, her golden eyes wide with curiosity. She sniffed Alex approvingly, then sat down on the sofa watchfully. When Alex started crying, Elvis looked up with what appeared to be almost maternal concern. I picked up the baby and rocked her until she calmed. Elvis didn't calm, either, until Alex was pacified. Thereafter the cat would always come running whenever the baby cried, standing watch like a sentry. I had never seen Elvis take so instantly to a newcomer, but I think she sensed this little being was different.

Fortunately, Nicki didn't explode when she realized the cat was still around. "I gather you're not giving her away," she said with what seemed a note of resignation, surprising me totally.

My mother left a couple days after Nicki came home, promising to return in a few months. By that time, Nicki's mother had set up shop again, and Nicki's sister was a frequent visitor, as well. Though my in-laws were polite to my mother, the atmosphere was uncomfortable. But their presence gave me a respite to spend time at the office. Though ordinarily I could do work at home, in the final stages of the Pension Building proposal the staff needed to work closely together.

Finally, the proposal was complete, and all of us were intensely proud of it, absolutely certain that it was the best work of which we were capable. The artist's rendition of the completed building was breathtaking. It appeared just like the building must have when it was first constructed, in all its grandeur. But the true beauty was in the details, from polished mahogany woodwork to gleaming brass railings. And with improved structural integrity, from electrical to plumbing to foundation, all behind the scenes, reflecting the enormous technological innovations that would enhance the building and allow it to stand proud for another century and beyond. It was by far the most ambitious project ever proposed by Horizon. If our design was selected, it would grace not only its immediate surroundings but the entire Capital City.

We submitted it on a Wednesday, and the next day the proposals were all set out for public display in the City Council building on Pennsylvania Avenue (another building that was sadly in need of restoration). The room was filled with architects, not only those who had bid on the contract but dozens more.

I was instantly filled with optimism. Three of the bids were positively feeble, little more than sandblasting the building, shoring up structural support, repainting the interior, and updating the plumbing and wiring. It constantly amazed me how little imagination most architects possessed, in a profession where possibilities were without limit. Two of the other designs were pretty good, both of them using the original building as a base to construct a modern facade, full of glass and marble. Not bad, but in my opinion, not what the building demanded. It was too grand in its own right to do anything other than faithfully and lovingly restore it.

Then there was ours, which stood out as a proud beacon, drawing the most attention.

As I watched, Rich Deeks tapped me on the shoulder. The look on his face was grave. "Come here, there's something you need to see."

He led me over to the one proposal I hadn't seen. When I looked at it I did a double-take: it was a replication of ours. Down even to the brass rooster on top of the bronze dome, a feature that had disappeared from the building half a century earlier. "What the . . .?" I muttered. As I examined the interior design details, the similarities persisted, but there were numerous differences. All of them shared a common denominator: they were cheaper. Wood veneers instead of solid mahogany. Brass and marble overlays. They could shave off half a million dollars on the final construction, though at a severe cost to craftsmanship. I glanced down at the cost estimate, which was two hundred thousand dollars below ours. They had built an extra quarter-million into their profit margin.

I glanced at the presentation plaque: Fielder, Steinmetz & Way. My blood boiled.

And then all at once I heard the nasal voice beside me. "Pretty impressive, huh, Gibbons?" intoned John Friedman Fergaman. "It beats yours by two hundred grand."

I wheeled around to look at him. "You jackass," I bellowed, causing several people to turn toward us, "you stole our concept!"

"C'mon, Kevin," he replied, "this isn't your concept. The whole idea was to restore it to the original, right?" Fergaman was standing so close that I couldn't help but smell the stale stench of cigars on his breath. He lowered his voice and smirked, "And besides, you gotta do what you gotta do, right?"

"You son of a—!" I growled and began to swing at his fat face; but Rich Deeks grabbed my arm and pushed me away, not stopping until I was out of the room. From there he led me out a side exit where no one would see us. "Goddamnit, Rich, that fucker stole our plans!"

"I know. I had a feeling those bastards were behind it, but we can probably never prove it. Fergie's right. We worked off the original design, and so did they. If we could get access to it, so could they."

"Fuck!" I slammed the side of the building so hard it nearly made my fist bleed. "I can't believe that after all that work, they're going to collect the profit."

He shook his head. "Our only hope is that enough of the details are the same that, combined with the break-in, we can sue them for appropriating our design. Sort of like stealing an idea for a song: if enough of the notes are the same, it's copyright infringement. They're probably way too smart for that, but it's our only hope."

"No. Our only hope is to win the competition."

"How? They underbid us by two hundred thousand."

"Yes, but the design committee will see through their shoddy workmanship."

"The City Council, though, will look at the bottom line," he said. "They won't be able to tell the difference in the designs. That's the brilliance of Fergaman's proposal. It looks the same, but they underbid us and still they make more profit. Besides, Ray Scott is in their pocket."

"Who's Ray Scott?"

Rich rolled his eyes. "Man, you really are naive to the ways of this city. Ray Scott is chairman of the City Council Design Review Committee. It's a small committee, five members, but lots of opportunities for graft. Scott controls the committee with an iron fist; half the other members don't even show up for meetings. And Scott is in Fielder, Steinmetz's pocket. They even use his firm for their law work. That's why they control half the work in this city."

"Isn't that a conflict of interest?"

"In any other city it would be, but in this town it's business as usual. Our only real hope is that the design committee doesn't pick theirs as one of the two finalists."

But that hope wasn't realized. When we received the call from the committee on Friday, both our designs were the finalists. The Council committee would make the final decision at its next meeting the following Thursday. Under the circumstances, our prospects were so bleak that I told the staff to leave early and enjoy a long weekend as best they could.

I went home, too. I was happy to find no one there but Nicki and Alex. Nicki was asleep, but Alex was cooing to herself in the bassinet. She was so tiny I could hold her comfortably on my forearm. I took her to the living room, where I spread a blanket on the floor. I started tickling her and, to my surprise, she made little giggling noises, more like hiccups, but definitely mirthful. She looked up at me, helpless, with big attentive eyes. Before I knew it, we were rolling over and over on the blanket, making her even more excited. I wondered if I should be doing this or whether I was rattling her brain or something, but she plainly loved it so I kept doing it. She'd managed to completely drain the stress from me. She truly was magic, and already I loved her more than I had ever loved anyone on Earth.

That night, I coaxed Nicki back to our room and the three of us fell asleep together, but later, worried that one of us would roll over on Alexandra, I carried her to the bassinet. Then, having just had a bolt out of the blue, I went to my office in the next room. I clicked on a lamp and saw that the clock read two-fifteen. I looked up Rich's phone number.

His wife's groggy voice answered on the third ring. Whispering, I apologized for the untimely call and asked to speak to Rich.

"What's up?" he asked.

"Rich, I have an idea, and if you agree, you'll need to get to work on it tomorrow. There are five members on the City Council's Design Review Committee, right?"

"Right."

"And Steinmetz, Fielder & Way controls the chairman, Ray Scott, right?"

"Right."

"Stay with me. That leaves four members."

"Yeah, but like I told you, Scott controls the committee."

"But not if we make it worth the while for the other members to buck him." I tried to swallow, knowing that once I uttered these words I could never take them back. My throat was dry. "I mean two can play at this game. I'm talking about spreading some money around."

Rich was silent for a moment before he responded. "I think we could do that." Rich's mental wheels were working. "Remember the building permit guy whose palm we had to grease on the Kalorama project? Now he works for the Design Review Committee. He could be our go-between."

"If he doesn't get cross-wise with Ray Scott."

"All these guys play both sides."

"Well, let's go for it. And Rich, whatever it costs, it's worth it. It's not just that we need this project. I want to nail that fucker Fergaman's ass."

THE WEEKEND WAS our first together as a family. Nicki was steadily regaining her strength. The weather was pristine, and we took Alex for her first stroller tide around the block, Nicki and I holding hands, admiring the brilliant spring flowers. We couldn't go far because Nicki's leg was sore, but the outing was good for us.

We also had reams of company to welcome baby Alexandra. One was Rich, and as he was leaving, he drew me aside and told me, "The process is underway. I don't know how it will work out. Our emissary says the other members rarely buck Ray Scott on design issues."

"So it will cost more than we expected."

"Of course. And no guarantees."

"Naturally. This is the District of Columbia." Rich and I exchanged knowing glances as other guests approached, saying goodbye.

While Nicki fed Alex, I brought up a subject I had wanted to raise for some time. "Nick, how would you feel about moving?"

"Moving where? New York? California? I know you have clients there, but I want to stay close to home."

"No. I mean someplace local, like MacLean, or Potomac, or even Bethesda."

"Why?"

"D.C. is driving me nuts. I hate the politics. Obviously I have to deal with it professionally, but I hate coming home to it. The potholes. Meter maids. The ridiculous taxes. Crime. Waiting three hours in line to register the car every year. The schools suck. This is no place to raise a child. We could live in one of the nicer close-in suburbs and have twice as much house for the same money." And, I didn't add, maybe the same-size house for less money. Our financial problems were an omnipresent concern.

"No. This is our house. You designed it for us."

"I didn't design it for us. I didn't even know we would end up together when I designed it."

"Yes, you did." And that, as far as Nicki was concerned, was that.

THURSDAY FINALLY ARRIVED. Rich and I represented Horizon at the committee meeting. It was scheduled to begin at ten, but predictably started closer to eleven. Several Fielder, Steinmetz & Way officials were there, including their rising star, John Friedman Fergaman, but wisely they sat on the opposite end of the committee chambers, away from us and avoiding our glances. Several members of the local media were present as well, including two cameras from the local cable access channels.

The Fielder, Steinmetz folks looked positively ebullient, clearly confident that the fix was in. By contrast, Rich had not heard anything definitive from our emissary, despite dispatching more than ten thousand dollars in bribes. For all we knew, not a dollar had reached its intended beneficiaries.

And then the meeting began. Chairman Ray Scott was the first to arrive, shaking hands all around, looking imperiously resplendent as befitting not only a senior member of the District's highest elected body, but a celebrated K Street corporate lawyer. Everything about him reeked of corruption.

By contrast, the other three committee members—one was absent, meaning we needed all three to prevail—looked every inch like hack politicians. Barbara Eddy, Simon Oliver, and Roger Williams represented three of the poorest wards in the city, and all were proteges of the mayor-for-life, Samuel Weaver. That ordinarily placed them at odds with the downtown establishment broker Ray Scott, but apparently not on his committee turf.

After several preliminary matters, the chairman took up the matter of the Pension Building, the largest design and construction contract the city would award during the forthcoming fiscal year. Scott talked about the history of the building, its central importance in the Second Ward—which had been represented for eighteen years by Councilman Williams—and the competition for the design. Finally he extolled the virtues of both proposals—which were virtually identical, he declared, except for their costs. He was clearly preaching to the media, and setting us up for a fall.

Then he asked the other members if they would care to comment. Eddy and Oliver demurred, but Williams obviously felt impelled to perform for the cameras. At first I hoped he might take the chairman on, but it turned out his comments were incoherent, making no point whatsoever except that he deserved all the credit for bringing this project to his ward.

Patiently waiting for Williams' ramble to run its course, Scott finally called for the vote. The chairman was called first. Scott prefaced his vote with additional remarks, again noting that both proposals were superb and nearly identical, but then stating that in view of the considerable cost advantage—along with the outstanding record of public works designed over the years by the esteemed architectural firm of Fielder, Steinmetz & Way—in the name of the public interest, he was impelled to vote for the Fielder, Steinmetz proposal. He went on to express profound (and, in my view, profoundly patronizing) hopes that Horizon would bid on future city projects. Yeah, I thought darkly, he'd be happy to have us provide a convenient cover for his corruption. I glanced across the room at Fergaman, who was grinning insanely.

Next up was Barbara Eddy. She made a statement about the importance of the contract, and seemed uncomfortable being cast in the second voting position. True to that appearance, she passed.

Then Oliver was called. He passed immediately, saying that he would defer to the representative of the ward in which the project was sited. That seemed to me an odd circumstance, given as how the chairman had already expressed his views. It gave me a surge of optimism.

But looking at the seemingly befuddled Williams, my hope faded. If this guy had ever talked straight in his lifetime, it surely wasn't any time recently. Again he delivered a lengthy and pointless diatribe, going on at length about how this was one of the most important buildings in the District.

And then I heard him say two words that made my ears perk up: Roscoe Smith. The elderly retired janitor who had helped us. It turned out Smith was one of Williams' constituents; the men had known each other for more than fifty years. And when Williams was deciding which design to choose, he consulted the one man who knew the building in question better than anyone else: Roscoe Smith. And Roscoe, it turned out, had a strong opinion on the subject.

All of a sudden, Roger Williams was making abundant sense to me. All the more when he cast his vote for Horizon.

Chairman Scott gavelled down the unruly audience which was murmuring surprise, and he called for a recess. But Simon Oliver suggested that the chairman's motion was out of order as a vote was pending, and Scott relented. Eddy was called and she voted for Horizon; then Oliver did likewise. Chairman Scott sheepishly announced the result: Horizon had won the contract, three votes to one.

Rich and I hugged each other. Instantly we were surrounded by the media, for which I was completely unprepared. "We are honored to have this contract, and pledge to restore the Pension Building to its original grandeur, making it once again the pride of southeast Washington," I said. I couldn't help but add with a grin, "I hope this will cement Horizon Architects as the premier renovation firm in the nation's capital."

As the media began to dissipate following spirited questioning, someone grabbed my shoulder. I turned around and saw it was Fergaman. "Oh, hi, Fergie!"

"What did you have to do to steal this contract away from us? We were the low bidder."

Frankly, I didn't know the answer to his question. Was it the bribes? Did they even ever reach Williams, and did they determine his vote? Or was our ace in the hole Roscoe Smith, and the committee's decision an exercise in civic virtue? To those questions we would never know the answer.

So instead, all I said to the incredulous Fergaman was, "You gotta do what you gotta do."

25

I AWOKE TO the same thoughts I had fallen asleep to, with ideas about the latest project cascading relentlessly through my mind. Great, I thought: now I'm building projects even in my dreams. That's all I need, as if fifty or sixty daylight hours every week weren't enough.

I glanced over at the clock and saw that it was only six. Theoretically, I could go back to sleep for another half hour. But I probably wouldn't fall asleep; I'd just lay there tossing and turning unproductively. So I may as well get up and make some money off my mental endeavors. I reached across and found an empty bed. Nicki must be up sculling on the Potomac River. I had to give her credit: I didn't think she would stick with getting up at five-thirty three times a week to brave the morning fog and chill of Georgetown and go rowing with a bunch of young athletes. But she was persisting, at least for now. It was her latest scheme to shed the last of the weight she had gained during her pregnancy. She'd had to abandon jogging due to her leg ailment, and sculling provided the benefit of an intense aerobic workout without stress on her leg.

Nicki hadn't yet returned to work, instead spending part of her days at home, and the remainder in a variety of volunteer activities, leaving Alex either to her mother or more frequently to Rita, our part-time nanny from El Salvador. But she was starting to send résumés around, feeling anxious to resume her career. Her conduct lately was both restless and aimless, a dangerous and irritable combination for Nicki, so I encouraged her in whatever she wanted to do, hoping she would find a clear direction soon. For now, the sculling occupied her energy and I was grateful for it.

I glanced at the little photograph of Alex that adorned the shelf over the toilet. I nearly burst out laughing, as I often did when I saw it. The photo was taken on one of our sojourns to a renovation site, to which Alex frequently accompanied me. There was my little girl wearing a construction hat—or, as she called it, her "fire hat"—which I had custom-made for her. Still, it was huge and nearly covered her eyes.

Last time I showed her around a project, I was explaining in the simplest possible terms the changes we were making. She peered up at me from beneath the cockeyed construction helmet, gave me a knowing glance, and asked, "Are they struck-chool?" When I realized the big-person term she was trying the use, I burst out laughing, and she had laughed too, just like she was in this picture.

Alex epitomized the word precocious, I thought. It amazed me that someone so little could have such a complex, fully formed personality already. It was like Nicki's in some ways, like mine in others, and completely unique in yet other respects. Alex was self-absorbed and generous like her mother, artistic and sensitive like me, and feisty and quick-tempered like neither of us. She accepted and bestowed affection freely; but withheld it when angry. All that and more in a pint-sized, pony-tailed package. The "terrible twos," they called it, and that's exactly what it was, except that mostly it was wonderful.

After my shower, I got dressed quickly and sneaked into her room. She heard the door open and stirred. I looked down at her. She may have inherited a bit of both our personalities, I mused, but her looks were all Nicki.

"Hey, Princess, wanna have breakfast with Daddy before he leaves for work?"

In a single fluid movement, she roused to her feet and lifted her arms toward me in reply. I lifted her high in the air, kissed both her cheeks, and lowered her to the floor. Her upraised hand barely reached mine as we scurried toward the kitchen. "Can have grogurt?" she asked in her little-girl voice. Grogurt was our term for the combination of granola and yogurt; in her case, cherry-flavored. Nicki eschewed traditional children's breakfasts in favor of healthier alternatives, and we were delighted that Alex's favorite was grogurt.

"Of course." We walked out to the kitchen hand-in-hand. Everywhere in the apartment there were little step-stairs to allow Alex to elevate herself to tasks and curiosities. Together we fixed our breakfast. Alex's job was stirring the granola and yogurt together, which she performed with a facility belying her two years and one month.

I made coffee for myself and poured some milk in a covered mug for Alex.

"Can I have chocklit in it?"

I glanced over at her. Nicki had warned me repeatedly that I would be able to deny nothing to Alex, and for the most part I had found that to be true. Seeing her hopeful expression, I said, "Okay, but don't tell Mommy, 'kay?"

"'Kay, Daddy." She snickered through her nose, a sound so like one that Nicki made that it caused my skin to tingle.

Alex had outgrown her high chair and now sat in a booster seat at the table, very lady-like. As we ate we talked, or rather Alex mostly talked. Even though her vocabulary was limited, she was a loquacious little girl. She recounted scene by scene what had happened in yesterday's *Sesame Street*, and speculated over what might happen in today's show. "Rita took me to get a shovel and pail for our bacation," Alex announced cheerfully. The nanny was a godsend, about thirty years old with four children of her own, but totally committed to her second family.

Our trip to Bermuda the following month would be our first true family vacation together. Nicki and I had taken off for two weeks the previous summer, leaving Alex for a week with each grandmother while we drove up the California coast. We had stayed as overnight guests in Jule Maguire's gorgeous new house, which I showed off to Nicki like a trophy. Now I had showed Alex where Bermuda was on a map, and she seemed excited but uncomprehending. "You know how you like to play in the sand-box at the playground?"

"Yes."

"Well, the beach in Bermuda is like having a *million* sandboxes, with big waves coming in and erasing everything you make."

Alex's light brown eyes widened in wonder. "The Count says that a million is the biggest number of all!" she said, instantly relating what I told her back to her favorite television show.

"And speaking of which, how would you like to go watch *Sesame Street* until Mommy comes home?" She answered by lifting her arms up.

I grabbed a second cup of coffee, then decided to ditch my plans to get some early work done. Instead, I went to the living room where Alex was occupying the center of the sofa, glued to the television set. Elvis was curled up next to her, and Alex was absently and gently stroking the cat's fur. Elvis's eyes were mere slits of ecstasy. Alex noticed me at last and patted the sofa on the other side. "Sit down and watch with me and Elvis, Daddy."

I sat down next to her, and instantly she reconfigured to lay her head on my lap. One big difference between Nicki and Alex was that Alex loved to be fussed with, and would always thrust her head or feet onto the nearest available lap; or both if two laps happened to present themselves. Often Alex would form a human bridge between Nicki and me, which I thought an apt metaphor. I wished that the daughter could teach her mother something about physical affection, but so far it hadn't rubbed off.

Alex explained in animated fashion everything I was seeing. She pumped her feet in excitement, which disturbed the slumbering Elvis and induced her to sulk off for a bite of cat food in the kitchen.

Then the front door opened and Nicki came in, exhausted, dressed in a windbreaker and sweats and wearing her glasses, her hair pulled back in a ponytail.

I extricated myself from Alex and busied myself in the kitchen, fixing something for Nicki to eat, then got dressed for work. As I came back out to the living room, Nicki was occupying my previous place on the sofa, with Alex on her lap. I kissed them both, and left for the office.

It was a busy time, growing busier all the time because of the improving economy and our growing reputation. We had grown to fourteen architects, half of them assigned to the Pension Building, which was nearing completion. We were thinking of opening a new office and deploying some of our staff to New York or Philadelphia, as our business had expanded in both cities. Rich, a partner now, was managing the office on a daily basis. We now occupied the entire floor of our building, and the overall staff had grown to twenty-two. My work was focused on designing our top-dollar projects, exactly as I wished it would be, but rather than shrinking my workload, it had increased. The firm was still identified as my alter ego, and clients demanded my personal attention.

By the time we left for the sunny Atlantic island, I was desperately in need of a break from work. On the flight over, Nicki referred several times to our previous trip to the island as if it had been one of our best experiences, and she seemed oblivious to my muteness in response. This time we stayed at a beachfront resort that had a children's program, which allowed Nicki and me to explore the island on mopeds while Alex was entertained with arts and crafts. Alex absolutely loved the crashing waves, to which I introduced her cradled safely in my arms.

One thing I love about Bermuda is the fact that everything is open-air. You can keep the shutters to your bedroom open at night and sleep in the lilting breeze. Restaurants and bars are open to the soft air, lending a mellow and romantic atmosphere.

I couldn't have been more relaxed as we sat down for breakfast in the hotel's beachfront restaurant, the sun bathing the white-sand beach in brilliant morning light.

"We should consider buying a time-share here," I suggested.

"I like the idea of exploring new places better," said Nicki. "There're a whole world of beaches out there."

As much as I loved Bermuda, I liked her idea better. The thought of the three of us beach-combing in exotic locations like Hawaii, the Caribbean, and Fiji made me positively ebullient. I was enjoying my life, very much.

Alex ate a few bites of breakfast, but the abundance of possibilities made her bored and fidgety, and she squirmed on Nicki's lap. Accepting the inevitable, Nicki let her down to run around.

Alex's absence gave Nicki and me a chance to talk about everything and nothing. Nicki was stressed over her inability to find a job. She wanted something part-time but professionally fulfilling, and that was a difficult mix. Plus, I had a feeling the hotel where she had worked most recently was blackballing her. It was vicariously frustrating, but as usual Nicki resisted my ideas and offers of assistance.

She complained about her leg. Nine months of rehabilitation had strengthened it, but left her with a slight limp and recurrent pain. It had also left her thigh swollen, a fact that Nicki commented upon now that she was in a bathing suit for the first time since her pregnancy.

My mind wandered, as it so often did when Nicki was talking. Once I realized it, I turned my thoughts back to the conversation. Nicki was talking about where we should have dinner and whether we should make reservations. "I think Papagallo's would be nice because that's the first place you mentioned something about getting married." Nicki's memory was amazing. "But the Royal Palm has a really nice buffet, and I think Alex would enjoy the opulence."

I didn't think our toddler could yet appreciate opulence, though her mom surely was working on it. "Whatever you think. Though maybe Alex would like the clowns at—"

My comment was suddenly cut off by a pile of dishes crashing to the floor from somewhere behind Nicki. Both of us winced at the sound, then Nicki stood bolt upright and rushed toward the sound. She had instantly sensed it was Alex. The mental connection between the two of them manifested itself so often that it was uncanny, and I shivered despite the warm air.

I stood too and all I could see was cacophony, waiters and busboys bustling frantically. Out of the midst of it, Nicki swooped Alex up and strode back toward the table. Alex's cheeks were streaked with tears and one of her feet bore a tiny rivulet of blood.

"Shh, shh, baby, it's all right," Nicki soothed her. She sat back down with Alex on her lap, and I sat down as well.

"Is she okay?" I asked.

"She's fine," Nicki replied, dabbing at the injury with a wet napkin.

"Make sure there's no glass in there."

"It's just a tiny scratch."

Alex was down to sniffling, though her eyes were red from crying. In the background, several hotel staffers were attending to the mess that Alex had created.

"Hey, young lady," I said to Alex, catching her attention. "That's what your Mommy meant about getting into mischief."

Alex looked at me sadly. Nicki retorted sharply, "Don't yell at her!"

I was taken aback by the unexpected fury of Nicki's reaction. "I'm not yelling at her. I was explaining to her that knocking over a stack of dishes is mischief, and that's what she's not supposed to get into." Nicki looked away from me, continuing to dab Alex's foot even though the flow of blood had stopped. "She really could have hurt herself, Nick."

Nicki turned and fixed her green eyes on me. "They shouldn't put the dishes so close to the edge. You should sue them."

I pushed back from the table. I would've thought she was joking if Nicki had that habit. "That's ridiculous, Nicki. They can't anticipate a little two-year-old running around creating havoc."

Now Nicki pushed back from the table. "Let's go, Alex," she said. "Your father doesn't like our company. We'll spend the day alone together." And with that Nicki whisked off, Alex on her shoulder staring back at me, her face devoid of expression and her thumb planted in her mouth.

Banished from their company, I spent the rest of the day sitting on a chaise lounge by the pool, pretending to read but wondering morosely how such an idyllic vacation had so utterly gotten out of hand. But by evening, Nicki and Alex were talking to me again as if nothing had happened other than a planned girls-only outing. Trouble was, my enthusiasm had waned, and we had only one more full day before we returned to Washington. It passed too quickly, though we did get to explore a lighthouse at the northern end of the island from which the view of Bermuda and the surrounding turquoise water was sublime. My spirits rekindled a bit, but not completely.

Before we knew it we were on the plane again. "Let's go back to Bermuda again next year, Daddy."

Echoing Nicki's earlier words, I replied, "There's a world of beaches to explore, Alex." At that, Nicki delivered a sideways smile. I knew that for her, at least, the incident was behind us. Whatever anger she had built up toward me recently for whatever reason was now spent, and now she was beckoning me back with sunshine.

As for me, however, I couldn't wait to get back to work. A week of Nicki's company was a larger dose than I could handle. At least in that respect, Bermuda had provided a needed tonic of sorts.

We returned to the penthouse late on Sunday evening. When we arrived, Alex was still high-strung from the trip and practically bouncing off the walls. Elvis, whose care had been entrusted to our housekeeper during our absence, came out to greet us. Suddenly and inexplicably, Alex fell to her knees and started pulling the cat across the room by her tail. Elvis wailed and tried without success to pull away from Alex's grasp.

"Alex, let go of Elvis's tail!" I yelled. I had never had occasion to use such a harsh tone with her. Alex recoiled and let go. Elvis swung around angrily and scratched Alex's hand. Alex immediately started screaming, even more intensely as she looked down and saw blood welling from her hand. Elvis sulked away as Nicki swooped in and picked up her hysterical daughter.

"Kevin, I told you to get rid of that awful cat!" Nicki bellowed over Alex's screams as she took the girl to the kitchen sink to wash her hand.

I stood by myself in the living room for a moment, temporarily dumbfounded. The whole scene was like *déjà vu* from only two days previous.

Then I snapped to and stomped into the kitchen. "Nicki, god-damnit, Alex knows better than to pull the cat's tail."

Overdoing the hand-washing in streaming water, Nicki glowered at me. "Don't use that kind of language in front of Alex."

"Oh, yeah, I forgot about your virginal Catholic ears," I sneered. I realized that my reaction reflected the accumulated irritation that had built up over the previous few days, but I couldn't contain myself.

Alex was still sobbing, surely stoked by the feverish emotional pitch surrounding her. "Don't you care about your daughter?" Nicki asked, projecting her view of the answer through the tone of the question.

"Yes, I care about Alex. And if she gets hurt I want to comfort her. But all of a sudden you're giving her positive reinforcement for misbehaving."

Nicki glared at me for a moment, then turned off the water and picked Alex up again. "Come on, sweetheart, Mommy will take you to the bathroom and put a band-aid on your boo-boo." As she strode off, I heard her say in a softer but still stern voice, "That bad old cat."

I knew it was going to be a rough night. As I brought our suit-cases to our bedroom and unpacked them, I could hear Nicki banging around elsewhere in the apartment and running bath-water for Alex, who by now had calmed down. I had no idea where Elvis went.

As I got ready for bed, I wondered if I would see Nicki again that night, or if she would punish me by sleeping elsewhere in the condo. I decided to venture out into the hallway. The door to Nicki's study was closed, meaning that I would be sleeping alone that night. I changed course for Alex's bedroom, and entered in the soft glow from her nightlight. She was sucking her thumb in her crib, just shy of falling asleep.

"How is your boo-boo?" I asked.

"It hurts. My foot hurts, too."

"Alex," I said, "you understand why Elvis scratched you, don't you?"

"Because she's a bad cat," Alex stated categorically.

"No," I replied, irritated at Nicki all over again. "You can't pull a cat's tail. In fact, it's wrong to hurt any animal. And if you hurt an animal, sometimes they'll hurt you back." Alex looked up at me without expression. "Elvis didn't mean to hurt you. You were hurting her and she wanted you to stop. She'll probably lick you tomorrow to show you she's sorry she hurt you, just like you're sorry, right?"

Alex said nothing.

"Right?"

Finally, Alex responded in a low and serious voice. "I don't like Elvis anymore."

I looked down at Alex for several moments. Her eyes were shiny but her expression willful. I reproached myself for expecting a two-year-old to understand complex emotions, particularly when her mother's reactions were utterly irrational.

As I crawled into bed, I was frankly grateful for the solitude Nicki had given me that night. Life with my wife could be very trying. I glanced at the clock: eleven-thirty. I hoped Nicki wasn't going sculling in the morning, so I could get to the office early. I wanted to vacate the premises as quickly as possible and get back to a world of greater normalcy.

I was awakened by shrill screams at dawn. Alex.

My heart pounded as I threw off the bedcovers. Alex sometimes experienced frightening nightmares, just like any child, but these screams were bloodcurdling.

As I rounded the doorway into the hall, Nicki emerged at the same time from her study. We both ran to Alex's bedroom.

As we entered, Alex was screaming, "Elvis! Elvis!" in between hysterical cries.

"Oh my God! What has that cat done now?" Nicki bellowed. She lifted Alex out of the crib, patting her back and trying to calm her down.

I had no idea what was happening. I looked frantically around the room and didn't see Elvis anywhere. Then looked inside Alex's crib and saw the cat's telltale white fur near Alex's pillow. Had Elvis jumped into Alex's crib? She had never even attempted to do that before.

Nicki saw her, too. "Get that cat out of there!" she demanded.

I pulled the pillow away, expecting Elvis to scamper off. But instead she lay there motionless. Finally I realized that the cat had suffocated beneath Alex's pillow. She was dead.

At some unknown point Alex's bedroom had descended into complete silence, so much that I could hear the pounding of my own heart. I lifted the cat from the crib, my head spinning in disbelief and incomprehension. "No, Ellie, no," I murmured, trying to deny the painful reality. My cat, my wonderful feline companion.

I stood there dumbly, my throat constricting, trying unsuccessfully to fathom what could possibly have happened. At last I glanced over at my wife and daughter on the other side of the room. They regarded me silently. Save for Alex's thumb in her mouth, their expressions were identical, completely impassive.

Tears suddenly clouding my vision, I clutched my cat's stiffening body to my chest and fled the room.

24

ALEX SCRAMBLED UP the hill, her blonde ponytail bobbing halfway down her back. "I'm gonna catch you!" I cried.

She convulsed with giggles. "No you're not!" she insisted. Then she looked back and screamed as I made a lunge for her. She scampered up, and gained a foothold on the top of the hill, whereupon she dashed forward.

What a fast little bugger, I thought, a four-and-a-half year-old bundle of energy. And her old man's slowing down, that's for sure.

I finally gained the top of the hill as well. I chased after her until I closed the gap, just as we reached Nicki, who was stretched out on our picnic blanket. Alex fell on her, still screaming and laughing, and knocked the wind out of her mother. I piled on, and now Nicki joined the screaming too as I tickled both of them. Nicki wasn't ticklish, but Alex was, helplessly so, and I took full advantage of her weakness.

"Help me, Mommy!" Alex begged between gasps for air.

"You're crushing me!" Nicki protested.

I grabbed Alex and pushed myself up to my feet. Then I took her arms and twirled her around and around.

"You're going to make her dizzy," Nicki said as she sat up on the blanket. But she merely smiled and shook her head as Alex and I spun around. Alex squealed with delight. Then we slowed and I set her down. She tried to take a step but then collapsed on the blanket, still giggling. "I'm too dizzy!" she exclaimed.

I was, too, and I fell down next to her, panting from the exertion. "You are silly," Nicki observed.

"We're the entertainment committee for your birthday," I puffed.

It was Nicki's thirty-sixth birthday, and the day happened to fall on a Sunday. We had decided to celebrate with a late autumn drive into the Virginia countryside, stopping at Linden Winery for a bottle of chardonnay that accompanied the picnic lunch Alex and I had assembled. My surprise contribution was salmon mousse, just like Nicki and I had enjoyed on one of our first dates; Alex had suggested gingerbread cookies for dessert, which happened to be her favorite. The day was gorgeous, the last throes of Indian summer.

Nicki reconfigured to lay on her back, and Alex leaned back against her breast.

"Okay, you two, it's such a beautiful day, I have to take a picture." With Nicki and Alex, one didn't have to ask twice. As I took out the camera, Nicki rose to her knees and gathered her daughter in her arms. The sun brought out the color of their eyes, Nicki's green and Alex's light brown. Their smiles beamed brightly and I snapped the picture.

Nicki kissed Alex loudly. "You're Mommy's little fashion model, aren't you?"

"Yes," Alex replied.

"All right, you two narcissists, we've got to gather up and make the drive home."

"What's a narcipiss, Daddy?"

I chuckled. "I guess it's someone who's self-centered and has a bad attitude, all at the same time."

"Kevin," Nicki scolded me, "you're going to confuse her."

"Oh, you'll straighten her out," I said. It actually was a good day for Nicki. She'd lost her part-time job at a family-owned travel agency over a personality conflict with the owner. Recurring pain in her leg had forced her to curtail sculling. But things were beginning to look up, it seemed. She had taken up some new hobbies, most recently shooting at the pistol range, which Nicki enjoyed although the thought of my wife with a gun in her hands terrified me. And a few weeks earlier, she had gotten a new job as advertising director for a college radio station in Maryland. She loved it and was crazy about the station manager, Gil Van Sant. I hoped for the best: when Nicki's life was going well, all of our lives were going well.

THREE MONTHS LATER, I found myself in an adrenaline rush as I drove home from the office. It was unusual to come home in the daylight hours and I exhilarated in it. Wednesdays were Nicki's late night at the radio station, filling in for the news producer, so I tried to come home early and spend time with Alex. It offered an enjoyable break from the usual routine.

But that day I was even more pumped up than usual. Even though I wasn't sure how to surmount the obstacles, the offer I'd received earlier in the day from Sally Kriegman, dean of the Cornell University School of Architecture, was enticing. I would teach a fall semester course in architectural renovation at their campus in Rome. They would provide an apartment in the heart of the city for the family, and we would have two weeks of vacation in October during which we could explore Italy. I had visited Rome as an architecture student and had loved it. To spend an entire four months in residence there—and to have the opportunity to visit Florence, which was one of my dreams—was head-spinning.

Still, it would require serious sacrifices. I would have to be away from the firm for a long time. But the teaching demands would be relatively light, and with FAX and modem, I could be in constant contact with the office. The staff was competent, and Rich ran the office anyway. On the other hand, I would have to prepare assiduously to teach the course.

Perhaps more problematic was Nicki's position at the radio station; her skills seemed to be in demand, so perhaps she could find another position if she gave this one up, or possibly the station might even hold her position for her.

Alex was supposed to start kindergarten in the fall, but this diversion certainly wouldn't disrupt her education. Indeed, one thing that made the offer attractive was the opportunity to introduce Alex to life in a foreign country at a formative age. Maybe she could even learn some Latin or Italian. The image of Alex spouting words in a foreign language—especially one so lyrical as Italian—made me smile.

Despite the logistical challenges—which might prove insurmountable—I wanted to make it work. But I tried to constrain my enthusiasm, because Nicki was definitely the deciding factor. Her moods lately had improved as she had regained a measure of confidence in returning to her professional roots in communications.

As I let myself into the house, I heard Rita puttering in the kitchen. What would we do with her if we went to Rome? Even though she was like a member of our family, she had kids of her own, and certainly couldn't spend four months away from home. And the market for competent nannies, particularly in Washington, was intense, so we would lose her for sure if we let her go temporarily. I guessed I would have to pay her, maybe lending her to Alex's nursery school, in order to keep her.

"Hello, Mr. G," Rita greeted me. She had moved to the United States with her children, after having taken care of her ailing mother until she died of tuberculosis. Try as I might to convince her to call me Kevin, the best I could do was to get her down to the first letter of my surname.

"Hello, Mrs. L." She sent me an amused frown. "Where's Alex?"

"She's in her room, drawing, I think."

"Did you guys have a good day?"

"Yes, mostly," she replied. "The *señiorita* went to nursery school, then we had an ice cream soda at Fagin's, the neighborhhod ice cream shop, then she played for awhile in the afternoon next door with Mrs. Beeman. They watched soap operas and Mrs. Beeman baked chocolate chip cookies."

Our elderly neighbor seemed to delight in Alex's company. We rationed Alex's visits because I didn't want Alex to wear Mrs. Beeman out. The odd-couple relationship summoned mental images of a female version of Mr. Wilson and Dennis the Menace.

"Oh great, an ice cream soda and chocolate chip cookies. Alex will be bouncing off the walls."

"Well, right now she's quiet."

I walked down the hallway to Alex's room, pausing outside her door. The room was vintage Nicki and Alex: busy and frilly and feminine. The room was strewn with Alex's huge collection of stuffed animals, which she favored over dolls and invested with distinctive and complex personalities.

Alex was sprawled lengthwise on the floor, facing away from me. Stretched out that way, it was striking how long her body was for her age, and how slender. Her blonde hair was fixed into a ponytail, bobbing slightly as she concentrated on her work. I entered the room quietly and looked over her shoulder.

Alex was sketching on a tablet. Her drawing skills were unbelievable, and not inherited from me or Nicki. I leaned down and kissed her on the back of her head, inhaling the scent of her hair.

She turned her head to see who it was. "Oh, hi, Daddy."

"Beautiful drawing," I said.

"Oh, thanks, Daddy."

"Why are Mr. Bear and Dragon smiling at the turtle?" I asked.

"Mr. Green lost his shell." I had forgotten the turtle's name. "See, there it is on the ground." Alex pointed to a curved object at the bottom of the drawing. It struck me as slightly macabre.

"But why are they smiling?"

"Because Mr. Green is homeless."

"But it's not funny for someone to be homeless."

"Mommy says when people are homeless, it's their own fault." She rolled over and cast a frown in my direction, as if telling me something I should know.

"But it's not Mr. Green's fault that he lost his shell, right?"

"Yes, it is. He didn't pay his rent."

I burst out laughing. "Come here." She scurried to her feet, giggling along with me now even though she wasn't sure why. I kneeled down and gave her a big hug.

Alex pulled away from me, still smiling. "Daddy, can you take me shopping?" Like mother, like daughter.

"Sure. Why?"

"I want to buy Tessie something." Tessie was her best friend, a beautiful brown-haired girl who was a year older than Alex but a couple inches shorter. Her parents had held her back from kindergarten for a year, so she was in Alex's preschool class.

"Is it her birthday?"

"No. You told me that if I like someone, you should give them presents even if it's not their birthday. Or even Christmas."

Alex had inherited her mother's impulsive generosity. "You're right and that's really sweet. How about if we go shopping on Saturday?"

"Can we go to Nordie's?"

"Good grief, you have expensive taste." I knew who she inherited that from, too. Alex looked at me expectantly. "Of course we can go to Nordie's." Alex flew into my arms and rewarded me with a hug.

Rita went home and Alex and I decided to wait to have dinner until Nicki came home around eight-thirty. It was late for Alex to eat, as we usually put her to bed around nine, but it would be a treat for Nicki. In anticipation, I had Alex bathed and in her pajamas by eight.

Nicki came home just as I was extracting a bottle of wine from our new temperature-controlled wine cabinet. Even though the radio station was informal, Nicki wore professional clothes every day, as befitting her status as the oldest (and presumably most mature) member of a very young staff. The clothes showed off her figure. She was more slender than at any time since I'd known her, and she looked fantastic. More like twenty-six than thirty-six.

Alex came flying out of the hallway into her mother's arms, chattering about her day and the fact that I would be taking her to Nordstrom's on Saturday. Nicki glanced in my direction, and though she was polite to Alex she seemed distracted.

"I don't feel like having dinner, or wine," Nicki said as I came over to peck her cheek. "I have a headache and I'm tired, so I think I'm just going to take a shower and go to bed."

That was a surprise. Usually when Nicki came home from work she was full of chatter about her day, and Alex and I could barely get a word in edgewise.

I glanced at Alex, who looked as disappointed as I felt. "Okay, we'll have dinner by ourselves."

"Okay," Nicki replied, and she disappeared into the hallway.

"Well, it's just you and me, then, kiddo." I reluctantly returned the wine to the cabinet.

"I'll have Mommy's wine."

I laughed. "No, I don't think so. But you can have Mommy's dessert, okay?"

"Okay!"

After she went to bed, I sat quietly in the living room; I hadn't had much time to myself lately. The solitude was so rare that I savored it. I ruminated on our life. Work was fulfilling and profitable. Nicki and I could aspire to anything, and nothing was unattainable. We would be able to send Alex to a good private school. We were entertaining regularly, and Nicki relished and excelled in the role of Washington hostess. All three of us were in good health.

Alex was a joy, for the most part. She experienced terrible temper tantrums, mostly when she didn't get her way. I was trying to teach her that she could get more from honey than vinegar. But Nicki often contradicted me, siding with her daughter constantly, no matter how irrational the outburst. The two of them shared an almost preternatural bond, often communicating without words. It was scary. They were in a sense closer than other mothers and daughters, yet lacking some essential emotional connection I could not identify.

It was after twelve when I finally went to bed, thinking about going to Italy. It seemed like no time at all had passed when the alarm clock started beeping. I took my time shutting it off because I knew Nicki would already have left for work. Thursday was her early day, which was rough because it followed her late Wednesdays. Maybe that was why Nicki was so grouchy last night.

But then I felt her stirring in bed beside me. "Shut off the alarm," she mumbled.

I turned over and looked at her, as if confirming her presence. Sure enough, it was Nicki.

"Turn it off!" Nicki ordered.

I fumbled for the alarm clock and switched it off, then rolled over to look at Nicki, who was facing away from me in a fetal position. I tried to organize my thoughts. "Nicki, don't you have work today?"

She turned just her head to face me. Her eyes were red. "I'm not going into work. I quit last night."

"What?!"

She had turned away from me again, and mumbled into her pillow. "Gil and I weren't getting along. I don't think he liked having an older woman around who knows more about radio than he does. He resents it."

I was stupefied. Nicki had raved about Gil Van Sant. He was a talented young man—but heck, at thirty, only six years younger than Nicki—who had managed to make a go of a tiny radio station. I thought Nicki loved her job. Though now that I thought about it, I realized Nicki hadn't been so ebullient about it lately. But now another short-duration employment? Her résumé was beginning to look like a battlefield. Not that we needed financially for her to work, but even with a heavy volunteering schedule, Nicki went stir-crazy when she wasn't working. And when Nicki was stir-crazy, it was contagious for everyone around.

"Are you sure it's not just a tiff, Nicki?"

"After the things I said to him last night, believe me, it's over." She pulled the blankets over her shoulder. "I want to go back to sleep."

As usual, Nicki was cutting off questions and accepting no comfort. So there was little to do but get up for work.

Rita was coming in just as I was writing her a note telling her what had happened. Instead, I told her. "Don't worry about it; she'll be fine."

I could tell Rita was unsettled by the news. She didn't like instability, and I think Nicki's mercurial temperament unnerved her. But she would brave it out.

The whole thing bothered me all the way to work. What was it with Nicki? Finally she was happy, and then she had to go wreck it by getting into an argument with the boss. Yet why was I assuming it was her fault? I had met Gil at one of our dinner parties, and though he seemed a little too politically correct for my tastes, he was clearly competent. But who could figure it out? Certainly, getting a straight story from Nicki wasn't in the cards. At about ten-thirty, I realized it was driving me to distraction and I had to do something about it. I picked up the phone, then hung it up again. Considering the matter for all of about a second, I launched myself out of my office.

The drive to College Park took forty-five minutes in midday traffic. Still, as I reached the radio station, I realized I hadn't even formulated the semblance of an objective, much less a plan. Nicki would be fit to be tied if she knew what I was doing, but I was tired of being kept outside of the inner sanctum of her life. On one hand, I was curious about why Nicki had lost another job. Her professional pattern paralleled her friendships: at first she was totally thrilled, everything was wonderful, then she started souring and finding faults. For weeks, everything was Gil this and Gil that. He was so talented, so nice, so funny. If it wasn't the same reaction Nicki had toward everyone, I would have thought she had a crush on him. Her relationships were like roller coasters, lots of hills and curves, but always seeming to end up at the bottom. On the other hand, perhaps Nicki wasn't at fault this time. She had genuinely loved her job, at least in the beginning; and she'd been totally committed to it. I hated to see her unhappy. Maybe it was the snot-nosed kid who was to blame. And if so, I intended to let him know how I felt about it.

I walked inside the entrance of the small building housing KMDC to the reception desk and asked for Gil. She called Gil as I looked around. There was Nicki's office door with the nameplate still intact: Nicole Gibbons, Ass't Mgr./Advertising. Her sudden departure appeared to have been unanticipated. Then the receptionist led me down the hall, past the two studios, to the door at the end. His nameplate brought a smile to myself for the formality of his name: W. Guilford Van Sant III, Station Manager. No wonder he had adopted a nickname.

I opened the door and Gil was seated behind a old wooden desk piled high with papers and compact disks. As always, he wore jeans and a crisp white shirt; his beard was neatly trimmed, his medium-length brown hair was slicked back, and he wore a diamond stud in his right earlobe. Not handsome, but very stylish.

"What can I help you with, Mr. Gibbons?" He did not rise to shake my hand.

"Why the formal manner?" I asked. "It was just Kevin the last time I saw you."

"I assume you're here to dispute your wife's dismissal."

"Dismissal? I thought she quit."

Gil made a snorting sound. "In a manner of speaking, she did. She took action she knew would lead to immediate termination."

Now I was glad I hadn't prepared a speech. This revelation would have knocked me off my stride. "What was that?"

Now Gil smiled, but it wasn't a happy smile. "I'm not surprised she didn't tell you, but I can't discuss it. It's the station's firm policy not to discuss personnel matters."

"Lookit, Gil, I'm not here to sue you, or threaten you. I just want to find out what happened." He stared at me without expression, taking my measure. "I'm concerned about Nicki. I promise, whatever you tell me will not leave this room. Even to Nicki." I could tell his resolve was softening. "Besides, I'm not the type to hire a lawyer. I hate lawyers."

His phone rang and he picked it up. "Yeah," he said. "No, tell him I'll call back in five minutes." He hung up and rubbed his face with his hands. Suddenly he looked tired, and older than thirty. Management will do that to you, I thought. That and dealing with Nicki. He put his hands behind his head and leaned back in his chair. "She didn't tell you anything?"

"Nothing. I thought everything was going fine."

"Well, it was, for a few weeks. She has enormous energy, and was running around the place, talking a mile a minute, getting our advertisers to double their ads. Even then, though, I thought she was manic or something. Then she had a couple of turn-downs from advertisers, nothing surprising, but she took it personally. She started insulting our clients. Insulting their intelligence. 'You must not know anything about advertising,' she'd say, 'because anyone who knew about advertising would double their budget with KMDC.' I couldn't believe it, but I heard the same story from several people. And, of course, instead of doubling their advertising, they cut it altogether. After two months, accounts were up seventeen percent; after four, they were down ten percent. We're a small station. We can't handle that kind of hit.

"At first I let it go, then a few weeks ago, we started having it out. It was difficult, because she's an older woman. She didn't make it any easier, treating me condescendingly, like a child. Even then, I would've tried to work through it. I've fired plenty of interns, but never a professional. But her other behavior was what really was driving everyone up the wall. She was hitting on every guy here, me included."

I was flabbergasted. "Hitting on you?"

"Don't get me wrong. She wasn't hitting in the sense that she seemed to be trying to have affairs. It was, how should I say it?—vicarious. She was just always talking to the guys about sex. Asking what they did on dates, how sex was with their girlfriends, talking about stuff guys do, very explicit. Totally inappropriate. Most of these guys talk about sex all the time, among themselves. But she's almost old enough to be their mother in some instances. We're talking college kids. And it made the female employees uncomfortable, too." I knew my face must be crimson, but Gil seemed oblivious. "I think she wanted to fit in, be treated like a college girl, and be considered attractive by all these young guys. She certainly is high on her own appearance, that's for sure, and she seemed desperate for reassurance. It was weird, Kevin. Pathetic. She was a walking sexual harassment lawsuit waiting to happen."

I was hoping Gil was through, but he wasn't. "So last night we had it out. There was one advertiser, Clover Dale Cleaners, who dropped an account, and I told Nicki about it and she freaked out. I couldn't even talk to her about the other stuff, she was too angry. So then she went on the air—you know Wednesdays are her on-air night, reading the news—and told listeners that we had pulled the advertisements for Clover Dale Cleaners because we had gotten too many customer complaints about them. Can you fucking believe that? I hauled her back into my office and fired her."

My head was reeling, but Gil still wasn't done yet. "I told her to pack her things and leave, and she did that, banging around like she was going to topple the studio over. But even after she left, she wasn't completely gone."

Gil pressed his fingers together into a pyramid. "I left the studio a couple hours later, and when I walked into the parking lot, a car that was parked there turned on its headlights. It nearly blinded me. Then this Ford Probe came tearing out like a bat out of hell, right at me. I barely jumped out of the way in time." I couldn't believe what I was hearing, yet he affirmed it. "Your wife nearly killed me," he said. Gil leaned forward and his eyes laser-beamed into me. "I hate to tell you this, Kevin, but you're married to a psycho."

25

GIL'S STORY FRAZZLED me beyond belief. I didn't want to go back to work and found myself driving aimlessly around parts of suburban Maryland I didn't even know, getting myself utterly lost. In the afternoon I stopped by a phone booth and called the office, telling my new assistant Wendy that I wouldn't be back that day. Eventually, I found myself in Great Falls, walking the trail alongside the Potomac. During the workday there weren't many people around, mainly a few joggers and mothers or nannies with small children.

I looked down at my gray Burberry suit and Calvin Klein tie. Left to my own devices, I'd prefer a Hugo Boss blazer and a mock turtleneck, befitting a successful architect, as opposed to the K Street lawyers' garb I was wearing. But Nicki preferred more conservative attire. So that's what I wore. As I thought about it, I realized that I'd conformed practically my entire life to Nicki. My outlets were my work—and even there, it was dictated in part by the need to make lots of money to support our exorbitant lifestyle—my thrice-weekly workouts at the gym, and to some extent my private time with our daughter. But everything else, down to my diet and my underwear, were strictly Nicki.

Was it wise to defer so much to someone as reckless and irrational as Nicki? I almost laughed out loud over that thought. Did I love Nicki? I supposed so. What stoked my despair was my complete acquiescence in the circumstances in which I found myself. I constantly suppressed my fears and my dissatisfaction. I concentrated on the things that made me happy—my work and my little girl—and accepted the facade of my relationship with Nicki as something akin to normal. More than that: I sometimes fancied ours a happy marriage. Placidity was a virtue; so long as Nicki didn't rock the boat, I ignored any danger signs. My long-ago discussion with Dr. Maguire—and his dire warnings—were deposited into a repressed mental databank. But no matter how much I ignored the realities, they were there, ready to surface whenever I grew too complacent.

I gave myself about six hours to brood, then I gathered myself and drove home. When I came in, Nicki and Alex were curled on the sofa locked in concentration, working on an embroidered tapestry for Doug and Karen's new baby. A fire was crackling in the fireplace and I could hear Rita puttering in the kitchen.

"See, doesn't that look nice?" Nicki asked Alex in her soft voice.

Alex admired their handiwork raptly, and looked up at me. "I like making gifts for people."

"It makes people like you," Nicki commented, finishing a stitch. "And it's good for people to like you."

"I'm gonna go see what's for dinner," Alex said, clearly not wanting to subject herself to adult conversation, and she ran off toward the kitchen.

I didn't know what to say to Nicki. I had rehearsed several options, ranging from confronting her about the radio station to demanding that we go to family counseling. But instead I asked her something I hadn't even contemplated. "How would you like to move to Italy for a few months?"

She looked up. "I've always wanted to go to Italy."

I think that was the first time in months that something I had said had truly excited Nicki. I guess timing truly is everything. I had been dreading raising the subject of Italy—and now here was Nicki, all eagerness. "I could take some art classes! I've always wanted to learn about Renaissance art!"

Her enthusiasm was contagious. Before long, my anxiety had subsided and we were talking about the specifics as if it was a done deal.

"You know, Doug and Karen have been looking for a nanny. We could let them have Rita while we're away," she suggested.

"So long as they don't steal her permanently."

"And Alex can delay starting kindergarten until the spring. She'll learn more in Italy, anyway."

OVER THE NEXT weeks we planned our trip in earnest. I had not seen Nicki so focused and enthusiastic since . . . she had gotten her job at the radio station. Getting ready to leave required long hours at work.

I think everyone at the firm had mixed feelings about me leaving for several months, both anxious about being rudderless, but eager to take on greater responsibilities. Still, it seemed like the tasks requiring my attention before we left were endless.

I needed to brush up on my studies. Every architecture student learns a great deal about the Renaissance period, but I had long consigned that knowledge to a memory dustbin. One evening Nicki and I had arranged to meet at Kramer Books so I could get some Renaissance books, and then we could have an early dinner. She was there when I arrived; she was going to leave after dinner to work the Bingo game at the church.

Nicki lifted her lips as I passed, and I paused to plant my own on them. Her kiss was warm, and her green eyes sparkled. "Hi, sweetheart. I love this place in the springtime."

Kramer's was one of our favorite places, one of the few true cafés in Washington, with a wonderful bookstore attached. Great reads and scrumptious desserts—what a delectable combination.

"Sorry, honey, that I'm late. It was tough finding a place to park."

"That's okay. But I was starving, so I ordered this bean dip. It's fantastic, try some," she insisted, pushing it toward me. I obliged, and found her assessment correct.

The waiter came by and I ordered a glass of the same wine as Nicki. My wife was pumped up, almost manic. "Guess what?"

"What?"

"I hired an au pair to come with us to Rome," she announced, her face beaming and her eyes searching mine for a reaction.

"You did what?!"

"I hired an au pair," she replied, as if my ears were defective. "A college student. From American University. Her name is Cassie. She's an art student from a small college in Kentucky, isn't it perfect?" Nicki was talking a mile a minute. "I know we have room in the apartment they're getting for us in Rome, and Alex met her this afternoon and really liked her, and this way I can take my classes over there and we don't have to worry about finding someone to watch Alex."

"I'm sure we could juggle our respective schedules," I said, knowing protest was futile. "My teaching load isn't that heavy."

Nicki took a sip of wine, then leaned forward, her chin resting on her hands and her eyes enormous. "Yes, but this way we can explore Italy during your two weeks off," she said. "And we can do it alone. Just the two of us."

I suddenly felt myself stiffening beneath the table. Nicki rarely affected a seductive look, but she was doing it now, all big beckoning eyes. It had been long since Nicki and I had been alone together for more than an errant weekend. She looked so incredibly beautiful, and the idea of a long sojourn into the Tuscan countryside was amorously alluring.

She could tell she had me; I could see it in her eyes. I couldn't remember the last time she had focused her fertile imagination on a romantic interlude, and I wasn't about to spoil the occasion—even as I silently calculated the extra financial costs we would incur with a fourth person in tow. But the waiter returned with my glass of wine, and then Nicki told him to bring an entire bottle, and the early evening turned into quite a celebration.

I was feeling the effects as well as I slid the key into the penthouse door back at the Parkside. Rita had agreed to stay late, and I could hear her banging around the kitchen as I entered the apartment.

As I stuck my head into the kitchen, Rita jumped and clutched her heart melodramatically. "I didn't hear you come in."

"Jeez," I replied with a grin, "you were making quite a racket. Where's Alex?"

Rita grimaced. "She's in her room. How you say, brouting."

"Pouting?" I asked. "Or brooding."

"Both," Rita said.

"Well, then, that's a good term for it. Brouting." I found it funny, even though Rita was obviously agitated. Rita loved Alexandra tremendously, but the little girl could get her babysitter's goat when she resolved to do so. "What happened?" I asked, trying to appear the concerned and responsible father.

"That stupid Cabbage Patch doll." Rita nearly spat the words. It was the latest fad, and Rita plainly didn't approve. "I took Alex to the park, and Tessie was there. Alex brought her doll. So ugly, that doll. I tell her to share, but she would not, even though Tessie want to play with her and the doll. So I took the doll away. Next moment I hear Tessie scream. She say Alex pull her hair, but Alex say no, and she refuse to say she sorry. So I take her home. Then I tell her she can not go see Mrs. Beeman, but she sneak out. I look everywhere. Alex, Alex, where are you, no Alex. Then I go next door and she there, so I drag her out and now it her turn to scream. She lock herself in the bedroom and not even come out for dinner."

I put my arm around Rita's diminutive shoulders and gave her a little hug. "Well, tomorrow's your day off, and I'd say it's well-deserved," I said.

"I go home now," she announced. "Leftover dinner is in icebox."

As Rita gathered her things, I walked down the hallway to Alex's room, finding the door closed. I tried the knob and found it locked, so I knocked. "Alex, open up," I called. Still feeling buzzed, I didn't really have the heart to punish Alex, but I needed at least to go through the motions.

I heard scurrying noises inside the room, then the latch being turned. What possessed me to design Alex's room with a lock? I wondered. When I opened the door, Alex was lying on the floor, her back to me. She was playing with her extensive collection of stuffed animals, which were gathered upright in a semi-circle, the Cabbage Patch doll prominently featured, as if holding court. Rita was right: that doll was ugly. Hardly worth fighting over.

I observed the scene for a few moments. Alex's hair was pulled back into a ponytail, with a flower sprig tucked into the rubber band, her latest fashion. She projected an amazingly wholesome image, reinforced by her soft voice, which she altered comically to create voices for her various characters.

I fought back a grin and said, "Hey, Alex, I need to talk to you." I walked over to Alex's bed and sat down, patting the spot beside me.

Alex looked up at me expectantly. It was remarkable how she could fix her gaze upon me without betraying any emotion whatsoever. Yet her light brown eyes would probe mine, as if fathoming my innermost thoughts. It was almost creepy.

I had to look away to gather myself. When I looked back, I tried to convey a tone that was more stern than I felt. "I hear that you pulled Tessie's hair today."

"I didn't pull Tessie's hair."

"Rita says you pulled Tessie's hair."

Alex frowned and shook her head. "Rita didn't see me pull Tessie's hair."

This wasn't getting us anywhere. "You have to learn to share your toys. They're your toys, and you get to keep them, but it's nice for you to share. And then the other children will share with you."

"But Tessie doesn't have any good toys."

I almost laughed. "Spoken like a true capitalist."

"What's a bapitalist?"

"A holy-roller. Don't change the subject."

"Daddy, *you* changed the subject."

"Tessie is your best friend. You have to treat her like she's your best friend. Didn't you learn about the Golden Rule in Sunday school?" I hoped at least she learned that; otherwise in my book Sunday school was a complete waste of time.

Alex's eyes narrowed suddenly, and her voice grew husky. "I hate Tessie." An angry furrow knotted her brow, and I realized that was actually a physical characteristic she'd inherited from me.

"That's not true. Tessie is your best friend."

"I don't want to play with her anymore," Alex replied, her face turning impassive again. "I'm not *going* to play with her anymore." She dropped back down to the floor, picked up the Cabbage Patch doll and started playing with it.

"Alex!" I said, "there are certain rules around here, young lady. Once you learn them, you'll find they allow you a surprising amount of freedom." I wondered if this concept was over her head. Sometimes Alex seemed so mature, yet other times she was stunningly irrational. I didn't know which Alex I was speaking to now.

"You don't set the rules. Mommy sets the rules. She says so."

"Oh, is that so? And what exactly did Mommy say about the rules?"

"Mommy says, 'I set the rules, and the rules are set by whim.'"

"What? Did you say 'whim'?"

"Yes," she replied seriously. "I don't know what whim is, but Mommy says she'll teach me."

No doubt she would. I looked at Alex, whose attention had returned to her Cabbage Patch doll. This conversation was surrealistic and obviously futile, and I could feel my temper rising precipitously. "It's time for your bath."

Nicki returned a couple hours later, after Alex was asleep. As I sat on the bed, watching her put clothes away that Rita had laundered during the day, I confronted her about my exchange with our daughter.

"Did you say that to Alex?"

"That's right."

I was incredulous. "How can you tell her that? What sort of example are you setting for her?"

"Kevin," she said, sitting down next to me and affecting the condescending tone she sometimes used with Alex, "Alex is a very special little girl. Exactly what I wanted: she has my looks and your brains and talent. It's a winning combination. And she has to learn how to use that combination to her advantage." She looked at me appraisingly, as if to determine whether I had mastered the simple idea she was imparting. "You see, when you're both beautiful and brilliant, the ordinary rules simply don't apply."

"You really believe that."

"Of course I do. It's true."

"What about right and wrong?"

She snickered. "Of course she'll learn about right and wrong. That's what they teach her in Sunday school. She'll learn about that at the same time I'm teaching her about the power she has at her disposal. And then she'll make her choices." Nicki smiled brightly and got up and left the bedroom.

Suddenly I felt like I had a pounding hangover, even though it had been hours since I had consumed any alcohol. I pulled off my clothes, tossed them sacrilegiously on the floor, and slipped beneath the covers. I turned onto my stomach, burrowed my face in the pillow, and let loose a primordial scream, a sound that emanated from my innermost depths yet was muffled through the goose down. It felt good, and when it was finished I rolled over, placing my hands behind my head and stared at the ceiling.

I felt like I was living in a lunatic asylum. One thing I knew for sure: leaving for Italy, escaping to completely new surroundings, couldn't possibly come fast enough. But one thing I couldn't know then, and indeed the thought didn't even cross my mind at the time: Alex never countenanced Tessie's friendship again.

20

WHY ON EARTH had I accepted such a challenging assignment? The Italian students who were taking the course had terrible English, particularly in written form. And now I had to suffer the penance, poring over paper after paper, trying to puzzle out what they were trying to say.

Still, I enjoyed teaching even more than I had imagined. The class contained two dozen budding young architects, about half American, half European. Among the latter, most were Italian, but there were a few French students and one adorable Brit named Helen Lumley. I had taken the class to an old building in the center of the city that was about to be converted into apartments. The building was five centuries old and had been everything—a livery, a broom factory, an apothecary, and an art gallery—but never before had it housed people. So it presented unique structural challenges, several of which I had presented to the class. But now I chastised myself for having them tackle the problems in writing rather than with drawings.

The early evening sun streamed through the ancient twin windows in the cramped living room of our apartment, illuminating the papers with uneven light as I read them. Although two air conditioners labored mightily in the living room and master bedroom, the thick humidity managed to seep through.

Two small, soft hands reached from behind and slid over the sides of my face to cover my eyes. Actually, given that my eyes were so strained, it felt good. "*Babbo*," she said, "*vorrei un gelato, por favor.*"

"How can I take you for ice cream if you're covering my eyes? You could be some sort of Italian troll masquerading as my daughter."

Alex giggled and removed her hands, scampering around the sofa and onto my lap, dislodging the papers in the process. "It's not a troll, Daddy, it's me!"

"Oh, it's little *pippola*!"

Alex kneeled on my legs and stared at me, her light brown eyes big and expressive. "*Vorrei un gelato*," she repeated, "please, please, please, *babbo*!"

I glanced at my watch, less to make a decision than to determine how badly it would ruin Alex's dinner. Pretty badly. But Nicki was at her art class and wouldn't return home until after seven. In any event, one of the things I loved most about teaching was the spontaneity it allowed, and I was not about to let the moment pass.

"Where's Cassie?"

"Buying groceries for dinner. I didn't want to go with her."

"And Paolo?" I queried, wondering where Alex's constant after-school companion was.

"It's Wednesday, Daddy, so Paolo has piano lessons."

"Well, then, *gelato* for *babbo* and *pippola*, it is."

"*Grazzi*!" she exclaimed with delight.

Our apartment was in a lovely though densely populated residential neighborhood of downtown Rome about three blocks from Cornell's small campus. It had taken Alex all of about ten minutes to discover the local ice cream shop to replace Fagin's Ice Cream Parlor, her favorite destination back home. She adored the texture and rich flavors of the Italian ice cream, and I wondered if Fagin's would ever regain its stature in Alex's ice cream lexicon.

At the ice cream shop, Alex ordered spumoni and I ordered chocolate. My diet had gone to hell since coming to Rome, and my exercise had fallen by the wayside. We sat down to enjoy our ice cream.

"I'll miss this ice cream when Mommy and I drive up to Florence."

A cloud passed over Alex's face. "I want to go with you."

This was terrain we had traversed previously, and it was precarious, but I wanted to firmly establish the certainty of it, which is why I brought it up. "No, Alex, Mommy and I haven't been alone together in a long time."

"Are you going to make another baby?"

I blushed, wondering how that thought could have entered her mind. "No, you know Mommy can't have any more children. You're the only one, *pippola*."

"Well, I still want to go."

"You and Cassie are going to have a good time."

"I don't like Cassie."

That was news to me. She and her *au pair* seemed to get along famously. At least up until the time that Alex was faced with the prospect of spending time with her alone. "Why? I thought you liked Cassie."

"She bosses me around. She's not my Mommy."

"Yes, but she's your *au pair*, so she's in charge when Mommy and I aren't around."

"But she's a kid, like me."

"No, she's a grown-up."

"No." Alex said this definitively, and in a certain respect she was right. Cassie was a slender, attractive girl barely out of her teens, and not terribly mature for her age. She had grown up in a pampered Southern household. Still, she accepted her relatively modest responsibilities along with the benefits of her stay in Rome.

"Well, you're going to have to make the best of it."

With a pout, she licked her ice cream but averted her eyes from mine.

"Hey, look at me." She did. I could see frosty resentment in her eyes, though the ice cream coating her chin took away some of her intended effect, and it almost made me laugh. "Tell you what, you and I will take a vacation together next spring."

Her eyes brightened. "Just you'n me?"

"Yeah."

"Can we go to Chincoteague and see the ponies?"

"That sounds like a great idea."

Alex slid off her chair, demurely dabbed at her chin with a napkin and tossed the remainder of the cone in a trashcan, then came over and threw her arms around me. I squeezed her in return, holding my ice cream cone away lest I get chocolate in her hair.

"I love you, *babbo*!"

"I love you, too."

Alex's mood remained remarkably upbeat as Nicki and I departed for Florence two days later.

Nicki had gotten a lot of Renaissance art under her belt from her class, and she was excited to impart her learning when we reached Florence. We had rented a little Fiat Spider convertible and were able to lower the top in the unseasonably warm drive along the western coast. The vistas were breathtaking, framing the coral blue waters of the Mediterranean.

We stayed the first night at a villa in a tiny town on the coast. The wind billowed the curtains from the terrace as we nibbled cheese and grapes and drank chianti. I think we had both been anticipating the chance to be alone together. Ever since Alex had learned to walk, our lovemaking was furtive and fleeting; and even then, Alex seemed to have an uncanny knack for walking in on us. I had learned how to give Nicki pleasure without making a big enterprise out of it. But I was not always so lucky on the receiving end.

At last, after being in this country where romance is displayed very openly, and inspired by our spectacular surroundings, we were in a position to make love with reckless abandon, and we made the best of it. It was exhilarating, and wonderful. I can remember every moan, every touch, and of course the lingering image of Nicki's eyes closed and her lips parted, in sweet ecstasy.

With rural Italy not having entered the modern communications era, we weren't able to check in with Cassie and Alex, so Nicki was anxious to do so as soon as we reached our hotel in Florence. As Nicki placed the call, I surveyed the magnificent view from our balcony. It seemed that almost nothing had changed from the time of the Medicis, one of the greatest periods of art and sculpture in all mankind. I was soaking it up through my every pore.

Nicki brushed against my shoulder.

"Isn't it breathtaking?"

Nicki didn't reply, and looked pensive. "There was no answer. I hope they're okay."

I looked her in the eyes. "Nick, they're fine. Let's start sightseeing, and we'll call them this evening when we get back. We only have two days to enjoy Florence."

We set out to explore the treasures of the city. It lived up to its reputation. Overcoming her dark mood, Nicki was positively buoyant, experiencing the works of art she had studied. We explored the streets and galleries, beholding one wonder after another. As we both were keen on Michelangelo, we made a pilgrimage of his major works in Florence. Just as in Rome, the standard of grandeur was stratospheric: what would qualify as a stupendous cathedral or a work of art in any American city merely blended into the montage in Florence. Mean-

while, as Nicki and I stared in awe at the splendor around us, the
Italian men gaped openly at my beautiful and (for them) exotic wife,
indifferent to my presence. I smiled in bemusement.

It was late afternoon by the time we grew tired, and in our excitement we had skipped lunch altogether. We managed to find a café that
was open and enjoyed some rich Italian pastries and cappucino. Nicki
chattered as I sat back and watched the people walking by the café. I felt
at once a crackling intensity coupled with complete and utter calm.

Later we continued to stroll in the balmy air, hand in hand,
and returned to our hotel near midnight. As we reached the desk to
retrieve our key—in old Europe, keys are massive affairs, and must be
left at the front desk—the attendant flashed a look of recognition and
pulled a message slip from the cubbyhole with our room key. "Mr.
Gibbons," the matronly attendant said in heavenly accented English,
"it says you must call home in Rome immediately."

"My God, is something wrong with Alex?"

"It only says to call home at once," the attendant repeated. "There
is a phone."

I raced over to it, Nicki jabbering on. "Shh!" I commanded, and
picked up the phone, barking the telephone number to an operator
who seemed maddeningly incapable of comprehending me. Finally
after what seemed an eternity, there was a distant ringing noise. After
two rings, the phone was picked up.

"Hello?" Cassie's distinctive Kentucky accent was unmistakable.

"Cassie, this is Kevin. What's wrong?" It sounded like Alex was
screaming or crying in the background.

"Stop it, Alex!" Cassie demanded. "Mr. Gibbons. Kevin. You have
to come back. I can't take this anymore. I'm leaving."

My panic subsided in favor of profound confusion. "What's
wrong?" Nicki was clawing my arm, asking the same question I just
had. I shoved her gently away from me, and she glared at me icily.

Cassie was saying something, but between Nicki to the side of me
and Alex in the background on the phone, I couldn't make out her
words. "What, Cassie?"

"I'm not going to spend another minute with this fricking
monster," she declared, her tone bordering on hysteria. "I'm booked
on the first flight out of Rome tomorrow morning. If you're not back
by then, I'm leaving her on her own."

"Don't do that, Cassie!"

"Let me talk to Alex," Nicki demanded. I waved her off.

"Listen, Cassie, we're coming back to Rome right away. Please don't leave. We'll get there before morning. Just stay where you are."

I could tell Cassie had placed her hand over the phone and was quarreling with Alex. When she came back, her tone was insolent. "Just get back here before morning."

"Just calm down. We'll take care of the situation as soon as we can."

And then the connection was severed on their end. I returned the receiver to its cradle. My blood was throbbing in my temples. I was grateful for the caffeine hit from the Cappucino as I tried to gather my thoughts. I mentally went through my Cornell colleagues who I might enlist to intercede before we reached Rome, but realized I didn't know how to contact any of them. It would just waste precious time anyway.

"What's going on?" Nicki asked. "I can't believe you didn't ask to speak to Alex."

"She's all right, I could hear her in the background."

"We don't know what this woman is capable of."

"You're the one who decided out of the blue to bring an *au pair* with us to Italy."

"Don't blame me! *You're* the one who decided to leave Alexandra all alone with her."

"I'm not blaming you for anything, except maybe for your genes."

Her eyes widened. "What's *that* supposed to mean?"

"Come on, we're wasting time arguing. Let's get out of here."

I went to the front desk to check us out, while Nicki returned to our room to throw our things in the suitcases. Within minutes, we were navigating our way out of Florence and onto the unfamiliar highway to Rome, a more direct route but different than the way we had come. Even in the middle of the night, the Italian drivers were reckless, and the roads were confusing, a situation exacerbated not only by the moonless night, but by the drizzle that started just as we left the city limits. We had to stop and put the Fiat's top up. That made the atmosphere inside the tiny car positively cloying.

"Cassie better not have done anything to my daughter," Nicole said into the darkness. "She'll pay for the rest of her life."

"Why don't you just reserve judgment until we find out what happened?"

"I don't care what happened."

"You mean, you don't care if your precious daughter precipitated it, right?" I retorted.

Nicki merely sighed, as if trapped with a buffoon.

My irritation and anxiety poured into my driving. Now it was I who was recklessly passing cars at breakneck speeds.

"Kevin!" Nicki cried, grabbing my arm after one especially harrowing maneuver. "You're going to kill us."

I clenched my jaw and said nothing. Nicki turned away in her seat. Before long I could hear her gentle snores even over the Fiat's revving engine. Remarkable: my wife had trouble sleeping in a calm bed, but no trouble doing so now. The hours passed in silence, interrupted only when I stopped to get gas. Even then Nicki did not stir.

We reached Rome before dawn. I had never seen the streets so deserted, and we wound through the residential section in no time. Nicki roused just as we were pulling up to our apartment building. No one was parked illegally in front of the entrance, surprisingly, so we did. Nicki had her door open by the time we reached the curb, and I had to hustle to catch up with her.

Nicki was the first inside the apartment. The living room was illuminated only by one lamp and the flickering images of the television, whose volume was barely above a whisper. As my eyes adjusted to the dimness, I could make out Cassie sitting on the sofa, surrounded by suitcases.

"What's going on?" Nicki demanded.

Cassie made a snorting sound. "Ask her," she said, gesturing with her thumb to the hallway at the opposite end of the room, where Alex stood, sleepy-eyed, clad in Minnie Mouse pajamas and her thumb in her mouth.

Nicki swept her up in her arms and kissed her. "Are you okay, sweetness?" Alex nodded, but did not remove her thumb from her mouth. It was a habit that annoyed me, now that Alex was five-and-a-half, but Nicki insisted that peer pressure would make her grow out of it. "Mommy's home now, everything's going to be all right."

I turned my attention back to Cassie. "We're not asking Alex what happened. We're asking you."

"Where do I start?" Cassie moaned, then the words seemed to pour out of her. "From practically the moment you left, Alex was misbehaving. She wouldn't do anything I told her. And she didn't want to do anything I suggested by way of activities. I knew she had separation anxiety, so I tried to be patient. But there was no satisfying her. Not the movies. Not the park. Nothing." That assertion had a ring of truth to it.

"She's a little girl," Nicki growled. "It's not like it's rocket science to entertain her." I waved for her to be quiet, though I agreed. I nodded to Cassie to go on.

"We got through Saturday, with one tantrum after another. I thought her screaming was going to pierce my eardrums. Then yesterday I sent her to church with Paolo's family, and they played afterward. When she came home, I thought everything was okay, finally. She was all sugar and spice. And then she asked to go for ice cream, and I figured sure, why not, positive reinforcement and everything."

I glanced over at Nicki, who was rocking Alex gently, not appearing to be paying attention to Cassie at all. I looked back at the *au pair*. She looked very young and fresh-faced, and very earnest, but not cut out for serious responsibility. So far, she seemed to have overreacted pretty badly.

"But as soon as we got outside, Alex let go of my hand and darted into the traffic. You know how it is around here on Sunday afternoons, like rush hour in Manhattan." I nodded. "So of course I screamed and chased after her. I would almost catch up to her and she would take off again, cutting in front of cars and buses. People were slamming on their brakes to avoid hitting her."

I swung my gaze to Alex. "Alex! You know you're not supposed to cross the street by yourself. Ever. It's too dangerous. How many times have I told you that?" She wouldn't look at me. "Alex! Look at me!"

She turned her face toward mine and leveled a gaze that was pure Nicki. Seemingly bereft of feeling, but nonetheless full of meaning.

"There was a point to it, Mr. Gibbons." Cassie's voice drew my attention back to her. "At that busy intersection at Santa Maria—do you know the one I mean?" I nodded—there was traffic coming from all directions. "At that intersection, she looked both ways and darted out. I raced after her and at the last second saw a truck. He couldn't stop. I had to roll to the ground to avoid it. He came within inches of hitting me."

I was aghast. Cassie continued. "Several people saw what happened and helped me up. When I stood up, Alex was waiting at the opposite corner, watching me and laughing. Laughing!" Cassie looked over at Alex then back at me. "She deliberately tried to kill me."

Nicki erupted. "How dare you accuse Alex of something like that! She's five years old!"

"I'm not accusing her of anything, Mrs. Gibbons. I'm *telling* you what happened. Alex deliberately tried to kill me, or at least get me seriously injured."

Nicki lowered Alex to the floor. "Go back inside your room and close the door 'til Mommy comes to get you, okay, sweetie?" she said softly.

As Alex scampered off, the tension hung in the air so thick you could slice it with a dull knife.

"Nicki," I said after I heard Alex's door shut, anticipating my wife's response to the horrible vignette Cassie had just relayed, "even if Alex didn't intend to hurt Cassie, what she did was terrible, and dangerous. Alex knows better than to run out into traffic. And Cassie risked her life to run after her. We can't have Alex doing things like that. She needs to be punished—severely punished."

"The whole thing happened because Cassie doesn't know what she's doing!" Nicki exploded. "She was driving Alex crazy. No wonder she wanted to run away. I know exactly how she feels! If Cassie had kept an eye on Alex, none of this would have happened."

Suddenly Cassie was on her feet, her rage matching Nicki's. "Your little girl—your precious little princess—is a monster!" she shot back. "She nearly got me killed, and you're blaming me!"

Nicki looked from Cassie to me and back again. She seemed like a caged animal, and finally she trained her venom on me. "Why are you taking her side?" she whined. "You're taking the word of some immature bitch over your own daughter!"

"Good grief, Nicki, I didn't hear Alex denying anything," I replied as calmly as I could, though I was shaking when I said it.

"I can't believe it!" Nicki spat. She turned her back to me and bolted down the hall. "Alex and I are flying back to Washington."

"That demon child isn't flying on the same plane as me!" Cassie shouted after her.

"Don't worry," Nicki retorted, "we'll be in first class!" Then a door opened and slammed.

Nicki's last missive nearly made me laugh out loud. I experienced once again the recurrent feeling that I was living in a madhouse. "Cassie," I said softly, "I'm sorry about what happened, and I'm sorry that this didn't work out."

"Whatever."

I followed Nicki's path down the hall and found the door to our bedroom closed. I knocked.

"What!"

I opened the door. Nicki already had two suitcases on the bed and was throwing her remaining clothes and Alex's into them. Alex was playing on the bed with her dolls, seemingly oblivious to all the commotion.

"Don't do this, Nicki. I can't leave and I don't want you and Alex to leave."

"It wasn't my decision. It was yours."

"Give me a break."

"You should have given Alex a break."

I watched her for a few moments, irritation welling inside me. Finally I announced, "I'm going for a walk." Nicki didn't even glance in my direction. I returned to the living room, where Cassie was moving her belongings outside to the cab that had arrived. I helped her, then started walking.

The morning was stirring in earnest. I rambled aimlessly, then stopped at a newspaper stand and picked up a day-old *USA Today*. I needed a normalcy fix. I took it to a café that was open and read it over a steaming cup of espresso. It was hard to concentrate but I forced myself. It looked like the Democrats were about to take back the White House after twelve years of Republican occupancy. Gee, the news was bad everywhere. I made the skimpy newspaper last a long time, poring over even the entertainment gossip. I didn't want my thoughts to wander back to my own reality.

Finally I glanced at my watch. Nine-thirty. Shit!—I had a class in thirty minutes. Wait, no I didn't. It was vacation week. That's right, I was supposed to be spending the second of two glorious days in

Florence with Nicki. Tomorrow we were set to begin exploring the lush vineyards of Tuscany. Another dream that would be left unfulfilled. I sat back in my chair and watched the Romans go about their day.

I couldn't believe that Nicki would desert me. She had wanted this sabbatical in Italy as much as I had. And after all, the source of her anger was gone now, on her way back to the United States.

Then I smiled ruefully, realizing that was wrong. Cassie wasn't the source of her anger. I was. Once again I had committed an apostasy, siding with someone over my wife and daughter. Or, excuse me, *Nicki's* daughter. Sometimes I wondered if Alex had any of my blood flowing through her veins.

I gathered myself to intercept my wife and daughter. I didn't want them to leave. Hopefully, the two of them were shopping somewhere, ringing up unconscionable credit card bills.

It was midmorning by the time I arrived back at our residence. I opened the door and called inside. "Nicki!" My call reverberated emptily through the cavernous apartment.

I walked down the hallway and looked first into our bedroom, then Alex's. Aside from my belongings and the furniture, both rooms were bare.

Nicki and Alex were gone.

27

I STILL HAD seven weeks remaining in the semester. I weighed cutting it short and returning to the United States, but didn't want to shirk my responsibilities. Anyway, it seemed like the distance—both time and geography—might allow me to gain perspective on the situation.

Oddly, my unanticipated new circumstances settled almost immediately into a routine. Nicki called when she reached home to let me know they had arrived safely. She acted as if nothing was out of the ordinary—and indeed, in Nicki's world, it probably wasn't. Although Nicki's conversation was terse, Alex was as sweet as usual, and like her mother, acted totally unruffled by their sudden trip home. She implored me to come home, as if I were the errant family member, and as if she had done nothing to precipitate a huge cataclysm that had torn our lives asunder. When I told her I couldn't come home, she accepted the news stoically, but assured me she missed me and promised to write and send drawings every week. I decided not to confront Nicki—or Alex—from such a distance, but resolved to do so, each in her own way, when I returned to America. Despite Nicki's (and apparently Alex's) habit of suppressing awkward memories, I would not allow this incident to pass as if nothing had happened.

Meanwhile, the news spread quickly among my colleagues and students that my domestic situation had changed. I think Cassie had been dating one of the students, so I can only imagine the story that got around. Immediately, one of the Italian professors in the program, Rocco Benigno, started inviting me out drinking after classes, which was a near-daily ritual with his students. I didn't know how he managed to teach class after drinking each night into the wee hours, and he was even older than I. I resisted a week of invitations, but finally I got tired of eating dinner alone and decided to join them.

The only problem for me was a truly practical one: what to drink.

I had always hated beer, and the Italian wines served at bars were swill, particularly for a wine snob like me. At the students' urging, I tried some exotic Italian liqueurs—I enjoyed Anisette, but after one glass found it too syrupy. Then I remembered Belvedere vodka, straight-up and chilled. It was smooth and delicious. And, combined with the overall experience, sublimely intoxicating. Over the next several weeks I must have consumed gallons of Belvedere vodka and tons of pasta and tiramisu. I couldn't keep up, so I reduced my nocturnal outings with the students to one or two per week.

I missed Alex desperately, even as her conduct disturbed me profoundly. In general she was an exceptionally affectionate little girl. I could easily imagine Alex running away from Cassie, but not deliberately imperiling her life. I thought that sort of cunning surely beyond the capacity of any five-year-old.

Where I was plainly at fault was in not setting down clear rules for Alex. I thought that I had, but I realized I put too many of them up for negotiation. I wondered if it would be the same if I had a son, instead; or if Alex had an older brother. That wistful thought darkened my psyche: were fate a bit kinder, Alex would indeed have had an older brother.

Nicki's penchant for contradicting me exacerbated the problem with discipline. That was simply going to have to change. I couldn't remember all the times I had implored Nicki that we needed to apply one common set of rules, not two. Yes, that would have to change.

As for Nicki, my feelings were far more complicated, and frankly I tried to think about her—or even communicate with her—as little as possible. Her conduct disgusted me. And it maddened me. What was the deal with her? She seemed to need me, yet seemed to need to repel me on a regular basis, all at the same time. What kind of warped marriage was this, anyway? I preferred to ride my roller coasters in an amusement park.

Our telephone conversations were even more superficial than ever. Because we had loaned Rita to Doug and Karen for the duration of the year, Nicki was forced to curtail her volunteering activities, except during the mornings when Alex was in school. She also had to delay her job search, which I knew she must be dreading given the debacles she had made of her last two experiences. But I found I really didn't care.

For our last class, I had a surprise for the students: I had arranged with the Vatican for a private tour of the Scavi, the magnificent Roman ruins beneath St. Peter's. They were discovered during some structural work on the cathedral a few decades before. Few of the students had seen them, and all (including me) were awestruck. It was a fitting crescendo to a wonderful semester. The students presented me with a magnificent drawing depicting an architectural rendition of the Colosseum, signed by each of them. It would occupy a special place back in my office.

Making the long journey home was bittersweet. I was going to miss Rome and teaching. I couldn't wait to see Alex, but I wondered what greater circumstances awaited me. This time, I vowed, I wouldn't leave my future to fate.

It was mid-afternoon on a cold winter Saturday when the cab from Dulles deposited me outside the Parkside, remnants of an early-season snowfall still covering the grass. I lugged my bags up the elevator and knocked on the door to the apartment. Immediately I could hear bare feet rapidly pounding the hardwood floors toward the door. It opened and Alex flew into my arms. She had grown an inch or two in my absence, and though she still couldn't be more than sixty pounds, the difference knocked me off my stride and literally off balance. We collapsed onto the floor.

"Daddy! Daddy! Daddy!" I laughed and we hugged intently. "I missed you!"

She helped me drag my things inside. The apartment was decorated for a Ralph Lauren Christmas, but there was no tree as yet. "Why don't you pull my suitcases down the hall into Daddy's bedroom, and look inside for your surprises?"

And then suddenly there was Nicki. "Hey you," she said, and leaned over and pecked my lips.

"Hi." As Alex started wheeling the bags down the hall, reminding me of Sisyphus rolling a boulder up a hill, I silently leaned back on the floor and regarded my wife. And realized, with a feeling of shock, that for the first time since the moment I had first laid eyes on her a decade before, I did not find her beautiful. Her pale skin was pasty. She had put on some weight since I had last seen her, and her face was puffy. She was wearing sweats and no makeup, with her hair pulled back.

But none of that mattered. Regardless of how she looked, I simply didn't find Nicki attractive anymore. She had driven it out of me.

And in that moment an epiphany swept over me: Nicki's hold over me was broken. This woman was not my ideal, my partner, my object of affection. She was a demon, a leech. Suddenly an image passed through my mind of those science-fiction movies, like *Species*, where the alien monster takes the human form of a beautiful woman. But lurking beneath the facade are a reptilian tongue, groping tentacles, and chomping mandibles. A chill ran through me as I watched Nicole, truly detached for the first time. Then the chill was supplanted by a different sensation: a feeling of giddy exhilaration, of liberation. What was it that Martin Luther King, Jr., said on the steps of the Lincoln Memorial? "Free at last! Free at last! Thank God almighty, we are free at last!"

But just as that feeling arose so swiftly, so was it replaced by another, diametrically opposed: I may have been freed from my obsession with Nicole, but still I was trapped by circumstances. It made me feel like a caged animal.

"Why are you staring at me?"

"I'm trying to fathom you."

"Gee, I'm glad to see you, too."

"Nicki, either you need to see a therapist, or we both do. The situation between us is intolerable, and I'm not going to sweep it under the carpet any longer."

"I don't know what you're talking about."

"Nicki, you don't just disrupt our lives, and take my daughter away from me for seven weeks, without major repercussions."

"We wanted to go home. We're here, waiting for you to come home." She pouted. "Why are you being so mean?"

That almost made me laugh. "Nicki—"

"And that reminds me," she interrupted, "we have Doug and Karen coming over for brunch tomorrow. And next Friday we have two Christmas parties we're invited to. And I've been working with your office to arrange the holiday party, which is a week from Wednesday. It's going to be wonderful, at the Willard, which I knew you'd like. Oh, and I can't wait to show you how I redecorated our bedroom, like I told you on the phone last week." If she had told me, I must have tuned her out.

"Daddy!" Alex exclaimed, returning to the living room. "Thank you for the art kit. I love it! And the new dress. It's beautiful!" She beamed. "Is there anything else?"

I laughed and swept her into my arms, kissing her ear. "You didn't find the earrings?" Nicki had gotten Alex's ears pierced when she was two.

"No, let me look for them!" And she squirmed from my arms.

"Hey, wait a minute. Why don't you get some shoes and socks on, and we'll drive to my office. You can find your earrings later."

"Okay!" she said cheerily, and ran back down the hallway.

"Well, I'm going to make a special dinner for the three of us," Nicki announced.

"Fine. But we need to talk about this, Nicki. It's not going away."

"Fine."

And then Alex was back, bundled in her down-filled jacket and practically pulling me out the door. "Let's go!" she demanded, and we did.

We spent the afternoon together, stopping first at the office, where Rich and some of the other architects were working. It was a nice reunion. It turned out that time had not stopped still while I was gone, and sure enough there was quite a pile on my desk and chair. As Alex played at the drawing board with one of the architects, I thumbed through a few of the papers. I knew where I'd be spending most of my weekends in the foreseeable future.

Afterward, Alex and I drove around to some of Horizon's projects, inspecting them from the outside. The already harsh winter had set back some plans, but nothing disastrous if the weather cooperated henceforth (it didn't). Then Alex asked me to drive out to the Pension Building, which she referred to as "Daddy's pretty building." It had metamorphosed from decrepitude to resplendence as Alex was coming of age to appreciate it, and she was drawn to it in a special way. It seemed she always wanted to check it to make sure there were no signs of decay. "It's still pretty, *babbo*," she announced as we inspected it from the street.

Nicki made a scrumptious dinner, but fortunately the twin tasks of unpacking and attending to Alex's demands for my attention consumed most of the evening. I found that I couldn't bear to be in

Nicki's company. And I was fast in jetlagged sleep by the time she came to bed.

Alex's loud arrival on the bed the next morning awakened me, and as I glanced at the clock on my night-stand I realized it was nine o'clock. Nicki was out of bed, and my sensitive nostrils detected a fritatta baking in the oven. I grabbed Alex and we snuggled. Left to her own devices, she was a late sleeper, and she liked to rise slowly. She put her thumb in her mouth, then yanked it out and lay quietly beside me. Good, I reflected, she's breaking that habit on her own.

Nicki popped her head inside the bedroom. "Time to get up," she announced. "Doug and Karen will be here at ten."

It was great to see them. Alex took instantly to their toddler and went off to entertain him. Doug and Karen had brought over a bottle of White Star champagne and fresh orange juice, though I hated to waste such fine bubbly on mimosas. So I took out a cheaper bottle from the refrigerator for mixing and we drank the White Star unadulterated.

Doug and Karen wanted to hear everything about Rome, having traveled there years earlier. It was awkward at first, not knowing how much Nicki had conveyed to them, or how accurately. But the combination of champagne and good company dissipated any anxiety on my part, and Nicki acted as if nothing strange had happened. In her mind, nothing strange probably had happened, I reflected.

Rita had worked out well for them, not surprisingly. Nicki offered to let her stay rather than coming back to us after the holidays, as we had arranged. Doug and Karen were ecstatic, but I was shocked.

"Gee, Nicki, I thought you were looking for a job," I said. Nicki was clearly irritated that I was revealing that her announcement had taken me by surprise. Frankly, I wasn't thrilled over Alex being under Nicki's constant supervision. Rita might not speak English fluently, but she was a good person.

"No," Nicki scolded, "as I told you, I don't think it makes sense to look for a part-time job while Alex is in kindergarten. I'll wait until she starts first grade next September."

If she had ever told me that previously, I must have ignored it. Our guests stayed until the early afternoon. As Nicki took Karen to our room to show off the new decor, I poured a last cup of coffee for Doug and sat down opposite him.

"Doug," I said, "I need to come by to see you. Professionally."

"I've been wondering what was going on," he replied, lowering his voice in turn. "Nicki gave some story to Karen about having to come back to the United States suddenly, but I thought it was weird." As usual, Doug was unstinting—and dead on point—in his assessment of Nicki.

"I do need some help."

"Well, stop by sometime this week and we'll discuss the options. You're going to want to wait until after Christmas to do something in any event."

I nodded just as Karen and Nicki returned.

I drove back to the office after they left for the rest of the afternoon to clear some papers from my desk before the week began. But also to get some space from Nicki. Before I had opened up to Doug, I hadn't even realized that I had already began charting a course of action. But for better or worse, I was resolved about the future. Our marriage was a sham, and clearly it wasn't going to get any better. What crippled me inside was the thought of leaving Alex. I didn't know how I could bear that, and I knew that Nicki would make life very difficult. She knew how much Alex meant to me, and there was no question she would use it as a weapon if I decided to divorce her. Doug was right. I needed the holidays to think things through. I shouldn't act precipitously. But I knew I had to act. Finally, at long last.

I delayed returning home until mid-evening, calling Nicki to tell her not to hold dinner for me. On the way home, I stopped at a fast-food place and ate alone, scolding myself for avoiding Nicki but finding it impossible to summon the desire to be with her.

When I finally returned home, it was Alex's bedtime. A new week of kindergarten would start for her the next day. For the first time in a long while, I was able to read her a bedtime story. It was Maurice Sendak's *Where The Monsters Are*. One of my personal favorite's, and Alex's too. She was both reading and writing well above grade level, but she still loved having stories read to her, and I obliged with exaggerated melodrama.

Finally I bade her good-night. I repaired to my study and waited out Nicki. After awhile she walked past to our bedroom without a word. After a few minutes the lights went out. I waited a half hour before going to bed, knowing it typically took Nicki a long time to get to sleep. As I was about to click off the light, Nicki rolled over and looked at me, her face inches from mine. The light from my nightstand brightened her eyes against her pale skin. I stared at her, my gaze meeting hers, saying nothing.

"Don't even think about divorcing me. I'll never give you a divorce. And if you try, I'll make your life a living hell."

Suddenly she smiled as if she had just told the punch-line of a joke; yet as mirthful as it was, her smile imparted no humor whatsoever. "As I told you when we were married," she continued, "you're stuck with me forever."

And with that sentence rendered, Nicki turned away from me and promptly fell asleep.

But I didn't fall asleep for a very long time. As I tossed and turned beside my slumbering wife, it occurred to me that I had never felt more lonely in my entire life.

28

INSTEAD OF GOING into the office refreshed and reinvigorated, I was zonked from lingering jet-lag and sleep deprivation. It would take a day or two to get my chemistry back to normal following my transatlantic return. I had a sneaking worry that my colleagues had learned to get along without me, so I was gratified to learn that everyone seemed to want some of my time. Following the staff meeting, Rich and I closeted away for a couple hours and caught up. Aside from a few minor glitches, everything was going well. We had increased our architects by two in my absence.

Given my absence, I decided not to take a bonus for 1996, and instead applied our profits to staff bonuses. Actually, part of my thinking was that if I was contemplating divorce, I shouldn't enhance my personal worth just then, but instead keep equity inside the business. I was my own personal amateur tax lawyer.

Around lunchtime, I called Doug's office and scheduled a racquetball game, followed by an hour of his professional time, for Wednesday afternoon. In the meantime I plowed myself into my work, putting in calls to our bigger clients and inviting them personally to our Christmas party.

Again I found that I wasn't excited about going home after work. On Monday, I stayed late. On Tuesday, I went out drinking with some of my colleagues. Both evenings I was home in time to read Alex a bedtime story. But she was getting irritated over my absences, even though Nicki didn't say a word. I think she was as happy as I was to avoid one another. On Saturday, Alex was going shopping for Christmas presents with Nicki and visiting her grandparents in Maryland, while I would spend the day at work; but she would spend Sunday with me. That worked, too, because I wouldn't have to spend either day with Nicki.

On Wednesday, Doug and I played racquetball. Even though he

had laid off the game in my absence, his concentration overcame my tiramisu-diminished stamina and he beat me soundly. Afterward we went out for coffee. I filled him in on what had transpired in Italy, then recounted the similar experience in Bermuda, as well as Nicki's turbulent employment encounters and other incidents. He listened without comment. "For me, the bottom line is custody. Is there any chance I could end up with Alex?"

He rolled his eyes. "Should you get custody? Absolutely. Will you get custody? Probably not. The District of Columbia is a pretty liberal jurisdiction, but the one area in which liberalism has stalled is child custody. The mother is still given a strong legal presumption." He took a long sip of coffee. "And right now Nicki is a stay-at-home mother, while you're a workaholic."

"She's a stay-at-home mother because she's too insane to keep a job."

"Well, if we're going to go down that route, it's going to be expensive and nasty."

"It's going to be one of the nastiest custody battles in history, regardless. Nicki probably won't even consent to a divorce, and she'd probably kill rather than give up Alex. There's not much that really matters to Nicki, but Alex does, above everything."

"What about Alex?"

"Alex is going to be scarred no matter what. After all, Nicki's her mother." I was surprised at the venom that was flowing from my mouth. "But I can't let Alex stay in that environment without a fight. All I'm asking is whether I have a chance. If not, then I'll figure out a way to cope, somehow. Move into separate bedrooms or something, rather than get a divorce. But if I do have a chance for custody, then let's go for it."

Doug regarded me intently. "You have a chance, but no more than that."

"Then start gathering our experts. We'll get through the holidays, and strike right after the first of the year. Do you need a retainer?"

He shook his head. "No. I just need you to build up your resolve, because this isn't going to be easy. Or pleasant."

"I'm ready. And when this is over, we'll celebrate."

It was tough to get through the rest of the week. Friday evening was worst of all. Two high-society Christmas parties, one sponsored by the Association of Washington Architects, the other by a Smithsonian patrons organization with which Nicki had gotten us involved. They were painful, utter charades. Nicki hung on my arm like a cheap date, telling all of my architect acquaintances and the museum socialites what a wonderful time we had in Rome. I barely said anything except when Nicki prodded me. But her smile beamed brightly the entire evening. As we drove home, Nicki was ebullient as if nothing was out of the ordinary and the evening had been one of the high points of her life.

When Nicki came to bed, I faked being asleep, but Nicki would have none of it. She wasn't finished critiquing the parties, and then she wanted to discuss the details for the Horizon Christmas party the following Wednesday, an event I was now positively dreading. How could Rich have allowed Nicki to insinuate herself so thoroughly into the planning?

The following day, Nicki and Alex bustled off to the mall first thing in the morning, two women on a mission. As they left, Alex was arguing with Nicki about which mall they should begin their shopping. I couldn't believe that my five-and-a-half year-old would have strong opinions about such matters, but after all, she was her mother's daughter.

I had a tremendous amount of work set aside for the day, but I procrastinated at home and didn't get to the office until close to noon. Then I puttered around and realized I needed a different outlet. I had already worked like a maniac for a whole week, and the stress over Nicki was driving me batty.

I was seized by a sudden inspiration. I heard Jen had moved to Centreville in the far suburbs of Virginia. Did I remember her married name? Yes. Should I call? No. But I did. After two rings, Jennifer answered the phone, her voice completely unchanged in the nearly seven years since we had last spoken.

"Jen?"

A pause. "Kevin?!"

"Yeah!"

"Oh my God! It's great to hear your voice!"

We caught up on our respective families. Jen's little boy was six and enjoying kindergarten. She was working part-time at a law firm in Fairfax, doing real estate work. Darren had opened his own surveying company. To me it all sounded idyllic. He and their son were visiting relatives in Charlottesville, giving Jennifer some private time.

I told her about my sabbatical in Rome, and about Alex learning Italian, and about how large my firm had grown.

"Every time I see something in the *Post* about a renovation project, I check to see if it's you, and it usually is. I'm really proud of you."

That meant a lot, and I smiled momentarily. The act of doing so made me realize how rare it was. "Well, I wish everything was going as good as my career." And with little prompting, I began spilling my woes to Jennifer.

"Hey, wait a minute," she said. "This is going to take awhile."

"Oh, I'm sorry, Jen," I replied, feeling mortified. How could I think that after seven years, Jennifer would have the time or interest to listen to my problems.

"No," she said, "I do need to go shopping, but I was wondering if you might be able to break away for dinner tonight, or brunch tomorrow. Then we could really talk."

"If we made it early, I could definitely get away for dinner tonight. Nicki and Alex won't be home 'til late."

"I'll make dinner for you."

I left at about four-thirty, and picked up a bottle of Bordeaux from the liquor store at the foot of Key Bridge, then sped out Route 66 toward the Virginia countryside. I arrived at precisely the appointed time, and not surprisingly Jen wasn't there yet. After about twenty minutes, she pulled into the driveway, peering sheepishly through her car window. I bolted from my car and helped her with the huge bundles of groceries and Christmas bags. We barely got into the house without collapsing, and then were greeted by an adorable mutt who looked like Ludwig von Beethoven. After Jen yelled at the dog to quiet down—Muttley, he was appropriately named—we hugged tightly.

We stood apart and took each other in. "You look great, Kevin."

"Less hair and more heft."

"Well, you look buff. You must be working out."

I nodded. "And you're beautiful, as always." It was true. She definitely had put on some years, but was very slender, perhaps too much so. Her attire was casual—jeans, sweatshirt, no makeup, her medium-length hair askew. But she looked radiant, and a wave of affection swept over me.

"Hardly." She grimaced. "I bought takeout so we can eat as soon as I get these things put away."

When dinner was ready, we settled into comfortable the living room, and Jennifer built a fire. Then we settled into the sofa and ate a delicious dinner and drank the superb wine. When we finished eating, we each reclined on our respective ends of the sofa. Jennifer had long since burned out as a litigator—the demands were incompatible with motherhood—but she had lost none of her keen skill at eliciting information. Slowly but surely she extracted the highlights of my relationship with Nicki, not commenting on anything I said but leading me back to the same conclusion I'd arrived at. It was cathartic just to relay the story, and when I was done, Jennifer didn't have much to say. I had pretty much said it all.

She looked at me, saying, "It's going to be tough, Kevin. Not just in the short-term, either. You're going to have to deal with Nicki for the next twelve or thirteen years."

"I know."

"But it would be even longer if you stayed with her and tried to live a lie, wouldn't it?"

"Yeah, but who knows, with Nicki that might be a possibility. When I think about it, we've been living a lie the entire time we've been married."

"The choices we make always have ramifications, good and bad."

I was puzzled. "Meaning, in your case . . ."

"Meaning, I think maybe I made a mistake, too. Not that Darren is a bad person, at all. Justin is a fantastic little boy. And Darren is a good father. They're inseparable. But my life just isn't what I dreamed about."

"How?"

"Well, we're just in a rut. Darren wanted a wife, and as soon as he got one, that was the limit of his ambition. He's settled down. He doesn't realize you have to work to keep a romance vibrant." She sighed and looked at me with misty eyes. "I want to see the world. When you told me about Rome, and Florence, for a moment I imagined what it would have been like to be there with you."

A shiver went up my spine when she said that, and I suppressed imagining it myself. I had to avert my eyes from Jen's, so I stared into my wine while she continued talking.

"Darren's idea of an adventure is renting a cabin and fishing. That's fine, and we have a good time. But there's never anything romantic. He hardly ever even remembers my birthday or our anniversary. He has absolutely no desire to step out of our little world, and there's so much more out there to see, to experience. Sometimes I feel trapped."

I knew what she meant. "It's weird. I have lots of friends, lots of people around, I'm almost never at home, almost never at a loss for something to do. But when I'm laying next to my wife in bed at night, I feel incredibly lonely."

Jennifer nodded. Neither of us said anything for awhile, sitting there quietly, sipping our wine and listening to the crackling fire. Finally I broke the silence. "I'm really glad that I was in love, once."

And suddenly she leaned toward me and we were kissing. Her taste was wonderful, familiar even after so many years. The kiss propelled us forward rapidly, without conscious thought but with deep-seated need. Quickly, we were removing each other's clothes, beckoning each other onward with our moans. I wanted so desperately to pleasure her, to validate physically the seminal place she would occupy forever in my heart. I touched her intimately, in ways that I knew she loved, and which I had never forgotten.

Before long we were making love with enormous energy, each of us thrusting as if to demonstrate a claim to superior need or desire. At one point the phone rang in the kitchen, and our ardor cooled a bit. We both knew that it probably was Darren, or Justin, calling Jennifer. That injected some guilt that I'm sure Jennifer felt far more strongly than I. After a few moments, we eased into a more gentle rhythm, knowing that there was no undoing our act, yet reveling in it as best as our respective consciences would allow. It was awkward, yet sweet. And when we finally pulled apart, sated, we embraced.

For a long time we said nothing. I thought that this was the first time in memory that I had truly made love to a woman. It felt idyllic to lay there, feelings of affection radiating from each of us. How long had it been since I had felt this way? Had I ever felt this peacefulness and contentment with Nicole? Ever? Regardless of the mixed feelings

I was experiencing, I refused to suppress the joy I felt over being with a woman I truly loved.

After a time, Jennifer sniffled, and I realized the pillow was damp. I leaned forward and lightly kissed her lips, which were warm and damp.

"What's wrong?" I felt like a puppy sensing his master was unhappy, but not really certain why.

"I don't know. I don't know whether I'm sad about what we just did, or sad about the reasons we did it."

We lay there for awhile longer, and finally I said, "I guess I'd better go home." I wished I could stay the night. And every night. But that was impossible.

We slowly extricated ourselves and sat up on the sofa. Both of us reached simultaneously for our wine glasses, making us chuckle. We each took a sip, lowered our glasses, and stood up. She walked me to the door and handed me my jacket.

We hugged again, but did not kiss. "Thanks for a great dinner."

"And dessert, huh?"

I took her chin in my hand and lifted it gently so I could see her eyes. Though they contained a shadow of mirth, they were mostly melancholy, as was her voice when she spoke again.

"This has to be the end," she said softly. "You know that, right?"

I tried to speak but found my throat constricted. I cleared it, then said, "Yeah, I know." Even though I didn't.

"We've both chosen other lives, and we have to give them our all, or they can't possibly work." I could barely meet her eyes, which looked at me expectantly. "We can't have temptations," she continued. "And you *are* a temptation."

That made me smile a bit, which was reflected instantly on her face. "Even after all these years," I said.

"*Especially* after all these years," Jennifer replied.

I looked at her beautiful face, knowing it was probably the last time I would ever see it. Finally I knew I had to leave. "Merry Christmas, Jen," I said at last.

"You too," she said, and she leaned past me to open the door and sent me out into the bitterly cold night. Jennifer turned the floodlight on to illuminate the walkway, and then closed the door behind me. I did not look back as I walked down the pathway to my car, passing a brightly lit Santa and snowman along the way. It mocked the lack of festiveness I felt at the impending holiday.

I glanced at my watch and groaned out loud when I saw it was after eleven. I had forgotten to call and leave a message, assuming I would get home before Nicki. Well, shit.

I raced home through the flurrying snow, but still it took forty-five minutes. When I opened the door to the apartment, it was pitch black. That was odd: usually Nicki stayed up late on Saturday nights, and sometimes allowed Alex to stay up, too. I didn't turn on a light until I was inside our bathroom. I brushed my teeth, peeled off my clothes, snapped off the light, and walked across the bedroom and slipped beneath the sheets. Nicki was quietly asleep on the other side of our bed.

I think I had briefly entered the realm of sleep when Nicki clicked on the lamp on her side of the bed and sat up. Groggily, I peered over at her, shielding my eyes against the light. Nicki was glaring down at me.

"I can't believe it. Not only couldn't you come home in time to kiss your daughter goodnight, you couldn't even wash your girlfriend's scent off your body." She threw the covers off her and stormed out of the room.

"Christ almighty!" I bellowed as she fled the room, but that was merely to mask my pounding heart. Nicki had to possess hyper-sensitive olfactory senses to detect that I had been with another woman. Or, more likely, she was guessing. I hoped.

My first instinct was to rush out after her. But what would I say? Dumbly, I hadn't even formulated a plan or a story on the drive home. But as I gave it a few moments' thought, I realized that anger was exactly what I wanted from Nicki. I wanted her to be as pissed off as I had been for the past several months. Maybe we were even now.

As I leaned out of bed to turn her light off, I could hear her down the hall putting sheets on the bed in her study. Fine. She had slept in that room many a night, confronting whatever demons robbed her (and sometimes me) of sleep. Now she could sleep there in self-imposed exile, and we would both be better off for it. Fuck it.

I returned to my side of the bed. Again, I banished the complex thoughts, and thanked the effects of an exhausting workweek and the red wine. Somehow, I was asleep again in no time at all.

WHEN I WOKE up with a throbbing red-wine hangover, I looked at the clock on the nightstand and saw that it was eight-thirty. I was disoriented and confused. Alex and Nicki were usually bustling around on Sunday mornings getting ready for church. But the apartment was silent.

I slid out of bed, found a bathrobe, chewed some aspirins, and checked the apartment. It was empty.

The morning wound on. By the time *The McLaughlin Group* finished at noon, Nicki and Alex still hadn't returned, so I called her parents' house in Maryland. Her mother answered. "Hi, Mrs. Petri."

"Oh, hi, Kevin."

"I'm looking forward to all of us coming over for Christmas dinner."

"Well, there's plenty of room."

"Mrs. Petri," I said, getting straight to the point, "Nicki and Alex aren't home from church, and I was planning to go shopping with Alex. Do you know where she is, by chance?"

"No, I have no idea. I haven't heard from her today."

"Well, if you hear from her, would you please ask her to call?"

"Yes, I'll do that." We hung up.

Well, this sucked. I busied myself in my study and passed the afternoon. But by five I still hadn't heard from them. I stretched out on the sofa to watch television, and before long fell asleep. I woke up some time later, groggy and disoriented. It was ten o'clock. Night or day, I wondered. Night. And the girls still weren't home.

I rummaged through our telephone book and found Nicki's sister's number. I dialed the number and Kim answered. "Kim, it's Kevin. Is Nicki there by chance?"

A pause, then a brisk tone. "Yes, Kevin, she and Alex are staying here. Nicki will get in touch with you when she feels like it."

God, how I hated her insolence. Probably because it mirrored Nicki's. "That's not acceptable. I was supposed to spend the day with Alex. Put Nicki on the phone."

"No. As I said, Nicki will contact you. Don't call back." Then the phone clicked in my ear.

I slammed down the phone. God*damn* it! I was sick and tired of Nicki leaving and taking Alex with her. Should I drive out to her sister's house and confront her? Then I thought, for gosh sakes, isn't this what I wanted? Nicki was driving me out of her life and now I was driving her out of mine.

By nine-fifteen Monday morning, I was behind the wheel of my car, driving up Wisconsin Avenue toward Annunciation School, the Catholic school that Nicki and I had chosen for Alexandra. It was a relatively small school with mostly middle-class students.

My plan was to take Alex out of class early, take her on our shopping trip, and then take her home. If Nicki wanted to see her, she could come home. I was trying to figure out what to do after that, because I understood two could play at this game. I did not want to use Alex as a pawn; I knew we would have to reach an accommodation. But the immediate objective was vital: I was not going to allow Nicki to take Alex away from me again. Period.

I pulled into the visitors' parking and walked into the office, which was small and austere as befitting a Catholic school. The matronly receptionist got up from her typing—amazingly, not only was she using a typewriter, it wasn't even electric—and walked over to me from behind the desk. "May I help you?"

"Hi," I said, trying to appear cheerful. "I'm Kevin Gibbons, Alexandra Gibbon's dad. She's in your kindergarten?"

"Whose class is she in?" the woman asked.

Ouch. I couldn't remember. Alex had mentioned her name a dozen times, but because I hadn't met her, the name hadn't stuck. "I'm sorry, I can't remember." She gave me a quizzical, disapproving look. "I just returned from Italy, and I need to pick Alex up." This wasn't going as I had intended it.

"I'm sorry, sir, but I'll have to ask you for identification," she said. I fumbled to get my wallet out, and pulled out my driver's license.

She scrutinized the license. "Please wait for a moment." She disappeared into an office whose door was marked, "Sister Bernadette Scanlon, Principal." A few moments later, the receptionist came out of the office, followed by Sister Bernadette.

"Mr. Gibbons, nice to see you again."

"Sister Bernadette. Happy holidays."

"Same to you," she said. "I understand you're here to pick up Alexandra."

"Yes. I've just returned from Italy, and need to pick her up early."

She gave me an appraising look. "You need to coordinate a little better with your wife. She called this morning to say that Alexandra wouldn't be in school until after Christmas break."

"So Alex isn't here?"

"No. As I said, your wife called this morning."

I tried to recover. "Oh, she mentioned she might be doing that, but you're right, we got our signals crossed. Well, I look forward to visiting Alexandra's classroom after she's back in school."

"We look forward to having you. Merry Christmas."

I left the building quickly and walked out to my car, sliding behind the wheel and closing the door, but not starting the car. I needed to collect my thoughts. The rage that had been accumulating inside me erupted. "SHIT!" I screamed, slamming the steering wheel violently.

Nicki had done it again. She had taken my little girl away from me.

20

I DROVE HOME and called Doug. His secretary told me he was in a meeting, but I asked her to interrupt him. Before long he was on the line, and I was telling him everything that had happened.

Doug outlined my options. He could call Nicki at her sister's house and urge her to act rationally. I could initiate divorce proceedings and ask the court for an immediate custody order. Or I could sit tight and wait for Nicki to take some action, whatever that might be. "Once this train leaves the station, there's no getting it back."

He was right. I decided to give it another night or two, perhaps try to contact her again. Perversely, if anything would lure Nicki back—and more importantly, get Alex back—it was the firm's Christmas gala scheduled for the day after tomorrow. It would take a lot for Nicki to miss that, given that she had organized the whole event.

I thanked Doug and told him I'd call no later than Thursday with some sort of decision. He reminded me that Christmas was only nine days away, and that if I was going to do something, I'd better act quickly. "Lawyers work the last two weeks of December, but judges don't."

I went back to the office, taking my colleagues by surprise. I was able to get some work done, including phoning some clients that I hadn't spoken to in quite awhile. I called Art Longley and chewed the fat with him. I could still feel some distance between us; although his corporation had expanded and he was buying and rehabilitating properties up and down the eastern seaboard, he was no longer our biggest client, and he was spreading some work around to different architects.

Fortunately, our year had been Horizon's third straight with growth in excess of twenty-five percent, and it should get even better the next year with the economy improving. But I assumed I was going to have to make some management changes, increasing Rich's partnership share to a full half. To put it mildly, I could not afford to lose Rich.

I went home at about seven. Still no Nicki. I was anxious but decided to wait until the next day to initiate calls on my own. I settled down to watch *Melrose Place*. I was tired, and found an intriguing-looking Dean Koontz novel and took it to bed with me. Eventually I snapped off the light.

Then I thought I heard sounds coming from the living room. Fortunately, the building was secure and the odds of a break-in virtually nonexistent. And usually if I really did hear sounds, it was either Nicki or Alex prowling around. But Nicki and Alex weren't home. And this time the sounds didn't seem like a middle-of-the-night hallucination.

I craned my neck to peer toward the doorway. It was pitch black. Our bedroom windows faced the park, so there was no reflected light from the streets; and when there was no moonlight, it was completely dark in our room. Like now.

Something odd caught my attention: a tiny red glow on the bed comforter. Where could that be from, I wondered, shaking the remaining cobwebs from my brain. Maybe a reflection from the little red light on the ceiling fire detector? Except that we didn't have one in our bedroom.

Then the light moved, horizontally across the comforter, until it stopped on my torso. My eyes widened in disbelief.

Something primordial inside me screamed to get out of there. As quietly as I could, I slid out from under the covers and dropped slowly to the floor, pulling my legs behind me. But I got tangled somehow in the phone cord, and it came crashing down to the floor with me, the ringer jangling loudly.

Just then a huge explosion roared, deafening me and practically lifting me off the floor in fright. Christ, someone had just fired a gun at me!

The shot had been followed by a thudding sound, suggesting that the bullet had buried itself in the mattress. Good God, what should I do? There was no chance of escape—the assassin was between me and the apartment's only exit. Perhaps if I lay there silently, he would think he had killed me, and leave. But I doubted it.

My heart thumped inside my chest as I gathered my thoughts.

Then a possibility occurred to me—the phone! I looked down and it was off the hook. I punched in nine-one-one, then slid the phone under the bed. I didn't dare even whisper into it. I just hoped that the emergency operator would figure out the situation and send someone. Fast.

Just then the overhead light flicked on. Footsteps muffled by the carpet sounded from across the room, coming toward where I lay cowering on the floor. Then a face.

Nicki.

She was clad entirely in black. Just, as I recalled perversely, as she had been dressed the first time I had seen her.

But her face this time was different. As she gazed down at me, her eyes were blazing with pure hatred. I looked up at her from my helpless position on the floor, almost more terrified of her eyes than of the gun she was aiming at me, police-style. It would have been a hilarious image, were it not for Nicki's deadly serious expression and the fact that I might be facing the end of my life. I realized stupidly that I had never detected real emotion in Nicki's eyes before. Until that moment.

"Nicki." I tried to gather myself up, but my legs were still tangled in the bed linens.

"Don't move." Her voice was hard, deep, guttural.

Remembering that the phone was off the hook, and praying that someone was listening, I said, "Nicki, please put down the gun." Her gaze bore into me. "You know that the Parkside has security. They're going to come up here."

"These walls are well-insulated. You told me that yourself."

Yeah, what a fricking terrific architect I was, I thought grimly. "Nicki, we can work this out."

"There's only one solution. That's for you to die."

Something inside me reacted to that. "You couldn't even abide a divorce! Doesn't murder stack up as a slightly worse sin?"

"This isn't murder," she said earnestly, her voice softening. But somehow that just made the sound of it more chilling. "This is an eye for an eye, just like the Bible says. One sin exchanged for another."

Great, she had this worked out theologically. Keep her talking, I told myself. "I didn't kill anyone."

"You killed our marriage. You betrayed me. Over and over again.

But when you betrayed our marriage vows, that was the final transgression."

She held the gun steadily, her hands not even appearing to shake in the slightest. Her shooting-range lessons had apparently paid off.

"What about Alex?"

"It's better that it's just the two of us, given the options. You've got tons of insurance, and your share of the firm. We'll do just fine."

"But it won't just be me she's losing. It will be you, too. You'll be in jail. They'll figure it out."

"I've got it all worked out. My sister will give me an alibi. I was there with Alex the entire time. And I stole the gun from the firing range. They'll never notice it, because I'll sneak it back. They'll think this was a burglary. I'll jimmy the lock, and take some things to make it look good." She smiled at her cleverness. That expression combined with her hate-filled eyes made her look stark raving mad. "And even if they do catch me, it will be justifiable homicide. I looked into it at the library this afternoon. You cheated on me, Kevin."

"I think they call that pre-meditated murder, Nicki."

She laughed out loud. "I told you when we met that I'm crazy. You just didn't believe me."

"Nicki, you can get some help. *We* can get some help. And even if you don't love me, think about Alex."

"I *do* love you," she exclaimed, her voice emotional now and her eyes moist. "You're the only person I've ever loved, aside from Alex." My throat constricted; amazingly, not from my heart-thudding fear, but from the words that had come from her mouth.

I thought maybe we were making progress toward defusing the situation, until her next words, which were spoken evenly. "That's why I have to kill you."

Gallows humor starting whispering in my mind: be careful what you wish for, buddy. You wanted out of your marriage, and this is the final exit.

I was about to try to reply when suddenly a loud voice yelled from the doorway, "Freeze!" It made both Nicki and me jerk in surprise.

Nicki turned her attention toward the doorway and her eyes widened, but she kept the gun aimed in my direction. I couldn't see a thing from my prone position on the side of the bed, and I didn't move a muscle.

"Lower the gun slowly to the bed, and no one will get hurt," the voice instructed.

Well, imagine that, I thought to myself. D.C.'s finest actually came through. But Nicki hadn't reacted to their commands yet, and I was still terrified. The voice sounded again, gentle but firm. "Come on, now, lady."

"Nicki. Alex needs you," I pleaded.

A huge sigh lifted Nicki's shoulders, and she lowered the gun onto the bed. She glanced angrily at me and looked miserable.

As soon as she dropped the gun, footsteps rushed toward us. Someone retrieved the gun from the bed. An officer grabbed Nicki's arms, pushed her face against the wall and frisked her. Another officer leaned over an extended a hand to me. "Are you all right, sir?" The first cop was white, the second was black. Both were big guys.

I let the officer help me to my feet. I was shaking uncontrollably. "Yes, I think I'm okay. Thanks for coming so fast."

"He cheated on me," Nicki bellowed.

The officer who was attending to her read Nicki her rights. I had only seen this in movies and on television, and the whole experience was surrealistic. Nicki sobbed loudly.

As the black cop pulled handcuffs off his belt, I urged him, "Please don't do that. My wife isn't dangerous." He looked at me incredulously. "I mean, she isn't dangerous anymore." He shook his head but replaced the cuffs on his belt.

The white cop instructed, "We'll need you to come to the station and make a report. Don't touch anything in the meantime. We'll send over some detectives to gather whatever information we need."

"Can I take a shower before I come over?" I was shaking uncontrollably.

"Sure," he answered. "It will take a couple hours for processing anyway. Try to get there by five. We go off shift at six." He handed me a business card.

"Sure, thank you." He nodded, then spoke into a radio and told the dispatcher that they were coming in with a two-twenty-nine. I guessed that meant Nicki.

She was looking humiliated, tears streaking her cheeks. I had never seen her look so forlorn. I couldn't imagine what would happen to her, but I knew it would not be easy.

She looked over at me, all traces of anger gone. Her face was pale in the harsh overhead light. "Thanks, Kevin," she said softly. I looked at her curiously. She lifted her hands. "About the handcuffs." I nodded. Her eyes glistened, and the semblance of a grin crossed her face. "You're the only one who gets to use handcuffs on me," she said meekly.

Her comment suddenly made my heart ache. I nodded dumbly in reply.

Then the officers were leading her through the apartment, turning on lights along the way. I threw on a bathrobe and caught up with them. Our front door was ajar. Nicki's gaze was downcast as the elevator door closed.

I went back into the apartment, still trembling, and got some coffee started. I would need it. Then I took a long hot shower until my shaking began to subside. It wasn't until I was back in the bedroom toweling off that it truly struck me what had happened. I walked over to the bed, and couldn't find a hole in the comforter but found one in the mattress. And continuing into the wall, right next to where I'd been lying. How the shot had managed to miss me, I couldn't imagine.

I picked the phone up off the floor and returned it to the bedstand. That is what saved my life, I reflected. I hoped 911 had gotten everything on tape.

I dressed with a tie and sport jacket, then poured myself some coffee. Three-thirty. I had some business to attend to before I left for the police station. I needed to arrange for a lawyer for Nicki. But first I looked up Kim's number and dialed. Kim's husband, Mitch, answered groggily. As a fireman, he was probably used to nighttime calls.

"Mitch, this is Kevin. Let me talk to Kim."

"What?" he asked. "Kevin, if this is about Nicki . . ."

"This is about Kim. Put her on the phone."

I could hear murmuring in the background, then Kim's irritated voice. "What do you want?" she asked.

"Your sister just tried to kill me."

"What are you talking about?"

"I don't know whether you were in on it, but if you weren't, you can check your sister's room. She's not there. That's because she's at the police station, under arrest for attempted murder."

"You're not serious," she said, but not convincingly.

"Believe me, I wouldn't kid about something like this. But to answer your first question, what I want is this: I want Alex back here, at the apartment, by nine a.m. Do you understand that?"

"I have to go to work," she protested ludicrously.

"Kim, damn it, let me tell you this once," I growled. "If Alex is not here by nine o'clock, I will have you arrested for kidnapping and for accessory to attempted murder. And if you don't believe me, try it. Do you understand?"

Pause. Then meekly, "Yes."

I hung up. No sooner had I put the phone down than it rang. "Hello?"

It was Doug. "Kevin, what's going on?"

"Doug, how do you know about this?"

"I just got a call from Nicki. From jail, for Christ's sake! I couldn't figure out what she was in there for, and asked if she had called you. That's when I got the surprise of my life. I mean, you weren't kidding about her, were you?"

"No, I guess not."

"Well, I told her she needed a criminal lawyer, and just gave one a call. He's on his way down there now. I didn't have the heart to tell her I'm already representing you."

Doug agreed to meet me at the police station. I drove down there before five. The station was awash in predictable chaos, all sorts of bleary-eyed suspects carted back and forth by grim-faced cops. It must've been a typically wild night in the nation's capitol.

I finally gave my statement, starting with my altercation with Nicki on Saturday but omitting the explanations. If Nicki wanted to fill in the details, she could.

Doug and I huddled afterward. "My thinking is that we agree not to press charges in exchange for an involuntary commitment to a psychiatric facility," Doug advised. "Or voluntary, though Nicki probably won't agree to it. Under the circumstances, she won't have much choice, especially with the nine-one-one tape."

"When could she get out?" I asked.

"We can only get ninety days prior to a complete evaluation, but given the violence, it will turn into a couple of years. And they might actually be able to help her."

"I hope so. Let's go for that."

Doug smiled. "I'll see what I can do." He touched my arm. "Do you need Rita back?"

"I'll manage. Between my mother and Mrs. Beeman, I'll have babysitters when I need them. And I need some bonding time with Alex right now."

He nodded empathetically. "We'll talk later today," he said, and we went our separate ways.

It was after eight when I came home. The detectives must have come and gone, for I found another business card on the kitchen counter. I called my mother and told her what had happened; again omitting my own embarrassing contribution. She was incredulous, but strong as usual and offering to help. I asked her to come down right away, and she promised she'd come on the first flight the next morning.

As I stood in the kitchen trying to think things through, I thought I heard a tapping at the front door. I opened it and Alex stood framed in the doorway, looking very tiny, a red stocking cap pulled down to her eyes and her Raggedy Ann backpack strapped over the shoulders of her red down jacket. My first thought was outrage that Kim had merely sent her on her own, without even bringing her up.

Then I noticed Alex's lower lip was trembling, and in a moment I was kneeling down and Alex swept into my arms. She sobbed.

I lifted her inside, removing her backpack and then her jacket and hat. I sat on the sofa and she climbed onto my lap, hugging my chest and still sobbing. She looked up at me with a tear-soaked face, so much like Nicki's had been only a few hours earlier.

"I don't like this," she hiccuped. "Mommy wouldn't even let me call you. She said I wouldn't ever see you again."

A chill ran up my spine as I contemplated how close that threat had come to reality. I held her tightly, and her intense crying resumed. I patted her back, whispering, "Shh, shh, it's okay."

When finally she quieted, she looked up at me, as if searching my face for an explanation. "Honey," I said as soothingly as I could, "Mommy's sick. Really really sick. So she went to a hospital, where they're going to help make her better. But we might not see her for a long time, while she gets better. Okay?"

Alex popped her thumb into her mouth, something she had not

done for a long time, and she stared ahead. I patted her on her back, rocking her gently.

Then Alex extracted her thumb long enough to look up at me again and make a statement. "I don't ever want to go away from you again," she said in the softest little-girl voice I had ever heard.

"Don't worry. You'll never have to go away again. I promise."

That assurance seemed to comfort her, and Alex burrowed her face into my chest, holding on as if for dear life.

30

THE PARTY LINE was that Nicki was seriously ill and had been hospitalized for an extended period of time. I declined to discuss the nature of the illness, and I think most people suspected it was leukemia or some other type of cancer. I did nothing to discourage that speculation. Rich was the only person outside my family, other than Doug, with whom I shared the truth. He was shocked, but understanding. I desperately needed his support if I was to have any chance of juggling the various responsibilities in my life.

My mother arrived on Wednesday and pitched in immediately. Though she had slowed down physically, she still took Alex by Metro to the Air & Space Museum. Alex was hesitant to go with her—for whatever reason, probably Nicki's influence, she didn't seem to care much for my mother—but she seemed placated when I promised that I would be there when she got home. I made a mental note to check out some child therapists, because I was sure that no matter how things turned out, Alex would need some help coping.

Meanwhile, the involuntary commitment hearing was set for Thursday afternoon. Doug had made a deal with the prosecutor to drop charges, subject to the judge agreeing to order the involuntary commitment. Nicki had hired a lawyer to fight the commitment, even though her lawyer was no doubt urging her to take the deal.

Doug had researched some facilities, and we found one in Towson, Maryland, that specialized in patients with borderline personality disorders called the Kreitzer Foundation Residential Clinic. Talking with one of their top psychologists, Dr. Alan Goldblum, Doug was satisfied that they would take her illness seriously, and recommend proper long-term treatment if that proved necessary. It was convenient to Nicki's family, and not too far away for Alex, or Alex and me, to visit once we worked that out.

On Wednesday evening, I somehow managed to play the host at

our Christmas party. There were three hundred guests, and it seemed that nearly every one asked about Nicki. Halfway through, I drew everyone's attention and mentioned how unfortunate it was that Nicki had become ill—I didn't indicate the seriousness—on the night of a party she had planned.

When I got home around midnight, my mother was sound asleep on the sofa, but Alex was still awake watching television, waiting up for me. I roused my mother and told her to go to bed, kissing her gently on the cheek.

"Brush your teeth and time for bed," I told Alex, exhausted both from the party and over the prospect of the ordeal that faced me the next day.

Alex usually used the bathroom down the hall, but she brushed her teeth in our bathroom so that Nicki could monitor her hygiene. When she was finished she scooted off to her bedroom and I told her I'd tuck her in momentarily; I had to use the bathroom first. I stood at the toilet and something amiss caught my attention at the bathroom sink. I wasn't sure at first what it was, but then realized it was the toothbrushes. Specifically, their order: Nicki's was at the end and Alex's little one was now in the middle, next to mine. Alex had changed the position of her mother's and her toothbrushes.

For some reason, that irritated me. I went to Alex's room, where she was conducting a conversation with a stuffed lion.

"Did you change the toothbrushes?"

"Yes."

"Why?"

"Because Mommy's not here, so my toothbrush goes next to yours."

"But what about when Mommy comes back?"

"Maybe Mommy won't ever come back."

I sat down on the side of her bed, trying to restrain my anger with her callousness. "Your mom is coming back, Alex. She's just sick. But she's going to get better. And when she does, she'll want her toothbrush in the right place. Understand?" Alex's jaw was set, but she nodded. "Okay, 'nighty-night." I leaned over and kissed her cheek, then waited, and she kissed mine back. I guessed that meant she was okay. "Sweet dreams," I said as I turned off the light.

I went back to my bathroom and switched the toothbrushes

back. As I was falling asleep a few minutes later, I realized, to my considerable surprise, that my reaction to Alex meant that I really did want Nicki to get better, and even to return. As horrible as the events were only two nights before, they carried the sliver of a silver lining: the prospect of Nicki finally confronting her problems, having some real professional help, and possibly overcoming them. If she could somehow bring out the best features of her personality and purge the dark side, she truly could be a wonderful person. A beautiful person, inside and out. And maybe, just maybe, we could build a normal life together.

The next day, I left close to noon and met with Doug before the hearing. He was optimistic that everything would go our way.

"Nicki desperately wants to avoid commitment to a mental facility. But of course she doesn't want to stay in jail, either. No one can get through to her that our offer is the best she's going to get. The prosecutor certainly isn't going to drop the charges," Doug said.

The thought of Nicki in jail, or even in a mental institution, troubled me. But the image of her standing near my bed, aiming a gun at me while bearing a look of pure hatred, troubled me even more.

"I'm really worried Nicki will feel trapped," I told Doug.

"This is for the best," he assured me. Having rejected his advice at a crucial juncture a long time before, I was inclined to accept it now.

The hearing was before Superior Court Judge Elwood S. Bryant. Several of Nicki's family members, including her parents and Kim, entered the courtroom and sat in the back. They cast frosty glances in my direction, and didn't make an effort to talk to me—nor I to them. When the case was called, Nicki was brought in by a police officer, accompanied by a tall, handsome man who was apparently her lawyer, Robert Kleniewski. I sat at counsel table with Doug. As the charge was a felony, in the District of Columbia it was prosecuted by federal rather than D.C. lawyers.

Nicki looked beautiful, but had lost weight during her brief incarceration. Her cheeks were sunken, which had the effect of making her look like a fashion model. She looked scared.

The prosecutor explained the situation to the judge: Nicole Gibbons was charged with attempted murder of her husband, but the prosecutor was willing to withdraw the charges if the court would remit Mrs. Gibbons to involuntary commitment for psychiatric care and evaluation for ninety days. The motion was supported by her husband, who was present and represented by counsel who had submitted the petition. The judge heard from Doug, who submitted an initial psychiatric recommendation and spelled out the prescribed evaluation protocol. Doug noted that Nicole had a daughter, and that the suggested course of action could reunite the two of them much faster than if she were prosecuted for attempted murder.

Nicki's lawyer was fairly polished but had a tough case. He pointed out that Nicki did have responsibilities for her daughter, and that the alleged assault (in his argument he downscaled the offense) was precipitated by marital infidelity. He offered to have Nicki testify to demonstrate her lucidity and remorse.

For a moment I worried that Nicki would get off. But Doug had assured me that even if the judge didn't grant the petition, Nicki still would be subject to criminal prosecution.

We played our trump card: the nine-one-one tape. It was only thirteen minutes long—I couldn't believe the police had arrived so quickly!—but listening to it made my blood freeze. At first it was difficult to hear because the dispatcher was trying to make himself heard. But then he was silent, and it was just me and Nicki. My voice was much louder; Nicki's more distant. The judge listened intently. I looked back at Nicki's family, and they sat stonily. I glanced over at Nicki, but she too sat staring straight ahead.

The judge waved to his attendant to cut off the tape. "I don't need to hear anything more. Frankly, Mr. Kleniewski, I think the government is being very generous here. Clearly they could prosecute Mrs. Gibbons. This way, she's in for ninety days. If she's sick, she stays longer and gets help. If she's not, she's released and pays nothing more for her actions." He gazed at Kleniewski, who said nothing. "As I said, I think that's generous. Do you agree?"

"Yes, your honor," Kleniewski said.

The judge pulled some papers together. "The court remands Nicole Gibbons to the Kreitzer Foundation Residential Clinic for an initial evaluation period of ninety days, with leave to renew the petition. The District shall dismiss all criminal charges against Mrs. Gibbons, with prejudice. I will prepare an order with my findings." Then the judge adjourned the proceedings and disappeared.

The courtroom rumbled, even though there were only about a dozen people present. Then from across the room, Nicki cried out again, "Kevin, don't send me there! I'll die in there!"

I looked across the courtroom, where Nicki was surrounded by family members, and her attorney and the bailiff were ushering her toward the door. But her eyes, gushing with tears, were fastened on mine. "Please don't do this to me, Kevin!" she shrieked. "I'll die in there!"

I was shaking when I left the courtroom.

ON CHRISTMAS EVE I spoke to Dr. Goldblum, who reported that Nicki was settling in. The facilities were fairly luxurious—they certainly were expensive enough—and she was assigned to a private room. At first Nicki was extremely agitated and the doctors were forced to sedate her. But after visits from family members, and discussions with her doctors, Nicki seemed to have reconciled herself to her situation. She asked repeatedly about Alex, and was told she could speak to Alex on Christmas day. Dr. Goldblum advised me to monitor the conversation very closely. If all went well, we could arrange a visit sometime after the holidays.

I was sleeping pretty soundly the next morning when Alex bounded in and jumped on my bed, announcing, "Daddy! Daddy! Santa brought lots of presents!"

My mother was making breakfast and Alex was playing with her new toys when the phone rang. I was surprised to hear Dr. Goldblum's voice. "Mr. Gibbons, I'm sorry to disturb you on the holiday," he said gravely. "Are you alone?"

Startled by his question, I glanced around and saw that both Alex and Mother were out of earshot. "Yes, doctor. What's wrong?"

He paused before answering. "Mr. Gibbons, I desperately hate to give you this news." Pause again. "I'm afraid that your wife died this morning."

"What?!" I couldn't believe what he was saying. "Are you serious?"

"I'm afraid so. She committed suicide."

"Oh, Christ," I said.

"It's not pleasant," the doctor continued. "Nicki filled the shower basin with hot water, and broke her eyeglasses to use them to slit her wrists. We found her just an hour ago, and there was nothing we could do." He paused. "We've only had a single suicide in our fifteen years, before this. We take precautions, Mr. Gibbons. Mrs. Gibbons knew what she was doing."

That part didn't surprise me. If Nicki had wanted to kill herself, she would find a way to do it. With perfect timing and in dramatic fashion.

I hung up the phone and sat in stunned silence. There was a touch on my shoulder. I jumped. "Kevin, what's wrong?" My mother, her coffee sloshing from my startled reaction.

She let me lead her into the living room. "Alex," I called to her, "come here."

"What?" she asked.

I wished I knew how to say this. "Alex, you know that Mommy was very, very sick."

I could hear my mother gasp, "Oh, no."

Alex nodded, looking suddenly very vulnerable and frightened.

"Honey, your Mommy died last night."

Alex's bottom lip quivered, and she looked at me with huge eyes. I could tell she was trying to determine whether to believe me, desperately not wanting to, but knowing inside that I wouldn't kid with her about this. Suddenly she plunged into my arms and burst into hysterical tears. I held her tightly and my mother hugged us both. Alex's sobs wrenched me to my core.

EVERYTHING HAPPENED SO fast after that. Calls to Nicki's family, fury and recriminations on their part, more tears and guilt. Arrangements with the psychiatric facility and a funeral home. My sister and her family coming in from Las Vegas, not finding the Christmas frivolity they expected, but instead preparation for a funeral. Doug, looking as guilty as I felt, and Karen, and my colleagues. Drew and Leslie Tournus driving up from New Jersey. And a blizzard, adding logistical nightmares to all the rest.

My friends and family didn't know what to say. They hadn't even known Nicki had been committed. I had kept everything a secret. They all suspected, I'm sure, that there had been problems. But I could tell from their awkward words and empathetic expressions that they hadn't even begun to comprehend the depth of those problems.

Alex clung to me, constantly. She grew nervous if I was out of her sight. I reassured her as best I could. But it was false assurance, for I wasn't feeling very confident about much of anything.

I did not let her come to the viewings at the funeral home. She stayed home with my mother. Alex's cousins were a precious distraction. At first they seemed awkward, not knowing what to do. But when they figured out that playing games with Alex not only wasn't forbidden but positively therapeutic, they went at it with gusto. I don't know how we could have gotten through those days without them.

Nicki was buried on Saturday. There seemed to be hundreds of people, many of whom I had no idea who they were. Nicki had such an amorphous past—hell, an amorphous present—that I didn't even know a lot of the people who were in her life. Nicki's family avoided me assiduously. I don't think they even said a single word. I told Mr. and Mrs. Petri and Nicki's siblings how sorry I was. They returned my words with cold glares.

Alex came to the funeral with me. The service was held at a Catholic church in the Maryland suburbs that the Petri family attended. The church where Nicki had been baptized, and had experienced her first communion. It was at the cemetery in Severna Park that Alex and I broke down again. It was excruciating to see Nicki's casket lowered into the ground with such utter and concrete finality.

As the cars in the funeral procession began to pull away, Alex and I parted company. We had discussed this. Nicki's parents had insisted on hosting a gathering at their home. I wanted no part of it and they wanted no part of me. My mother and sister agreed to take Alex to the Petris' house and then bring her home. That would also give me several hours to be alone.

I walked Alex back to the limousine in which we had driven over. As we reached the car, she looked up at me. Though her eyes were red, her face was resolute. Alex pursed her lips and said, "It's just you and me now."

That almost got me crying again, but I nodded and leaned down and hugged her. Then my mother and sister were there, making their way slowly up the snowy path. I kissed Alex's cheek and straightened up. My sister took Alex by the hand. Alex turned away, her long blonde hair swishing from beneath her hat just as I had seen Nicki's do so many times.

Drew and Leslie dropped me at the Parkside. The snow was falling again and had further darkened a dreary afternoon. I walked over to the bathroom and flicked on the light. It was time to freshen up and face the future.

Something seemed out of place and I searched the bathroom to discern what it was. Then I figured it out: beside the sink, the toothbrushes had been rearranged once again. Like before, Alex's little toothbrush had been moved next to mine.

But this time, though I searched for it, Nicki's was nowhere to be found.

PART THREE

alex

31

I HAD CHOREOGRAPHED this moment in my mind so thoroughly and repeatedly that I couldn't believe it finally was really happening. As I stood at the door, I'm sure my face bore what in technical parlance might be called a shit-eating grin.

I rapped loudly on our apartment door.

From the other side of the door, I could hear the patter of bare feet running along the hardwood floor, then the sound of the deadbolt opening, followed by the door itself, opening just a crack to reveal huge hazel eyes. "Daddy?"

I smiled. "C'mon over by the elevator."

Alex and I practically tiptoed toward the elevator, where a medium-sized cardboard box sat on the floor. It seemed to be quivering.

She leaned over and pulled away the lid. The puppy practically pounced out of the box. Alex recoiled in surprise, then exclaimed, "Daddy, it's a puppy!"

"Happy birthday!" I said, and walked toward the two of them. For the puppy, apparently, it was love at first sight, for he was bathing the little girl's face with kisses. Alex squealed with laughter, trying to hug the puppy as he squirmed away, his tail wagging a mile a minute and still kissing her. It made Alex giggle. "He's so sweet, Daddy!" she cried out. "It is a 'he,' right, Daddy?"

"Yes, he's a boy-dog," I replied, taking in the scene. It was exactly as I had imagined it.

Alex gave me a final hug, then turned her attention back to the frolicking puppy. He was a little Cairn terrier, which the puppy farm folks recommended for its intelligence, small size, and happy disposition. The puppy's scruffy fur practically covered his eyes.

"What shall we name you?" Alex asked as she kneeled down to scratch him. "We shall name you Benji, just like in the movie," she said.

"Benji is a good name," I agreed.

Rita appeared at the door. Fortunately her tenure with Doug and Karen had ended, and she was working for me full-time again. "What is all this noise out here?" she asked with a smile. Rita and I had discussed the proposition of getting a puppy, given that the task of taking care of him would fall primarily on her shoulders. "The little girl needs a puppy," she had advised me, and I thought she was right.

As if on cue, the other door in the hallway opened. It was Mona Beeman. "Oh!" she exclaimed. "What a beautiful little puppy!"

"Mona, Rita, look at what Daddy brought me!" She picked up the squirming puppy and held him close so that he could kiss first the housekeeper, then our neighbor. Then me, too, for good measure. "I love him, Daddy!"

"That makes me very happy," I said. And it did.

Eventually we gathered up the puppy and his belongings and brought him inside. Alex immediately wanted to take him for a walk, and we put on his little collar and leash and took him outside. Not a moment too soon, it turned out. I marveled that such a little puppy could hold so much liquid.

Unsurprisingly, throughout the evening Alex and Benji were inseparable. Alex ran up and down the hallway, her ponytail and Benji streaming behind, Alex giggling and the little dog yapping excitedly. When it was finally bedtime, Alex was sweaty and seriously needed a bath. Benji stood sentry with his front paws perched on the ledge of the bathtub, intrigued and slightly frightened by the bubbles Alex sent in his direction.

I had determined not to let Benji sleep with Alex, but of course acquiesced immediately upon Alex's entreaties. The people at the puppy farm assured me he was housebroken—a quality for which I gladly paid a premium price—and I took him out for a walk again just before bedtime. Alex was waiting near the elevator when we returned, but both little girl and puppy seemed worn out. I read the two of them a bedtime story—even though Alex was already reading at a second-grade level, she preferred my pre-sleeptime storytelling—then turned out the light.

I stood by the doorway and watched them both fall quickly to sleep. It was difficult to spot Benji among all of Alex's stuffed animals.

But my growing daughter was prominent among them, her long blonde hair shrouding the pillow and her fingers gently entwined with Benji's fur. It was a precious tableau, and I smiled as I walked back to the living room.

Given the catastrophe that had produced our circumstances, it seemed remarkable how easily Alex and I had settled into our new life. Over the weeks following Nicki's funeral, Alex sometimes had awakened at night crying. She would repeatedly sneak from her own bedroom in the middle of the night, and I would wake up in the morning to find her sleeping beside me. At those times, I would get out of bed, gently extricate her thumb from her mouth, and carry her back to her own bed. On the occasions that I perceived her arrival during the night, though, I didn't have the heart to send her back to her room until morning. And frankly, sometimes it was nice to have company.

I wanted to move to Potomac or McLean, where there would be playmates in the neighborhood, but Alex wouldn't hear of it. I didn't press the issue, not wanting to further uproot Alex's stability. But we had redecorated much of the apartment. We turned Nicki's study into a playroom, and I let Alex pick out new wallpaper for the playroom and both her bedroom and mine. Not surprisingly, considering her maternal lineage, Alex had well-defined and mature taste. But different from her mother's: while Nicki was strictly Ralph Lauren, Alex preferred Laura Ashley. So my bedroom turned out a bit more frilly than I would've liked, but it always made me smile to think about the five-year-old decorator who had selected it.

Now that decorator was six, and growing fast. She was one of the tallest children in the kindergarten. Very athletic, and tough. As I watched her on the playground, she always seemed to organize activities and exert leadership. Her first instinct was to cajole, the second was to coerce. Usually she successfully goaded other children into following her lead. I would interfere only when she turned nasty, which sometimes happened. I didn't like that quality in her, at all. But generally, the other children seemed to admire her leadership qualities and imagination.

Work was fantastic lately. Of course, I had had to curtail my hours fairly significantly, but a project had captured my fancy, and we had bid on it and won. In my opinion, Ford's Harbor would become the signature of my career.

Although apartment renovation remained Horizon's specialty, increasingly we had branched out into new construction. Even there, our emphasis was not new housing developments, but construction in established residential and historical neighborhoods.

A few months ago, a small newspaper article had caught my eye and fired my imagination. A developer had abandoned a project on one of the few undeveloped parcels in Old Town Alexandria. It was the site of an old, long-abandoned Ford automobile factory that had been designed in 1931 by Albert Kahn, a legendary art deco architect. The building was an historical landmark, and any development required that the building be salvaged. But it was crumbling, and this developer was the second to abandon a project there.

We took a look and determined that we could preserve the building's facade and build condominiums, surrounded by townhouses occupying the remainder of the 9.7-acre parcel leading to the edge of the river. It was prime property, and the townhouses overlooking the river would command more than one million dollars apiece. It would mark the largest new development in Old Town since the 1940s, and it would make our firm rich.

Remarkably, the usually prickly Architectural Review Commission loved the concept, especially after having been burned by two previous proposals. We had the preliminary go-ahead. If our final plans were approved, we would be designing for much of the duration of the year, with construction to begin the following spring. The project had gotten my juices flowing more than any previous one, save perhaps the Pension Building. But that project was nearly complete, and no longer commanded much of my attention. This one would occupy my thoughts and talents for some time to come.

THAT SATURDAY WAS her birthday party. Ten children from Alex's kindergarten class had accepted her invitation, nine girls and one boy named Kyle. Personally, I thought he would be a lucky little boy to be surrounded by girls, but at age six or thereabouts, I doubted he'd feel that way. Although Alex had never indicated an interest in the opposite sex, I wondered about her insistence that Kyle—but no other boys—attend her party.

Fortunately, Rita was able to come over and give me a hand. Invariably, the children were dropped off by their mothers, who regarded me curiously. The kids were adorable. Kyle turned out to be a little prince, with jet black hair and bright blue eyes. He seemed very shy, at least in this company, but Alex was very attentive to him. It made me feel whimsical to think that Alex might have her first schoolgirl crush.

I also finally met Alex's new best friend, Ashleigh. She was a striking little girl who actually could be Kyle's twin. She was very quiet, and when Alex wasn't fussing over Kyle, she and Ashleigh would huddle together in secretive conversation.

I had hired a magician, who proved entertaining enough, performing some clever tricks (including, to the girls' squealing delight, producing a live bunny who seemed remarkably calm) and creating clever balloon animals for all of the children. We played pin-the-tail-on-the-donkey. The cake from the local ice cream shop was delicious. Alex loved her presents and was appropriately appreciative, and everyone seemed to have a good time.

After everyone went home, Rita and I cleaned up while Alex took Benji for a walk; Alex had proved to be very responsible about the dog.

The next morning after breakfast, Alex and Benji and I took a drive to Old Town Alexandria to look at the site for Ford's Harbor. I pulled her toward me and walked with my arm on her shoulders as we toured the development. I pointed out where everything would be, and I could tell Alex was applying her keen imagination to visualize it.

Afterward, we went to Ben & Jerry's for ice cream and strolled around Old Town. Walking there made me miss it from my bachelor days. I wondered—silently—whether Alex would entertain the possibility of moving there. We could live in one of the grand townhouses overlooking the Potomac. Eastern exposure, beautiful surroundings—and a clean break from the past.

Looking up from her S'Mores ice cream, a little dab of vanilla at the corner of her mouth, Alex announced earnestly, "I like Old Town, Daddy, but I would never want to move here." Shades of Nicki, reading my mind.

52

FOR A LONG time after Nicki's death I lost romantic interest in women. I didn't spend much time thinking about it, but I found that even when I interacted with especially attractive women, it was with almost clinical detachment. It didn't bother me, because the main focus of my attention was, and had to be, Alex.

I didn't realize how much I missed female companionship, of an adult if platonic variety. I found it in an unexpected venue: Kramer Books, where I was browsing one Saturday evening when Alex was having a sleepover at her grandparents'.

"I almost didn't recognize you on this side of the Atlantic," a voice beside me said in a British accent.

I turned and at first thought the woman beside me must be speaking to someone else. But her intense starre, through glittering green eyes, left no doubt I was the object of her comments. Obviously enjoying my discomfort, she laughed and said, "You don't remember me, do you?"

I blushed and stammered, "Of course, great to see you again."

She wouldn't let me off the hook. "So, then, who am I?"

I ad-libbed. "If you don't know, I can't help you." She laughed a mirthful sound.

"Helen Lumley," she replied. "One of your students in Rome."

"Oh, yes!" And indeed I remembered. She was an adorable, preocious student. We had shared drinks together with other students after Nicki and Alex had made their exit. Now, Helen was all grown up, strikingly pretty and no less forward than she had been in Rome.

We ended up getting a table in the Afterwords restaurant at the rear of the store. She was working at a small design firm in Bethesda. I caught her up with the events in my life, which she received empathetically. The minutes dissolved into hours, and I realized how starved I was for good conversation. Helen and I resolved to meet there again, for dinner, in two weeks when Alex spent the weekend away again.

It was after eleven when I returned home.

I noticed the light flashing on the message machine in the hallway when I came in the apartment. It was unusual to receive messages on a Saturday night. But I had four.

Alex. "Hi, Daddy, we're watching *The Muppet Movie*, it's really great!" A mile a minute, just like her mother. "Where are you, Daddy? I called your office, and you weren't there, either. What did you have for dinner? I had ice cream. Not for dinner"—giggle—"but for dessert. Daddy, I have to go shopping for a present for Ashleigh. It's her birthday party next Saturday. Can we go shopping tomorrow? I know exactly what I'm going to get her. Call me back, Daddy. Love you! Bye."

A surge of guilt washed over me. The second message exacerbated it: Alex again. "Dad-dy! Where are you? Call me back. It's Alex." Then a giggle, and a click.

The third time the voice was different, grown-up, reproachful. "Daddy, Grandma Petri says I have to go to bed now, and you can't call me back"—sigh. "I guess I'll talk to you tomorrow. Goodnight."

And the fourth, just a click. I sighed realizing that it was the first time since her mother died that I had not bade my daughter good-night.

Poor Benji actually had to bark—or what passed for a bark for him—to wake me up the next morning. Nine-thirty—yikes, I never slept that late! The previous night's occurrences came flooding back, accompanied by a pounding hangover. I crawled out of bed, downed some Tylenols, and threw on some clothes to take Benji for a walk. I maneuvered him a few blocks to pick up some bagels and coffee to bring back. Benji didn't mind waiting outside, knowing that he would get a favorite treat of blueberry bagel. The puppy had unusual tastes.

After finishing breakfast I took a long, hot bath. I had just gotten dressed when I heard Alex at the door. She now had a set of her own keys which she took with her on her weekend forays to her grandparents'. I rushed out to greet her, opening my arms for a hug.

Alex diverted course and walked right past me. I was crestfallen. She disappeared down the hallway in her bright blue Sunday dress.

I followed her, but she slammed her door in my face.

"Al-ex," I called to her. "What kind of welcome is that?"

"I'm getting changed," she replied through the door.

"Well, get dressed in shopping clothes. You and I have to shop for Ashleigh's present."

I heard drawers opening and slamming. An editorial comment, but no words accompanying it.

Finally the door opened. She was dressed in jeans and a Winnie the Pooh sweatshirt, her long blonde hair streaming over her shoulders. She looked up at me with hurt in her hazel eyes. "Daddy, I don't like it when I can't find you when I need you."

Her words were so much like Nicki's that a chill ran up my spine. I leaned forward and hugged her, taking in her scent. To make it a family threesome, Benji arrived on the scene and started whimpering for Alex's attention. She leaned down and scratched his ears.

"I went out for a drink with one of my colleagues, and lost track of the time."

"That's okay. But now we have to buy Ashleigh a really nice present."

WHEN I CAME home after work on Friday, Rita was waiting for me anxiously. "Alex is in her room, very angry," she announced. "She had a fight with her friend, Ashleigh."

I tossed my blazer on the sofa and went into Alex's room. The door was closed. I knocked and Alex told me to come in. She was lying on her bed, face toward the door, brushing Benji, who was submitting to it patiently.

"Hello, young lady," I said, leaning over to peck her on the lips.

"Hello, Daddy. I hate Ashleigh," she said angrily. Her tone made me recoil.

"Look, whatever happened, you're best friends, right?" But of course we had been through this before. Alex had a constantly replenishing supply of best friends, just like Nicki had. I wondered if Nicki had experienced such tumult in her relationships as a child. I wished there was someone I could ask. "What happened, Alex?"

She sniffled. "Ashleigh stole Kyle away from me," she said through clenched teeth. "They were holding hands at recess. I asked her and she said he was her boyfriend."

Aww, I thought. Poor Alex's first broken heart. This wasn't going to be easy.

I sat down on the side of her bed and stroked her hair. "Sweetheart, sometimes you have to put things in perspective. And forgive people when they do mean things. Friendship is a really important thing. You'll be sad if you and Ashleigh aren't friends anymore."

"No I won't," Alex responded, not looking up at me. "And I'm not going to her stupid birthday party tomorrow."

"That's okay. I understand, even though I hope you'll change your mind." I knew she wouldn't.

"And I'll get her back, too."

"Alex," I said, my tone sharper. "You will do nothing of the kind. Do you understand me?" I lifted her face toward mine. "Do you?"

"Yes."

Alex didn't eat much dinner that night, but her mood improved as we spent the weekend together. We took in an IMAX movie at the National Air & Space Museum, and played frisbee in the park. She didn't mention Ashleigh once, even though the fact that she was missing the birthday party weighed heavily though remained unspoken.

Monday was busy as usual, and the time got away from me without my realizing it. I had planned to work out at the gym but it was almost time to go home for dinner, and I liked to be on time whenever possible to eat with Alex. As I was preparing to leave, my assistant Wendy called in and told me there was a man named Ben Gilman on the phone. I didn't recognize the name. "He's from the Bethesda Swim Club," she said.

That news was alarming. Bethesda was the club where Alex took swim lessons after school. Had something happened to her?

"Mr. Gibbons," he started, "Ben Gilman from the swim club. We have a little problem, and we need for you to come by right away, please."

"Is Alex okay?" I asked, my heart beating rapidly.

"Yes," replied Gilman in an even tone, "fortunately, everyone is okay. But you'll need to pick up Alex. I would prefer not to discuss it on the phone."

I agreed to come right over, though the long drive up Wisconsin Avenue would take awhile in the rush-hour traffic. Something must be seriously amiss. It took a half hour to get there. The pool was crowded and it took some time to finally get directions to Gilman's office. It turned out he was the assistant manager. When I arrived at his small office, Alex was inside, dressed in school clothes, with her swim bag sitting next to her chair. Her hair was still wet.

A thirtyish-aged man with brown hair and a mustache was seated behind the desk, attending to paperwork. "Mr. Gilman?" I asked.

He leapt out of his chair. "Yes. Mr. Gibbons?"

"Yes."

"Sit down," he instructed, motioning to a chair alongside Alex's. "Thanks for coming."

"What's the problem?" I asked, glancing at Alex, who was avoiding looking at me.

Gilman rubbed his hands together. The scene seemed hauntingly reminiscent of a similar conversation not all that long ago at a radio station not very far away. The image proved prescient.

"Mr. Gibbons, when the girls' class was over, and before the next class came in, the instructor, Alicia Gomez, noticed that two of the girls were missing. Your daughter and Ashleigh Kubrick. Alicia went back to the pool, and at first didn't see them. But then she realized that they were underwater, in the deep end of the pool, where they're not allowed without an instructor. And they weren't coming up. Alicia dove in and discovered that Alex was at the bottom of the pool, holding the ladder with one hand and Ashleigh's ankle with the other. Ashleigh couldn't get to the surface. When Alex realized Alicia was there, she let go, and went to the surface herself. But Ashleigh could have drowned. When Alicia got her to the surface, she was coughing up water."

I was flabbergasted. I looked at Alex, who looked up with red-rimmed eyes. Apparently she was crying.

"Did you do this, Alex?" I asked sternly. Whatever her answer, I knew the truth.

"We were playing," she mumbled.

Gilman interrupted. "Ashleigh was terrified. She said it started out as a contest, but then Alex pulled her into deeper water and held her under. Apparently Ashleigh can't hold her breath as long as Alex can." He sighed. "Mr. Gibbons, I have to tell you that Mrs. Kubrick may press charges. And Alicia is certain about what she saw."

"I'll call Mrs. Kubrick," I said, thinking dimly that I might have to call Doug as well in light of possible legal action. "And in the meantime, I'll take Alex home."

Gilman rose as I did and looked at me sternly. "Mr. Gibbons, I hate to say this, because before this, Alex seemed like a nice enough little girl. But Alex is not welcome back here at the swim club."

"I understand." I looked over at Alex, who was fidgeting with her swim bag and sniffling. "Let's go, Alex." I got up and walked out, knowing she would be several paces behind.

As I walked through the doorway, suddenly my vision grew momentarily black. It cleared after a moment, but I was left with a dire realization.

The nightmare was beginning all over again.

33

THE DRIVE HOME was silent. In the seat beside me, Alex's face was shrouded in darkness, save for an occasional flickering illumination from oncoming headlights. Even then I could not bear to look at her. I was filled with surging emotions, alternating between anger and terror. Alex said nothing in her own defense.

When we arrived at home, I told Alex to get ready for bed, and took Benji out for a walk. It turned out to be a long one, as I needed time to attempt to collect my thoughts and rein them in. By the time I returned home, Alex was in bed, apparently asleep. I looked in at her from the hallway. Though she was growing like a willow, tonight she seemed tiny in her bed, surrounded by her stuffed animals, which stood sentry by her side. Benji joined them. I moved toward my own bedroom, then reversed course and entered Alex's bedroom and kissed her lightly on the cheek. She did not stir as I did so.

Once in bed, I tossed and turned relentlessly, for hours. Finally sleep subsumed me. Sometime toward dawn, I felt the stirring of Alex climbing into bed with me. I was so sleepy that I did not respond initially to her presence. She snuggled next to me and put her arm around my shoulder. I opened my eyes and through the darkness saw that her eyes were already closed. The thumb on her other hand was lodged in her mouth, a phenomenon that, along with Alex climbing into bed with me, I had thought fallen by the wayside. Apparently not.

I awoke groggily to the smell of coffee. At first I thought Rita was making breakfast, but then realized that she shouldn't be there yet. But the smell of fresh coffee was unmistakable. I sat up and looked around, still feeling dislocated. Alex was no longer in the bedroom. I pulled myself out of bed and made my way toward the kitchen. There I found Alex standing on her step-stool, mixing granola and yogurt, and amazingly, brewing a steaming fresh pot of coffee. I blinked in disbelief.

"Good morning!" she exclaimed brightly. "I thought I would make breakfast for you!" She blew me a kiss and returned her attention to the cereal. She was dressed in overalls, looking ready to go to school.

"How did you know how to make coffee?"

"I watched you a bunch of times. I even got the half-and-half out for you. And I already took Benji out for his morning walk." The dog was off in the corner of the kitchen, munching contentedly and loudly on the dry food in his bowl.

I poured myself a cup of coffee. It was delicious, just right. "This is great, Alex." She beamed.

We ate in the breakfast nook. Alex had the morning newspaper set out but I ignored it. "I think we both need to take a day off today," I announced.

Alex nodded earnestly. "I figured we needed to straighten out this problem."

I almost laughed. I was amazed at how grown-up she sounded, and knew that was the image she was trying to project. Someone as mature as Alex couldn't have done what she was accused of, right?

"And what 'problem' is it that we have?" I asked.

Alex pondered that for a moment, chewing her lip absently. "That Ashleigh and I don't get along."

I shook my head. "Lots of people don't get along with one another. They don't try to hurt one another, though. And that's what you did. That's our problem."

"Daddy, people try to hurt each other all the time."

"Yes, but it's wrong when they do. People are supposed to solve their problems without hurting other people."

"But even in the Bible, they have wars, and sometimes they're okay. An eye for an eye."

Yikes, I thought. That was the wrong argument with me. "The Bible teaches lots of good and important things, but that's not one of them. Do you remember about Jesus saying to turn the other cheek?"

Alex frowned. "I wasn't trying to hurt her, Daddy. I told her I could stay down longer, and she didn't believe me."

"You were holding her down, Alex. You could have hurt her, badly. She could have drowned."

Alex's eyes flashed. "But I didn't."

"Only because Alicia discovered you."

"But I didn't, Daddy. Hurt her."

My temper was rising dangerously. I shook my head again. "Alex, I'm going to call Dr. Purcell today. We need some help with this problem." Purcell was the therapist who had counseled Alex after her mother died.

"But Dr. Purcell said I was okay."

"But obviously you're not okay."

Alex rolled her eyes. "It wasn't a big deal, Daddy."

I grabbed her wrist and squeezed it, then with my other hand lifted her chin so she would look me in the eye. "Stop rolling your eyes." It was the first time I had ever exerted any physical pressure on her. Alex averted her eyes. "Look at me," I commanded. She finally did, but her expression was insolent. "I don't like what you did. It was wrong. It was inexcusable. You will never hurt anybody, or anything, again. Do you understand that?" Her eyes welled up, but the tears didn't spill over, and Alex held my gaze without blinking. "You need to find some other way to express your anger. And we'll start with Dr. Purcell, as soon as we can get an appointment."

We looked at each other in a standoff. Finally I released her wrist, realizing I was squeezing it too hard. As soon as I did, she scurried down from her chair and ran off, announcing she was going to watch *Sesame Street*. Her back was to me and I suspected she was finally crying. Or perhaps I hoped so.

I wasn't hungry. Instead, I walked over to the phone and called Sister Bernadette, the principal of Alex's school. She took my phone call immediately. "Alex won't be coming in today," I told her. "We had a mishap last night with one of the other students that we need to straighten out." I didn't know how much to tell her.

"The Kubricks have already been in to see me, Mr. Gibbons. They've asked that Alexandra be removed from the school. They told me that a Mr. Gilman will corroborate their recounting of the incident at the pool."

Oh no, I thought to myself. Alex couldn't lose her school. "Sister Bernadette," I said, "please don't expel Alex. She loves the school. It's good for her. She needs the discipline." That was for sure. "And I'm getting help for her. It would be awful for Alex if she couldn't go back there."

"Calm down, Mr. Gibbons," the principal instructed. "We generally do not expel students for incidents that occur outside of school grounds and school hours. But this is serious enough that we'll have to change her class. It won't do to have Alexandra and Ashleigh in the same classroom anymore. Alexandra will be transferred to Sister Callista's class. She'll have to make up any different work they've done there." The principal wasn't finished yet. "Alexandra will be on disciplinary probation for the remainder of the year. If there is even a single incident, she'll be removed from the school, no questions asked."

Next I called my office to ask Wendy to cancel my appointments and let everyone know that I'd be in the following day. Finally, I called Dr. Purcell's office. After I explained we had an emergency, they were able to squeeze us in at five.

When Rita arrived, I gave her the day off. Alex and I kept our distance over the course of the day. She and I took turns walking Benji, and Alex watched television, played quietly in her room. I could now hook up with the office via modem, and spent my day putting finishing touches on a plan for a small office building. Finally it was time for Alex's appointment. On the drive over, I recounted what Sister Bernadette told me, and rendered a strong admonition of my own that Alex needed to be on perfect behavior for the remainder of the school year. She pursed her lips but nodded. She seemed unhappy that she would be switching to Sister Callista's class, but she accepted the news without complaint.

Alex stared straight ahead as we drove. I cast a sideways glance at her and noticed the sun illuminating her hazel eyes in profile. For the first time, I thought I glimpsed the vision of what Alexandra would look like as a woman. Already at this tender age she was pretty enough that boys were self-conscious in her presence. But as a woman she would be devastating. Tougher looks than her mom's, but more wickedly intelligent, as well.

We did not have to wait long after our arrival. I spoke to the psychologist first. Dr. Purcell was a well-dressed, middle-aged woman who projected an air of calmness and authority. I told her what had happened.

"Well, we don't know what would have happened, so it's important that we not jump to conclusions. If Alex told you she wouldn't have hurt Ashleigh, that's reassuring. She knows the mode of expected behavior now, and she's attached herself to it."

"But she did hurt Ashleigh."

"Alex may not have realized that, or the danger. After all, she might have expected that Ashleigh could hold her breath longer than she did." I must have cast back a dubious look. "But I'm glad you brought her in, Mr. Gibbons. She obviously needs help."

"Will you be able to let me know what you're finding out?"

"Do you mean can I divulge Alex's confidences?" Dr. Purcell corrected. "On some occasions, I can. It's different than with an adult patient. But even with a child, if she asks me to keep a confidence, or tells me something that in my judgment shouldn't be shared, I will retain confidentiality."

I nodded, thanked her and shook her hand. Then Alex came in, smiling sheepishly. Alex was in there for nearly an hour. Finally, Dr. Purcell emerged, her arm around Alex's shoulder. Alex was carrying a Beanie Baby. "Thanks for giving me Batty," Alex told her cheerfully.

"Take good care of him," the doctor instructed. To me, the psychologist said, "Please call me tomorrow at ten. I'll be between patients."

I nodded, and Alex and I departed. On the way to the parking garage, I asked to see Alex's Beanie Baby.

"It's a bat," Alex said, holding it up for me to inspect. "I guess Dr. Purcell gave him to me because she thinks I'm batty."

My first instinct was to reassure Alex, but her comment struck me as so funny I burst out laughing. Alex did, too, and it was a joyful sound. I tousled her hair and we walked the rest of the way to the car hand-in-hand. We didn't talk about her session, and stopped at a Chinese restaurant on the way home for a scrumptious dinner.

The next day I dropped Alex off at school, first stopping to meet her new teacher, who was indeed a stern nun. Then I proceeded to the office, and at ten I called Dr. Purcell. She took my call immediately. "Well, Mr. Gibbons, there's no question there's some deep-seated anger. It's not surprising that it took her awhile to act out from her mother's death. Sometimes the reaction takes time to manifest itself."

"What's the prognosis?"

"I can't be sure yet. I think she'll need some regular therapy. My recommendation right now is a weekly session, about forty-five minutes each time. She's a complicated and troubled little girl."

"Any insights at all?"

"Certainly Alex is resentful of her mother leaving her. That's not surprising. Alex doesn't understand why she did it."

I voiced my deepest worry. "Is there any chance that Alex will do the same thing?" I asked in a hushed voice. I hadn't even realized that question was nagging my subconscience.

Dr. Purcell hesitated before answering. "At this point I don't see a concern. That's one of the reasons for suggesting the regular sessions. I want to probe her thoughts on that issue. But for now, I think Alex can't understand why anyone would do such a thing. She seems relatively happy. But, she is insecure about you."

"About me?" I asked.

"Yes. She senses that you weren't there when your wife needed you. And she's wondering if you'll be there when she needs you. It's very important that you reassure Alex of your love for her, even when you're appropriately angry with her."

"I try to do that." I sighed. "Do you think she's borderline?"

Again the doctor considered her response before speaking. "I do think so, yes, probably. But that doesn't help us very much, because we don't know very much about the disorder."

"Is it hereditary?"

"It appears it can be, yes."

"Can it be effectively treated with medicine?"

"The main treatment is therapy, but I think I'll prescribe Remeron, a fairly new S.S.R.I." I had no idea what she was talking about. This was sounding hauntingly like Nicki's situation. "Selective serotonin reuptake inhibitor," Dr. Purcell went on. "In other words, it regulates the chemicals that cause mood swings. It should moderate any serious anger if it erupts. It shouldn't have any side-effects, but should make the lows a little less severe."

I was grateful for that. "Do you think she'll be all right?"

"It's too early to say that with any assurance. But I think so. Really, her reaction is not unusual for a young girl who has just lost her mother to suicide. You have to keep that in mind. It's hard to imagine anything more traumatic than that, at this stage in Alex's life. Also, she loves you desperately. She wants to please you. That may be the most important thing we have going for us."

I promised to schedule the next appointment, and thanked Dr. Purcell for squeezing Alex into her schedule on such short notice.

The remainder of the week passed, fortunately, without incident. Alex was scheduled to go with her aunt and cousins to Gettysburg over the weekend. I looked forward to the respite. I considered telling Kim about what had happened, but couldn't think of a good reason to do so. Kim probably would find a way to blame me somehow. I did call my mother one evening after Alex went to bed. She was comforting, as always, but had no framework to draw upon to render any real assistance. It was nice to know that someone cared, though.

On Friday evening Alex and I went shopping at Tysons' Mall. For once, she had nothing on her own shopping agenda, but instead insisted that we buy clothes for me. I went home with three new sweaters, a casual shirt, and a tie. All in impeccable taste, thanks to Alex.

The next morning we packed Alex's bag—filling it with an amazing collection of clothes and shoes for a mere weekend—and I dropped her off at her Aunt Kim's house. I stocked up on my wine selection, which was one of my favorite pastimes. It was too cold and rainy to go bicycle riding. So I worked on some fanciful architecture sketches—thinking about teaching again, perhaps—and made some long-overdue calls to friends.

That evening I met Helen again. Dinner was sublime, the conversation even better. Helen's accent was scintillating.

Was there attraction? Maybe a bit of flirtation. But Helen spoke (mostly disdainfully) of guys she was dating, and I think it went without saying that I had not yet even come close to recovering from Nicki. But I savored Helen's company.

After dinner I invited her over for wine. My collection was growing because I had few occasions to enjoy it.

Helen loved the apartment, admiring aloud the renovation features. She stopped at a photo of Alex. "Your daughter is beautiful," she remarked.

"Just like her mom," I replied, regretting the words instantly. But Helen seemed to take no note.

After enjoying a bottle of Riesling together, I suggested coffee, and went out to the kitchen to grind some beans. Over the racket, I thought I heard Helen's voice from the living room.

I stopped the machine and called out, "What?" Then I realized the phone had been ringing, and Helen had asked whether she should pick it up.

And I thought: no.

Too late, I bolted to the living room, where an agitated Helen was speaking into the phone.

"No, no, this is his friend, Helen. I'll get your daddy for you straight away." She held the phone away from her ear and turned around, looking relieved to see me. Holding her hand over the mouthpiece, she said, "It's your daughter, I believe, and, ehm, she sounds a tad upset." Her face was grave.

I strode over and picked took the phone from her. "Alex?"

"Daaa . . . deeee?!" Alex yelled, her voice a screech.

"Alex, it's okay, honey. Are you okay? That was just a friend of mine. Everything's okay."

"Daaa . . . deeee!!!" she screamed, so ear-piercingly I had to take the phone from my ear. Helen looked up in alarm. I put the phone back to my ear and tried to say something. But Alex's screams turned into wails.

"Alex, stop!" I beseeched. But her wails escalated into a high-pitched, hysterical keening. The sound was primordial, relentless, more like a wild animal than a human. I glanced over at Helen, standing now looking at me with huge eyes.

"Daaa . . . deee!!!!"

I couldn't bear it. "Alex!" I said sharply, but I knew she couldn't hear over her own din.

Suddenly the phone was snatched away from her. Kim's voice now. "Kevin?"

"Kim, what's going on?" Alex was screaming incoherently in the background.

"What's going on with you?" Kim responded, trying to make herself heard over Alex's hysteria. My ear rang from Alex's shrill screams. "What did you do this time, you idiot? You've got your daughter very upset!"

"Kim," I beseeched, but it was to the sound of a click. The phone instantly grew quiet.

I held it there for a moment. Finally I returned the phone to its cradle, my heart thudding in my chest.

I did not hear back from Alex again that night. And after Helen left, I did not see her again, or for that matter, any other woman, ever again.

34

I WAS ENGROSSED over some drawings with one of our young architects. Trouble was, I couldn't remember his name. The guy seemed bright, a real engineering whiz, but a total nerd. The architecture schools seemed to be turning out socially dysfunctional graduates these days. Nordhut, or Nordlinger, or whatever this guy's name was, wasn't catching any of my jokes. Worse yet, he didn't understand you were supposed to laugh at the boss's jokes, even if they weren't all that funny. Sheesh.

A voice sounded on the intercom on the guy's desk. "Owen?" Oh that's right, I thought: Owen Nordsten. Fresh out of the University of Oregon. Rich had hired him. It seemed like we were hiring and firing all the time, and Rich did it all. I was merely the creative guru, the wise sage.

"What's up, Wendy?" I asked.

"Kevin, Dr. Purcell is on the phone," Wendy advised.

"Okay, I'll take it back in my office, if she can hold on," I replied.

At long last I was no longer nervous when I received a call from Dr. Purcell. Alex had made good progress over the past nine months. She had survived the probation period at Annunciation, with only a couple outbursts of temper, which quickly dissipated and were followed by what seemed sincere contrition. Alex seemed to be learning right from wrong, and internalizing it. She also received all A's, including deportment, and was reading at a third-grade level. We had decided, however, that Alex would start second grade at Quaker Day School the following fall. The school had smaller classes and was within walking distance of the Parkside. And Alex's latest best playmate, Tommy Hempster, attended school there. Alex seemed to be looking forward to a fresh start, where none of her classmates knew her history—or looked at her with suspicion or fear.

"Dr. Purcell," I greeted her enthusiastically.

"Mr. Gibbons."

"What can I do for you?"

"I understand you and Alex are leaving for Key West today. She's really been looking forward to it."

That comment made me smile. We had been reading travel guides together, drawing our route from Miami to the Florida Keys on a map, and getting increasingly excited as the time for our departure approached. "Yes, we head out in just a few minutes."

The doctor went on. "I'm going to cut back Alex's intake of Remeron, from thirty milligrams to fifteen a day. I think it's a good time. She likes spending time with you, and you'll be there to observe any side effects. But I think she's ready for a reduced dosage."

I regarded the doctor's news as wonderful. But she wasn't finished. "I think Alex is adjusting well. And your ability to spend more time with her has helped." Indeed, I had cut back my hours in the office to about thirty per week. Although I still worked at home sometimes in the evenings, I was usually at Alex's school to pick her up every afternoon. "I think we can even cut back the visits to one a month," Dr. Purcell added, "just so I can continue to monitor her progress."

The doctor went on to explain about Alex's revised prescription. Finally the conversation ended, and as I signed off I glanced toward my door.

Alex was framed in the doorway, her eyes boring into me intensely. I wondered how long she had been standing there, listening. Then a metamorphosis took place, and she gave me a bright smile. She looked beautiful standing there in a flowery sundress and sandals. "Are you ready to go?"

I strode over to her and gave her a hug, receiving a wet kiss on my cheek in return. "I'm ready!" I announced. "How did you get in here?"

"The driver walked me in. He's waiting outside to take us to the airport for our trip to Key West. And I asked for Wendy, who let me into your office." Precocious little Alex definitely knew the ropes, and who to talk to in order to secure the desired result. It made me grin again.

And then we embarked on the first of our vacations together, just the two of us.

A WEEK BEFORE it, Alex and I chatted about the party for her eighth birthday, scheduled for the following weekend. She had invited about a dozen children to go paddle-boating on the Tidal Basin, followed by a carousel ride at the Smithsonian and a picnic on the Mall. That was the benefit of having an early springtime birthday in Washington. Even the parents would enjoy the festivities. Monday was actually her birthday, and Alex was excited that I was taking her to Citronelle for dinner. I had started introducing her to fine cuisine, and she enjoyed the luxury and elegance of the experience. It was funny hearing her talk about her favorite restaurants, with a sophistication that even the *Washington Post*'s food critic, Phyllis Richman, would envy.

The weekend was delightful and relaxing. Fortunately I didn't have to go to work, and spent the entire time with Alex, save for Saturday afternoon, when she went to the movies with Tommy Hempster, and Sunday evening when she watched "Murder, She Wrote" with Mrs. Beeman.

The day started off uneventfully enough. "How does it feel to be eight?" I asked her over breakfast.

She scrunched her face in concentration before answering. "Actually," she said with an air of maturity, "I think I won't really feel eight until my party next weekend."

I laughed. "Then I'll be taking a seven-year-old out for dinner tonight?"

"No, I'm really eight. I just don't feel that way yet."

I tousled her hair, which used to amuse her but now irritated her because it messed up her appearance. "Daddy, don't!"

"If you didn't say cute things, I wouldn't mess up your hair."

"Okay, I won't say any more cute things." She snickered through her nose.

My heart skipped a beat. Her mother used to do that constantly. At most, Alex would have been only subconsciously aware of her mother's habit. Could a person inherit a habit?

I brushed that disturbing thought away. Alex and I packed up some cupcakes we had made for her class to celebrate her birthday, and I dropped them off at school along with Alex, kissing her atop her head and wishing her a fun day.

Arriving twenty minutes later at the office, I started the workweek with a fairly unremarkable staff meeting. Since our staff had mushroomed, we had winnowed the Monday morning meetings to senior employees, but that still meant sixteen people gathered around the conference table. Our biggest new project was a major renovation of the National Portrait Gallery. It was a massive project, updating the grand dame museum's ancient wiring and plumbing, and converting office space into extra exhibit space. Fortunately, my exposure to renovations of classical buildings in Rome had come in handy on restoration work in the District of Columbia. If you could restore a building that was a thousand years old, a mere hundred was a piece of cake.

Following the staff meeting, Rich asked to speak with me privately. "My office or yours?" I asked.

"Yours."

As I shut the door I started in with familiar banter. "The Dodgers look good this season," I said as we sat down opposite one another on my sofa. Rich was a Dodgers fan, having grown up in Los Angeles. I was a diehard Yankees fan, creating a playful intraoffice rivalry, though the Yanks and Dodgers hadn't faced each other in post-season competition in decades. "Kevin Brown is one serious ace."

"After last season, I don't think anyone can catch the Yankees. But hey, Kevin, I need to talk to you about something."

Rich was even more serious than usual. I leaned forward. "What's up?"

Rich sighed. "There's no easy way to say this, Kev, so I'm just going to say it. I'm leaving the firm."

I wasn't sure I had heard him correctly. I *couldn't* have heard him correctly. "What're you talking about?"

"I've had an amazing offer, and I had to accept it."

"An offer? With whom? Another architectural firm?"

Rich cleared his throat. "Fielder."

I jumped up. "Fielder? Come on, Rich, you've got to be fucking kidding me!"

He jumped up too and gently grabbed my arm to pull me back down, but I shrugged him off and stood with my arms crossed. He sat back down and leaned against the arm of the sofa.

"Rich, if this is a joke, it's a bad one. We've been partners for practically ten years. You run this place. You can have anything you want. Why on earth would you want to go to a place like Fielder?"

"They made me the proverbial offer I couldn't refuse."

I laughed. "That's their style, all right." I glared at him, still not sure this wasn't a joke in exceedingly bad taste. My heart pounded as my subconscious weighed the horrible ramifications of what Rich was telling me.

Rich frowned. "They offered me a half million a year, plus bonus incentives. And a half million signing bonus up front." He paused and looked at me directly. "Plus twenty-five thousand for every architect I recruited, and a percentage for every client I bring in."

"What? What? Don't tell me you're taking some of the architects with you!"

"Thirteen."

"What? Who?" I demanded. He named them. He had nabbed the best architects in the firm. Leaving me the deadwood. The only silver lining, I noted ruefully, was that Rich was taking Owen Nordsten. At least the firm's biggest nerd was leaving. He would fit in well at Fielder. "And clients?"

He listed some of our biggest ongoing accounts. He finished with Art Longley.

"Art? You're taking Art?" I started pacing, and could feel my face turning crimson. This was a nightmare.

"You haven't been paying much attention to him recently."

"I didn't know I had to," I retorted. "I didn't realize you were cultivating him for your new firm."

"My first contact with Fielder was a month ago. I hadn't contemplated leaving. Ever." He rose and I stopped pacing. "You know I wanted to retire in ten years. This will make it five. I'm not going to throw my heart and soul into Fielder, the way I would have here."

"So for the past month you've been working for the enemy."

"I'm not going to take any salary for the past month. Even though that's when we cinched the National Portrait Gallery contract. That's a big contract, one that Fielder would've salivated over. My absolute loyalty has been to Horizon."

I just sighed. It was clear that Rich had this all worked out. "All the loyalty in the world, and you're decimating this place." I couldn't even look at him. "Well, when are you leaving?"

"We're packing up today. We'll leave after closing hours."

"The surreptitious escape. Well, I'm going to have to announce it. Even though I'm the only person who probably didn't know."

"I'm really sorry. I couldn't turn them down. But I've really enjoyed our partnership. You've been a tremendous teacher."

My eyes glistened, and I managed to meet his eyes. "You too, Rich. Even though I can't remember being angrier in my whole life, I will miss you tremendously." We eyed each other regretfully. "No way I can change your mind?"

He shook his head slowly but firmly. "There's nothing a firm of this size can do to match an offer from a place like Fielder."

"Except integrity."

Rich stared at me, then extended his hand tentatively. I shook it, firmly. Then turned my back as he left.

I sat down at my desk, staring into space. Then slammed my fist on the desk so hard I was sure I had broken blood vessels. "Fuck!" I muttered sharply. Then pressed the intercom for Wendy.

She entered my office with huge eyes. "What's going on? Are you all right?"

"Rich is jumping ship. Along with thirteen others."

"Are you serious?"

"I wish I wasn't. Listen, ask Rich for a list of the people who are leaving. Then round up everyone else for an emergency staff meeting, pronto."

My intercom buzzed. "Mr. Gibbons, a reporter from *Washington Architecture Journal* is on the line, something about the Fielder raid," the receptionist said.

I could feel my blood pressure rising. Christ, the media was onto this already? I could picture John Friedman Fergaman's leering grin as he picked up the phone to make the call first thing that morning. No doubt the *Washington Post* would be next. "No calls for the duration."

"Who should I refer her to?"

"No one. Hold everyone's calls. We're going to be gathering for a staff meeting."

When I terminated that conversation, Wendy asked, "Are you going to be all right?"

"I have no idea, Wendy. This is slightly outside my frame of reference."

She sighed and announced, "I'd better get to work." And left me alone with my tortured thoughts.

Where to start? I needed to call the firm's lawyers and obtain immediate counsel. Then our accountants to get them started on assessing the hit we would take. I knew instantly that the amount of the accounts Rich was taking dwarfed the salaries of the architects who were leaving. And as soon as the news got out, we'd lose more clients as well. We would be left with too much office space. True, the National Portrait Gallery was a plum project, but it wouldn't occupy twenty-some architects, not for very long. And who would supervise them, make the place work? Rich was indispensable.

I put in calls to the attorneys and architects and set up meetings in the morning and the afternoon.

In the meantime, there was the staff meeting. As I looked at the assemblage, I realized I didn't even know many of these people. Yet they were all dependent on me, and whatever actions I would take, for their livelihoods. I could tell that about half of those present already knew the news; the remainder were shocked. Emotions ranged from anger to fear, which in that case were flip-sides of each other. I didn't know what to tell them, how to assess the damage. So I told them to sit tight, that once I evaluated the situation I would give them a report.

"What about those of us who are working on projects for clients who are leaving?" one architect asked.

"How many of you are there?" I queried. Roughly fifteen of the remaining twenty-five architects raised their hands. Shit.

I glanced at Linda Bloom, our office manager, who was standing with her hands on her hips, a look that could kill on her face. "Linda and I will figure all this out. Everyone get me a list of their assignments by the end of the day. Most of you will probably switch to the National Portrait Gallery. And unless you're working with a supervisor who isn't leaving, report directly to me in the interim." I looked around at the faces to see where I could detect looks of eager leadership, of confidence. None. Rich had cleared the place out. If anyone was going to save this firm, clearly it would have to be me.

Suddenly a soft little voice sounded in my mind. It was Alex, admonishing me the previous summer that I should give everyone a raise. A smile suddenly played on my lips, though one that held little merriment, and the words that emanated next were pure Alex. But I was grateful for them. "Everyone who makes it through this hellacious week gets a thousand dollar cash bonus. If you put in overtime, it'll be one-five." Some of the stern faces in the crowd softened a bit. "Just to demonstrate that life goes on."

But that brief mental interlude was the only bright spot in an otherwise utterly dismal day. My meeting with the lawyers was not very optimistic. Unless the departing architects had stolen firm secrets—something I still didn't believe Rich would do—we had no recourse against them. Not that I wanted to get back at them, for the only crime of which they were guilty was disloyalty. Suing Fielder, on the other hand, was a tempting prospect, but apparently unavailing. Stealing architects—and clients—was fair game. We had no exclusive contracts with our clients, and had compelled none of our architects to sign non-competition agreements. We were, in other words, SOL. The meeting confirmed why I hated lawyers.

The accountants' meeting was worse. They seemed even more alarmed than I, making it obvious if not explicit that they were suddenly afraid that one of their biggest clients was going bust and—perish the thought—might not be able to continue paying their exorbitant fees. I told them straight up that they were our accountants for the bad times as well as good, and it was their job to tell me what I needed to do to keep us financially viable. They informed me it would take a week of several accountants' time, at the usual rate of up to three hundred dollars per hour. If we weren't destitute when Rich walked out the door, we would be when our accountants were finished with us.

The biggest hit was Rich's draw, to which he was entitled upon leaving the firm. He was owed six hundred thousand dollars. We didn't have that in the bank. Rich was an advocate of investing our equity in expansion. Because neither of us was planning to cash in— ha!—that didn't seem unwise. But we didn't have that kind of cash lying around. We would have to work something out with Rich, and possibly even borrow it. But against what collateral?

In the midst of the big meetings were myriad small ones—punctuated by guilty-looking architects stealthily tiptoeing out with armloads of boxes. Linda burst into my office at one point, beside herself. "They're walking outta here with half our supplies!" she exclaimed.

"Take an inventory and send an invoice to Fielder," I deadpanned.

Linda put her hands on her hips in what I feared was becoming a permanent position. "You're just going to let them leave with our stuff? What if they leave with plans and drawings?"

"Linda, those things belong to our clients. They've paid for them. If these guys are allowed to steal our clients, they can steal our clients' plans, too. I'm sure Rich has gone over everything with them."

"Well, at least we should dock their last week's pay. That's when I gather the mutiny took place."

I smiled morosely at my loyal office manager. "No. I may even send them Christmas bonuses at the end of the year. This'll be the last time in their careers that someone treats them decently. That's the only revenge I can have against them."

Linda grimaced. "Those fuckers." I laughed. It was the first time I had ever heard her swear. "What?!" she asked.

"I'm glad you're still here, is all."

"Well, none of us is going to be here much longer if you keep handing out thousand-dollar bonuses and Christmas bonuses and letting people walk away with our plans and drawings."

"Whatever. I'll figure it out tomorrow." I glanced at my watch. Five-thirty. Rita would have picked Alex up at school when I didn't call to tell her I would be there. I should probably think about heading home for dinner.

But that wasn't in the cards. A constant flow of architects streamed through my office, asking questions I wasn't yet prepared to answer. Considering how creative these people were supposed to be, they were remarkably like sheep, waiting to be herded. I gave them guidance as best I could.

In the midst of one meeting my private line rang. I looked at my watch again. Seven-thirty. Shit, where had the time gone?

"Excuse me," I told the architect whose name was Lennie something. "Hello?"

"Mr. G, this is Rita."

"Rita, I'm tied up."

She seemed perplexed. "But have you forgotten?"

"Forgotten what?"

"It's Alex's birthday. You were supposed to take her for dinner."

Oh no. I had completely forgotten. The headache that had been flirting around the periphery all day suddenly hit with full force. I looked at my watch again, willing it to run backward. Our reservations had been for seven.

"I'll call the restaurant and see if we can still go," I said, regretting instantly the thought of keeping Alex out so late on a school night.

"No, Mr. G, the restaurant call and say you can not come unless by seven-thirty," Rita informed me.

Damn. "Can you put Alex on?"

"She go next door," Rita replied.

"Well, will you ask Mrs. Beeman to come over and watch Alex if I'm not back before you have to leave?"

"Yes, Mr. G," she said.

I returned the phone to its cradle and looked up at the architect who was waiting for me. My headache pounded. "Okay, Cheryl, show me what you have so far."

And she did, and so did the next architect, and the next. It was nine o'clock before I was finally able to leave.

But before I did, I walked around the suite, which was quiet as a tomb and bereft of human habitation save mine and the cleaning people, stopping at each office that had been cleared out during the day. I finally reached Rich's office, the venue for so much constructive synergy over our years together.

Empty. I pulled the door closed, then retraced my steps and closed the doors to the other abandoned offices as well. My idea of closure, I guess.

Finally I retrieved my car from the garage. The weather was unseasonably warm, so I put the top down to clear my head. What an awful day. As I neared the Parkside, I noticed lights on at Fagin's. The ice cream parlor was still open. Remarkably, there was a parking space in front. It was past Alex's bedtime, but I would buy her some Rocky Road ice cream, and if she was asleep, wake her up for it. I didn't think she'd mind—if she could bring herself to forgive me.

I arrived at home maybe fifteen minutes later, ice cream in hand. Mona Beeman was sitting on the sofa watching television, and my arrival seemed to startle her. I think she must have been dozing off.

"You are home!" she exclaimed. "Alex is asleep."

"Thank you so much, Mona, for watching her for me. We had an emergency in work today."

"Oh, it was my pleasure. She is such a delightful little girl."

"She's very fond of you, Mona," I replied. It wasn't an exaggeration. Alex spent as much time there as she could, and would probably stop by every day if I didn't restrain her out of concern for the elderly woman's privacy.

"I gave her a pair of earrings for her birthday," Mona said. "She is always admiring my jewelry."

For some reason her remark evoked a tinge of irritation. "Mona, you don't have to give Alex any presents. Certainly not your jewelry."

"Ach," Mona tutted me, "I am an old woman. What do I need with so much jewelry? She is an adorable little girl, and so sweet." She rose to leave.

"Can I offer you some Rocky Road ice cream?" I asked, holding the bag aloft.

"No thank you, it is close to my bedtime."

"Well, thanks again, Mona." I bade her good night. I detoured to the kitchen to put the ice cream in the freezer, then made my way down the hall to Alex's room.

I opened the door quietly and a shaft of light illuminated part of her bed. Benji was sleeping at the foot of the bed and lifted his head, then wagged his tail. I entered the room and scratched his ears. He licked my hand appreciatively.

Alex did not stir upon my entrance. I sat down on the side of her bed. Alex was facing away from me, clutching one of her stuffed animals. She was breathing peacefully. The light from the hallway fell on her hair, which cascaded around her pillow.

I nudged her shoulder gently. Nothing. Then again. "Hey," I whispered. Still no reaction. She had to be awake. I leaned forward and nuzzled her hair, kissing it lightly. "Hey, if you're awake, happy birthday." I straightened up and regarded her in the semi-light. I sighed. "Alex, I am so sorry that I missed our dinner," I said, still speaking quietly. "We had a really bad day in work today, and I couldn't break away. You know almost nothing on earth would keep me from coming home on time for your birthday, but this was really, really bad."

Alex shifted slightly, but did not turn over. From this angle, I could not see whether her eyes were open. Absently I stroked her hair. "You know my partner, Rich Deeks, right, sweetheart? I know you do, he gives you a present every Christmas. Well, he quit today. And a bunch of the other architects left with him. They're going to another firm. You know that firm where that big fat guy works, John Friedman Fergaman? I shouldn't say mean things, I'm sorry. But anyway, it made lots of turmoil. I had to spend the whole day trying to fix it and make sure no one else left. And the hours passed and all of a sudden it was seven o'clock."

I looked down at her again but she was still unresponsive. I leaned over and kissed her again. "I'm sorry. Can we go on Saturday night, instead?" I shook her shoulder gently then tickled her, hoping to make her laugh. "Hey, I have Rocky Road ice cream in the fridge. From Fagin's. I made them stay open. Wanna stay up late, even though it's a school night?" I shook her shoulder again. "Alex?"

Finally she rolled over and opened her eyes. The were red and glistened in the light from tears. The sight made me heartsick. "Ah honey, I really apologize." Her eyes searched mine, but were impassive. She blinked away tears and sniffled. "Will you forgive me?"

Alex looked away for a moment, as if considering her response. I waited expectantly.

Finally she looked back at me. Her face was utterly transformed, as if someone else—someone much older—had replaced Alex. Her eyes were suddenly clear, as if she had never been crying. In fact they were ablaze, amplified by the shaft of light streaming through the open door. They bored into mine. She cleared her throat. For some reason, a shudder passed up my spine and I was terrified to hear what she was going to say.

My fear proved prescient. When Alex finally spoke, her voice was deep and guttural, the words pronounced with an acid tone and steely gaze, almost like she were rendering a death sentence. And as far as my heart was concerned, it had precisely that effect.

"*I hate you.*"

And with a final angry, glaring glance, she rolled over and dismissed me for the night.

30

THE NEWS FROM the accountants had been bad. Devastating, in fact. Factoring in the clients Rich had taken, fixed costs exceeded anticipated revenues by nearly three dollars for every two. We had very few assets—except for our reputation, which was rapidly dissipating in the harsh glare of the media spotlight. Fielder, Steinmetz & Way had pulled off the architect heist of the decade, and everyone was hearing about it.

I wasn't sure what we had left by way of talent. Over the weeks since Rich had taken his leave, I had divided up assignments, but found myself and a handful of other decent architects constantly performing remedial work for the younger and less-skilled architects. At the same time, I had to nurture our remaining clients, but two significant ones had bolted to other firms before I could even contact them. Our lawyers had helped stop the hemorrhaging: they had convinced Rich that in order to collect his share of firm assets in a timely manner, he would have to agree to not solicit our remaining clients for at least six months. I knew some would follow him anyway—like rats off a sinking ship, I thought ruefully—but at least he wouldn't initiate the contact. It made sense from his perspective, because if we went under he would never collect his take.

For the short-term, the bottom line was that I would have to put two hundred thousand dollars of my own savings—nearly all of my own net wealth, apart from the slender equity in the condominium—into the firm just to meet payroll and expenses over the next six months. It was a "loan," technically, but if we couldn't pull out of the nosedive, it would all be lost in a year. The thought of going to work for someone else was abjectly depressing. And even with the cash infusion, the firm would have to trim its sails. I knew I would have to lay off some architects—it was clear that some of them could never carry their own weight—but I dreaded it.

I sat behind my desk, fingering the scrap of paper I'd gotten from a colleague the previous evening. My heart palpitated as I considered making the call. I ruminated over what to say, an exercise quickly interrupted by a torrent of memories. Finally I brushed them away and dialed the phone number on the paper.

A professional voice answered crisply after two rings. "Good morning, Jeager Jablonski Architects."

"Samantha Benjamin, please," my voice croaked.

"Who may I tell her is calling?"

"Just tell her it's an old friend."

There was a delay before any further response, as I expected. Finally, a distant yet familiar voice. "Samantha Benjamin. May I help you?"

"Wow," I said, "I can't believe a partner at Jaeger Jablonski would take an anonymous call. I'm impressed."

A pause. "Kevin?"

"That's me."

"Kevin Gibbons?"

"How many Kevins do you know?"

She giggled. "One. Actually, none."

"Aww, don't give me a hard time. It's only been like, what, ten years or so?"

"Something like that," she replied. "What are you doing calling me?"

"Oh, I just heard that you made partner, and wanted to call and congratulate you."

Samantha laughed. "I made partner three years ago."

"Oh, well, I heard that you moved to Chicago."

"Kevin, I moved to Chicago *seven* years ago."

"Oh. Well, in that case I called to offer you a job."

Another pause. "Really. Pray tell."

Our conversation lasted more than an hour. I waved Wendy off several times, attempting to interrupt me with other phone calls. Whoever they were, clients, creditors, media, they would have to wait. Mostly Sam and I caught up with our lives. She had heard about Rich Deeks' defection—I was amazed and depressed that news had already traveled to the Windy City—but she didn't know that Nicki had died, or even that I had a daughter. She seemed sincerely sympathetic over our travails. Meantime, Samantha's career had gone well, but she had ventured in and out of relationships, and had yet to find true love. Our conversation was easy and pleasant, almost as if no time had passed or that no conflagration between us had ever erupted.

Finally I came to my point. "Sam, I need your help. I need you to come back, take Rich's place. Whip this place back into shape, make it the lean, mean, hungry, talented boutique it was in the beginning."

Samantha sighed. "I don't know; it sounds tempting. But I love Chicago."

I smiled, feeling hopeful. "Sam, I can't pay you a whole lot. I can match whatever salary you're making. Give you profit-sharing bonuses. And a half share of the partners' equity—same as me. If we turn this place around, you'll deserve that and more."

Samantha had to wind up the conversation because she had a client coming in, but she promised to consider the offer. As we were about to conclude, I said, "I know I have no right to say this, but I really need you. I have nowhere else to turn."

She sighed. "I really wasn't looking to move back to DC. Too many unhappy memories. And it is a pretty big risk."

"Hey, don't forget the good memories, too."

"I have to admit, it might be nice to put the old team back together again. JJ is a pretty big bureaucracy."

"Now you're singing my song!"

Detecting a glimpse of sunlight on the horizon after my conversation with Sam, I left my office to collect messages from Wendy. Several were from clients, but one caught my attention: Mrs. Robles, Alex's second-grade teacher. The message asked that I call her after school hours. I set about returning other calls, and buried myself in my work.

Around three-thirty my memory jogged, and I pulled out the message slip from Mrs. Robles. I hoped she would still be there, then remembered that private school teachers usually stayed late. I dialed the number and was connected with the teacher. Apart from two routine parent-teacher meetings and a chance encounter with Alex in the grocery store, I had had no contact with the teacher, a kindly middle-aged Hispanic woman.

"Mr. Gibbons, thank you for calling."

"Of course, Mrs. Robles. How can I help you?"

"Ordinarily, I would ask you to come in. But I take it from Alexandra that you're very busy."

I was taken aback. Had Alex been complaining to her teacher about my work hours? Slightly annoyed, I said, "Mrs. Robles, I can come in if you think it's necessary."

"Well, not right at the moment. But perhaps if the problems persist."

"What problems?"

"Alexandra's schoolwork."

"There's a problem with her schoolwork?" Alex was consistently an A student, bright, imaginative, and punctilious.

"She hasn't handed in a number of her assignments over the past few weeks. On her last spelling test, she handed in a blank piece of paper. And her comportment is unsatisfactory. Last week she pulled Hillary Tompkins' hair. I had to send her to the principal's office. She's to sit inside during recess for the next two weeks so she learns manners."

This revelation hit me like a ton of bricks. "Mrs. Robles, are you sure there's no mistake? I check her assignment pad every night and make sure she's completed all her homework."

"Either Alexandra is not writing down all her assignments, or she's not finishing them, Mr. Gibbons."

"I just don't understand."

"Mr. Gibbons, is there some sort of trouble at home?" she asked.

I hesitated before answering. "No. No, there's trouble at work. I've had to work long hours lately, and weekends. It's disappointed Alex."

Mrs. Robles pondered that, and I felt like she was sitting in judgment. "I think you'd better have a talk with her, Mr. Gibbons. In the meantime, I'll check the assignment pad before she leaves each day, to make sure she's copied everything. Then you can check it on your end."

"Thank you, Mrs. Robles. Please let me know if the problems persist."

I vowed to go home earlier than usual that evening. Lately, about eight was my norm—too late to have dinner with Alex. Usually she was at Mrs. Beeman's next door, watching television. I hated to burden the elderly woman, but Rita had to leave by six-thirty at the latest to get home to her own family. Alex would sit at the dinner table as I ate my warmed-up meal, her head on her hands as she gazed at me through hazel eyes and recounted her day. She did seem a little forlorn, but frankly I was too tired and distracted to pay close attention to the nuances. Clearly that would have to change. Often after she went to bed at around nine-thirty, I would work some more in the study. Now that I thought of it, during the hour-and-a-half of supposed quality time I was able to squeeze in each evening with Alex, my thoughts were usually still preoccupied with work. I went to sleep thinking about it and awoke to it. If it didn't stop, I would drive myself to an ulcer.

But it didn't look like it was going to stop anytime soon. To the contrary, I was going to have to throw heart and soul into my business to have even the slightest chance of keeping the firm alive. I guess subconsciously I assumed that Alex understood. But really, how much could I expect an eight-year-old to grasp the depths of crisis? And I tried to put the best possible face on the situation when I was in her company. I had a million things to do. But I picked up the phone and called home, leaving a message for Rita not to cook dinner, and to tell Alex I would be bringing Chinese takeout home.

The rest of the day was a typical blur. One client called to cancel a condominium conversion project that we had already started work on. We'd get to keep the deposit, but we'd already invested far more than that amount into it. We could sue for breach of contract, but that would just mean more money for lawyers. The cancellation meant that two of our architects literally had nothing to do. We would have to spread the remaining work even more thinly.

At around four, Wendy interrupted a phone call with a note that Art Longley was on the line. My heart skipped a beat. I hadn't spoken to him since he deserted the sinking ship with the mutiny party. I quickly signed off my conversation with a vendor who was complaining about a late payment—the type of call I hadn't had to make in years, but was making frequently now—and picked up the other call. Wendy closed the door behind her.

"Art! Great to hear from you!" I sounded too eager, I realized.

"How're you, buckaroo?" he asked gregariously.

"Well, life sucks, but other than that, everything's great."

"Yeah, I guess it must be pretty tough right now."

"I've known you well enough, long enough, to tell you that's an understatement. Fielder, Steinmetz took our best architects and our best clients. Including you."

"C'mon, I've never known you to gripe like this." I could tell he was taking a puff on his cigar. Art was not one to honor the District of Columbia's authoritarian ban on smoking inside office buildings, or even the national ban on Cuban imports. "Besides, I'm not going to be a Fielder, Steinmetz client for long."

"You're not?"

"Heck no," he replied. "The architects from your place who're over there now are completing projects for me. After that, no way. To a firm like Fielder, Steinmetz, I'm nothing. Chump change. That's why I like the boutiques. More creativity. More personal attention." Another puff. "As you know, I demand personal attention."

"I know."

"But I hadn't been getting much from you the last couple years, Kevin. Starting to feel you were getting too big and important for your old clients."

I started to protest but then thought: Shit. That was true. We *were* too big. I sighed. "Art, you always manage to separate the wheat from the chaff."

"Or the shit from the crapper!" he bellowed, laughing uproariously. "Well, listen, Kevin, I guess you guys qualify as a boutique again, huh?"

I chuckled ruefully. "Yeah, I guess you could say that. I'm definitely getting back to the basics."

"You're good at the basics, Kevin. The best."

"Thanks, Art. That means a lot." It really did.

"Well, old soldier, how's about we get shit-faced this evening and talk about a couple of projects."

"That sounds great, Art."

"Six-thirty, University Club."

"Great." Then: "Shit! Wait, Art. I can't do it tonight. How about tomorrow night?"

"Can't. Leaving for Europe tomorrow with the new bride." Oh my God, that's right, Art had gotten married again. I hadn't even been invited to the wedding.

"What about later tonight, then? Like eight or eight-thirty?" Perhaps I could get a babysitter, or maybe Mrs. Beeman could come over.

"Can't, Kevin. You know, I live in Middleburg now. And the flight's early in the morning."

I sighed again. "Okay," I said resignedly. Then, "No. I can't, Art. It's important to Alex. I can't miss it." There was silence. "Can we schedule something right now for when you return?"

He puffed again, this one long and loud. "Don't think so, Kevin. Got a full schedule. But I'll give you a call if I can squeeze you in." It sounded like a brush-off.

"Please do, Art. I promise you won't regret it." I wondered if my words sounded as pathetic to him as they did to me.

"I wonder, Kevin, I wonder."

I couldn't think of anything worthwhile to fill the silence, so I bade him a good trip, and we signed off. Then I stared at the phone for awhile, blankly, feeling utterly disgusted with myself. All at once I sank into a state of utter, total, take-no-prisoners depression, like I hadn't felt since the days of Nicki. I realized I had been staving it off for a long time, ever since Rich had presented me with the *fait accompli*. But now it was hitting, big-time. And all I could do about it was to sit there, letting the torrents of despair wash over me.

After awhile, there was a knock at my door. Wendy came in, a big expectant smile on her cherubic face. But it disappeared as soon as she saw my expression.

"Hi, Wendy."

"What's wrong?" she asked innocently. "I thought that might be good news from Art Longley."

I exhaled deeply. "It might have been good news. But I couldn't hearken to his beckon call. I have home responsibilities. So he's taking his business elsewhere."

The traffic on the drive home ordinarily would have annoyed the hell out of me, but I barely noticed. I was preoccupied by what seemed an insoluble dilemma at work. I was still focused on it as I picked up the Chinese food, but when I reached the penthouse, I tried to brush those thoughts away.

Rita greeted me at the door, and seemed pleased that I had arrived at the promised time and that she could go home for what passed these days for early. She looked tired, and I wondered as I often did how she could manage two households when I could barely manage one.

I put the food on the dining room table and walked down the hallway to Alex's room. She was lying on her bed, her ears covered with Walkman headphones, playing with Muk, her Pokemon doll. It was her latest obsession.

We wolfed down the food: General Tso's chicken, Szechuan green beans, meat dumplings, and fried rice, which Alex called "fly lice." For such a dainty, feminine little girl, she could be pretty gross sometimes. I also didn't know where she packed all the food in a seventy-pound body. Unlike her mother, who had struggled with her weight all her life, Alex seemed only to grow up, not out. She was already up to my chest, and I figured she would surpass me in height by the time she was thirteen.

My appetite gave way before hers. Then I was astonished when she asked, "Can we go to Fagin's?"

I groaned. "You can eat ice cream after this?"

She grinned back at me. "Dad, I can *always* eat ice cream."

"Well, I will watch you in wonderment, but I surely can't eat any myself." It turned out to be a fib: I ate a small portion of rainbow sherbet while she downed a cherry sundae with French vanilla ice cream.

The neighborhood hang-out was packed with college students and other families. I finished but Alex was still working on hers. As I looked at her I noticed something dangling from her ears. "Where did you get those earrings?" I asked. They were much bigger than anything I had seen on Alex before, much too large for her ears. I couldn't believe I hadn't noticed them before. I must've been too occupied with dinner.

"Mrs. Beeman gave them to me. Aren't they pretty?" She cocked her head so I could look at them.

They were garish, heavy silver with pearls. "They're for a grown-up, Alex," I replied. "An old one at that. How did you get them?"

"I was over there today and asked for them. She has lots of cool jewelry; this is the second pair she's given me," Alex reported matter-of-factly. "She's going to give me a beautiful ruby ring too, when she dies. I told her I would like to have it before then, and she said she would think about it."

"Alex!" I exclaimed, appalled. "You don't go asking for gifts."

"Dad." She put down her spoon and looked up at me, her white mustache depriving her of the earnestness she was trying to affect. "She doesn't wear much of it anymore. She says she likes to share with me. She says I'm her favorite little girl."

"I'm sure you are, Alex. But I don't want you asking her for gifts. I'm going to have to give them back."

Alex pouted. "Dad, I've had them for a *week*. I wore them every single night, and you didn't even notice. You weren't ever home to notice."

I sighed and extended my hand across the table. She took it with hers, which was cold from cradling the ice cream dish. "Let's go for a walk."

"Okay," she replied, taking one more spoonful of sundae for good measure. She dabbed her mouth with a napkin, and then we were off into the balmy night. I put my arm around her slender shoulders as we walked around the park.

"It's a really tough time at work right now. Ever since Rich left, I've had to work really hard. They really need me right now." I looked down at her, but her face was inscrutable, her eyes staring ahead.

"But I need you too, Dad."

"I know, honey. I want you to know that tonight I turned down— well, I just know, sweetheart. It's just really tough right now, and I'm going to try harder to get home on time. I promise this won't last for long. If it does I'll quit and get another job. Okay?"

She pulled away and took my hand, squeezing it gently. "I understand, Dad. But not for long, right?"

I squeezed her hand back. "Not for long, I promise." Then a thought occurred to me. "Where would you like to go for summer vacation? I know we talked about Montreal, but that's not set in stone."

Alex looked up at me. In the gathering dusk her eyes were shrouded and dark. "Can we go anywhere?"

"Anywhere," I replied.

"Can we go to the Grand Canyon? And ride mules down to the bottom? I saw it on National Geographic."

I smiled. "Sure. That sounds like a great idea. Um, I spoke to Mrs. Robles today. She said you haven't been handing in your work lately." No response. "So what's going on?"

Alex sighed. Good grief, she sounds like me, I thought with a start. The weight of the world on her little shoulders. "I have been so forgetful lately." She sounded very contrite. "Sometimes I forget to write it down, sometimes I forget to hand it in, or just lose it. Mrs. Robles says she'll check my assignment pad. And I know you do." She sighed again. "I'll try harder. I really like school." She looked up at me hopefully.

This was good under the circumstances, I thought. No denial. No tantrum. She was admitting the problem and resolving to do something about it. "I'll do whatever I can to help you."

"Maybe you can come home before I go to bed, and check my homework with me."

Ah. Now we were getting to the root of the problem, I suspected. "Yes," I assured her. "From now on, I promise."

The rest of the walk was uneventful. We talked about the projects I was working on—none of which were all that interesting—and about recent birthday parties in her class. Tommy Hempster's was coming up, and Alex was resolved to buy him a Play Station. She even offered to spend half her own savings—about fifty dollars. It was an extravagant present, but Tommy was the best—and longest-lasting—friend Alex ever had sustained. So I agreed to kick in the rest of the money.

It was a typical act of Alex's generosity. I had to admit, as I thought about it, that she was thoughtful with regard to Mrs. Beeman, and Rita, too. She searched the Internet for a source for Mrs. Beeman's favorite teas, and demanded that we go into a Salvadorian grocery store we passed one time to pick up some native specialties for Rita. Maybe it wasn't so bad that Mona Beeman gave Alex the earrings—I just didn't want Alex asking for things.

As we got home, I came back downstairs to walk Benji after running a bath for Alex. When I returned we checked her homework. It was all complete, and looked accurate. "Don't forget to turn it in."

"Okey dokey," she said with a smile. Then I put her to bed, Benji jumping up and settling in by her feet.

"What a great idea to go to the Grand Canyon," I told Alex as I tucked her in. "I'll get some brochures from the travel agent tomorrow," I promised.

We hugged tightly, and I suspected Alex was already heading

toward dreamland as I clicked out the light. She needed sleep, if for nothing else to digest a massive dinner. I smiled as I walked up the hallway toward the living room.

Well, I think we had a breakthrough, I said to myself. I had to get my life in order. If I had to work extra hours, I would sneak in on the weekends, when Alex was with her aunt or grandparents, or at Tommy Hempster's house. But I had to make time, every night, and every weekend. Or she would act out in ways unpredictable and probably self-destructive.

I sank down into the sofa. Alex's backpack was waiting for her to take to school in the morning.

On impulse, I pulled it over to me and glanced inside. Yes, her homework was there. And a hairbrush. Plus stickers, and bubble gum, and a packet of Pokemon cards. What a collection. Then I saw some papers deep on the bottom, folded together. I pulled them out. It was a thick stack. Hmm, had I found the missing homework? I unfolded it, but the mystery deepened. Sure enough. English. History. Math. Latin. Probably six or seven assignments. And each with a thick black "X" in crayon. An angry mark. Alex hadn't lost her homework, she had trashed it. And had lied, defiantly.

Rage welled inside me. God-fucking-damnit.

I went through the homework again, my anger building. I would not let this little girl play me for a fool.

I shoved the bag aside, clutching the papers, and strode loudly down the hallway. I pushed Alex's door open and flicked on the light. Benji blinked his eyes, took one look at me, and jumped off the bed.

"Goddamnit," I yelled as I walked over to her bed and leaned over, my face less than a foot from hers. "You lied to me! I found your missing homework! You put an X through it!" Alex burst instantly into tears, moving to burrow her face into the pillow. "Hey, look at me, Alex!" I grabbed her chin and turned it toward me. "Look at me!"

"Ow," she bellowed, "you're hurting me!"

"You deserve for me to hurt you, Alex. Maybe I'll spank you first, then ask questions later."

"Don't hurt me!"

"Don't lie to me!" I hollered back. She slid her face, wet with tears, out of my grasp and back toward the pillow. "Goddamnit!" I yelled again, and grabbed her shoulder and wrenched it around so she had no choice but to face me.

She looked up at me, her eyes rimmed with red, her countenance brimming with insolence. But her voice was icy calm. "Are you going to make me die, like you did to Mommy?"

"What?"

"You know what I mean."

"Who planted that idea in you?" Alex pursed her lips and I grabbed her face and shook it. I had never been so enraged with her. "Who said that to you? Was it your Grandma Petri? Your goddamned aunt? Who?!" I demanded, yelling now, feeling my slim self-control slipping.

"Stahhhp!" she demanded, pulling away from me and slinking to the edge of the bed.

I managed to calm myself slightly, still gazing furiously at her. "Who told you that, Alex?"

Alex was no longer crying, though her eyes were bright. "Mommy told me that," she replied.

I squinted with confusion. "When did she tell you that? Do you talk to her in your dreams or something?"

"No," Alex replied, rolling her eyes. "Mommy's dead. She doesn't talk to me in my dreams." She searched my face as if for a measure of understanding, then finally explained. "She told me before she died."

I looked at her incomprehensively. "What on earth are you talking about? What did she tell you before she died?"

"Mommy told me she was going to die. She told me that one day you were going to kill her."

37

AMAZINGLY, I HAD managed to keep my vow to restrict my work to relatively reasonable hours over the next several months. The main reason was Samantha: she had agreed to come back, and had wrapped up her work in Chicago and made the move back to the District of Columbia in about two months. She immediately exerted a settling impact—mainly on me, but also on the firm in general. By the time she arrived, the situation had stabilized somewhat and at least we were no longer hemorrhaging. We were forced to lay off most of the holdover architects and now once again had a small, talented crew. Several new small clients had come in. I think that our free-fall among establishment clients had the unexpected but salutary effect of emboldening smaller clients to seek our services. We were happy to have them; and frankly, the work was more interesting and fulfilling. The situation was still precarious, but Samantha had taken the helm firmly, allowing me to take over creative management. My work was demanding but manageable, and I was actually beginning to enjoy it again. That allowed me to get home on time to Alex, and she seemed to flourish with it. On the few occasions when I couldn't get home, I would call her and explain, and usually negotiate some unexpected extra time with Mona Beeman or Tommy Hempster, who were her two favorite people, even though they were about seventy years apart from one another in age.

For awhile, everything looked golden. Especially at work. We received news that we'd won a bid for the conversion of a warehouse on U Street into a condominium complex. It was the largest project to date for the new firm, in an up-an-coming District neighborhood. The project suited us—our prices were lower than the major firms, and our reconstituted firm was on the rebound, just like the new neighborhood. Cutting-edge. Or at least I hoped so.

But the new project would mean longer working hours for

awhile. I wanted the firm to stay lean and mean. The thought of hiring new architects and running the risk of laying them off was more than I could bear. So Samantha and I had agreed not to take on more work than we could handle, and to shoulder the work ourselves as best we could.

And indeed things went along very well for awhile. My workload amounted to about fifty hours per week, but it was manageable and most nights I was home for dinner with Alex. The few nights I had to work late, she usually watched television with Mrs. Beeman or spent time at Tommy Hempster's house, either of which seemed fine with her. Alex started third grade and seemed to like her new teacher, Mrs. Finnegan. In fact, Mrs. Finnegan sent a note home asking my permission for Alex to take reading classes with the fourth grade, which was fine by me. She suggested Alex might even skip fourth grade if all went well.

The fall in Washington was unexpectedly blustery, and by early October, we were wearing jackets. The season seemed to be in a rush to get on with things.

It seemed after all to be an omen. A few months after returning home I received a call from my sister with very bad news. My mother's cancer, in remission for several years, had returned. She didn't yet have a complete prognosis, but it sounded pretty bad. I didn't realize my sister had traveled to Pennsylvania to be with my mom, who wasn't feeling up to talking to me. As usual, my mom had kept her concerns to herself, not wanting to trouble me but willing to confide in my sister once she had no other choice.

"She's lost a lot of weight, and isn't eating well," my sister reported. She sounded scared.

"Do you want me to come up?"

"I'm leaving next weekend. How about the weekend after that?"

I told her that was fine. I was sure Alex's aunt or grandparents would be happy to have Alex for the weekend. I didn't want Alex to see my mom if she was really sick. I did tell Alex about it, though, to prepare her for the possibility that I'd be away on some weekends. She seemed matter-of-fact about the news.

"I could just stay here with Benji, and hang out with Mrs. Beeman."

I rolled my eyes. "You're too young to take care of yourself, and Mrs. Beeman is older than your grandmother."

"I cook for you sometimes."

Frankly I was pleased she wasn't so keen to spend time with Nicki's family, but considering the alternatives it was the only choice. So I was firm with Alex and she acquiesced.

When I finally spoke to my mother that week, she was depressed and negative. She didn't want to go through another surgery, or radiation or chemotherapy. It seemed like nothing I could say would brighten her perspective. My sister had warned me that Mom was in bad spirits, but I'd never seen her this way. But she'd never had cancer twice before, either. The woman who had been my rock since I was a little boy was beginning to crumble. I spoke to her doctors. I had never been particularly keen on the quality of medical care in her vicinity, and my conversations with her doctors didn't improve my assessment. The cancer was advanced and I couldn't understand why they didn't catch it earlier during her check-ups. I wasn't optimistic that they could treat it adequately.

The prognosis was grim. The cancer had spread to her lymph nodes. It was now so widespread that surgery was not an option. With radiation and chemotherapy, they told me, her life expectancy would increase from six months to perhaps two years.

That wasn't enough. My mother was otherwise healthy, in her mid-seventies. She led a fairly vigorous lifestyle, traveled abroad every year or two, visited my sister and me at least once a year each, and indulged her passion for slot machines at least six times a year in Atlantic City. I didn't want her to have to give that up, either for a short time or forever. And selfishly, I didn't want to lose her, either for myself or for Alex. She was always a port in a storm. And for Alex, she was her only normal grandparent, even if Alex had never exhibited much warmth toward her.

I took an afternoon off from work to research her condition. I learned that Georgetown Medical Center had developed a cancer protocol that, although intense, could drive my mother's type of cancer into remission and double life expectancy, from two years to as many as five. That seemed to me a huge difference. If only I could convince her to do it.

I called Georgetown and found out there was an opening the following month if she could get a referral from her own doctors. The treatment would require three months of intense treatment at Georgetown, plus extensive recovery time. That was fine: she could move in with Alex and me. Frankly, it would be nice to have her around.

I decided not to tell Alex about her grandmother's condition until I had an opportunity to get things set. I took off for the weekend and drove up to Pennsylvania, leaving Alex in the dubious care of her Aunt Kim. When I arrived Saturday afternoon, a premature winter storm was approaching. But my mother and I went out to our favorite diner and took in a movie. Though she had lost weight, otherwise she looked like her usual self and seemed to be in better spirits. When we left the movie theater, it was snowing, and the flakes were beginning to stick. My mother urged me to drive back home so I wouldn't get stranded, but I suspected that her ulterior motive was to avoid the conversation she knew was coming.

"Hey, do you want to get rid of me already?"

"Of course not!"

"Well, I'm just going to bunk down at home then, and hope school is cancelled tomorrow."

"Kevin, it's Sunday tomorrow, there's no school."

"And you know what? I'm grown-up now, and don't have to go to school anyway!"

"Well, I admit sometimes I still think of you as my baby."

"It's funny, Mom, I was just having this same conversation the other day with Alex. Sometimes she seems so mature and I forget she's just a little girl."

My mother laughed knowingly. Though she occasionally inquired about how Alex was handling things, I rarely intimated much about Alex's occasional emotional problems. My mother was such a stoic person, having handled my father's death so bravely many years before, that I don't think she could relate too well to someone who was emotionally more fragile.

And besides, the immediate concern now was my mother's problems. I rose early in the morning and cooked a big breakfast for the two of us, casting an occasional glance at the still-falling snow outside. Six inches had accumulated during the night, with several more on the way. The major highways were closed and it looked like I might have to stay over a second night.

At the breakfast table I brought up the subject of treatment. My mother was adamant. "No radiation. No chemotherapy. Whatever time I have remaining, I don't want to go through that awful stuff."

She was stubborn but I was resolute. I told her about the Georgetown program. Three rough months of treatment, but maybe five good years afterward. She seemed surprised that her own doctors had given her only six months without treatment. "I don't want this to be our last Christmas together, Mom."

After a lengthy back-and-forth, she began to relent. "We'll see."

"You'll let me speak to your doctors about a referral?"

"I'll think about it. But, I don't want to be a burden to you and Alex."

"A burden? Mom, for goodness sakes, it would be great to have you around."

"Who's going to take care of me during the treatments? They take a lot out of you. You can't do much for yourself."

I was glad to hear her considering the possibility; but I hadn't thought this part through. "I'll take you to the treatments, and we'll hire someone to take care of you." But as the words came out of my mouth I started mentally calculating the costs. It was going to be tight; our household account didn't have much of a margin these days, and the extra time burden was going to eat into the time available for work. But it was Mother, and I quickly banished those errant thoughts from my mind.

"We'll see," she said again. And that ended the conversation.

We spent the rest of a pleasant day watching football and some movie rentals from Blockbuster. Around five it was clear I couldn't make it back to Washington, so I called Kim and asked if she'd drop Alex at school the next morning. She was uncharacteristically pleasant, perhaps because it gave her more time to indoctrinate her niece. I asked her to put Alex on the phone.

"Hey, Dad, where are you?"

"I'm still at Grandma's. There's a big storm and I can't get back tonight, so you're staying over at your aunt's one more night, okay?"

Alex's mood changed immediately. "I don't want to stay here. I want you to come home."

"I can't. The roads still aren't clear. I'll drive home tomorrow as soon as they're plowed."

"What if you're not home tomorrow night?"

"I'll probably be home before my regular time, but Rita will be there after school and you can stay with Mrs. Beeman if I'm late." There was silence on the line. "Alex? Listen, I'm sorry, your grandma is sick, and I'm stuck here. But I'll be home as soon as I can."

"I don't like Mrs. Beeman anymore."

I was stunned. "What are you talking about? When did this happen?" Alex had been Mona Beeman's little shadow for as long as we'd lived next door to her.

"I just don't like her anymore."

"Alex, this doesn't have anything to do with her jewelry, does it?"

"Dad, she keeps telling me she's going to give me rings and necklaces and earrings after she dies, but she's not using them now and I can't understand why she won't give them to me now. It's not like she wears it or anything. She doesn't *need* it."

I lost it. "Alex, I can't believe you're still saying all this nonsense. I told you never to mention wanting her jewelry again. Mrs. Beeman is incredibly nice to you. She doesn't owe you anything!" I was practically shouting over the telephone, hoping my mother wouldn't hear me from the living room.

"Dad, I'm her *friend*, don't you think she owes me for that?"

"I can't believe these things are coming from your mouth. We're going to talk about this when I get home. You can count on that."

"There's nothing to talk about. I don't like her anymore!"

"If you were rude to her, you're going to apologize as soon as I get home."

"No I'm not!"

"Yes you are!"

"Damn it, Dad!" she screeched, her voice now choking with sobs. "I hate Mrs. Beeman! Do you get it? I *hate her*!"

And then she hung up, severing the connection and leaving me shaking with rage and disbelief.

Sometimes I thought Alex had lost the capacity to shock me, but I staggered away from the phone. How could my world with Alex be so topsy-turvy? She was at once the most thoughtful, sweet, adorable little girl and at the same time a selfish, spiteful, nasty little monster. I made a pretense at watching television with my mother—answering her queries about how Alex was doing with soothing platitudes—but soon I excused myself, kissed my mother on the cheek, and went to bed.

The following morning I was up early and made a light breakfast for my mother and me before leaving. Again she promised to think about my proposition, and it seemed she was reconciling herself to it. I considered the mission nearly accomplished.

It took me a half hour to shovel out the car. The folks from the apartment complex had plowed during the night, leaving a mound of snow behind the car. But unlike the preceding day, I now had a strong sense of urgency about getting home. The drive home was treacherous. The Saab inched along the Pennsylvania highways, choked with massive traffic jams caused by numerous accidents. Around four I had finally reached Maryland and left the snow behind. I stopped at a McDonalds for a coffee and bathroom break, and called Rita to let her know I'd be late. I told her to leave Alex in the apartment alone after Rita made dinner, that I'd be home shortly thereafter. Given Alex's fracas with Mrs. Beeman, I didn't want to suggest her staying with the next-door neighbor, but I felt she could handle being alone for an hour or so until my arrival. Alex cheerfully confirmed that fact when I spoke to her briefly. As usual, it was as if nothing untoward had happened between us.

Unfortunately, the Beltway was gnarled in horrendous rush-hour traffic, and it took me even longer than I anticipated to arrive home. When finally I did, I was utterly frazzled. And I was starving. I was ready for a stiff drink, something to eat, and a good night's sleep.

I slid the key into the door and opened it. Inside the living room, the television was blaring, and Alex did not run to the door to greet me. I put my overnight bag down and strode toward the kitchen to see if Alex was in there and to find something to quiet my rumbling stomach.

As I reached the threshold of the kitchen I suddenly halted. Alex was kneeling on the floor, barefooted and wearing a colorful jumper and playing with her Pokemon. I did a double-take: her face and the floor around her was smeared with a red substance that appeared to be blood.

"Hi, Daddy," she greeted me, turning around to face me and smiling sweetly, gruesomely.

"What is that on your face?"

"It's blood. I drank Benji's blood." She giggled innocently, returning her concentration to her doll.

I glanced around and saw no evidence of the dog. My heart pounded as I stared at her first with incomprehension, then disbelief. I felt like I was about to pass out; but I stood there, dumbly, trying to make sense of the situation, watching Alex play with her Pokemon doll as if nothing was out of the ordinary.

She looked up and watched my expression raptly. Then all at once she pealed with high-pitched laughter and ran over to me, wrapping her arms around my waist. I couldn't find it within myself to embrace her in return, looking down at her like she were something inhuman. Finally, she looked up at me. "Daddy," she said, convulsing with giggles, "it's not real blood! It's cake decoration! Benji's asleep by the fireplace!" She lowered her head again and giggled hysterically.

I pushed her away from me, gently but firmly, and grasped her shoulders. Finally she calmed, though she couldn't look at me without smiling and snickering.

"I don't think what you did was funny," I said, my heart still thumping like it was ready to burst.

She shook her head as if trying to fathom me. "Daddy," she said, her voice now all maturity. "I would never drink a dog's blood. How could you believe that for a minute?"

Now she smiled at me knowingly, as if sharing a joke; and her sincerity made me calm down a bit. But the words that came out of her mouth next quickly dispelled the momentary calm. "A *human's* blood, maybe," Alex said earnestly, "but never a dog's."

38

SOMEHOW, I MANAGED to collect myself and haul Alex to the bathroom to clean herself off. Then I made her wash the floor while I took Benji—who had been curled on the living room sofa the entire time—out for a long walk. I think I needed to let off some steam more than Benji needed to relieve himself.

When I returned, Alex was apologetic. "I'm really sorry, Dad," she said, now acting very mature in stark juxtaposition to the demon child who had found so much humor in the situation a few minutes before. "When Rita made a cake this afternoon, I thought it looked like blood, and my imagination just got going and I'm really sorry I scared you." She looked and sounded so sincere that I was willing to forgive her. Though to say that the morbid experience had shaken me would be an understatement.

Over dinner we talked about her shopping outing the previous weekend with her aunt—which apparently had been a nonstop expedition—and about her day in school. She had picked up a birthday present for Amy Ridenhour, a classmate whose party was two weekends hence. After I packed the dishes into the dishwasher, I went to Alex's bedroom, where I found her playing with Muk, her favorite Pokemon doll. It had to be the ugliest toy ever invented, but Alex absolutely loved it.

"Don't you have any homework?"

"Only spelling today, and I finished it after school. It was easy."

"Okay, so tell me about Mrs. Beeman."

She fell back onto her pillow. "Do we have to?"

"Yes, we do. She was one of your best friends and suddenly you 'hate' her. That's not supposed to happen."

Alex put a hand over her eyes. "Dad, she's an old lady. She can't be one of my best friends."

"Anyone can be your best friend, no matter how old or how young.

After my dad died, I had several close friends—mentors, maybe is the better term—who were older than my father." I looked over at her, but she still had her eyes covered. "And Alex, you're one of my best friends in the whole world, despite the slight age difference between us." No reaction. "Aren't I one of your best friends? After Tommy Hempster, anyway?"

She pulled her hand away and cast me a devastating look with her bright, light-brown eyes. "That's different."

"I don't think so."

"Dad, I'll tell you what. I'll go over there. Just not right away. Maybe in a few weeks, okay?"

I smiled benignly. "Are you a little embarrassed, maybe?"

She frowned. "Yeah, maybe a little."

"And when you go over there, you'll apologize?"

This time, a pout, accompanied by a sigh. "Okay. I guess so."

I gave her foot a squeeze. "That's my girl." Then I decided to go for broke and bring up the other touchy subject. "You didn't ask how your grandma is."

She picked up her Pokemon again and started playing with it. "How's Grandma?"

"Thanks for asking," I replied, my sarcasm appearing to miss its intended mark. "She's not doing very well. The cancer has spread really badly. The doctors say she may have only six months to live."

I glanced over to see if Alex was reacting to my words, but her concentration seemed focused on the doll. "Well," she said matter-of-factly, without lifting her eyes from the doll, "old people die."

I could feel the recently vanquished irritation returning. "Your grandma is still a relatively young woman." Funny, I thought to myself, how one's perspective on such matters changes as one gets older. If I were Alex's age, I would think her grandmother was ancient. Heck, I would think her *father* was ancient. "There's a special treatment she can get at Georgetown Hospital that could help her live for five more years. So grandma may be moving in with us for a few months starting next month."

This finally got Alex's complete attention. She put the Pokemon doll down and looked directly at me. "Grandma's going to live *here?*"

"Yeah. Maybe. It's really important for her to come to Washington for this special treatment. We can help extend her life by several years. And have some really special time to spend together." It was difficult to read Alex's expression. "But it's going to be tough. The treatment will make her really sick and weak."

"But who is going to take care of her? And where is she going to stay? We don't have room for another person here."

I snorted. "Alex, we used to have another person living here. We can convert your mom's old office into a bedroom for your grandma. We can put a television in there and everything." Alex averted her eyes from mine and picked up her Pokemon again. "And we'll hire someone to be with her during the day. A nurse. But of course we'll have to help take care of her." No reaction. "That's fine with you, isn't it?"

"Not really," she said matter-of-factly.

"What do you mean, 'not really'?"

"Dad," she replied, looking up at me over Muk, "this is our house. I don't want someone else moving in."

"You know what, Alex?" I said, rising from the bed and pacing back and forth. "This is our house, that's right. But things change, sometimes, and sometimes we might bring someone into our home. We've shared it with other people, including grandma and your aunt and uncle and cousins, and even Tommy Hempster when he's slept over. If your mom and I had had another baby, you would've had a little sister or brother living here, too." Alex cast me a sudden sideways glance that made me think she had never before contemplated that thought. "And we invited Benji into our home. Right? Benji didn't used to live here."

"Benji's a dog."

"So, we have a zoologist living in the house. Thanks, Dr. Gibbons, for that astute observation. The fact is, Alex, that grandma is a part of the family, and she needs to live here for a few months."

"A few months?" She looked at me again.

"A few months isn't a long time, Alex. And we're talking about your grandma. She's been really good to you your whole life. She's loved you and spoiled you from your very first moment. So it's not a big deal for us to help take care of her for a few months. Not a big deal at all."

"Can't she stay at the hospital? We could visit her." I went back to her bed, peeled away the Pokemon, and tossed it onto the floor. "Be careful!" she whined. I couldn't stand that she cared more about the stupid doll than her grandmother.

"Alex," I said as I stared down at her, "I really need your cooperation. Sometimes you can be the sweetest, most cooperative person on Earth. Other times you're so selfish, it's disgusting. It's a really tough time. We're all going to have to make some sacrifices. This is your grandma, my mom, and she needs our help. I need you to promise to help me, to pull together with me. And not to act out in some way. Like pretending you're a fricking vampire or something. Do you understand?" Her features seemed to have softened a bit. I continued in a softer tone. "I need you to be the lady of the house, which you became when your mommy died. Okay?"

All of a sudden her lower lip trembled and her eyes welled with tears, which I could tell she was struggling to hold back. "You mean you need me to be like Florence Nightengale?"

I smiled. "Yeah, a little bit." I leaned over and kissed her forehead. "But just a little bit. Do you think you can do that, sweetheart?"

She smiled back. "Yes, I think so." She sniffled. "I help with Benji."

"You certainly do. You take him out for walks twice a day, and you give him lots of love and attention. And your grandma's going to need help like that. She won't be able to take care of herself. But just for a little while."

Alex nodded, but a tear ran down her face.

"Let's go get some ice cream at Fagin's," I said. And her face lit up even more. I glanced down at my waistline, which had been expanding of late, but decided this was a pretty small price, too.

I could tell over the next few days that Alex was brooding, but she was keeping it pretty much to herself. I figured she needed some time to make the mental adjustment. Mostly I was too busy to notice. Every spare moment it seemed I spent making phone calls. My sister agreed to help persuade Mother to accept the treatments. I secured the requisite referral from her home-town doctors. I spoke to George-town Hospital to begin making arrangements. I began interviewing nurses for my mother's daycare. The biggest hassle was dealing with Blue Cross, which seemed an impenetrable mammoth bureaucracy, divided into smaller multiple bureaucracies at the local level. I was grateful I hadn't become a lawyer, having to deal with that type of nonsense on a regular basis.

And at work I needed to make every second count. Our workload was increasing just as the demands on my personal time were growing more acute. It meant I had to start taking more work home, because I was determined to spend most of my nights and weekends at home. It was especially difficult because Alex wasn't spending time any longer with Mrs. Beeman––a subject I did not bring up again, opting to allow Alex to deal with it in her own time, as she had promised––so Alex demanded more of my attention at home. I was grateful that she had taken to spending an hour each night on the phone with Tommy Hempster.

But mostly the increasing demands meant that I was sleeping less. The anxieties took their toll on the quality of my sleep, too. I found myself dragging at work, picking myself up with copious amounts of coffee, and then suffering caffeine high when I was trying to get to sleep. It was a vicious cycle that would only get worse.

And worse it did get, with an unexpected giant lurch in the form of a telephone call one day from Mrs. Scanlon, the principal at Alex's school. I heard from her rarely, and then only for one of two reasons: a discipline problem or fundraising. In this case, I would gladly have exchanged a hefty contribution for the problem that Mrs. Scanlon was bringing to me.

"Mr. Gibbons, you need to come to the school to pick up Alexandra."

"Is she sick?" I asked. Given the alternative, I actually hoped the answer would be yes.

"No. She's had another discipline problem. This one is particularly serious. We'll discuss it when you arrive. Can we expect you in a half hour?"

I didn't even bother to look at my watch. "Of course. I'll be right over."

I glanced at my phone and saw that Samantha was on her line. I gathered up some materials, shoved them into my briefcase, and went out to Wendy.

"Are you going somewhere?"

"There's a problem at Alex's school. I'm not sure if I'll be back. Please tell Sam she may have to cover the meeting with the construction team on her own, okay?"

I was worried about the amount of work I was placing on Samantha's shoulders. The firm was at the make-or-break point in terms of demonstrating its ability to deliver on a major project. But I was not carrying my share of the burden. Samantha assured me that she understood, and I was sure that she did. But if I couldn't pull my weight, at some point the strain would fray her nerves, and the firm's performance would suffer.

In other words, problems at Alex's schools simply weren't tolerable at this point.

I entered the Spartan administrative office. Mrs. Scanlon's assistant didn't need an introduction. "She's helping with the bake sale. I'll go get her." As she left the office, she looked back and added, "Alexandra is in Mrs. Scanlon's office."

Uh-oh, I thought, they hadn't even sent her back to class. Well, whatever was going on, I silently thanked the divinities for the firm disciplinary standards enforced by Alex's school. Alex needed clearly defined, consistently enforced rules desperately.

Finally, the middle-aged stern-faced principal entered the office, her assistant trailing behind. I always considered Mrs. Scanlon's energy remarkable. She glanced at me, strode into her own office, and left the door ajar, apparently expecting me to follow. She was an intimidating lady, so I cautiously stuck my head inside before entering.

"Come in, Mr. Gibbons. Sit down."

I did. Alex was sitting in a seat in the corner, her eyes red from tears.

The diminutive principal folded her hands atop her desk and leveled a stern gaze at me. "Mr. Gibbons, Alexandra has had another incident. She choked a classmate with a jump rope during recess. It left a very nasty burn and sent the girl to the hospital."

"It was an accident," Alex protested plaintively from her corner.

Mrs. Scanlon shifted her gaze in Alex's direction. "I did not give you permission to speak. I've heard everything you have to say. This conversation is between your father and me." Alex rolled her eyes, which were shiny with tears, and emitted an exaggerated sigh. "I don't need to hear a sound from you!" Mrs. Scanlon snapped, bringing about the desired silence.

"Is the girl okay?" I asked.

"We'll see. We sent her with her parents to the emergency room at Georgetown Hospital."

"Who was it, Mrs. Scanlon?"

"It was Jennifer Mulcahey. She's in Mrs. Finnegan's class with Alexandra."

I recognized the name and associated it with a tall, pretty, athletic girl with strawberry-blonde hair and freckles. Who, of course, Alex disliked. "Are you certain it wasn't an accident?"

"Quite. Apparently Alex and another girl were holding the jump rope, and when it was Jennifer's turn, Alexandra twisted the rope around Jennifer's neck and pulled. Even after the other girl dropped her end of the rope and began screaming, Alex pulled her end tightly. Several other children witnessed the incident. I inspected the marks. The burn surrounds her entire neck and is quite deep." She paused. "Yes, Mr. Gibbons, I'm quite sure it was no accident."

My heart sank. I looked over at Alex, who was looking down at the ground, shaking her head in what I took to be denial rather than disbelief. Sitting there in her uniform of khaki skirt, blue blouse, and matching knee-high socks, she looked wholesome and innocent. It was difficult to fathom the malice that lurked beneath the surface.

"I'm sorry, Mrs. Scanlon. Please tell me the ramifications for Alexandra." Hearing myself use my daughter's full name, which I almost never did, heightened my realization that we were in a very serious straits.

"Mr. Gibbons, we have no choice but to ask you to find another school for Alexandra. Considering the incidents before she came here, we cannot risk our other children's safety. Alexandra is not welcome back at this school."

Though I think I suspected that outcome, I was mortified. The school was an important part of her foundation. "Please reconsider. Alex hasn't had any disciplinary problems for a long time. It's clear she's remorseful. She loves it here. She absolutely loves it. All her friends go here."

"I'm sorry, no. Alexandra knows the rules, and the necessary consequences of her atrocious behavior. We admitted her despite concerns about her past behavior, but it's clear that we were wrong to do so."

"How about just a few weeks, until we can find another school?"

"Alexandra is a threat to the other children. We cannot tolerate such behavior or the risks it presents for a minute longer. I suggest you seek professional help for her. If you'll excuse me now, I have other business to attend to."

Alex was immediately at my side as I arose. We walked to the Saab in silence. Once inside and driving home, Alex broke out into loud sobs. "Dad, it was an accident. I didn't mean to hurt her. The rope just got twisted around her neck." She looked at me pleadingly. "Why didn't you stick up for me?"

I tried to control my anger. "Alex, I don't know what to believe. But your past behavior, along with the witnesses, and the fact that I know you don't like Jennifer Mulcahey, make a pretty strong case for expulsion, no matter how you look at it." She wailed even louder. "I don't have any idea what we're going to do now, Alex. No idea."

We drove home in relative silence, only the sounds from Alex's sobbing accompanying the noise from the street. Once upstairs, Alex announced she was taking Benji for a walk. I was glad to have her gone.

I burrowed into the sofa. My head was pounding. What the fuck was I supposed to do now? Where would Alex go to school? The image of an old-fashioned reform school flickered into my mind, and for a moment it was a pleasing thought.

I called Dr. Purcell. I guess the anxiety was obvious in my voice because the receptionist quickly put her on the line. I told her about the incident, making my tone hushed as Alex came back into the apartment and padded off to her room. Then I told her about the gruesome incident with Benji, about her sudden parting with Mrs. Beeman, and finally about her reaction to my mother's forthcoming stay.

"Has anything happened lately to upset Alex, other than the news about your mother?"

"No, really, things are—were—about as stable as can be. I was hoping she was making progress."

"Well, it certainly seemed that way," Dr. Purcell agreed. "I've found her lately to be a delightful young woman. She evidences the normal adolescent feelings about other children, both good and bad, but nothing worrisome. Her apparent behavior is contrary to my observation."

I wondered at Dr. Purcell's use of the word "apparent." I hoped she wasn't siding with Alex. "I'm worried about what this disruption is going to do to her," I said. "And in a few weeks my mother will be here. I've got to focus on her needs for awhile."

"Well, you need to focus on Alex, too. I'll add an extra visit this week, tomorrow, if you like, and try to get to the bottom of this. You and I can chat afterward."

"Do you have any recommendations about school?"

"You can try the learning disabilities program in the District of Columbia Public Schools. Or home instruction with a tutor, until you can find something more permanent. Other than a residential facility, I'm not aware of schools in the area that are likely to take Alex in, given her expulsion and prior record."

I thanked the doctor for her time and signed off. I was skeptical that the doctor could help her, given that Alex obviously had convinced her that she was the picture of a normal adolescent girl. Occasionally she had convinced me of that, too, but I wasn't a psychologist.

Later that afternoon I told Alex she was grounded, including phone calls from Tommy Hempster. She took the news stoically. After Rita arrived, surprised to find Alex and me home, I went out and bought some computer CDs in reading and mathematics to keep Alex's studies going on what I hoped would be a short-term basis. I stayed home the remainder of the week, interspersing work with phone calls relating both to my mother and Alex. I told Samantha to hire a new architect to pick up the slack, with the salary coming out of mine.

The District of Columbia Public Schools were, predictably, a morass. In order for Alex to qualify for a learning-disability label—which of course was a misnomer, but apparently a catch-all designation that covered all manner of problems, including behavioral dysfunction–she would have to undergo a battery of tests. And the waiting list was two years. In the meantime, I could sign her up for a regular public school. Not a chance.

I contacted several private schools to no avail, then was referred to an educational consulting firm. I made an appointment and went in to see them. After recounting the situation, I was informed that the only suitable schools in the area had long waiting lists. I could get Alex on the lists and perhaps something would open up, but even then there would be no guarantee the school would accept Alex given her record. They suggested that I opt for home instruction or, as Dr. Purcell had suggested, a residential placement. I considered the latter a last resort—not only did I not want to give Alex up, but I didn't want to shake her foundation even more. Instead I told them I'd pursue in-home instruction, and they gave me the names of several tutors. The price was staggering: a minimum of one thousand dollars per week for twenty hours of instruction. But it seemed the only viable alternative for the time being.

That afternoon I took Alex to her appointment with Dr. Purcell. After their hour-long visit, I went in to meet with the doctor. She sat behind a huge desk in her office. The degrees on her wall were so numerous and impressive it was actually intimidating. "Well, without violating confidences, you're right, Alex is in a bit of a tailspin. She's distressed about your reaction to her argument with Mrs. Beeman, about the disruption your mother's visit may entail, and about the possible loss of her friends. She tells me you've forbidden her to see her friend Tommy."

"No, she's just grounded. And she was dis-invited to a birthday party of one of her former classmates. I know that was pretty unsettling."

"Well, I don't think it's a good idea for you to deny contact with Tommy. Or to do anything that's going to unsettle her more. She wants to please you. Desperately. But she also doubts your love for her, and it makes her insecure and angry."

"What? She doubts my love? I love her like crazy." I realized I had used an inapt term in the presence of a psychologist.

"She loves you more than anything, Mr. Gibbons. But she was very distressed that you didn't believe her version of the events at the school."

"I didn't believe her version of the events because it wasn't true."

The doctor regarded me with a look that registered disapproval. "Sometimes you have to stand behind the person you love, right or wrong. At least that's how Alex sees it. Very much so."

"And sometimes you have to set standards of behavior for your children, and demand that they meet them, whether they're psycho or not." Now the doctor's disapproval was palpable. "I'm sorry, I didn't mean that. Exactly."

"She's very special, but just because she sees things a certain way doesn't mean it dovetails with reality as the rest of us understand it. That is, after all, the essence of psychological illness. Our job is to understand her perceptions as best we can, and give her as much support as possible to reconcile herself to the real world."

"I understand all that, but there's a lot of stress coming up, and there's not much I can do to change it. I can't afford to have Alex going off the deep end while I'm trying to take care of my mother and my business. So what can we do?"

"I'm putting her back on Remeron, to modulate her mood swings. It seemed to temper the situation before. Beyond that, I should see her once a week, to provide an additional outlet during the difficult period."

We discussed the school situation, and Dr. Purcell approved of the idea of a home-based tutor until something more permanent could be arranged. "But you may want to consider a residential placement for awhile," she suggested.

"Actually, Dr. Purcell, I really don't want to do that. I might feel differently if it weren't for her mother. I think Alex would view it as the same situation, and it would be like the end of the world for her. And I would be worried sick the entire time. Waiting for the call—like Nicki."

The doctor nodded reassuringly. "I understand, Mr. Gibbons. But this would be decidedly different, and it would be important to characterize it that way. This would be a school, not a sanitarium. The psychological evaluation and therapy is secondary. I'm thinking in particular of a place in Maryland about an hour from Washington called the Cacoctin Institute. It's an excellent school. Most of the students are girls, and a high percentage are diagnosed with border-line personality disorder. Borderlines typically have extremely high intelligence. That helps to make it difficult to diagnose and treat–the patients are adept at persuasion. At Cacoctin, the focus is on intellectual stimulation and genuine self-esteem. The headmaster is an excellent psychologist by the name of Habbyshaw Jenkins. I've written down his name and phone number, and taken the liberty of copying

Alex's records in case you call him for a consultation. I think you should check it out, just to have an additional option."

Options were one thing I desperately needed. "All right, I'll take a drive out there."

REMARKABLY, THE NEXT few weeks made it seem like none of that would be necessary. Though the stress seemed non-stop, Alex became my little partner. She helped me interview tutors, and we jointly (and enthusiastically) decided on a bright and sweet twenty-something exchange student from Finland named Hilda, who was pursuing a graduate degree in education at American University. Despite having only lived in the United States for two years, Hilda spoke flawless English, and she and Alex seemed to bond instantly.

Alex and I also interviewed nurses for my mother. It was gratifying to see Alex take such an interest in the matter. We finally settled on a middle-aged black woman named Trudy, who seemed both tough (which my mother needed sometimes) and empathetic. Trudy would come in three mornings a week following my mother's twice-weekly treatments.

Meanwhile, Hilda would come by to tutor Alex each day from ten until two. I would work at home in the early mornings, except for the days I needed to bring my mother in for her treatments. Alex would be on her own with my mother (who would presumably be sleeping) after two each day, until Rita arrived at four.

Alex agreed that we should redecorate her playroom, Nicki's old office, for my mother's arrival. First we re-painted the room a pale pink, chosen by Alex. Then we put up frilly borders, again chosen by the young designer. Of course we had to select matching bed linens. Alex's taste was impeccable and I began to envision her as an interior decorator. We added a television and a tape deck with an assortment of books on tape, and picked up two overstuffed rocking chairs for visitors.

My mother arrived a week before Christmas, and my sister and her family arrived the next day to celebrate an early holiday. My mother was frail, but had pushed off the treatments until the week after Christmas. We managed to have a fantastic time, I suspect because of the sudden awareness that we might not have many holidays left with my mother. The kids played together very well, and the gift exchange was delightful even if it was before the official day.

The treatments began the following week. At first she took them very well, with few side effects except weariness. She encouraged Alex and me to go out and celebrate the Millennium new year on our own, and we did so. I took Alex to Geranio in Old Town for a big-girl dinner. It was an unseasonably balmy evening, and Alex wore a beautiful, long, midnight-blue dress she had bought for the evening. Afterward we strolled to the waterfront and watched the fireworks over the city of Washington. I kissed the top of her head from behind, and she looked up at me with her big brown eyes and said, "I think this is going to be a really great century, Dad."

But it got off to a bleak start. My mother's treatments started generating adverse consequences. She began losing her hair and experiencing debilitating nausea. When she was awake, she would scold Alex for the slightest infractions, from making too much noise to not responding promptly enough to her needs. She also coughed incessantly, keeping everyone up at night. Alex seemed to be making the best of it, but I could tell that the experience was unnerving her. I began to wonder whether I had inflicted too much responsibility on the two of us.

At work, despite hiring an extra architect, we were falling behind on our projects, to the irritation of our clients. Samantha's nerves were fraying and we were losing our tempers with each other. And with an array of personal distractions, I wasn't able to contribute my best work in the limited time I had available for it. I knew it couldn't go on this way for long.

My personal finances were in a total free-fall. The expenses for the tutor and nurse were breathtaking. Fortunately, interest rates were low, so I was able to re-finance and take out some of the equity in our condominium, and the resulting mortgage payments were about the same as previously. That gave me some momentary cushion.

In mid-January, I took an afternoon off to drive out to the Cacoctin Institute. It was housed in a stately old mansion in the rolling hills of western Maryland. There I was ushered into the office of the Institute's director, Dr. Habbyshaw Jenkins, who ended up being an elderly black man with a tremendous air of gravitas.

He was thoroughly familiar with Alex's file, so we were able to plunge instantly into the details. Echoing Dr. Purcell, the director told me that Cacoctin could offer Alex individualized instruction at a high intellectual level, while tending to her emotional needs. "Our goal is to help our students become self-sufficient, fully functioning members of society. Most return to regular schools. Our graduates have gone on to Harvard, Yale, Brown"—then, smiling broadly—"and some good schools, too."

I expressed worries about having Alex so far away, and terror about Alex following her mother's example. Dr. Jenkins was reassuring but blunt. "We can't make any guarantees. But we have never experienced any suicides. We provide a very positive, affirming environment. This is a school, not a mental institution. And Alex would spend her weekends with you. Life in the outside world will be viewed as an achievable, positive goal. It will just require the enduring positive behavior that we want Alex to develop."

We visited some classes. As Dr. Purcell had described it, they were mostly made up of girls. I wondered if that would impel Alex to feel competitive over the small number of boys. But overall, the students seemed bright, serious, and most of all, wholesome and normal.

I left with a better feeling about the prospects if I decided Alex needed to be placed there. But I hoped we could avoid it. Alex's studies with Hilda were proceeding nicely. They seemed to enjoy each other's company immensely. They went to museums together, and Hilda was teaching Alex to speak Finnish. My hope was that after several months with Hilda, a place would open up in one of the local private schools that accepted troubled students.

But socially, I worried that Alex was atrophying. Her girlfriends (or more likely their parents) had ostracized her. I tried to get her to join Girl Scouts, but she had no interest. Fortunately, she still had Tommy Hempster, but he was her only outlet.

As I ARRIVED home one wintry Friday afternoon ready to collapse after an exhausting week, I noticed an ambulance with a flashing light in the driveway in front of our building. I hurried up the elevator and saw that the door to Mrs. Beeman's apartment was ajar. Several medical personnel were inside, speaking loudly, but I couldn't hear their words. I opened the door to my own condo to an even rowdier commotion. Alex was screaming somewhere inside the apartment and Rita was yelling at her.

I found them both in the kitchen, where Alex was hysterical. "What's going on?"

"Alex lost her Pokemon doll," Rita replied.

"I didn't lose it!" Alex retorted. "I think Grandma took it. I looked all over her room, but she hid it!"

Rita looked at me glumly. "Mrs. Gibbons was very upset. She tell Alex she don't have her doll."

"She's lying!"

The nonsense got to me instantly. "Stop it, Alex, and go to your room!"

"But Dad!"

"Go to your room! We'll sort this out later. You'll probably find your Pokemon in there anyway."

She stamped off furiously. I looked at Rita. "Do you have any idea what's going on next door at Mona Beeman's?"

"The lady from her church knock on the door and ask have I seen Mrs. Beeman, she miss her Bingo game today. I ask Alex, she tell me she no see Mrs. Beeman for days. So I think she have a heart attack."

"Oh no," I said. "The poor lady, all alone. Have you seen her son?"

"They call him, I think he there now."

I sighed. "I hope she's all right, but I don't have a good feeling about it." Rita nodded knowingly. "Well," I continued, "I guess I need to talk to Alex."

I walked down the hallway to her door and knocked quietly. No answer. I opened the door and saw Alex reading on her bed, Benji at her feet. I sat on her bed and tried to pull the book away, but Alex resisted and kept it in front of her face. "You know your grandma didn't steal your Pokemon. I don't think she has the energy to hide a doll."

"She sure has enough energy to yell at me."

I smiled, despite myself, but stifled it. "Honey, you know your grandma is really ill. She's going to get worse before she gets better, but she will get better. And she'll be a lot less grouchy when she does."

"I hope so," Alex replied, her face still in the book. "I can't wait for her to leave."

A surge of anger welled inside me, but I suppressed that, as well. I looked at Alex for a few moments, then finally said, "Well, Alex, I'm really tired. I'm going to have the nice dinner that Rita made for us and then go to bed. Tomorrow we can go see a movie, get out of the house, okay?" No answer. "You can come out and join me for dinner if you like. Or not."

There was still no response, so I left the room and ate dinner alone after Rita's departure. I checked on my mother, who was sleeping comfortably. I awakened her to give her some medication, but she retreated quickly into sleep. I checked Alex's room, and she had fallen asleep as well.

I wanted to also, but now I was restless. I picked up a paperback from my nightstand, took it into the living room, poured myself a glass of cabernet, and settled into the sofa. It was utterly quiet now. Not a sound from inside the house, or from next door. Eventually Benji padded out, apparently liberated from Alex's room. I'd have to take him outside before I went to bed.

Around nine there was a knock at the door. I looked through the peephole and recognized the middle-aged man outside our door as Mrs. Beeman's son. I opened the door. "Please, come in."

"No thanks. Carl Beeman," he said, extending his hand.

I shook it. "I know. How's your mom?"

His eyes grew moist. "She passed away. Apparently yesterday. A heart attack." His jaw trembled. "They found her on the floor, collapsed in front of her rocker."

"Oh, I'm so sorry. She was a wonderful lady. A wonderful neighbor, and a real friend to both Alex and me."

"I know," he replied, swallowing hard. "She was old, though. She knew she didn't have much time."

"Is there anything we can do?"

"Her funeral will be on Monday, with a viewing tomorrow evening."

"Alex and I will be there."

"She adored your little girl. She called her an angel."

I smiled. "I know. Alex loved her, too."

He nodded sadly. "That's why I came by. I think I found something in the apartment that must belong to her, and I didn't want it to get mixed up among my mother's things."

And then he presented me with Alex's missing Pokemon doll.

50

WITH SO MANY demands, the days and nights of the following weeks passed in a blur.

One evening in the grip of insomnia, I tiptoed through the darkness of my mother's room carefully, trying not to awaken my sleeping mother. As I reached her nightstand, I groped around its surface until I finally found the paperback novel I had left there a few hours earlier when I had read silently by her bedside as she napped. Picking it up, I turned and began to retrace my steps toward the equally darkened hallway.

And then stubbed my toe on the leg of her bed, really hard.

"Ow," I muttered, instantly regretting it.

My mother stirred. "It's okay, Kevin. I was half-awake anyway."

Her voice was feeble, but nonetheless seemed marginally stronger than it had been. She seemed to be regaining her strength, bit by bit, now that her chemotherapy had ended. Even her hair was growing back, though it looked a bit like the buzz-cuts I had gotten as a boy. These days my mother bore an uncanny resemblance to Sinead O'Connor, albeit a bit older.

"Why don't you turn on the lamp?" she asked.

"Are you sure?" But suddenly I realized I was eager for the company and didn't await her response. "Cover your eyes," I instructed, and flicked on the small lamp next to her bed.

The light amplified the shadows of her sunken face. My mother, robust in healthier days, was emaciated. Fortunately, she was eating soup occasionally, and of course her beloved ice cream. She didn't have any more weight she could lose.

"You couldn't sleep again?" she asked.

"No," I mumbled. She patted the side of her bed and I sat down. "Your hair is really growing back."

"I'm going to wear an earring and start a rock band."

I chuckled. "That's exactly what I was thinking. And heck, we can use the money."

She smiled. "I wish you didn't worry so much, Kevin. You're going gray. Everything's going to turn out all right."

I sighed. "I suppose, Mom. It's just rough."

"Well, we passed the New Year without any big disaster. I mean, weren't all the computers supposed to crash? And the son of Satan was supposed to appear, leading us to Armaggedon?"

"There you go, reading all those horror novels again."

"And what's that in your hand?"

I glanced down. "Oh yeah. Stephen King."

She smiled, but turned serious. "I hope you're not worried about me."

Of course I was worried about her. Her prognosis was not good. The treatment had been a failure. Her cancer had spread beyond the curative capacity of chemotherapy. The hospital had offered a different experimental chemical regimen, but my mother had refused it, along with any further treatment. "I wish you'd let the doctors try the new therapy," I protested, for about the hundredth time.

My mother's chin jutted out, as it always did when she was drawing some sort of line. I supposed mine did that too when I was feeling obstinate. "No," she said. "I'm not doing that."

"Mom . . ."

"Maybe I have a few months left. Maybe a bit longer. The treatments aren't going to cure me. They're going to make me sick. I can either spend my last few months feeling sick or feeling good. In a few weeks maybe I'll feel well enough to visit your sister in Las Vegas. Maybe even gamble." She looked me in the eye. "That's how I'd like to spend my remaining good days. Not in a bed, feeling horrible."

I could understand her logic. What I couldn't accept was the futility. And the prospect of losing the woman who not only was my mother, but truly my best friend.

"What else is bothering you?"

I looked down at my toes and considered my response. "Alex."

It was my mother's turn to sigh. She didn't know the details of what had been going on, but she didn't have to. She had sensed it, even in the midst of debilitating illness. "What are you going to do?"

I shook my head. "I don't know, Mom. I just don't know. I'm at my wit's end."

"You need help with her, Kevin. You can't handle it alone."

"I know, but I don't know what to do. Some of the things she does are scary. Really scary. And sometimes I feel like I don't know the half of it. I worry that's she's capable of unthinkable acts." I sighed. "Yet other times I feel guilty for thinking that. I think I'm imagining things. It's like something out of a horror novel." I tapped the book. "I mean, she can be the sweetest little girl. Sometimes. But other times . . ."

I let the sentence trail off. I wanted to tell her more. I wanted to tell her about the suspicions I harbored about the dark acts I feared my daughter had committed. And yet, I couldn't voice those fears, even though they haunted my every moment. They were truly unspeakable. Even to my mother.

And so we sat in silence. Above us I could hear the beating rotors of a helicopter. The president, perhaps, returning from a midnight tryst somewhere.

"Kevin, there's something I should tell you. I overheard Alex talking on the phone today to Tommy Hempster. She was saying something about playing with a gun. It sounds like Tommy's father has a gun somewhere in the house, and they found it. I confronted her about it, but of course she got angry and slammed the door to her bedroom."

"Ah, jeez," I said. "That's all I need, my little psycho daughter playing with a gun." I slapped my thigh. "Well, I'll speak to her about it. And I'll call the Hempsters and tell them to put the gun in a safe place. Or get rid of it." For all of my reactionary politics, I wasn't much of a fan of guns. If the District of Columbia police could get their heads out of their asses and do their jobs, people wouldn't feel like they needed to arm themselves. But I still didn't want my daughter playing with a gun.

"You need help dealing with her."

"I know, I know. But for Christ's sake, I don't know what to do. Dr. Purcell isn't helping. Drugs don't seem to help. And I can't afford to put her in Cacoctin. This place is mortgaged to the max. We're barely making ends meet at the firm. I don't have a cent saved for college for Alex. I just don't know what to do."

"I can give you some money."

"Mom, you've hardly got anything, and whatever you do have I want you to gamble away in Las Vegas, enjoying yourself."

"I've got a little bit of insurance."

"No, I'll handle this on my own."

"No, you have to let someone else help you."

"Anyway, it's not just that."

"You don't want her to go away. You're worried because of what happened to Nicki when she went away."

I nodded. Tears welled in my eyes. "What's wrong with her, Mom? What's wrong with me?"

She reached out and took my hand, and as always her skin was amazingly soft. "There's nothing wrong with you, Kevin. You're a terrific father."

The tears were streaming now, choking my voice. "I remember so many years ago, when you told me you wanted me to get married and give you some grandchildren," I said. "I guess I really blew it."

And with that, my mother drew me to her, and I cried like a baby; like I hadn't cried in her presence in years and years. And it had the same effect that it had when I was a child. It uncorked me, giving release to the accumulated fear, and worry, and grief. Eventually I stopped crying, and I pulled my head up, feeling a bit embarrassed. "I love you, Mom. Thank you."

"How about giving the old lady a kiss, and trying to get some sleep?" I smiled, then leaned over with a hug and gentle kiss on her cheek. "Sweet dreams, and don't forget Stephen King."

I smiled weakly. "That's a bit inconsistent, don'tcha think? Thanks again, Mom. Goodnight." I leaned over and kissed her again, and snapped off the light.

"Don't trip on your way out."

I laughed. But this time I was careful to avoid any hidden obstructions.

THE FOLLOWING DAY was actually productive. Samantha and I conferred for awhile, and our various projects seemed to be proceeding apace. The old partnership juices were flowing again. It felt good to be perceived as a contributing partner, rather than as a welfare case. I still needed to pick up the slack, but I felt capable of doing so, which was a nice change.

At lunchtime, I checked on Alex, and told her I might be a bit late. Then suddenly, I remembered. "Does Tommy Hempster's father have a gun?"

Silence. Then hesitatingly, "Yes. How did you find out?"

"That doesn't matter. Alex, I don't want you playing with guns, do you understand?"

"How did you find out?"

"I don't want you playing with a gun. Do you understand me?" No answer. It was amazing how Alex's mood could turn on a dime. "Alex, it's not a toy. It's dangerous. I'm going to call Mr. Hempster and tell him to lock it up."

Now Alex's voice sounded distant. "That witch. She was listening to me talking to Tommy on the phone."

"Alex, it doesn't matter. Get it?"

"I gotta go."

"Alex!" Click. "Goddamnit," I seethed into the phone. That little girl really had my number.

I hit re-dial, then thought better of it. I hung up the phone, then looked in my Rolodex and dialed another number. After two rings, Tommy Hempster's mother answered.

"Natalie? This is Kevin Gibbons."

"Hi, Kevin. Are you calling about the sleepover?"

I had forgotten that Alex was due to spend the night at Tommy's house that weekend. I supposed that would let me out of the good-parenting roster in William Bennett's book, letting my daughter sleep at a boy's house. But it was supervised pretty closely. I didn't think Alex was quite that precocious. But then, what did I know.

"Hi, Natalie. No, I guess we're all set. I just wanted to ask you something."

"What's that?"

"Does Neal have a gun?"

Natalie hesitated for a moment, then said, "Yes, actually he does, in the nightstand next to our bed."

"Well, I think Alex and Tommy have been playing with it."

"Are you serious? I don't think Tommy even knows about it."

"Apparently so. My mother overheard Alex talking about it with Tommy on the telephone."

"Oh, I'm so sorry. I'll take it out right now, put it in a safe place. I don't even like to touch it."

"It was probably Alex snooping around, anyway. But please, if you don't mind, put it somewhere they won't find it."

"I will, Kevin. I promise. I'm sorry."

I assured her it was not a problem, and confirmed that Alex would be over that Saturday. I was grateful for the respite. My mother and I could rent a movie and chill out.

A few hours later I left the office and went to my car. It was an unseasonably warm February day—the entire winter so far had been unseasonably balmy—and I put the top down on the convertible. The car was an extravagance, but with lower interest rates it had cost no more than my previous lease. And the warm air felt sublime.

By the time I got home I was feeling better than I had in a long time. Alex met me at the door. "I'm sorry."

"About what?" I asked.

"About playing with the gun, and not telling you."

I kneeled down. Alex was so tall now that I was no longer at eye level when I kneeled down, but I was able to look up at her downcast eyes. "That's okay, honey. Just don't do it again, okay?"

"Okay," she murmured.

I stood up. She put her slender arm around my waist and steadied me as we walked toward our respective bedrooms, with deep slumber awaiting.

40

THE NEXT TWO months were a time of change. Rita left our employ, returning to El Salvador to tend to a sick father. Her departure was heart-wrenching, especially for Alex. But it was time that we weaned ourselves away from her. Alex was old enough to take care of herself after tutoring each day. I was exploring options to enroll her in a full-day summer camp and to find a new school for her the following fall. I had hired a housekeeper to clean our apartment twice a month. And my mother, who was continuing to regain her strength, would provide a transition for another month or so, before she went to Las Vegas, where in all likelihood she would live out her last months with my sister and her family.

My mother and Alex had reached something of a grudging truce, essentially going their separate ways during the day, and coming together only during family time such as dinner and to watch DVDs. Alex still clearly resented it whenever her grandmother criticized her or told her to do something—and, to be sure, my mother was not exceptionally patient with her—but both of them seemed to be biding the time before my mother's departure. I was dreading it, knowing that the next time I would see her would probably be when she was approaching death. But I was grateful that the two principal women in my life were making the remaining time as pleasant as they could.

We had a going-away party for Rita for which Alex and I did our best to prepare some of Rita's favorite Salvadorian foods. Alex presented her with a parting gift that she had worked on assiduously yet kept a secret even from me. It turned out to be a poster-sized collage of photographs of our years together. Of course it made Rita cry immediately, which got everyone else crying as well. Rita invited Alex and me to visit her in Central America, and we promised that we would.

As she was leaving, Rita took me aside. "Alex is a very special little girl."

"I know." I nodded. "Though she's not so little anymore. She's as tall as you."

Rita laughed. "Big in size, but still little in years. She is not a bad little girl. I know she does bad things sometimes, but she is not a bad little girl." She looked into my eyes, as if trying to read my response, a skill I was sure she had mastered over the years. "She just needs more love than other little girls."

I hugged the diminutive woman ferociously. "We are going to miss you, Rita."

I called over to Alex, who had been playing with Benji in the kitchen, and together we walked Rita out to her car, saying goodbye and not knowing for sure whether we would ever see her again.

I began making plans for a party for Alex's ninth birthday. It was a bit tough to scrounge up guests, but I invited several girls from her dancing class, a couple from Sunday school, and of course Tommy Hempster, who would be one of the few lucky princes among princesses. My mother called around to find a clown who performed magic tricks. I wasn't sure whether the kids were too mature for that, but Alex had suggested the idea.

And of course it was springtime. My mother had rarely ventured outside since her chemotherapy, but the three of us took a drive to see the cherry blossoms around the Tidal Basin, which were absolutely splendid. With the convertible top down, the delightful fragrance and warm sunshine pervaded our senses. It was impossible not to be in happy spirits.

We drove to Old Town Alexandria, where the third and final phase of our waterfront townhouse community was nearing completion. We made an obligatory stop at Ben & Jerry's for ice cream and strolled around the development. My mother had never seen it before, and her enthusiasm for it filled me with pride. We had constructed a large number of residences on a fairly small amount of land, but had preserved a sense of openness amplified by views of the Potomac.

Alex was licking her pistachio ice cream cone thoughtfully. "I agree with Grandma. This really is a cool place. Have you ever thought about us maybe moving here?"

I stopped in my tracks. Would I? The thought had recurred to me constantly as the development took shape. I would love it. A new, fresh beginning in a wonderful new—well, old—place. A place that belonged only to Alex and me. But I had never dared even suggest the idea, for fear it would erode Nicki's sense of permanence. In fact, she had warned me against such a thought. "Would you want to do that?"

She shrugged. "Sure."

I assessed her expression, which appeared entirely sincere. "Wanna look at the ones that are still available?" I asked. "Pick one out? You know, tentatively?"

"Sure!" she agreed. And we found a shaded park bench for my mother to relax on while Alex and I went house-hunting.

There were only four unsold townhouses, and the one we wanted was obvious immediately. It was an end unit in the second row back from the water, with an unimpeded view of the water and green space on three sides, including a fenced back yard and a second-story deck. Two of the bedrooms—Alex's and mine, of course—had balconies with Potomac views. It was perfect. And soon it would be our new home.

Alex was so excited that she dragged her grandmother to see it. I could tell my mother was exhausted, but she feigned enthusiasm nonetheless. Alex's excitement was contagious, and as we drove home I couldn't recall how long it had been since my spirits had soared so high.

And happily, we could afford it. The townhouses were over one million dollars, but our penthouse condominium had escalated in value, so it would be an even swap. And taxes were considerably lower in the Old Dominion. Alex and I were going to become Virginians.

Still, in the back of my mind was the question of Alex's future. When my mother left, I would have to deal with her mostly on my own, with some help from her tutor, at least until we could get her into a school. I didn't know whether I was equipped to do that. I didn't want to send her away to Cacoctin, that's for sure. In fact, I shuddered at the thought of it. Nicki had been institutionalized, and Nicki had died. I did not want to institutionalize Alex. Period.

And yet. The psychiatrist didn't seem to be able to get to the root of the problem. I wondered whether the problems ebbed and flowed—didn't crazy people's emotions correlate with the moon and the tides?—or whether Alex was merely an amazing con artist, able to manipulate even skilled professionals.

I guess that at the core of it, I reasoned, or at least convinced myself, that despite my feeble abilities to fathom or control the dark side of Alex's personality, I had as good a shot at it as anyone. Better, in fact, because I had all the motivation in the world.

"Do you like the fuchsia or the magenta?" she asked, rousing me from my thoughts. Alex sat beside me on the sofa, tugging my sleeve to draw my attention to one of the decorating books that occupied much of my attention these days.

Instead of glancing at the book, I looked at my daughter's earnest face. She was wearing her brand-new glasses. They were tortoise-shell, and I wondered if she realized that they were almost exactly like the ones her mother had worn. Subliminally, she knew, I was sure, even if not consciously.

Alex's eyesight had deteriorated, probably as a result of reading in bed at night with insufficient light. Once we learned she needed glasses, she hadn't hesitated. She didn't seem to mind them at all. Perhaps because, as with her mother, they somehow managed only to enhance her beauty.

"Da-ad, which is it?" she asked again, looking up at me and frowning when she discovered that my attention wasn't on the book.

"I don't even know what magenta is," I replied.

"*This*," she said, pressing her thumb on the page, "is magenta. You're an architect. Don't you know that?"

I laughed. "Sweetheart, the only colors I need to know are black and white. I leave the color schemes to professional decorators like you and Marsha."

She closed the book and removed her glasses, looking at me seriously. "Do you think we could go into business together some day? You know, you as the architect, me as the decorator?"

That made me smile hugely. I leaned over and kissed her cheek. "Nothing in the world would make me happier than that." She beamed back at me. "Except that I thought you were going to be a gymnast."

Alex had taken to gymnastics as an outgrowth of her dancing classes. I still didn't know from whose side of the family she had inherited her athleticism. But she was more than decent at it. A couple of weeks earlier, my mother and I had attended a gymnastics competition, and Alex had earned third-place overall in her age group. The pink ribbon sat in a frame decorating a wall of her bedroom. Afterward Alex had convinced me to enroll her in a gymnastics camp at Georgetown Country Day School that summer. It was all she talked about.

Given all that, she flabbergasted me with her response. "Oh, gymnastics is a passing phase. What I really care about is decorating." My eyes must have widened. Alex deadpanned, "And clothes." At that, we were both on our feet, with me chasing her around the sofa and then down the hallway.

"Hey!" my mother yelled as we ran past her room. "It's past Alex's bedtime."

Alex came to a dead halt at the end of the hallway, panting heavily and grimacing. "What are you now, a freakin' hall monitor?"

I had stopped too, trying to catch my breath. "Alex!" I gasped. "Don't speak like that to your grandmother."

Alex looked at me indignantly, as if I had switched sides on her. "She doesn't want anyone to have any fun." And with that she turned and called Benji to go out for a walk, slamming the door angrily as she left.

Still huffing and puffing, I stuck my head into my mother's room. "I'm sorry, Mom."

She was reading in bed. "It's just so loud."

"I know. I'm sorry. She is only eight years old, though."

"Almost nine."

"Almost nine."

"Well, I'll be leaving soon, then she can run up and down the halls all she wants."

"Ah, Mom," I replied, "cut her a little slack. And please don't act that way. We don't want you to leave."

"You may not want me to leave," she retorted, "but she does. She hardly says a word to me when you're not around. She ignores me. And it's not much better when you're here."

That was true, but I wasn't in the mood to deal with it. "I know, Mom. I'm sorry." I walked over and gave her a kiss. "Sleep tight." And I headed for my own room.

But that was the only discordant note before her birthday party. Alex had invited ten children, three boys and seven girls, mostly from swimming class. Naturally, Tommy Hempster would be there. Along with the clown. I'd searched back issues of *Washingtonian* magazine until I had found some reviews, and hired the best clown I could find.

That morning at the breakfast table I gave Alex her gift. For the first time ever, it consisted only of an envelope.

"A Nordie's gift certificate?" she exclaimed with anticipation.

"Why would I get you a gift certificate when you already buy anything you want there?"

"Good point," she answered. "Well, what is it?" Without waiting for a reply, she ripped it open. She read the paper that was inside. "Cooking lessons," she read aloud. "For two!" She looked up. "Me and you?" I nodded. "Wow, what a great idea!" She got up from her chair and gave me a big hug. "That is, perhaps, my best birthday gift ever!"

"Perhaps."

"Are you making fun of me?"

"Do you know what 'precocious' means?"

She pondered that for a moment. "Is the root word 'precious'?"

I laughed. "You might say that." She looked at me quizzically, and I just smiled.

"I'm going to look it up right now," she announced, and padded out of the kitchen.

The party was scheduled for two. Alex's tutor, Hilda, came over at noon to help decorate. My mother wasn't feeling well, and told me she was going to stay in her room to save energy for when the crowd came. Two of the parents were going to stay as well, Mrs. Hempster and Mrs. Smiles. Or, rather, "Miz" Smiles, as Alex had informed me earlier that week, a single mother.

Tommy Hempster and his mother came over early, and Natalie and Hilda made an excellent team getting the house together. I spent some time with Tommy and Alex, who were playing computer games in her room. Or actually, I merely observed them, as if they were oblivious to my presence. I marveled over their relationship. They were completely compatible. So far as I knew, they never exchanged a cross word. They were both bright, and interested in many of the same things, but lately mostly computer games. Not Dungeons and Dragons, but puzzle games and quizzes. Very cerebral stuff. Unlike most boys his age, Tommy didn't seem fazed in the slightest by Alex's looks. Maybe that's why she respected him. Whatever the explanation, it was comforting to note that she was maintaining a healthy and enduring friendship, even if it was the only one.

One by one the children arrived, their parents dropping them at the door. All except one, a little brown-haired girl accompanied by her mother, who came inside with her. Her mother was unbelievably hot . . .

"Hi," she said, extending a slender arm, "I'm Kristen Smiles."

. . . and southern. An accent to die for. And looks to match. Tall. Blonde. Athletic. Clad in jeans and a silk sweater.

I shook her hand.

"You must be Kevin, Alex's dad."

I realized I had been standing there dumbly and hadn't even introduced myself. "Oh yeah. Yeah, that's right." What an impression I was making. Somehow, my mother, Hilda, and Natalie had all materialized behind me, standing there silently but with expectant grins. I turned to introduce them. "This is my mother, Mrs. Gibbons, and . . ."

And suddenly I blanked out on the rest of their names.

"I'm Hilda Merkoski. I've only been Alex's tutor forever." She smiled. Natalie introduced herself as well.

"Um, I think I'd better go pour some sodas for the kids." I could hear peals of adult laughter competing with the kids' as I made my awkward exit. Duh, Kev, I told myself, you are so out of practice. What an impression you made on Kristen. Who is beautiful.

And single.

The party was raucous. There hadn't been so many screaming kids in our condo in a long time, maybe ever. They played Twister, and scoured the apartment finding hidden treasures, and played all sorts of other games. All the while I studiously avoided looking at Kristen.

Then it was time for the clown, who surely looked the part. Then it was on to cake and milk. After that, the games dissolved into cacophony, and I was eager for it to be over.

As I stood silently by the counter in the kitchen, I heard a voice beside me. "Pretty neat party."

It was Kristen.

"Hey, thanks for bringing Patricia. And, um, for staying."

"Can I help you clean up?" I glanced at the clock. It was five, the time when the party was supposed to be ending. The other parents would start arriving soon.

"Oh, thanks, I can get it."

"So, you're an architect?"

"Yes. I renovated this building, in fact."

"It's nice."

"And you?"

She smiled. "A lawyer."

"Uh-oh."

She laughed. "No, not that kind, whatever kind you're thinking of. I'm a public defender."

"You mean a criminal lawyer?"

"Well, I represent people accused of crimes."

"Who never commit them."

"Exactly," she said, and we both laughed.

"That must be hot," I said. "Hard! I mean, that must be hard!" I could feel steaming color in my face again.

Kristen threw her head back and laughed again. It was a delightful sound, even at my expense. "It can get pretty hot sometimes, too."

And then words were coming out of my mouth before I even could think of them. "Hey, you know, it's pretty loud here, do you think sometime you'd like to go to a quiet place for a glass of wine, or something?"

She glanced at my finger and saw no ring. "Well, sure. That would be great."

And then, from down the hallway, a sudden eruption of yelling and screaming. It had a quality different from the childish screaming that had pervaded the party. "Excuse me," I said, and bolted toward the commotion. I heard Kristen's footsteps following mine.

I pushed my way past small bodies into Alex's crowded room. I heard my mother's voice sharply saying, "Alex!" And Alex's peals of laughter.

Near a wall sheet of Pin the Tail on the Donkey, Alex was spinning a small boy, Adam, around and around. He was no longer wearing his glasses, but was blindfolded, stumbling, and obviously dizzy. But Alex kept twirling him. The other children stood smiling, but silent.

My mother was standing next to Alex. She was barely taller than her granddaughter, and not much heavier. "Alex, stop it!"

But Alex wouldn't. She kept squealing with laughter, twirling the boy around and around. He was shrieking, and not with joy. The spectacle immobilized me.

Finally my mother strode forward and slapped Alex hard across the face. Adam fell down onto the floor. Apart from the boy's sounds, the room now was utterly silent. Alex's face reddened where my mother's hand had struck it. No one ever had slapped Alex before. Ever. And then Alex screamed like a banshee. As the scream trailed off, everyone in the room looked at her in abject horror, Alex broke for the door. I wrapped my arms around her like a linebacker trying to stop a charging running back, but she slipped from my grasp. As she reached the door, she turned back and looked at my mother. "I hate you!" she shrieked. She bolted from her room, turned left, and ran to the bathroom, where she slammed the door.

I looked around and caught Kristen's gaze. Her face bore the unmistakable emotions of shock and pity. I ran out of the room.

"Alex!" I called. I turned the knob of the bathroom door, but it was locked. "Alex!" I shook the knob. Inside I could hear violent sobbing, mixed with animal screams. And then the sound of glass breaking.

"Alex!" I yelled, pounding on the door.

Then Hilda and my mother appeared at my side. My mother's face looked positively ashen. Hilda looked terrified. "What's going on?" my mother asked, her voice frail.

"She's locked herself inside, and she broke some glass. I'm worried about what she might be doing in there." I tried to gather my thoughts. "Listen, Hilda, get everyone out of here. Can you bring all the kids down to the lobby and wait with them 'til their parents get here?"

"Sure," Hilda replied, obviously grateful to have the chance to get out of there.

"Do you want me to stay here?" my mother asked.

"No. Please give Hilda a hand, okay?"

I turned back to the door. Inside I could hear Alex sobbing. What the hell was going on in there?

I banged on the door. "Alex, open the door!" No answer. More sobbing.

I looked at the door. Alex was obstinate and could stay inside there for hours. I considered my options. The hinges were inside the bathroom, so I couldn't open the door by removing them. And the lock was a genuine bolt, so I couldn't slide a credit card to get it open.

I looked blankly at the door. In the distance of the apartment, I could hear people being shuffled out the front door. Inside the bathroom, Alex's sobs subsided, and then it was silent.

Then I remembered the glass. What had Alex broken? More importantly, why had she broken it?

Suddenly the image came pouring into my mind: Alex lying inside the tub, deep gashes in her wrists, blood cascading out of her veins.

"Alex!" I screamed. "Open the fucking door!" I started pounding again. Then I placed my ear against it. Silent. Oh my God, I thought, she is slitting her wrists. Like mother, like daughter.

I smashed into the door with my shoulder. Shit. It looked so easy in the movies. Again. Some give this time. Again, pain coursing down my side.

"Alex, please!" From somewhere tears were streaming down my face.

I retreated into the hallway and charged the door. This time it lurched inward, but held. Again, splinters breaking away from the bolt. Over and over. Each time I struck the door, I cried out Alex's name, but there was no answer.

Then I turned and squared my left shoulder, my right so numb it was useless. This time the door nearly gave. One more shot would do it.

I charged again and the lock gave way, the door crashing open. The force was so great it knocked me backward onto my butt.

I scrambled to my feet dizzily, dreading what I would find inside. I pushed the door aside and walked over the splinters into the bathroom.

Where Alex was sitting quietly on the toilet, seat down, reading a book.

She looked up at me as if I had interrupted her, no evidence at all of her previous hysteria.

And in a perfectly innocent nine-year-old voice, she asked, "Did I do something to worry you, Dad?"

41

WE SAT AT the coffee table in the living room, the darkness of the
surrounding depths of the apartment shrouding the brightly lighted
room. An empty hot chocolate mug sat in front of Alex; an empty
coffee mug in front of me.

We had been going over and over it for what seemed hours. I felt
like I was interrogating a prisoner. In a sense I was. But both of us
were wearing down.

After the incident, I had dragged Alex by the arm into the kitchen
and sat her down. In the background I could hear my mother and
Hilda straightening up; then Hilda leaving; then my mother retreat-
ing to her room. Both had given Alex and me a wide berth.

"I just don't understand why I can't go to camp," Alex whined.

"As I've told you, actions have consequences. And you've got to
start taking responsibility for your unacceptable behavior."

"But there's nothing I want more than to go to gymnastics camp
this summer. Nothing."

"That's exactly the point. It's something you value. It's the only
thing I can do to get through to you."

"But it's not my fault," she protested. "I wasn't doing anything
wrong. It was *her*."

I sighed tiredly. "See, that's the problem. Instead of feeling
remorse about your actions, you project them onto other people. It's
never your fault; it's always someone else's." I glared at her. "Your
grandmother is dying."

"No she's not. She's better."

"I wish she was better. But she's not. She never will be."

"She had no right to slap me."

"She had every right to slap you. You were scaring Adam."

"I wish she would leave."

"She will leave, Alex. And we may never see her again."

Alex fiddled with her mug, avoiding my gaze.

"I want you to make up with your grandmother. And I mean, really make up with her. I want her last remaining weeks here to be nice. And if that doesn't happen, I am going to ground you. Not that anyone wants to play with you anyway, or that their parents would let them if they wanted to. And if you don't behave, you can forget about decorating your room in our new house. You'll have to learn to live with white walls."

We sat in silence for several minutes. I hoped that my threats were sinking in.

Finally she looked up, her face impassive. "I'm tired. I want to go to bed."

I searched her face, but as usual I could not read her emotions when she didn't want me to. I nodded. "Okay."

She slinked off. "I'll take Benji outside." In the living room, the dog stirred to his feet upon hearing his name.

"I'll take him out."

She turned and trotted down the hallway to her bedroom.

I had taken a brief bathroom break during our conversation, and noticed that Hilda and my mother had swept up the splinters and glass from the bathroom floor. But of course the door was a wreck. That would probably make an impact on Alex. She wouldn't be able to enjoy her usual bathroom privacy. I figured she'd probably use my bathroom instead.

From down the hallway, Alex's voice. "Don't forget Benji needs to go out." In the darkened living room I heard the dog stir again at the sound of his name. Fortunately, we had a dog that was not only patient, but apparently possessed a large bladder. I fetched his leash and took him outside.

The late-night air carried with it the lingering memory of winter, but that would soon dissipate. The traffic on Cathedral Avenue was heavy, befitting a spring Saturday night. My thoughts went back to my single days, before Nicki. I would be a part of that Saturday night activity back in those days. Probably dancing to rock 'n roll at the Insect Club or the 9:30 Club. I didn't even know if those places existed anymore. It was a different, distant universe.

I was so mentally exhausted by the day's events that I fell asleep as soon as my head hit the pillow. My sleep was long and deep. Almost as if I were drunk when I fell asleep, though in fact I hadn't had anything to drink. When I finally woke up, bright sunshine was pouring through the windows. Why had I designed the apartment with my bedroom facing east? It did provide insurance against sleeping in late, though an overcast day would have been more merciful. My hand brushed against my chin. The rough stubble evidenced that the time was even later than I had first thought. I turned and looked at the clock. After ten.

I heard voices. As I strained to hear them, I realized they belonged to my mother and daughter. And they were angry. Shit. I'd thought that today was going to provide a respite, per usual following one of Alex's periodic outbursts. Apparently not this time. I swung myself out of bed and strode down the hallway. As I did, the voices grew louder.

"Grandma, I told you that I'm supposed to be at Tommy's at ten o'clock. I don't care what you say. I'm going," Alex insisted.

Then my mother's voice, tired but firm. "Alex, all I told you was you need to wait for your father to get up."

Alex's voice rose to a shriek. "I'm going, you old witch!"

I wheeled around the corner of the kitchen and saw Alex's back to me. My mother's eyes flickered at the sight of me. I grabbed Alex's ponytail and yanked her backward, evoking a scream and nearly knocking her off her feet.

"Don't ever, ever talk to your grandmother like that!" I yelled once she was facing me. "Now get to your room and don't come out the entire day. I've had it with you."

Alex looked at me insolently. Though her eyes were moist she was successfully stanching the flow of tears. Instead, her gaze bore white-hot hatred. Finally she turned and bolted off. A few moments later the door to her bedroom slammed. I hoped we wouldn't have to repair two doors, though I thought grimly that maybe we could get a quantity discount.

It was amazing: in nine years, Alex had never been struck in anger. Not once. Now, in the space of two days, she had been slapped and yanked by her hair. I knew that a boundary had been crossed, and there was no going back.

I let my breath out slowly. "I'm sorry, Mom."

"That's all right."

"No, it isn't." I walked over and hugged her. She was still skin and bones. "Let's go out for brunch," I suggested.

We did, and somehow it was pleasant. I was distracted by Alex, but resisted my mother's attempts to talk about it. My thoughts were racing, though. As the day went on, I reached a conclusion that I had long been resisting. And I realized I had resisted it for selfish reasons. I didn't want to face the loneliness of life without Alex, even temporarily. I had rationalized it by convincing myself that Alex needed the stability that our home life offered. But it was painfully obvious that whatever Alex needed, I was powerless to provide it.

The fact was that Alex was beyond my capabilities. It wasn't "help" I needed. I had been helpless with Nicole, and now I was helpless with Alex. I needed to send her somewhere where professionals could deal with her and hopefully straighten her out. And I needed to do it immediately, before something horrible happened.

Unwittingly, Alex's antics the previous day had taken away the one objective reason not to send her away. I was desperately afraid that if she was institutionalized, Alex would follow in her mother's footsteps and commit suicide. But yesterday Alex had implicitly threatened that anyway, in the sanctuary of our own home. If that was on her mind, in her bag of psychotic tricks even at home, there didn't seem to be much greater risk in sending her away. Particularly to a place where people were trained to deal with her.

The next morning I went to the office to call a handyman we'd used at the Parkside. I explained that we needed to have a door replaced, because a kid had gotten locked in there during a birthday party and we had to smash the door to get him out. The handyman was polite enough not to inquire why a nine-year-old didn't know how to unlatch the door. He promised to take care of it that day.

Then the more difficult call, to Dr. Habbyshaw Jenkins at Cacoctin. He wasn't available when I called, but returned my call a half hour later.

"Mr. Gibbons," he said with his baritone voice.

"Do you remember my daughter and me?"

He chuckled. "I am blessed, or cursed as the case may be, by a memory that never forgets a patient, or even a prospective one. How is your daughter?"

I went on to recount in great detail the events of the past few months. He listened quietly, interjecting an occasional question.

"Do you think intervention is warranted?" Good grief, since when did I talk like a psychologist?

"Actually, I do. She's exhibited violent tendencies previously. But this is the first time, if memory serves, that she has manifested overtly suicidal tendencies. Or at least acted them out. She could be facing a difficult period."

"But you think you could help her?"

"I know we can help her."

"But how can you know that? She's amazingly good at convincing people, even doctors, that she's fine."

He chuckled again. It was a reassuring sound. "We specialize in treating borderline personality disorder. People who suffer that disorder tend to be highly intelligent, and they tend to be exceptional actors. We've seen it all. And we've been able to help them overcome their problems and lead normal lives. Alex won't fool us, I assure you."

My spirits suddenly rose. "So you can take her in?"

"Unfortunately, not at the present time. We expect that one of our patients will leave in about a month, but we couldn't accommodate her until that time."

"What do I do until then?"

"I really don't think you'll have a problem since, as you say, Alex usually follows an outburst with a period of model citizenship. I think with your mother leaving in a few weeks, and the prospect of moving into a new house that she's helped decorate, will provide positive reinforcement for good behavior. I think you should ease off the discipline a bit, so she doesn't resent your mother even more. Once she's here, I think that the prospect of returning to a new home, a fresh beginning, will serve as a beacon while she's here, as well."

I hadn't thought of that, but it made sense. I made arrangements with the doctor to notify me as soon as the opening occurred.

And then, just as the doctor predicted, over the next few weeks as the time approached for my mother to leave, life resumed a semblance of normalcy. Indeed, better than that: Alex seemed to turn over a new leaf, going above and beyond what I had expected. Her comportment was ideal; not just toward me, but with Hilda, my mother, and others with whom she had regular contact. She no longer retreated to the sanctuary of her room when she was alone with her grandmother, and even stayed in the same room. As the weather assumed its spectacular springtime warmth, the three of us took walks to the park and to Fagin's for ice cream when my mother felt up to it. One evening as I was chatting with my mother in her bedroom, I noticed a framed drawing of my mother, Alex, and me, all holding hands. A going-away present, my mother explained to my astonishment.

And, fortunately, Alex still had the outlet of Tommy Hempster. Even as she managed to scare away most of her friends, Alex somehow retained Tommy's devotion. Maybe it was because he never judged her. Apparently, his parents were willing to overlook Alex's occasion-ally asocial behavior and to allow their son to spend copious amounts of time in Alex's company. I hoped that the friendship would endure, maybe even after Alex went to Cacoctin. I reckoned that more than anything else, what Alex needed was a friend.

Alex recently had taken to asking me if I needed help with the work I brought home. I managed to come up with some simple tasks, which delighted her to no end. I found myself explaining endlessly what I was working on, her wide eyes staring intently at my sketches. She seemed to take intuitively to architecture, even if her real passion seemed to be in interior design. Several times I went to sleep imagin-ing Alex and me in business together, a recurrent fantasy. After all, aside from her periodic outbursts—gee, Mr. Willickers, is that an elephant in your living room?—we got along famously. Her conver-sation was so mature, her observations so astute, that it was easy to forget that she was only nine years old.

And easy to put out of my mind what was necessarily to come. Every time I thought about it, I would push the thought aside. The decision had been made, and was based upon all-too-powerful evidence of need. I couldn't allow myself to be lulled into a false sense of sanguinity. Because I knew that eventually reality would come roaring back, and make me regret it all over again.

Still, the possibility that Dr. Jenkins might not call with an opening was not without appeal.

One balmy evening as Alex and I were walking in silence back from the park, Alex's soft voice interrupted my errant thoughts.

"Dad," she said, "may I ask you a question?"

"Of course."

"I was wondering, well, if you might reconsider your decision about gymnastics camp."

The question took me by surprise. Frankly, I had forgotten all about it. Given my plans for Alex, camp was outside of my frame of reference. And so I had no response handy.

"You know I've been trying hard," she continued, "and I don't like to make you angry. Or anyone else. I'm really sorry about how I behaved."

"Have you apologized to your grandmother?"

Alex was silent for a moment before responding. "Well, I guess I should. I've tried to be really nice to her."

"She's leaving in a week and a half. And we might not see her after that. At least not with any degree of health."

"I know. And I'm going to miss her." I hoped her remark was as sincere as it sounded.

We continued in silence, pausing to await a green light to cross the street toward our building. The traffic made conversation difficult, and I used the time to collect my thoughts. I didn't want to create false expectations. But I didn't want to set off alarm bells, either. Alex had a sixth sense about her, and I assumed that she suspected that something was going on. Indeed, that might have been the motivation for her good behavior.

After we crossed, she said, "It really means a lot to me." We were both staring ahead, not looking at one another.

A sliver of doubt trickled down upon me, but I resisted. I sighed out loud. "No, Alex. No, I'm sorry."

Now Alex looked over at me, her eyes shining. "But why? Haven't I been good?"

I looked back, trying to project the empathy that I felt. "Yes, Alex, and I'm very glad of that. But it's important to learn that actions have consequences. And big actions have big consequences." She looked forward again. "But I promise we can talk about it for next summer." Well, I thought, at least I wasn't lying. I couldn't bear to do that. It might be optimistic, but perhaps Alex would be ready the following summer. And I could reward her. "Do you understand?"

She looked up at me, and for the briefest moment a flicker of anger crossed her countenance. But then it was gone.

"Yes," she replied in a monotone voice. "I understand. Perfectly."

I wasn't surprised that Alex went to bed early that evening, or that she was a bit aloof over the weekend. Still, she was polite, even with her grandmother. On Sunday, Alex spent several hours at Tommy Hempster's house. When she returned she seemed to have shed her momentary moroseness. Indeed, she seemed positively buoyant, goading me into baking cookies together, serving them to one and all (including Benji) with glasses of milk, and kissing both her grandmother and me at bedtime.

As I went to bed that evening, I finally allowed my feelings of doubt to wash over me. Maybe Alex was beginning to come to grips with her problems. Maybe I was beginning to figure out how to deal with it, through a system of rewards and punishments designed to bolster her own growing self-discipline. Maybe Alex had taken my comments to heart, and was working on improving her behavior over the long-term. Perhaps she was starting to sort out her priorities, and to realize that she was her own worst obstacle in having the life that she seemed so desperately to need and want. Maybe I should postpone her commitment to Cacoctin and try some positive reinforcement instead, relenting on my stubborn decision about dance camp. Maybe we could manage on our own together. I fell asleep, mired in doubts about my decision, wanting like crazy to come up with an alternative, and fearful of the horrible potential consequences if I was making a mistake. She was trying, wasn't she? How could I banish her to some faraway institution?

42

THE NEXT DAY roared in, as Mondays so often do. I was so absorbed in the work that lay ahead during the week that I barely noticed my commute in. We began with a weekly staff meeting, which reminded me that I hadn't even thought of half the things I needed to do. Indeed, I had forgotten completely about a mid-week client deadline that I had taken upon myself to complete. I brushed off Wendy and Samantha's questions about my weekend and holed up inside my office.

Fortunately, the usual phone calls didn't materialize as I pored over my drafting table; either that or Wendy sensed that she should hold my calls. Finally one came in. I glanced at my watch. Twelve-fifteen. My stomach rumbled in protest as I picked up the phone.

"Kevin, it's Hilda," Wendy said. "Hey, do you want me to pick up some lunch for you?"

"A chicken salad from Au Bon Pain would be great. And pick something up for yourself, too. Just so long as I get change from my five dollars." She chuckled and put Hilda through.

"Kevin?"

"Hey, Hilda. What's going on?"

"No problem. I just called to ask if Alex spent any time playing this weekend."

That question took me by surprise. "Um, yeah. She spent the whole day at Tommy Hempster's yesterday."

"Well," Hilda explained, "somehow she managed to complete her math workbook. Six weeks of lessons. We went over them and everything was right."

"Good grief. Did she stay up all night or something?"

Hilda put her hand over the phone, but I could hear her asking. "Your dad wants to know if you stayed up all night."

Then Alex's voice. "I just wanted to get ahead, y'know? So I stayed up late last night." She emitted a little-girl giggle.

I hadn't even realized that Alex was up. She amazed me sometimes. Actually, more than sometimes.

Hilda returned to the phone. "Well, anyway, I hadn't planned to get another workbook for a few weeks or so, and now she's out of problems. So I was wondering if it was okay for me to leave early today to pick up the next series at the University of Maryland bookstore."

"Sure," I answered. "Is Alex going with you?"

"No, she wants to stay here with her grandma. I think she's earned a few hours off."

"Me too. Is that okay with Grandma?"

Again Hilda put her hand over the phone. "She says it's fine."

"Well, let them know I hope to be home at my regular time. Though I may have to follow Alex's model and pull an all-nighter."

As I hung up I wished Wendy was back. I was ravenously hungry. When she returned I didn't even leave my drafting table, but wolfed down the messy sandwich with one hand while drawing with the other.

Around two the phone rang again. I was even more perplexed this time because it was Mrs. Hempster, Tommy's mom.

"Natalie?"

"Kevin, I'm sorry to bother you."

"Hey, thanks for having Alex over yesterday," I said.

"No problem," she responded, sounding a bit distracted. "She's always a perfect young lady."

I smiled, but waited for her to continue.

"Kevin, this is probably nothing. Well, it is something, but I'm hoping it's nothing. It's probably nothing."

A huge wave of dread hit me along with her words. "What's wrong? Did Alex do something?"

"Well, I don't know. I just stopped by Tommy's school, and he swears he knows nothing about it."

"Natalie, what?" The tension from the project was fueling my impatience.

"Well, my husband's gun is missing. He just noticed it this

morning. It could've been any time over the past week. But it also could've been yesterday, when Alex was here."

My blood froze. "Is it loaded?"

"Well, no, but a box of ammunition is missing, too. That's what makes my husband so certain he didn't misplace the gun."

"Jesus Christ."

"I'm sure Tommy doesn't know anything about it, and I would think that he'd know if Alex touched it."

Not if Alex didn't want him to. "I'll check into it right away and call you back." I hung up, then picked up the phone again and started dialing my home number. Good God, what is Alex up to?

The phone rang. Once. Twice. Then an icy, "Hello."

"Let me speak to your grandmother."

Silence. "She's in the bathroom."

Oh, Christ. Fear gripped my heart. But then I heard my mother's voice in the background. She sounded cross.

"Let me speak to your grandmother. Now!"

My mother's voice again in the background. I could make out some of the words. " . . . your father on the phone? Let me . . ." Then a hand covering the phone, and Alex yelling words I could not understand. Two raised voices, to which was added my own. "Alex, damn it!"

"No!" screamed Alex, and it sounded like there was a struggle over the phone. "No! Leave it alone!" Alex's words were clear, though not addressed to me.

Then she was back on the phone with me. "I hate her. She's evil." Alex's voice was seething with self-righteous anger. I could picture the familiarly defiant look on her face. But what turned my blood cold was not the words, or the tone, but the voice. It wasn't Alex. It was Nicki.

"Don't speak about your grandmother like that," I said with a firm but quavering voice. I was groping for the right words to say. I felt helplessly remote from a situation I could only guess at. "I'll be home in a couple of hours. We'll talk about it, okay? Let me talk to Grandma." I desperately wanted to find out if Alex had the gun, or at least alert my mother to the possibility so she could try to stabilize the situation until I got home.

Silence. Had Alex hung up? No, I could still hear movement, as if Alex were leaving the room with phone in hand.

I tried to stay calm, but my heart was racing, my palms sweating. I knew hysteria was seeping into my voice. "Alex," I said, trying to control myself. "Alex, did you steal a gun from Tommy Hempster's house?"

Still silence. Then she spoke, her voice Alex's again, but preternaturally calm. "I have to go now."

"Alex!" But my entreaty was to no avail—she severed the connection.

I re-dialed the phone number. It rang four times, then went into voice-mail.

I slammed my fist on my desk. "Shit!" What to do? Hilda was on her way to College Park. The apartment next to ours was still vacant. No one to call. And I didn't know what was going on. But the possibilities were dire.

I had to get home. Fast.

I bolted from my office, slamming the door open and racing down the hall. Wendy blanched. "What's wrong?" she exclaimed.

"Trouble at home," I said as I ran past her. I stopped at the door and whirled back around. "Please keep calling my house, and tell my mom or Alex that I'm on my way."

"Okay!" I heard Wendy say as I ran out the door. It was apparent from her reaction that Alex *had* stolen the gun, which meant she had thought about killing someone, or at least throwing a serious scare. Would she know how to use it? Almost certainly not. To my knowledge, Alex had never seen a gun fired. That was somewhat comforting, at least.

Clearly she had calculated to get to this moment, storing up her fury at my mother. But why? Thinking about it from Alex's tortured perspective, I could come up with multiple indignities. The slap across the face. The accompanying humiliation in front of her friends. Betraying Alex's secrets. My decision not to allow her to go tto summer camp, which she could have blamed on my mother. Her mere existence in our lives, taking precious time with me away from her.

And now Alex had a gun.

As I raced through traffic, my thoughts speeding faster even than the car, it suddenly occurred to me that I should call the police. I glanced down at the passenger seat and realized I hadn't brought the cell phone. Damn! Should I pull over at a phone booth and call 911? And tell them what: that my nine-year-old girl, all of about seventy pounds, had threatened to murder my mother? With a gun! It seemed preposterous, it probably *was* preposterous, and in any event the cops' arrival would terrify my mother.

If she wasn't terrified already. Why had I thrust her into this situation? She was so frail, no match for Alex. For God's sake, my mother was barely twenty pounds heavier than Alex at this point. I had rationalized it in terms of having her around so that I could take care of her. But I knew that it really was *I* who needed help. Just like when I was a little boy and found myself in a bind, and I would burrow my face into my mother's shoulder and everything would be okay again.

Except it wasn't okay, because this time my mother's life was in danger, and this traffic was so damned unbelievably SLOW!

I wiped sweat from my brow as I waited for a light to turn green. The car was stifling even with the air conditioning going full-blast.

The light changed. I slammed my horn and the driver in front of me actually moved over to the side of the street, obviously grasping my hysteria. I zoomed past. It was too late now to pull over and call the police; I was only a few blocks from my destination and they couldn't possibly get there before me now anyway.

I floored it for the last two blocks, slowing hardly at all for the stop sign. The wait for the garage door to open seemed interminable. I drove inside and stopped the car in the loading zone near the elevator, making a mental note to come back for it later.

The elevator came right away, but it stopped again at the lobby. Herb, one of the maintenance men, boarded the elevator and pushed four. He took one look at me and gasped. "Everything all right, Mr. Gibbons?"

"Everything's fine," I replied, knowing I must look a total wreck. "Just kind of a stressful day." I looked away to cut off further conversation. The elevator stopped at the fourth floor and Herb got off. I pounded the penthouse button and the doors closed again.

My brain flooded with horrible possibilities. What if, what if, what if. I had no plan of action, I realized, and no time to formulate one.

I reached into my pocket for my keys as the elevator reached my floor, noticing my own dank stench of perspiration. Deodorant failure, I thought darkly.

The doors opened and I ran to our apartment. I tried the door but it was locked. I knocked, loudly. "Alex! Mom!" No answer.

I fumbled with the keys, dropping them onto the floor and retrieving them, then unlocking the door and throwing it open.

Except that the chain was on, and the door caught with a cracking sound. Shit. I pounded on the door. "Alex!" I screamed.

From inside—not too far away, it seemed—I heard my mother scream. "No, Alex!" she called.

I pushed against the door and peered in. The narrow aperture framed Alex, her back to me, her hair pulled back in a benign ponytail. She was clad in a blue corduroy jumper and white blouse, barefooted, as if interrupted from playing. She was looking away from me, and I couldn't see what she was doing. "Alex!" I screamed again through the opening, but she took no notice of me.

Then there was a shot, the unmistakable sound of a gun being fired. It was so loud and sudden it made me jump. Yet what terrified me even more than the unexpected sound was the sight of Alex's slender shoulders arching violently at the same time the shot rang out. Alex remained standing there, not turning around.

"Alex, let me in!" I screamed. I thrust myself against the door, once, twice, to no avail.

Finally Alex turned around. I saw that she was holding a gun, which looked obscenely large in her slender pale hand. Seeming to notice me for the first time, she walked calmly toward the door, pressed against it and removed the chain, and pulled it open.

I pushed her out of the way and ran toward my mother, who was crumpled unconscious on the floor near the sofa. Blood ran freely onto the carpet from a gaping wound in her arm.

"Goddamn it, Alex," I screamed, turning around to glare at her. "Get some towels, quick!"

At first Alex didn't respond, and I barked at her again. "Now, damnit!"

Finally she ran off, then returned from the kitchen with several dish towels. I wrapped them around my mother's arm. The blood was pumping out, but by applying pressure it seemed to stanch the flow. I found a pencil on the coffee table and twisted the towel into a makeshift tourniquet. The flow of blood halted, but my mother was starkly white. I grabbed a pillow to prop her head and gently turned her fully onto her back. She looked so small, so helpless. "Mom, please don't die," I murmured beseechingly. "Please don't die."

I suddenly realized I should call an ambulance. I turned again. "Alex, get me the phone." Dutifully, she complied. I punched 911, reported that there had been a shooting, and requested an ambulance.

My mother was breathing, but barely. There was so little left of her anyway that a single bullet fired at such close range could easily kill her. Her eyes were tightly shut, a painful grimace on her face. Good God, I thought, Alex may have snuffed the fleeting life out of her.

I held my mother's hand, which was growing cold. I felt her wrist. There seemed to be a pulse, but it was weak.

I deliberately ignored the hideous monster who was standing behind me, making not a sound. Finally I lowered my mother's hand to the floor and slid around to face the little assassin.

Alexandra stood silently a dozen feet away, eyeing me silently, the gun still clutched in her right hand but pointing now toward the floor. I hadn't even noticed she was still holding it, and realized I should have grabbed it from her. I couldn't interpret her expression. Was it sullenness? Regret? Triumph? Did she even fathom the gravity of her act? Its possible immutability? Or was she monitoring my reaction, waiting so she could derive joy from my misery? Had she drawn me down to her plane now, both of us hating our wretched existence?

As if she could read my thoughts, Alex leveled her gaze at me and spoke to me, her voice husky and her tone defiant. "Don't be angry at me." It was not a plea but a command.

Her words almost made me laugh out loud, not only for their absurdity, but because they brought to mind the moment a decade before when her mother had commanded me not to judge her. If only I had, I thought ruefully.

That vivid recollection was quickly replaced by a feeling of utter revulsion that washed over me as I stared at the insolent little girl. Never before had she so much resembled her mother, and I hated her for the genes her mother had implanted within her. I wanted to rise and strangle her to death. Put an end to this demonic possession. And finally consign Nicki's ghost, in the form of her daughter, to the hell she so richly deserved.

We remained there regarding each other for some time, a standoff of some sort. Her jaw remained taut, her gaze rigid.

But then all at once the petulance vanished from her face, her features softening as if released from some alien grip. Finally her voice broke the heavy silence. Even though they were delivered by a voice that belonged to a little girl, her words shocked me.

"Can we go for ice cream?" she asked.

My gaze must have turned from contempt to utter incomprehension. How much more surrealistic could the situation get? But somehow, Alex looked back at me with the same hopeful expression that she always wore when she was asking for some special treat. And equally absurdly, it stirred inside me the usual gentle response.

"Alex," I said firmly but as calmly as I could, "you've just shot your grandmother. We're not going for ice cream. We're waiting for the ambulance."

She regarded me silently, a passive expression on her face. I wondered if she would transform into yet another personality.

But instead, without changing her expression, Alex slowly lifted the revolver to her face, and slipped the barrel into her mouth, then brought her other hand up so as to hold the gun with both hands.

My breath stopped, and I think my heart as well. Oh, Christ, no, I thought. Not again.

My head spun, and I nearly lost my balance as I pushed myself to my feet. "Don't," I took a tentative step toward her. Then I spoke more firmly: "Take the gun out of your mouth and put it down."

She retreated a step, looked at me dolefully and did not remove the gun.

The words were flowing now without the benefit of forethought. "All right," I said, "we can go get some ice cream. Just take the gun out. Please." I stared at her raptly, barely breathing, waiting to see what she would do.

At first she just stared back at me, not moving. Then abruptly she removed the gun from her mouth, her expression instantly transforming from melancholy to innocent expectation. "Okay. I'll go get my windbreaker." She turned to go, then abruptly turned back, her face serious again. "But I'm taking the gun." And with a whisk of her ponytail she was gone.

The living room was engulfed in near-silence, the central air-conditioning humming, the sounds from the street barely echoing in the distance. I reached over to the sofa and pulled off the blanket that my mother used to fend off the chills. I still couldn't even hear sirens in the distance, and I hated to leave her, but apparently Alex was leaving me no choice.

Footsteps sounded from the hallway. "Ready to go," Alex announced cheerfully. She was wearing a powder-blue windbreaker, one side weighted down with a bulge in the pocket. "C'mon," she said impatiently, as if I were cleaning a spill on the floor rather than ministering to my dying mother.

I tried to regain control over the situation. "Let's wait for the ambulance to come first."

"No," Alex reasoned, "if we wait, we won't go. We have to leave now, before they come. They'll be here any minute."

I looked down at my mother's face. Suddenly her eyes flickered open. She winced with pain, then looked at me, her gaze unfocused but alert.

I squeezed her hand gently. "Mom, help is coming." I did not want to leave, but Alex's impatience was palpable. "I have to take Alex away, Mom, 'kay?"

She closed her eyes but nodded, almost imperceptibly.

I leaned down and kissed her lightly on the temple. Her skin was cool and moist, but at least I knew she was alive, and hopefully she could hold out another few minutes until the paramedics arrived.

I sighed. "All right," I said to Alex, "but we have to come right back." I stood up and reached for Alex's hand. She pulled away from me, offering her other hand, away from the pocket that contained the gun.

I frowned but let it pass. "Let's go," I instructed.

I left the door ajar as we left the apartment so that the paramedics could tend to my mother. I would have to figure out later how to explain my absence.

The elevator was empty as was the lobby when we arrived there. As we emerged into the bright sunshine I could finally hear sirens in the distance. I considered trying to force Alex to wait with me, then decided to play along with her until I could find an opportunity to safely disarm her. The last thing I wanted was more bloodshed.

Alex acted as if nothing had happened, chattering about the nice day as we walked the block to Fagin's Ice Cream Parlor. The place was empty and we slid into a booth near the window. Even though the air outside was hot, Alex did not remove her windbreaker, reminding me of the omnipresent danger. But otherwise there was no indication that Alex was thinking about what had happened. She glanced out with little reaction as a police car sped past, then an ambulance, sirens blaring. Their arrival brought me at least fleeting comfort that my mother's life would be saved.

Alex ordered a pistachio sundae and I ordered a cup of coffee. It tasted bitter as I sat there sipping it bleakly, staring silently at her. But Alex ate her ice cream with her usual dainty enthusiasm.

Alex talked cheerfully about school, about what games she had played at Tommy Hempster's house, and even about the Jell-O she and her grandmother were planning to make for dessert, as if life would go on as normal, just like her mother would have. I listened to her talk, yet I heard nothing. I wondered what I would do, what I could do. Alex finished her ice cream and the waitress brought the check. The woman did not seem to notice that anything was amiss in the slightest, and I wondered how she would react if she knew that the crew of the ambulance that had screamed past minutes before was now tending to my dying mother and that the wholesome-looking little girl to whom she had just served pistachio ice cream was a cold-blooded would-be murderess.

And with that thought came the tears I had been holding back. They came flooding, and I couldn't stop them, and I buried my chin in my hands and looked at her through my tears.

Alexandra stopped talking and regarded me curiously, her big light-brown eyes locked onto mine. And I wondered: could it possibly be that she doesn't realize what grievous act she has committed?

But then all at once tears erupted from her eyes as well, and she pushed out of her side of the booth and rushed into mine and we held each other and cried.

After awhile our crying began to subside, and Alex pulled slightly away from me. She looked up at me with reddened eyes, and I thought I could see a look of shame on her face.

She reached down into her jacket and pulled out the gun, giving me a momentary start, but then she handed it to me. I quickly put it into my own pocket, out of sight and away from her reach. I thought darkly that I hoped the safety was on and that I wouldn't shoot myself in the leg.

Then I turned back to her; she was staring at me expectantly. Even against the backdrop of the horror I had witnessed, somehow at that moment I thought Alex had never in her life looked more innocent. It almost tugged me into the illusion that all was right, that it was just a normal, wonderful, bright summer day and I was playing hookey from work and enjoying a special outing with my little girl. But that was never to be again.

"I think we should go now," she said. "People are looking at us."

And indeed, as I looked around I realized there now were patrons at other tables, and along with the waitress they assiduously were pretending without success to ignore the spectacle at our table.

Clearing my throat, I replied, "I think so, too," but first I handed Alex a napkin. She wiped her eyes and delicately blew her nose. I wiped my eyes with the back of my hand, and we got up to leave. I patted the gun in my pocket and made sure it was securely inside.

We emerged into the humid day and Alex took my hand. Her hand felt small and warm inside mine.

We walked back toward our building, as we had done a hundred times before. I could see flashing lights surrounding the entrance, as if awaiting our arrival.

As we stopped at the corner waiting for the light to change, traffic streaming past in a mocking sea of frenetic normalcy, Alex tugged at my hand, drawing my thoughts back to her. "Daddy?"

She hadn't used that word to address me in a very long time. I looked down at her, the bright sunshine shimmering in her eyes, and saw she wore the same hopeful expression as when she had asked to go for ice cream.

I raised my eyebrows, unable to bring myself to speak but beckoning her to continue.

"Daddy?" she asked hesitantly, her voice soft and her expression earnest, a vulnerable little girl again. "Can you take me to somebody who can help me?"

All at once the heat of the day combined with her words made my vision go dark and my head reel. I closed my eyes momentarily to clear my vision, feeling the sunlight beating against my eyelids. When I opened my eyes again, I looked down at my little girl, who in turn was looking up at me expectantly, hopefully, the moistness of her eyes glistening in the sunshine. She wasn't Nicki anymore. She was Alex.

Before I knew it, I was kneeling down, hugging her with all my might, feeling her fierce embrace in turn. "Yes, Princess," I whispered urgently, nuzzling my face in her hair and feeling the tears spill freely again. "Yes, Princess, I can do that."

And I hoped desperately that I was right.

Printed in the United States
70613LV00003B/46-48